To my family

By Robin Burcell

WHEN MIDNIGHT COMES
EVERY MOVE SHE MAKES
FATAL TRUTH
DEADLY LEGACY
COLD CASE
FACE OF A KILLER
THE BONE CHAMBER
THE DARK HOUR

Coming Soon
THE BLACK LIST

ROBIN BURCELL

THE DARK HOUR

HARPER

An Imprint of HarperCollinsPublishers

HARPER

An Imprint of HarperCollins*Publishers*
10 East 53rd Street
New York, New York 10022-5299

Copyright © 2012 by Robin Burcell
Excerpt from *The Black List* copyright © 2013 by Robin Burcell
ISBN 978-0-06-213347-2

First Harper mass market printing: December 2012

HarperCollins ® and Harper ® are registered trademarks of Harper-Collins Publishers.

Printed in the United States of America

Visit Harper paperbacks on the World Wide Web at
www.harpercollins.com

10 9 8 7 6 5 4 3 2 1

Acknowledgments

For Their Expertise and Guidance

As usual, there were many people along the way who helped me with details, advice, research, and support, allowing me to bring this book to life. If any errors are made, I plead my standard excuse, as the fault is mine: It's fiction.

To Susan E. Crosby. I'm not sure what I'd do without you.

To FBI Special Agent George Fong (Ret.), who still answers my e-mail in the middle of the night (don't you *ever* sleep?) to make sure my FBI agents are top-notch.

To DP "Doug" Lyle, MD, for taking time out of his own writing to help me regarding stab wounds to the heart and intramuscular injections of morphine to the thigh.

To former EOD diver Matthew "Pat" Whalen, for assisting me with diving, shooting, and explosions in the water.

To Steven Kerry Brown, PI, for providing me with information on diving as well.

To all the lurkers at CrimeSceneWriters, who pop up to answer questions as we writers need them.

To my mother, Francesca, who helped me remember the places we visited so that I could get the details right, and whose imagination helped shape a few scenes.

To my cousin Monique l'Hoir and her husband, Dirk Willink, of Winterswijk, The Netherlands, who graciously made us feel at home during our visit, allowed me to use their names and their house for my secret agents and safe house, and vetted my Dutch phrases. And to my Uncle Paul, for picking us up from the train station, driving us around, and taking us out for the great fried fish meal, which I also used in the book.

To my agent, Jane Chelius, for always being there for me.

And last but not least, to all the wonderful folks at Harper-Collins, and especially to my editor, Lyssa Keusch, who braved a downpour walking the piers of San Francisco with me, sans umbrella, while we discussed this book and how to make it better.

For a Worthy Cause

To Julie H. Boucher, for her *very* generous donation to Rotary Club of Stockton in exchange for a character named for her daughter, Madeline "Maddie" Boucher.

Dedication to duty has a price.

The central belief of every moron is that he is the victim of a mysterious conspiracy against his common rights and true deserts. He ascribes all his failure to get on in the world, all of his congenital incapacity and damfoolishness, to the machinations of were-wolves assembled in Wall Street, or some other such den of infamy.

H. L. MENCKEN, 1936

1

November 19
Ten miles off the coast of the Cayman Islands

"I'm not kidding. There are ruins down there. I saw them."

April Robbins lifted her scuba mask to get a better look at her diving partner's face as he treaded water just a few feet from her. Martin Hertz was a know-it-all, in her opinion, always spouting off that his father was a former navy SEAL—which made Martin think he was the resident expert in diving. He was twenty-two, a year older than she in age, but light years younger in emotional maturity, and she was fast losing her ability to feign politeness around him.

"Ruins? You mean rocks?" she said.

"Where would rocks come from out here? They're ruins."

She glanced back toward their boat, the *Random Act*, and the rest of their team, who were diving very near it, searching for signs of a sunken ship—even though they were all supposed to be studying the effects of global warming on ocean life. Frankly, she wanted to be there with them, not Martin, but he'd insisted on exploring in the opposite direction.

She lowered her mask, about to swim back to the boat,

when he clasped his hands together and gave her a hangdog expression. "Please . . ."

"For God's sake, Martin. If those were ruins, someone would've discovered them by now. The professor definitely."

"He didn't see them. Just come with me, and if there's nothing there, go back and join the others. I'll leave you alone for the rest of the trip."

She turned around, glanced toward their friends, who didn't seem to notice the approach of a cargo ship. There were four other divers gathered around the *Random Act*, with their professor remaining on board, the dive flag up. The offshore wind carried the sound of their laughter toward her, and she wished herself there, until she saw Tim reach out and caress Diana Walker's face. At least it looked like a caress. Hard to tell with the water bouncing them up and down, and she suddenly wondered if that wasn't half her annoyance with Martin. *He* wasn't Tim. Great. Who was the mature one now?

"Fine," she said to Martin. "Where exactly are these ruins?"

He pointed in the opposite direction of the boat. Toward the open ocean.

"Out there?"

"About fifty yards."

April looked at the sky, thinking they might have another couple hours of sunlight. "Let's go see what you found." She put in her mouthpiece, dove, then followed Martin. As they neared the location, she took a frustrated breath, thinking that her first instinct was right. Just a bunch of scattered rocks, probably left over from some ancient volcanic activity.

She was about to rise to the surface when Martin tapped her on the arm, then pointed to where a shaft of sunlight lit up the ocean, the light becoming dimmer the farther down she looked. At first glance, it appeared to be more of the same barnacle- and algae-covered rocks, everything in hues of green, blue, and gray. But she watched in fascination as Martin directed her attention and she realized what she was looking at was a broken column. She followed him down farther, and saw another column, almost intact, as well as part of an arch, as though an ancient temple had come crashing into the water—which didn't make sense, since there was no land nearby for it to come crashing down *from*.

She wasn't sure how long she remained there, staring at the ruins, lulled by the sound of her air tank as she breathed in and out, as well as the muted rumbling of the freighter off in the distance. Her gaze caught on a school of tiny fish darting through the shadows of the ruined structures, and she swam closer, finding what she thought was the arm of a statue half buried in the ocean floor by the arch.

She dug in slightly, scooping out a handful of sediment at the bottom, then let it slip through her fingers. Something small and round fell. Envisioning a ceramic bead that had withstood eons under water, she caught it with her other hand, then kicked up closer to the surface and the light to see if it was anything significant.

A snail shell. She almost laughed at so anticlimactic a find. Still, she'd gotten to see the ruins. And though there was so much more she wanted to see, she checked her diving watch, noting they had less than ten minutes left of air, then signaled to Martin that she was ready to surface. He nodded, and together the two swam the rest of the way up.

"It was amazing," she shouted over the wind, after she pulled out her mouthpiece.

A loud whistling pierced her ears. She and Martin turned toward the sound. The air rocked with an explosion. A fireball lit up the horizon, then dissipated.

April jerked back. It was a moment before she recovered, then, "Oh my God!" She started swimming in that direction. "Where's the boat?"

Martin grabbed her arm, stopped her. "Pirates."

She froze, heart thudding as she bobbed in the water. The freighter they'd seen earlier was positioned about fifty yards beyond where the *Random Act* had been. A small inflatable boat jetted from the larger ship toward the flaming debris. Two men sat within the boat, both armed with long rifles aimed toward the water. If these were pirates, they weren't bothering with any survivors for ransom.

"What do we do?" she asked.

"How much air do you have?"

"About ten minutes."

"Swim as far away as we can. Under water, we'll have a decent chance. They might not know we're here."

She jammed in her mouthpiece, and just before she submerged, caught a glimpse of the pirates circling the area. She prayed that they hadn't been seen, that nobody bothered to notice two divers had escaped. And that ten minutes of air would be enough time for them to find a way out.

2

December 3
Interstate 395
Washington, D.C.

FBI Special Agent Sydney Fitzpatrick turned on her
windshield wipers, clearing the gray splatter from the dirty
snow that edged both sides of the highway. She was driving point on a surveillance, partnered with her ex-boyfriend,
Special Agent Scott Ryan, who'd asked her to fill in at the
last minute. Their mark was a tan Hyundai, about three cars
up in the fast lane, a couple of would-be bank robbers, and
so the last thing she expected in the middle of their operation was to field a call from her mother. She handed her cell
phone to Scotty. "See what she wants?"

"Hey, Mrs. H. Oh. Hey. Uh, we're a little tied up . . ." He
listened, then, "No . . . Oh my God . . . Yeah. Yeah, she's
here. Hold on." He pressed the speaker function of the phone
and set it in the center console, so Sydney could talk.

Imagining any number of emergencies, everything from
her eleven-year-old sister, Angie, being deathly ill, to her
stepfather having a heart attack, she gripped the steering
wheel in anticipation. "Mom? What's wrong?"

"It's not Mom, it's me!" came her sister's overly dramatic reply. "And *everything's* wrong."

Syd glanced over at Scotty, who mouthed, *Forty-niners lost.*

Great. "Angie, we're really busy right now."

"Are you chasing bad guys?"

"Two in fact."

"That is *so* cool!"

"Aren't you supposed to be in school?"

"Mom's taking me to the dentist. She wants to know if you're coming home for Christmas."

"Of course I'm coming home. Can we—"

"And she says you better book a flight if you want a good price." Her voice was singsong, implying that their mother was probably in the background, telling Angie what to say.

An SUV pulled onto the freeway in front of her car, blocking her view. "Tell Mom that—well, I'm sort of in the middle of something. Okay?" As much as Angie loved Sydney's occupation, their mother did not, and Syd found it best to keep her from hearing about the more dangerous aspects of her job, like hurtling down the freeway after possible bank robbers. "Call you later?"

"Okay."

"Love you." Syd turned her attention back to the road, did some quick maneuvering around the SUV, clearing her line of sight. "Is the info on this Hyundai legit?" she asked Scotty. They'd been following it for ten minutes, with nothing suspicious to back up the claims.

"Called in this morning anonymously, so hard to say." He turned on the FM radio. "You got any news channels programmed in? Senator Grogan's talk is coming on pretty soon."

"Wouldn't want to miss *that* exciting entry in the annals of political speeches."

"Trust me. This one you'll want to hear," he said, adjusting the volume of the talk show he'd found, keeping it low enough to still hear the police radio. "I think he's prepping to drop a bombshell at the upcoming global summit meet."

"What bombshell?"

"He wanted to reopen the LockeStarr investigation."

A political nightmare was the first thing she thought. Two years ago, LockeStarr Management was being considered by the Senate to manage and secure the control of U.S. ports of entry. The bid was backed by several key politicians who were in favor of turning over the running of the ports to a private entity to free up much needed tax dollars. And it would have slid by the Senate hearing without a hitch had one of them not inquired about who actually *owned* LockeStarr.

Apparently there were more foreign investors than U.S.

And still, even with that knowledge, the Senate was prepared to award the contract to LockeStarr—until *60 Minutes* ran their piece about foreign entities running U.S. ports. The public outcry was instant. LockeStarr pulled its bid, and it was seemingly forgotten, except for the investigation that was quietly opened, then closed when nothing turned up.

"So why now?" she asked, glancing over at him, then back to the road.

"Those college kids who were killed by the pirates."

"What does that have to do with LockeStarr?"

"Just that it backs up Senator Grogan's reasoning to tighten security, not just in the ports but in our shipping lanes. The bombshell, though, is he wants to see if someone in the U.S. helped facilitate the attempted takeover of the U.S. ports by LockeStarr. He thinks that whoever owns LockeStarr is behind it."

The Hyundai suddenly swerved from the fast lane to the slow. She pulled her foot off the gas pedal.

Scotty grabbed the mike. "They're exiting!"

"Stay on 'em," Special Agent White radioed back. "The intel is the job's going down today. We're about a minute behind you."

Sydney eyed her mirrors, saw nothing but big rigs behind her, the exit coming up fast.

"Go!" Scotty said. "Go! Go!"

She braked until her vehicle was directly parallel to the space between two of the semis. Foot over the accelerator, she stabbed it, yanked the wheel over, wedged her car between the two trucks, then veered to the off ramp. The Hyundai driver, thankfully, didn't seem to notice her maneuver and she kept a good distance between her car and theirs, as she weaved in and out of the thick traffic on the surface streets.

Scotty keyed the mike. "We're still on them," he said, calling in their new location as Sydney followed the Hyundai into the parking lot of a shopping center.

White radioed, "What the hell are they doing there?"

Scotty looked up at the sign posted over the grocery store entrance. "There's a bank branch inside the grocery."

"Ten-four," White said. "I do *not* want them going in. Intel says they're armed. The driver's on searchable parole. I say we take them down and do a search."

"Ten-four." Scotty looked over at Sydney as the Hyundai cruised slowly up the parking lot. She sped around the perimeter, pulling in behind the car, then hit the lights and siren as he called in the felony stop of two possible armed suspects.

Within moments Special Agent White's Ford Interceptor skidded into the parking lot behind her car, siren screaming. Sydney slammed on her brakes, angling her vehicle for the stop, and she and Scotty jumped out, drew their weapons.

"FBI!" Sydney yelled, her gun pointed at the two men.

The passenger bolted from the car, then slipped on a patch of rock salt, and fell facedown on the ground.

"I've got him," Scotty said, then moved in that direction as Special Agent White ran up from behind to take Scotty's place, his gun aimed at the driver.

"Get your hands up where I can see them!" Sydney shouted.

The driver exited his car as ordered, but then reached for something. Sydney pressed her finger on the trigger, felt that first initial click. A hairbreadth away from firing. Then she focused on his eyes. Saw something. Not anger. Not desperation.

Terror. As though he knew in that moment his life wasn't his own.

And for an infinitesimal moment they were connected. The same. Pawns in a game. "Hands up!" she said.

He raised his hands. Empty.

Sydney released the trigger.

"Jesus," White said. "We almost killed him."

She held the man at gunpoint, ordered him onto the ground beside the passenger as the air pulsated with the sirens of a half-dozen patrol cars that flooded the parking lot. Scotty cuffed both men, patted them down, then searched the car.

Not a gun to be found.

Anywhere.

And with half the Metro Police force staring at the four agents, probably wondering what all the fuss was about for two unarmed men. The radios blared to life: "Shots fired! Shots fired!"

Sydney heard chaos and screaming in the background, and then a panic-filled voice transmitting from the radio. "It's the senator . . . Senator Grogan's been shot!"

Then a faint voice, her sister's, coming from the speakerphone in her car, saying, "Mom! You'll *never* guess what happened!"

Great. She could hardly wait to get her mother's phone call.

3

December 3
Big River Discount Electronics
Washington, D.C.

The moment Alvin "Izzy" Isenhart heard the break-ing news about Senator Grogan's murder on every television in the store, he knew he was in big trouble—bigger trouble than any nineteen-year-old should be in. And though he tried to look away from the TV screen mounted beside the others, he couldn't move. He stood there transfixed, telling himself over and over, *This can't be happening.*

"Where are the video games?" The sound of someone clearing her voice, then, "Hel-lo-o?"

Izzy turned toward the woman, and it took a moment for him to realize she was speaking to him. "The senator was shot." He nodded toward the screen.

She glanced up at the TV, watched for a few seconds as the camera panned over the community college where the speech took place, then said, "The video games?"

"I'm sorry. I—what did you want?"

"Vid-e-o *games.*"

He pointed her in that direction, then, ignoring another customer who wanted to know if they still had the Sony fifty-two-inch TV on sale, he walked toward the front of the store, where the manager stood at a computer, looking up an item from some list on his clipboard. "I need to go home," Izzy said.

The manager never took his eyes off the monitor. "You can't. We're shorthanded."

"I don't feel good. Like, I think I'm going to be sick."

"Can't you at least wait for the next shift?" his boss said, finally turning toward him. "Jesus. You look like hell. Get out of here. And for God's sake, *don't* throw up in the store."

Izzy walked straight out the door, not even bothering to clock out. He pulled off his vest as he crossed the parking lot to his car, unlocked the door, started the engine, then sat there for a full minute, his hands sweaty, his underarms sticky even though it was in the mid-thirties outside and his heater had not yet kicked in.

Think.

Could any of this be traced back to him?

Oh God . . . What the hell was on Hollis's computer? The very thought sent his heart racing, and he started to back out just as a white florist van drove behind him. He slammed on the brakes, shaken that he was too upset to even drive.

Idiot! If he hit someone, that would bring the police and then where would he be? He didn't want anyone to see him, and waited until the van turned into the next row before he pulled out of the parking lot, wondering if he should drive to Hollis's, wipe the computer clean in person before the cops got there. But then what if they were watching Hollis's place? Not willing to chance it, he drove to his own apartment instead. Because he was thoroughly spooked, he parked behind the complex, then walked to his own building. Trying to shove his key in the lock, he dropped it twice before he managed to get it in the door, then bolted it behind him.

His desktop computer, the one that linked to Hollis's, was in the living room. It was where he spent the majority of his time, and he sat in his chair, booted up his computer, then swiveled around to turn on the TV, wondering if there had been any more information.

Every local channel was covering the shooting as Izzy sat

there in the safety of his apartment, remotely viewing Hollis's computer, meticulously going over every file, making sure there was nothing left to identify him with. No records of chats, no programs or viruses. Nothing but the desktop background photograph of a girl Hollis had been friends with, Maddie. Izzy had a crush on her, but it never seemed right, asking her out. Not when it was clear that Hollis liked her—why else leave her photo on his machine? he thought, as the TV reporter began discussing the arrest of the man responsible. Izzy glanced over in time to see them leading someone in handcuffs to a patrol car.

Hollis. They'd arrested *Hollis*.

No time. Concentrate . . . Izzy turned back to the computer, poised his hands over the keyboard, getting ready to access Hollis's e-mail folder, when suddenly it disappeared from the screen.

Izzy looked down at his fingers, then at the mouse. Still untouched.

Someone was in Hollis's computer.

He ripped the Internet router from the wall, worried that they would see him poking around in Hollis's files. And then he realized that they'd already seen him. If they were in Hollis's computer, they *knew* who he was. That meant they could find him. Looking around the room, he wondered what he could salvage, what he should take, his gut twisting the whole time.

Izzy threw some clothes in a duffel bag, packed his laptop into a backpack, then ran a program to wipe the desktop computer clean. He had no idea how long they'd been in his computer. Even with all his firewalls, they'd gotten to him.

Probably with the program that Hollis had on his own damned machine.

He should never have listened to the guy. And now Hollis was in jail for murder . . .

Forget Hollis. What else did he need? He made a quick walk through of the apartment, figuring he had what he needed, and more importantly, wasn't leaving anything vital behind. He grabbed the duffel and backpack, then his keys. It was by chance he glanced out his front window through the two-inch parting in the curtains, and saw the white florist van with two men in it, cruising through the parking lot.

He froze.

It was the same van he'd seen at his work.

Izzy pulled the curtains tight. Maybe it was nothing. This was a big complex. Someone else could be getting flowers. But somehow he doubted that and he walked over, turned the TV back on, hoping they would think he was inside, listen in first to see if they could hear what he was doing. If he was lucky, that might buy him a few seconds.

How to get out? The patio door, then jump over the fence? Bad idea. Someone watching from the front could see the patio. And on every cop show he ever saw, they always covered the doors. Not that he thought these guys were cops. But he figured they watched the same shows, so he decided to go out his bedroom window instead. They'd have to walk all the way around the building to see back there.

The cold air hit him as he opened the window, then popped off the screen and lowered his duffel to the snow-covered ground. He checked to make sure he had his car keys. The moment he started out himself, he heard someone knocking on his front door. As quickly and quietly as he could, he closed the window, replaced the screen, then walked through the complex to his car.

4

December 3
ATLAS (Alliance for Threat Level Assessment and Security)
U.S. Headquarters, Washington, D.C.

The moment Special Agent Zachary Griffin saw Mar-
lene, the division secretary, walk past his door with a sheaf of
papers toward the copy machine, he slipped into her office,
leaving an envelope with a Visa gift card on her desk. She
was leaving at the end of her shift for two weeks. Vacation,
she'd said. Truth was that she was driving cross-country to
pick up her daughter and new grandson, who were moving
back home. And though Marlene tried to downplay the situation, Griffin knew financially it would be a strain, because
she'd already helped her daughter pay for a much needed
divorce attorney.

She was not, however, the sort to accept charity, hence the
anonymous gift, and before she was even finished, he was
back at his desk, adjusting the volume on his scanner, listening to the officers at the scene of Senator Grogan's murder.
They'd made an arrest, and were now directing the CSIs on
what they wanted cordoned off, then processed.

Griffin expected the FBI would be looking into the investigation, due to the top secret clearance Grogan had involv-

ing national security. And sure enough, about five minutes later, as Marlene knocked on his open door, he heard one of the officers asking for the FBI's ETA. She crossed the room to his desk, carrying a packet of papers. If she'd seen the envelope, she gave no sign. "The security plans for the upcoming global summit haven't come in, but I made you three sets of your briefing on the stolen AUV for your meeting this morning." She handed Griffin the packet, then tapped his phone. "And you might want to turn your ringer back on. There's a call holding for you on line one from Amsterdam."

As he reached over to switch off the scanner, she leaned down and kissed him on his cheek.

"Thanks," she told him. "You shouldn't have."

"Don't know what you're talking about," he said, trying not to notice the shimmer in her eyes. He picked up the phone, saying, "Griffin."

"Zachary Griffin?"

He didn't recognize the woman's voice. "Yes."

"My name is Petra Meijer. I think you know my uncle, Faas Meijer."

It took a few seconds for the name to sink in. Faas Meijer was an old informant, one he'd not heard from for quite some time.

Two years, in fact.

His gaze flicked over to a framed photo on his bookcase, one of Griffin and his late wife, Becca, skiing in Gstaad six months before she'd left him. A year later she'd been killed in an operation she and Griffin had worked together. It was Faas who'd provided the needed intel to Becca that had sent the two of them on that fateful mission.

"How is he?" Griffin asked carefully, wondering not only why Faas would be using his niece as a go-between, but why the man would even be trying to contact him.

"He's fine, thank you," Petra replied. "He asked me to inform you that he recently received something you'd be interested in. His expertise is in small antiques at the Rijks-museum in Amsterdam."

"I remember."

"His feeling was that this would be . . . something you'd

want to see in person, something he felt you had been looking for the last couple of years. It might answer the who and why."

Griffin stilled. Several seconds passed by, his grip on the phone so tight it was a wonder the thing didn't snap. Then again, what if he'd heard wrong? It had been two years . . .

"Are you there?" the woman asked.

He shook himself. "Yes. Did he say anything else?"

"Just that you'd know what he meant. Oh, and that he was worried about other buyers finding it, and so wanted to meet as soon as possible."

"I can be there tomorrow."

"He won't be able to meet you until after six when the museum closes."

"That'll be fine."

She gave him her contact number, then disconnected. He dropped the phone into the cradle, sat there, replayed the conversation in his mind, going over each detail, trying to ascertain what wasn't spoken, as well as what was. Two years. He'd been waiting for this information for two years . . .

"Zach?"

He drew his gaze from his late wife's photo and saw Marlene watching him from the doorway. "Yes?"

"The stolen AUV? Your meeting's about to start."

He glanced up at the clock, unaware until that moment how much time had passed. His boss was expecting the report on MI5's investigation of the *Amphitrite*, an autonomous underwater vehicle used for scientific expeditions that had been stolen from a British port. ATLAS had been called in due to the potential threat should the robotically controlled underwater vehicle fall into terrorist hands, and this report on the AUV was the first lead they'd had since it went missing a month ago. Not much to go on, he thought, taking it with him. He paused outside the partially closed door of McNiel's office, checking to make sure he had the number of copies he needed. It was then he chanced to hear his name.

"Griffin's not going to be happy if he figures out why you're doing this." The voice belonged to his partner, James "Tex" Dalton.

"Griffin doesn't run this division. I do," said their boss, Ron McNiel III, as the phone rang.

Not sure what had prompted the conversation—never mind that in this business, there was always something going on that wouldn't make him happy—he knocked on the door.

McNiel answered the phone as he walked in. Tex was sitting in a chair opposite their boss, and with him was Marc di Luca, an agent they'd worked closely with in Italy a few weeks ago. Normally he wouldn't think twice about Tex being holed up in McNiel's office, if not for the oddly guilty look on Tex's face and the bit of conversation he'd overheard.

McNiel thanked his caller, then hung up the phone. "They've confirmed the arrest on Senator Grogan's shooter. That's all we know. No clue if his murder is related to anything we're working on, but the early reports indicate it to be an isolated event."

"Isolated?" Tex said. "Ten bucks says that early reports are wrong."

"We'll let the investigation determine otherwise," McNiel replied, always the voice of reason. He looked over at Griffin. "You have the report from MI5?"

Griffin handed each of them a copy, then took a seat. "Nothing definitive, because on the surface it appears that we're dealing with ordinary pirates."

"How so?"

"They're basing their analysis on a tentative connection to a freighter that went missing a couple weeks before the *Amphitrite* was stolen. That and some pirate activity off the coast of Jamaica. We received a naval report about a couple of college students on an oceanic field trip who mentioned seeing a cargo ship in the area that matched the freighter's description just before the students' boat exploded. At first they thought it accidental, until they saw a motorized raft being driven by men with long guns coming from the direction of the freighter."

"What's the theory?" McNiel asked. "Using the freighter to transport the AUV to search for gold?"

Tex tossed his copy of the report on the table. "You don't steal a long-haul freighter, sail it for two weeks to some godforsaken coast to look for sunken treasure. There's enough of it at the bottom of the English Channel where the AUV was stolen from. What they were looking for was right there where those students were shot, and they sure as hell didn't want witnesses."

"I have to agree," Griffin said. "The ocean floor drops off pretty deep out there. Which means we can't rule out the use of the *Amphitrite*."

McNiel pinned his gaze on di Luca. "We need to investigate this further. I want you in Jamaica, heading the dive team. Find out what the hell was going on out there."

"Lucky me," Marc said.

McNiel leaned back in his chair, a look of frustration on his face, one that was no doubt shared by every intelligence head in the alliance of nations that worked closely with ATLAS and the other U.S. intelligence agencies. The hypotheses from the various think tanks as to what might be achieved by someone who had possession of the AUV ran the gamut from piracy to spying on naval fleets to planting underwater explosives in order to take out entire ports. What the hell someone might need an AUV for in deep water channels, other than scientific exploring, had them stumped. "Let's get moving on this."

"I'll check for satellite images," Griffin said, then stood to leave.

"No," McNiel said. "You won't be assigned to that part of this investigation. I'd like you to accompany di Luca to Jamaica."

Griffin stopped in his tracks, turned, eyed Tex, who once again refused to meet his gaze. Even Marc looked distinctly uncomfortable. "To Jamaica?" Griffin asked. "I thought you wanted me to head the global summit security team."

"That was before Grogan's murder," McNiel replied.

"You just told us that his murder appears to be an isolated incident."

"I said early reports seemed to indicate such. What I didn't mention was a secondary MI5 report on the assassination attempt on a member of Parliament, who was also sitting on a committee to tighten port security. In fact, he used the growing threat of pirates as his impetus to increase funding for maritime security. Once Grogan heard that, he approached the Senate committee to reopen the LockeStarr investigation before the global summit started, intending to bring it up there to tighten security in international ports and shipping lanes, too. Rumor has it that was what his speech was about today, or would have been, had he finished it."

Reopen the LockeStarr investigation . . . "What was MI5's analysis?"

"They believe the Black Network may have been behind the attempt."

The Black Network was set up as a conduit for terrorism funding, arms trafficking, drug money laundering, sale of nuclear technology, and the bribery of public officials in order to infiltrate governments. They also specialized in the takeover of corporations that would further their goals. LockeStarr, a mega corporation with one of its many holdings involved in shipping port management, was believed to be one of the Network's conglomerates, though no tangible link had ever been proven.

Griffin needed no proof.

Publicly, everyone believed that the LockeStarr investigation was merely about it being controlled by foreign investors, which was not the ideal solution for running U.S. ports. ATLAS and the CIA, however, knew different. Griffin's wife had learned from her informant, Faas, that someone in the U.S. had tapped into and passed on the information containing every security measure and flaw of every U.S. port to the very company trying to take it over. She was killed following up a lead on LockeStarr.

That LockeStarr was the recipient of the stolen port data, Griffin had no doubt. The question the various intelligence agencies had never been able to settle on was why? If, as they suspected, LockeStarr was really a front company for the Black Network, it was for one of two scenarios, both favored by the Network: A false flag operation in which some Network terrorist activity on home soil was blamed on foreign terrorists. Or it was the sale of the information to the highest bidder, one who might be interested in knowing the weaknesses in port security that could be exploited for arms and drug running.

In either scenario, the Network had the same goal. To show that the various intel agencies and top governmental officials in the U.S. were incapable of dealing with the threats posed by other entities. Similar false flag operations run by the Network had allowed them to move their own people into positions of power when they'd come up with solutions to the problem or pointed the finger at those who allegedly had allowed such disasters to happen.

Unfortunately, after the death of Griffin's wife, the port data had never been recovered, and the investigation quietly closed when no other evidence had been found linking LockeStarr to the theft or to the Network.

No wonder McNiel wanted him out of the way.

It also explained the guilty look Tex gave him earlier, and he glanced at the report on the missing AUV, his thoughts spinning. Senator Grogan's murder, the phone call from Faas's niece, and now this. "Has anyone tied in the *Amphitrite* with LockeStarr?"

"Obviously that's one of the things you'll be checking into on the Jamaica mission with di Luca. Tex will be heading the LockeStarr team from here."

Normally Griffin would've been heading the team. His wife's history with LockeStarr precluded that, and the conversation he'd overheard was suddenly very much in context. "I'll get back to work, then," he said, and left the room, ignoring the relieved look on McNiel's face as he shut the door.

Work was the last thing on his mind. Back in his office, he sat at his desk, went over flight schedules on the computer, even as he wondered if the information from Faas's niece was legitimate. The caller, Petra, had intimated that their meeting was time sensitive, whether because the source would disappear, or someone was watching Faas, Griffin didn't know. If the latter, it also meant someone could be monitoring the Netherlands airports, and he decided that he'd take a red-eye into Brussels, then a train into Amsterdam. He wasn't about to allow this lead to slip through his fingers should it be legit, and he most definitely wasn't about to take chances should it be a setup.

Tex knocked at his door as Griffin was verifying his flight and train schedule. "Look, Griff. I would've said something earlier, but McNiel was worried about—well, the emotional toll."

Griffin stared at his computer, mentally going over everything he needed to take care of before he left. Two years . . . He'd been looking for—

"Griff?"

It took him a moment to gather his thoughts, realize that Tex was talking to him. "Sorry. You were saying?"

Tex narrowed his gaze. "We were talking about Locke-Starr."

"I'm sure you'll do an admirable job tying them into the Black Network without me."

"You didn't think that two years ago when McNiel pulled you from the case."

"I have something else to occupy my time."

"Bullshit. The only thing that would—" Tex suddenly turned, swung the door closed, then crossed the room, his look one of accusation. "There *is* nothing else. What have you heard?"

Griffin contemplated not saying a thing. But he knew he'd need someone on his side, and when it came to allies, there was none better than Tex. "Faas's niece called."

"I didn't even know Faas had a niece."

"Apparently he does."

"Or someone wants you to think he does."

"Trust me. I've thought of that. Bottom line is, Faas has some information for me."

"The only reason this information would come out now is to lure you into the open. LockeStarr's suddenly on our radar, and out of the blue, a sleeper agent contacts you? Hell. Not even a sleeper agent. His damned niece."

"I don't care if it was his neighbor's second cousin twice removed. I'm going to Amsterdam."

"What about Marc and the dive team?"

Griffin hesitated. Leaving his team shorthanded was not something he'd ordinarily do. He could not, however, let this potential lead get away from him. He had no family of his own. Becca had been it, all he'd had left, and they'd taken that away from him. "Tell Marc I'm sorry. I can't go. He'll understand."

"And what the hell am I supposed to tell McNiel?"

"Tell him whatever you want," Griffin said, scooping up his keys and walking toward the door. "If it's the last thing I do, I'm going to find out exactly who it was who killed my wife."

5

December 4
The White House, West Wing
Washington, D.C.

Miles Cavanaugh, a deputy national security adviser
to the president, looked at the number on his cell phone. Chet
Somera. Finally, Miles thought, answering the call. "Well?"

"The kid got away. We missed him. Both places."

"How?"

"He works at one of those electronics superstores. TVs
displayed on every wall, every one of them showing the
news about the senator's murder. When I went inside, asking
for him, the manager said he went home sick."

"So why didn't you get him at his place?"

"Somehow he must've figured we were there. We've been
sitting on his apartment all night. He hasn't been back."

"If he was spooked, then he knows. I want him found.
What about the other computer? The one belonging to
Hollis?"

"Cloned, then erased."

"Find out if he had any other friends, anyone else he might
have told."

"Will do."

Miles disconnected, then started pacing the room. More loose ends. This was the last thing he needed right now.

Someone knocked on his door, then opened it without warning. Ian Thorndike, director of the Special Activities Division, the black op arm of the CIA, walked in. "This has gone too far," Ian said, closing the door behind him.

"Too far?" Miles replied. "That's the goddamned understatement of the year. The senator's dead and that item you were so keen on keeping under wraps is missing, so does it really matter?"

"What matters," Thorndike said, "is that we start on damage control. Recover the item. We know where it was sent. We know who it was sent to, and we have a fair idea who the intended recipient is."

"Who would that be?"

"Zachary Griffin."

Miles stared at Thorndike. "What the hell is ATLAS doing involved in this?"

"ATLAS isn't involved. For him it's personal. I have a feeling someone thought they were doing him a favor by passing the information on."

"And let's say this package is . . . delivered to him."

"He'd be the last person we'd want it delivered to. We'd have to shut everything down."

"Or shut him down. Hypothetically speaking, how hard would it be to tie his hands? Make him ineffective in the field?"

"Hypothetically? Not impossible. And if the package is recovered before he sees it, unnecessary."

"We can't take any chances. You know what you need to do," Miles said.

"This conversation is over," Thorndike replied, walking toward the door. "I'm not about to rock my kingdom so that you can attempt to build yours."

"Don't forget it's your agent out there you want to protect."

"Is that a threat?"

Miles forced himself to breathe evenly when he saw the flash of emotion in Thorndike's eyes. "No. I'm just reminding you of what you have to lose."

Thorndike stood there for several seconds, then, "I can't burn Griffin unless I have a good reason to."

"Maybe you're just not looking hard enough."

"*If* it happens, understand this. You'll be left to clean up the mess on your own. You have *no* idea what this man is capable of."

"You think I'm afraid of him?"

"You should be," Thorndike said, yanking open the door. "Did I mention he's ex–navy SEAL? A walking killing machine. And that was *before* we got ahold of him."

Miles waited until Thorndike left the office, then closed the door and returned to his desk, picking up the phone to make a call. When it was answered on the other end, he said, "He thinks Zachary Griffin will try to pick up the package. Some sort of personal connection. He didn't say what."

The silence on the other end of the phone seemed to stretch forever, then, "I don't like that Griffin's involved."

"Neither did Thorndike. I think I have him convinced to blacklist Griffin."

"Thorndike didn't question why?"

"No. I have a feeling he'll do anything to keep his operation going. Whoever he has out there, he wants to protect."

"We'll make sure something comes up on Griffin. Was there no mention of the identity of Thorndike's agent in the field? That information would be invaluable."

"None."

"Should it come up, I need to know immediately. No matter the hour."

"Of course."

Miles disconnected, leaned back in his chair, certain this would eliminate most of their issues. Within a short time the CIA would have more than enough evidence on Griffin, and he discounted Thorndike's seemingly dire warning about having to clean up any mess. Griffin was about to be burned, and once that happened, Miles doubted the man would be capable of much at all.

6

December 4
Amsterdam, The Netherlands

Zachary Griffin, backpack slung over his shoulder, bought a map of Amsterdam from the bookstore at the Central Station, passing the clerk a five-euro note. "I also need a tram ticket," he said to the cashier, a short woman with curly red hair.

"How many strips?"

"Just one."

"Cheaper to buy five."

"One please."

She shrugged, handed him the tram ticket, then his change.

"Thank you," he said, but she had already moved on to the next customer, a man in a blue overcoat, who was buying a newspaper.

Griffin shoved the unneeded map into his backpack, gave a casual glance toward the man, recognizing him from the train, then stepped out in front of the brick-fronted Victorian-like building that served as a hub for Amsterdam's streamlined blue and white trams that ran along tracks throughout the city. The snow-covered *plein* was crowded with people bracing against the frigid December wind. Pedestrians, hooded and muffled, rushed toward the first tram that would take them into town. A few bicyclists rode through the swirling flurries that had added several inches to the snow already on the ground. Griffin barely noticed, his mind on his upcoming contact and a meeting where everything seemed wrong—as though the whole thing was being orchestrated. And if it was a setup? Whoever was responsible knew exactly what would bring him out into the open, no matter the cost.

And still Griffin had come.

He crossed the snow-blown street to the comparative warmth of the tram shelter. The Number 5 tram arrived about three minutes later, and he filed on amid the other passengers, handing his ticket to the woman in the booth at the back. Outside the swaying car in the growing dusk, the snow-topped bridges over the *grachten* and canals formed a picturesque backdrop, unappreciated by those who braved the cold, clutching their coats tighter as they quickened their pace. At last he heard his stop announced, Hobbemastraat.

Faas's niece was supposed to be waiting in the bar at Sama Sebo, a restaurant located a short distance from the tram stop. The diamond-paned windows at the bar entrance gave it a quaint, old world appearance, perfect for its location near the "Fifth Avenue" of Amsterdam, where well-heeled customers shopped at designer stores. He pushed open the door, then gave one last look outside, noticing a man in a long black overcoat across the street, hovering in the doorway of a shop, smoking a cigarette. He didn't move, simply stood there. Even so, the hairs on the back of Griffin's neck prickled, though he had no reason to suspect their location had been compromised. The stranger could be waiting for anyone . . .

Stomping the snow from his shoes, Griffin stepped into the warmth of the restaurant and was greeted by a man in his late forties, tall, dark brown hair, and dark eyes. "*Goeden middag,*" the man said.

"*Goeden middag,*" Griffin replied, his Dutch somewhat rusty. "I'm meeting someone."

"Petra?"

"Yes."

"She said you'd be coming in. This way." He showed Griffin to a small table in the bar, where a young blond woman sat by the window, drinking beer from a tall glass.

"May I take your backpack and your coat?"

"My coat, thanks."

Griffin hung his backpack on the chair, then sat opposite the woman. She was about ten years younger than Griffin, late twenties, petite, with short hair and blue eyes. She reminded him of a pixie, not an art dealer—though he doubted she'd appreciate the comparison.

"You are Faas's niece?" he asked, addressing her in English. "Petra?"

She nodded.

"Zachary Griffin," he said, shaking hands with her as a waiter appeared with a beer for Griffin as well as an order of *sateh babi*, skewered pork drenched in peanut sauce.

She plucked a skewer from the plate, bringing with it the savory scent of grilled meat. "Help yourself," she said.

"No thanks." He looked out the window, through the falling snow, saw the man across the street toss his cigarette into the gutter. "We should go."

"The museum is just down the block," she said with barely a trace of an accent, "and we're not expected for at least an hour. It closes at six."

"It's the getting there that has me worried. Did you happen to notice the man standing in front of that shop?"

She glanced out the window. "He is waiting for his wife. I ran into the two of them on the way over, and he asked if I could recommend this place for dinner and if it was expensive." She laughed as she reached for her beer. "I expect his wife is now spending all his money in the boutiques. I heard her asking him for his credit card as I was crossing the street."

"When did you last speak to your uncle?"

"This morning."

"Did he tell you anything further?"

She cocked her head, gave Griffin a small smile. "Whatever it is, he insists on telling you in person. He did say he was very sorry and he wishes that he could change things."

Griffin wasn't sure what to believe, and he dug some euros

from his pocket, dropped them on the table. "I'd rather not wait."

She took a last sip from her beer, then stood. Griffin accompanied her to the coat check, and as they put on their coats, the man who had seated him walked up. "You're leaving so soon, Petra?" he asked.

"Off to meet my uncle. When we have time, we'll have to come back for the best *rijstaffel* in all of Amsterdam." Petra leaned forward, giving him air kisses, cheek to cheek. "I will call you very soon."

Griffin and Petra stepped outside into the cold. The man who had been lurking in the doorway across the street was gone, but Griffin's unease remained.

Petra directed Griffin to the left, and they continued down Hobbemastraat. "The Rijksmuseum is not far from here." She looked over at him. "You have come a long way for information that may or may not help you."

Griffin didn't reply. He hadn't seen Faas in years. They'd been friends, but that was long ago. A different time. And now that he was about to get the answers he'd been searching for, he didn't quite know how to feel about it. The weight he'd been carrying all this time, the guilt . . .

The snow came down faster and the wind from the North Sea gusted, swirling the powdery crystals about the darkening air. Except for the two of them, the street seemed deserted until they neared the grand arch leading into the museum grounds, its wrought-iron gate standing open. Looking through the arch, just inside the grounds, Griffin saw a man walking toward them, his camel overcoat flying open in the wind as though he hadn't had time to button it against the biting cold. Suddenly the man stopped, turned from the path, and looked at something or someone behind a tall conical topiary. The bush blocked Griffin's view.

"Isn't that your uncle?" Griffin asked.

"He shouldn't be here. We were supposed to meet him inside the museum."

"Maybe he misunderstood."

"No. He was very clear." She quickened her pace, yelling, "Uncle Faas!"

Faas looked their direction, stepped backward, holding something close to his chest. And then he stumbled toward them, his breaths rushing out in short, fast vaporous bursts. Whatever he held against him, it seemed he wasn't about to let go. His gaze flicked from Petra to Griffin, and he gave a slight shake of his head, trying to warn them off.

Petra ran straight toward her uncle. Griffin tried to stop her. Failed.

"Go," Faas said. "Get out of here."

"What's wrong?" she asked him.

"Go!" he said, then lurched past her directly to Griffin. With his free hand he grasped Griffin's arm. "It was I . . . I . . . sent her. The both of you."

Griffin's pulse pounded in his ears. This was not what he'd expected. "What are you talking about?"

"You . . . wanted to know . . . about Becca? How you two . . . ended there . . . the explosion? She had to die . . ."

Griffin felt the world closing in on him. "Why?"

Faas said nothing.

"You know?" Griffin grabbed him by his shoulders. "Tell me."

Only then did Griffin notice the ashen tone of the man's skin. The stress in his eyes.

Faas looked down, lowered the hand he'd been clutching to his chest. And Griffin saw the slender hilt of a knife lodged beneath the man's sternum, the upward tilt of the weapon. In the lamplight Griffin saw the hilt's intricate pattern of gold on ebony. Faas had been holding the dagger in place as he walked.

"Don't let them get it," Faas said, wrenching the knife from his chest. He stumbled and fell against a statuette of a lion, the blade slipping from his hand into the bushes. "I dropped it. Find . . . Before they kill . . ."

"Kill who, Uncle Faas?" Petra asked.

"Everyone . . . This . . . from Atlant . . ." He grasped at the sculpture, then stumbled toward the gate. Griffin caught him.

"Oh my God!" Petra cried, spinning around, looking for someone to help.

Griffin lifted the slight man, carried him to the street

corner, then lowered him to the ground. The bell of an approaching tram rang out as Petra knelt by her uncle's side, sobbing. She looked up, saw the tram, crying out for someone to call an ambulance.

But Griffin saw the blood on Faas's shirt, saw it spread, tiny snowflakes landing in it, melting. He wanted to scream at Faas. He couldn't die. Not without telling Griffin what he needed to know.

Petra looked at Griffin in disbelief. "Who? Who did this?"

"Stay with him. I'm going to go look." He returned to the garden grounds, walked under the arch, retraced the path that Faas had taken. He stopped at the topiary where he'd first seen Faas. And noticed the disturbed snow where someone had stood, lying in wait. Whoever it was had fled out to the street, probably when he and Petra had run up to assist Faas. The trail in the snow led straight to the wrought-iron fence that bordered the property, and Griffin followed it, hopped over the fence just as the killer had done. He stood there on the sidewalk, the museum grounds at his back.

Footprints in a shallow snowdrift on the sidewalk indicated that someone had recently walked to the corner, starting from where Griffin now stood. He looked over in alarm, at the stopped tram, the group of passengers gathering around Petra and her uncle's body. The snow swirled down from the sky, faster and faster. Distant sirens grew closer. And there, among the onlookers, was the man in the long black overcoat, his hat shadowing his face. The same man who had been lurking across the street from the restaurant. Suddenly he pointed at Griffin, shouting, "There he is! He killed him!"

7

December 4
FBI Academy
Quantico, Virginia

Sydney opened her office door, saw the twenty-five applications on her desk from various law enforcement agencies, and thought about turning right back around again. The packets belonged to officers and civilians who hoped to attend the next forensic art course, of which she was one of the instructors. Normally she would have had each one vetted by now, except that she'd agreed to assist Scotty on that bank surveillance job. The suspects they'd taken down on the afternoon of Grogan's murder a few days ago denied trying to case banks for a robbery. The matter was still under investigation—one she was grateful wasn't hers, she thought as her phone rang.

Her mother. "Do you realize I just got a call from Angela's teacher? That Angela got up in front of the *entire* class for show-and-tell, informing them that she *witnessed* Senator Grogan's murder."

"Mom, I'm sorry—"

"For God's sake, she's eleven. There's already enough violence in the schools, and now every one of her classmates is probably running home, telling their parents what *my* daughter is being exposed to, and that *we're* allowing it! What were you *thinking* letting her overhear something like that?"

"How was I supposed to know she was eavesdropping?"

"You know how she is when it comes to your job. You should have anticipated it."

Sydney closed her eyes, wondering how long it would be before her mother let her live this one down. "I don't know how many times I can apologize, Mom. I'll try to be more careful."

"Try?"

"I have to go. I love you," she said, then disconnected before her mother could think of anything else to say.

Apparently she thought fast, because the phone rang not ten seconds later.

"Mom, I'm really—"

It was not her mother, it was Scotty. "Still pissed, is she?"

"To say the least."

"I thought you were going home early today."

"I've got to finish reviewing these applications," she said, tucking the phone beneath her ear, then picking up the pile of papers, shuffling them for effect. "Backgrounds to get through for the next forensic art course."

"Any chance you'll finish in the next couple hours? There's this new Thai restaurant I want to try."

Scotty, unfortunately, wasn't good at the whole we're-no-longer-dating thing, and as many times as Sydney had tried to reinforce the fact she liked him as a coworker—period—she'd failed. For all his tough exterior, he was vulnerable, and the last thing she wanted to do was hurt him.

"Wish I could," she said. "But you know what a stickler Harcourt is for getting these things done."

Not surprisingly Scotty changed gears, his usual tack of working his way back to his original quest by quizzing her about other areas of her life. Thankfully before he returned to the dinner option, the very supervisor she had blamed for having to work late appeared at her door.

"You got a minute?" Harcourt asked.

"Gotta go, Scotty. Harcourt's here now."

"Call me."

She dropped the phone in the cradle. "I know you wanted these applications finished—"

"Actually I'm not here about that. There's a reporter asking to see you. From the *Washington Recorder*."

"The *Recorder*?" That, she never expected. The *Washington Recorder* was a front for an extremely covert government agency called ATLAS. An agency she had no desire to work with again anytime soon. Harcourt wasn't even aware of its existence, which showed how ballsy ATLAS's operatives were, since this was the second time someone from ATLAS had entered Quantico under a false identity. On the first occasion a man she knew as Zachary Griffin had sauntered in, posing as an FBI agent. That encounter led to her assisting on a covert operation in Rome with Griffin, during which she'd felt as though they'd . . . formed an attraction of sorts. Apparently the feelings were on her side only, because he'd stood her up for a date a few weeks ago on Thanksgiving, not even bothering to call, and she hadn't heard from him since. "Any indication what this reporter wanted?"

"A sketch. Apparently one of their foreign correspondents witnessed a murder and they'd like your assistance as soon as possible."

"Are they bringing the witness here?"

"No, they want you to go there. I've gone ahead and approved it, since they're footing the bill."

"And where would *there* be?"

"Amsterdam."

So much for worrying about how to avoid Scotty for dinner.

James "Tex" Dalton was waiting in the lobby near the guard's desk. Tall, blond, and broad-shouldered, he looked more like a linebacker than a reporter. His suit, however, was straight from the rack and just ill-fitting enough to pass muster for something an underpaid reporter would be wearing, and the touch wasn't lost on Sydney. She well knew ATLAS's attention to detail, which meant that Tex would also be acting as though they'd never met, when in fact he had worked closely with her and Griffin in Italy.

She smiled as she approached him, holding out her hand. "Hi. You must be from the *Recorder*? I'm Special Agent Fitzpatrick."

"Nice to meet you," he said, shaking her hand. "I'm assuming your boss informed you of our request?"

"He did."

Tex nodded, his brows raised. "And?"

"Why don't we step outside." She held her hand toward the lobby doors, indicating he should accompany her out. The moment the glass door shut behind them, Sydney said, "Are you serious? Do I even want to *know* what's going on in Amsterdam?"

"The basics?" he said, his breath visible in the cold air. He peered around her into the glass doors, no doubt to see if anyone was watching them. "Griffin and another woman witnessed a murder. He can't identify anyone, but the woman he was with may have seen the killer's face. It's a quick trip. If you can sleep on the plane, you'll be able to do the drawing tomorrow, enjoy a little Christmas shopping, then fly home the next morning. I've even booked you in first class."

"The answer's no."

Tex gave her a thorough appraisal. "You're not still sore because Griffin didn't make it out for Thanksgiving, are you?"

"Sore? Hardly." Except that her mother had grilled her about the mysterious guest to no end, then wouldn't let it go when he hadn't even bothered to let them know he wasn't coming. After all they'd been through together in Italy, Syd had been looking forward to seeing Griffin, was hurt when he'd failed to show. Since they weren't dating, technically weren't even an item, she'd done her best to downplay the matter to her mother. Griffin was now merely an event in the past, not someone she expected to see again. "But a phone call would've been nice. You know, something like, 'Sorry I can't make it to dinner.'"

"I'd tell you he's not worth it if that would make you feel better."

"It's no big deal."

"Good. So you'll do it?"

"I'll *think* about it."

"I'll have a ticket waiting for you at the airport."

"I haven't agreed."

"What if I told you someone's trying to blame him for the murder, so he's keeping a low profile?"

"If I thought I could trust anything you guys say to me, I might believe it. But tell you what. I'll check my schedule."

"One other thing you should know. This whole thing's under the radar."

"Isn't it always with you?"

"Not like this one, darlin'."

He left, and she was annoyed at herself for not sticking to her guns. She looked at her watch, wondering what she should do. Fly off to Amsterdam, just because Griffin wanted her to? Hell . . .

Shivering in the cold, she took out her cell phone and punched in Tony Carillo's number, her former partner when she'd been assigned to the San Francisco field office, where he still worked. He was one of the few people who knew of her involvement with ATLAS. "Tony, you busy?"

"Just about to order lunch. It's Taco Bell, so not to worry."

"I need your opinion," she said, then told him what Tex was asking.

"A drawing for Griffin in Amsterdam?" Carillo said. "When the hell you two lovers gonna quit dancing around each other and get down to business?"

"Since we're not lovers, I'm going to ignore that question."

"Yeah, right. Either go or don't. What's the big deal?"

"I don't know. The way Tex said it was under the radar."

"That's how it always is with government spooks. Standard disclaimer. It's why you don't see these things in any budgets when they're making a report to Congress. It'd kill 'em in a tax audit. No one would ever be reelected. The question is: You want a free trip to Amsterdam or not?"

She told herself that was the clincher. She'd never been to Amsterdam. Besides, it was only for a couple of days. A quick sketch, see a few of the sights, and fly home before the week was out, all on Griffin's dime. No muss, no fuss.

More importantly, as Tex said, she probably wouldn't even see Griffin. What could possibly go wrong?

8

December 4
San Francisco

No sooner had FBI Special Agent Tony Carillo dis-connected from his call with Sydney than two CIA spooks walked into the restaurant. He had nothing against the CIA. Except maybe when they decided to show up unannounced at his favorite Taco Bell in the middle of his lunch break demanding a meeting that was off the record. The off-the-record part he had no problem with. The messing-with-his-lunch-break part really ticked him off. He liked his tacos piping hot. Even so, he was wise enough to put a congenial smile on his face and act like he was used to secret agent types showing up at the fast-food restaurants he frequented. "Taco?" he asked, waving to his tray.

"No thank you," one of the agents said. Carillo recognized Jared Dunning from a case he and Fitzpatrick had worked a couple of months ago involving her late father. "Trying to eat healthier these days." Dunning's expression remained neutral, not that Carillo could tell much behind the guy's shades.

"You realize it's cloudy outside?"

Dunning slid off his sunglasses, dropped them in the inside pocket of his impeccable black suit. "Helpful to the last, Carillo."

"Yeah. Part of my sweet nature. What are you guys doing here?"

"You might get a phone call from Pearson over at FCI, asking if you'll help look into the murder of Senator Grogan."

FCI, the Bureau's Foreign Counterintelligence squad, was not something Carillo wanted any part of. He liked his cases clean, uncomplicated, and, more importantly, close to home and without the top brass looking over his shoulder. "Not to worry. I'll pass."

"We were hoping you'd say that."

"See? We can play nicely." He took a sip of his soda, eyed the two men. "What's your interest?"

"No interest. Just if you hear any familiar names, like ours, maybe act surprised."

Dunning and his partner left, and Carillo watched them walk out of the restaurant into the parking lot. After a cryptic conversation like that, there was no way he was turning down the assignment, if for no other reason than to see why the CIA was so fired up to keep him off the case.

And as he got up, dumped his trash in the receptacle, and left the tray on the counter, he knew he'd been played. A little reverse psychology to make sure he did take the case.

No one could say his job wasn't interesting.

Pearson, who headed the Bureau's FCI squad out of Washington, D.C., personally called Carillo at his desk that afternoon, asking him to look into the senator's murder, not only because of Carillo's experience in homicides, but because Carillo was as far removed from FCI as an agent could get. "We'd like to keep this low-key," Pearson said. "Preferably someone not recognizable from our unit."

"Why me?" Carillo asked, leaning back in his desk chair, waving at Doc Schermer to get his attention.

"Your name came up in a couple past investigations we've been following. In this case, your skills at bending the rules seemed . . . like an asset."

The only other investigations worth noting that he'd been involved in of late had to do with Sydney Fitzpatrick.

Which told him everything he needed to know.

This was no ordinary murder.

Well, these days the act of murder might be ordinary.

The victim sure as hell wasn't.

"When do you want me to get started?"

"I'd like you on the first flight out you can get. I'll clear it with your boss."

"The report?"

"I'll e-mail it to you now. And I'm sure it goes without saying, this is one rule that doesn't get bent. Tell no one."

"I'm on it." Carillo disconnected, just as Michael "Doc" Schermer walked up. "Well, look who's here. No one."

"I've been called worse," Schermer said, running his fingers through his white hair.

"Gonna have to cancel those dinner plans we had."

"We didn't have any plans."

"Well, if we did, they'd be a moot point right now. I'm on my way to HQ."

"For what?"

"Can't tell you."

Doc grinned. "Wouldn't be connected to your visitors at lunch, or maybe a certain wayward agent's impending trip to Europe, would it?"

"Hard to imagine it's not," he said, checking his e-mail. His new investigation had ATLAS written all over it, he thought, opening the attachment containing the report. CIA, the capital, a murder being looked into by the FBI's counter-intelligence squad, and Sydney Fitzpatrick's little jaunt to Amsterdam? He'd bet a month's salary she'd soon be knee-deep in whatever this was. What didn't make sense was the senator's murder being part of this package. "One important note," he told Doc, "should anyone ask, you didn't hear anything from me."

"Carillo. Silent as the grave."

"Hand me that report," Carillo said, nodding toward his printer.

Doc leaned over, grabbed the stack of papers, flipping it

over to read the top line with the victim's name, his brows rising just before he handed the documents to Carillo. "Okay, then. Glad you're not telling me about any of this." He crossed his arms, eyed Carillo. "You're not like Fitzpatrick, are you? Gotta call at all hours of the night?"

"Why would I call? You're not supposed to know what I'm doing. And, unlike Sydney," he said, dropping the crime report into his briefcase, "I can tell time."

9

December 5
Schiphol Airport
Amsterdam, The Netherlands

Sydney cleared customs, then strode toward the exit, where a driver was supposed to be waiting. A strong feeling of being watched came over her and she stopped, looked around. Sure enough a man approached. "You're the artist?" he asked.

She nodded, then introduced herself.

"Detective Paul Van der Lans, KLPD," he said, shaking hands with her. "You have only this one bag?"

"This is it," she said, patting the soft-sided carry-on slung over her shoulder, which contained her sketchbook, pencil case, and a change of clothes. "Quick trip. In today, out tomorrow."

He led her through the airport to where his car was parked. The air was chilled, crisp. Snow covered anything not moving, and she pulled her coat tight, glad she'd packed gloves and a scarf.

"Have you a hotel?" he asked. "My wife has invited you to stay with us."

"Actually, my partner recommended a bed-and-breakfast.

De Zeven Kikkertjes," she said, pronouncing with some difficulty the name of the establishment that Carillo had texted to her.

"Your Dutch is excellent!" He grinned as he opened the car door for her. "A nice place near a not-so-nice place. The famous red-light district. You have heard of it?"

Figured Carillo would direct her there. "I have."

"Our witness's home is not too far from your hotel. Just over a couple of canals," he said, getting into the car and starting it up. "Perhaps a ten-minute walk."

The drive into Amsterdam took about twenty minutes, and the farther in they traveled toward the city center, the more the city's charm became apparent. Snow rested on the spires of churches and the gables of tall brick houses that graced the canals and streets. Some of the rooflines were built like steps, others scrolled in elaborate curlicues. As he drove, Van der Lans acted as temporary tour guide. "Do you see the hooks at the top of each house? They are used to haul up furniture because the buildings and stairways are too narrow."

"That would be enough to keep me from moving very often."

"I feel the same." Van der Lans skillfully negotiated the car around some bicyclists who apparently didn't mind the cold. Eventually he drove over a bridge that arched across a canal bordered on either side by narrow streets, lined with tall houses, their brick façades contrasting darkly against the snow. He parked beneath a bare-branched tree, his car separated from the icy waters only by a low guardrail.

Sydney gave a dubious look at the barrier as she got out of the car and followed Van der Lans to a brick building opposite. Above the entrance was a blue diamond-shaped sign that read POLITIE. "The police station," he said. "My apologies, but I need to run in and pick up some paperwork. And I shall be able to offer you hot coffee and a quick breakfast in the café next door if you so desire."

"Coffee sounds wonderful."

An hour later they were back on the road, a ten-minute drive to the witness's home. Van der Lans slowed his unmarked police car, pointing to a street on the left. "The famed red-light district. You can see some of the women in the windows. Even when it snows they have customers."

Sydney caught a glimpse of a woman, barely draped in black lace lingerie, posing inside a window glowing with garish red neon lights. A man walking by eyed her, but apparently wasn't interested and continued down the street.

"Not too far away," Van der Lans continued, "is where your hotel is. The Zeven Kikkertjes, Seven Frogs." They drove over yet another bridge and he pointed. "There."

Sydney looked down the tree-lined avenue and the tall row houses, thinking that Carillo hadn't done too badly after all. Old world charm right on the edge of the red-light district. Give her something to talk about when she got back to the States.

A few blocks farther, Van der Lans double-parked in front of a narrow gabled structure with tall windows—typical of the area—about four stories high, red brick with cream-colored trim. A corner house, on one side it overlooked a bridge that crossed the canal, and on the other side, the street in front of the canal.

"This is where our witness Petra lives," he said. "It was her uncle who was killed."

She wondered if he knew about Griffin's involvement in the case—not that she was about to bring up the subject. As far as Sydney was concerned, she was merely there to do the sketch. Nothing else mattered, she thought, getting out of the car, throwing her bag over her shoulder, then shoving her hands into her coat pockets as the snow drifted down in large, feathery flakes. She followed the detective to the front door. He knocked, and a moment later, it was opened by a young woman with short blond hair and a narrow face. Her blue eyes were red and puffy, her skin mottled from crying. Van der Lans introduced them, and Sydney shook hands, offering her condolences.

"Thank you," Petra replied. She stepped aside, allowing the two of them to enter. "I thought we could work in my office," she said. "There is a fire to keep us warm."

"Unfortunately," Detective Van der Lans told her, "I have an interview I need to take care of. How long do you think you will need for the sketch?" he asked Sydney.

"About two to three hours."

"I'll come back then. Petra has my cell phone number." The detective apologized once more, then left, and Petra closed the front door after him. She led Sydney down a dark hallway into an oblong room with windows at one end overlooking the canal. A gleaming parquet floor bordered a large intricately patterned Turkish carpet, and Sydney noticed that smaller carpets of similar design were draped across the tabletops. Their rich crimson contrasted with the mahogany paneled walls, which were lined by shelves of leather-bound volumes. Dominating the long wall opposite the entrance was a gigantic mantelpiece which framed an inset of blue and white Delft tiles. In front of these a gleaming black wrought-iron stove radiated heat. Two scarred leather chairs, facing each other, had been drawn up in front of it. A massive desk occupied one corner of the room, its surface covered with papers and books. Petra directed Sydney to the other corner, where she saw an antique card table, topped in brown leather with gold trim and four high-backed chairs placed around it.

Sydney pulled her sketchbook and pencils from her black overnight bag, which she hung with her coat over the back of her chair, then looked around, admiring the warmth of the space, the dark beams that crossed the ceiling, and the richness of the paneled walls. "I love the woodwork. This is an amazing house."

"The room has quite a history," Petra said, taking a seat at the table, looking around as she fidgeted with her handkerchief. "There are hidden doors in the paneling. One opens to a closet that the former owners made good use of during the war, hiding resistance fighters and Jews from the Nazis. The other panel merely leads to the back hallway and the bathroom." Petra gave a small smile. "But you are not here for the history, are you?"

Sydney smiled in return, opened her sketchbook. "I know this can't be easy. But I need to walk you through the events leading up to the murder." She tried to think of the best way to describe the cognitive interviewing process to explain why she'd be asking about information that had nothing to do with the actual crime, and then dissecting what Petra had no doubt gone over ad nauseam with the police. "Even the tiniest things, the weather, noises you heard, what you were thinking. This process helps to recreate the events in your mind. Helps you remember more salient details about the man you saw."

"It all happened so fast," Petra said, looking down at the small square of cloth she held. "I'm not even sure if the man I saw is the killer. And even if he was, I didn't see his face all that well. He was wearing a hat pulled very low. But Zachary Griffin seemed interested in him. Worried, even."

"Why? What was the man doing?"

"Nothing really. Smoking a cigarette," Petra said. "I really had a better look at his wife. At least I assume she was his wife, since she asked for his credit card."

"What were you doing just before you first saw them? Let's start with, say, about an hour before you arrived. Everything you remember."

And Petra described her walk to the restaurant, the weather, the things she saw, where she was to meet Griffin, then encountering the man and woman, the man asking her if she could recommend the restaurant. Their conversation was brief, and then Petra left, crossing the street, just as the woman asked him for his credit card. "And that was all. Maybe twenty seconds of conversation. He might have been American. I could be wrong." She wiped her eyes with her handkerchief. "He was standing on the opposite corner from where my uncle was walking. I don't know what made Griffin notice him, or why he thought the man was involved."

Sydney had learned that Griffin's sixth sense was something that shouldn't be ignored. "Can you describe him?"

"As I explained to the police, to everyone," she said, appearing frustrated, "I really did not see his face. Only his nose and his mouth. He wore his hat very low, and he also wore a scarf around his neck, which covered his chin."

Sydney wasn't sure what she could do with half a face, and wondered if anyone realized the futility of attempting a drawing. "What about the woman?"

"The woman?"

"Could you describe her?"

"I—well, yes. But I thought they wanted the man's picture."

"Maybe if we identify her, we can find out who he is. We could do a sketch of her, and when that is done, maybe what you remember of him?"

Petra seemed to relax at the suggestion, and nodded. "I think I could describe her. She was tall and thin. She had a square face, wide-set eyes, and a thin nose. Pretty. Like a model. And her hair was short, like mine. But dark brown."

Sydney jotted notes in the top left corner of her sketch-book to reference later, then, using a soft pencil, proceeded to sketch the shape of the face, showing it to Petra. "Is this what you mean by square face?"

Petra gave a doubtful glance at Sydney's preliminary sketch. "I guess. But not her jaw." She reached out, traced the jawline with her finger. "More like this," she said. "More round at the chin. Softer-looking."

Sydney erased the original jawline and sketched in the correction. They continued on in the same manner, Sydney pausing every so often to show her progress to Petra, asking what changes she would make, careful to keep her questions open-ended. Petra responded, sometimes specifically describing a change, other times showing Sydney by applying her finger directly to the paper. Sydney held it up one more time, and Petra narrowed her eyes, tilting her head. "I think the nose is wrong. Too straight. Hers had a bump on the bridge, like it had been broken," she said, touching her own nose to show Sydney. "But on her it added character to a too pretty face."

Sydney sketched the small knot at the bridge, and Petra nodded, saying, "Better."

About two hours passed, the drawing was nearly complete. Everything was done but the shading of the hair and the planes of the face, a process that was slow and tedious while Sydney sketched. And as she ran her pencil across the paper, she glanced up, saw Petra's eyes welling with tears.

Petra turned away, her tears spilling onto the brown leather tabletop. "I'm sorry. I—I just need a moment . . ."

"Maybe this would be a good time for a break," Sydney

said, lowering the sketchbook onto the table, then standing. "I could use the bathroom right about now."

"Of course." Petra stood, walked over to the far paneled wall, and pushed. Sydney heard a faint click as the panel swung open, and cold air rushed into the room. Petra started to close the panel. "There's another bathroom upstairs. It's warmer. I can show you—"

"This is fine," Sydney replied, since what she really wanted to do was allow Petra some time to herself, to gather her thoughts.

"The bathroom is down at the end of the hall."

"Thanks."

Sydney closed the panel door behind her, shivering as she walked down the short hall. She used the bathroom, washed her hands in the icy water, then shut it off. The white tiled room was more than cold, it was frigid, no doubt due to the inefficiency of the double-hung window. The snow came down in swirls outside, and as she dried her hands on the towel, she heard Petra cry out.

Sydney opened the bathroom door, listened. The hallway was empty, the panel door leading to the office still closed. She moved silently down the hall. As she neared the hidden door, she heard a man's voice, deep, gravel-edged, and no trace of an accent. "Where is it?"

"Where is what?" Petra asked, sounding frightened.

"Hey. Look at this," came another man's voice, this one not as deep. "Dead ringer for the boss's girlfriend."

"Who drew this?" the first man asked.

"I—the artist. She's . . . upstairs. In the bathroom."

Upstairs? About to push open the panel, Sydney froze at the clear warning. She had no weapon. Her cell phone was in her bag on the other side of the door . . .

"Find her," the man said. "Maybe she has it."

"Has what?" Petra asked. "I don't know what you're talking about."

"She looks like she's telling the truth," the second man said. "I don't think she knows anything."

"That makes it easy. Kill her."

10

December 5
Amsterdam, The Netherlands

Sydney's heart jumped at the sound of the gunshot.
She stepped back. Stared in horror at the closed door. And
prayed that whoever had fired that weapon was not familiar
with this house and its hidden panels . . .

"Search upstairs," came the gravel voice. "I'll check this
level."

She wasn't sure how much time had passed. A few seconds. A few minutes. Her pulse pounded so loudly in her
ears, she had difficulty hearing whether they'd left the room
to look for her. If by chance Petra was alive, her only hope
was in Sydney escaping, getting help. Petra had to have
known that, or why else would she send them on a false
errand looking for her upstairs?

Sydney returned down the hall, eyeing the frost-covered
panes of glass, wondering if she could get the window open
without them hearing. It was just large enough for her to fit
through. With no other options, she stepped up on the toilet
seat, unlatched the window, and pushed up. It stuck at first,
then made a creaking sound as wood scraped against wood.
Please don't let them hear it, she thought.

Large flakes swirled from the sky, landing on the sill. She looked down at the base of the house, hoping the snowdrifts were soft or deep enough to break her fall.

"You hear something?"

"Yeah. Right behind this wall."

A knock on the paneled door. And then someone kicking it, causing the walls to shiver. Now or never, she thought, hearing the sound of splintering wood down the hallway.

She clambered through the window, then dropped. Landed on the rock-solid snowbank, sliding onto her butt. The palms of her hands burned from scraping the ice. Ignoring the pain in her tailbone, she picked herself up. The house stood on the corner, which meant she could be seen from either direction. She ran across the narrow street, then ducked behind a parked car on the canal side, the low metal railing the only thing keeping her from falling into the water. The snow fell fast and furious, sticking to the windows of the car, offering her some concealment. She dared a peek over the hood, saw one of the men exit the window she'd jumped from. He hesitated, looked down the street, then turned the corner walking quickly toward the front of the house.

She waited as long as she could stand the cold, not daring to move until she felt certain they weren't lying in wait for her. Not that they needed to. It would take about ten seconds for them to determine her identity, whether from her name on the cover of her sketchbook, or her business cards in the bag she'd left behind.

Shivering, she took another look. It was damned freezing out here without a coat. And now she was standing in a foreign country she'd never been to, with no money, no phone, and someone bent on killing her.

She glanced down the street, wondering if she could backtrack, find the police station from here, and then she thought about Van der Lans and how he'd left them. On purpose? Or was this a crime of opportunity *because* he'd left? And if so, were they expecting her to go to the police, because that was the logical thing to do? Just about everything she thought of was logical, and she had the gut feeling that she needed to be very illogical about her next steps if she was to survive.

Griffin's enemies tended to be on the sophisticated side, a far cry from the usual bank robber or serial killer with whom she was used to dealing. And that limited whom she could turn to for help. Every contact number she needed was in her cell phone in Petra's house, including any means of contacting Griffin or Tex.

Think. Van der Lans had driven her past the red-light district and also her hotel. She thought she could find the bed-and-breakfast at the very least, and there would certainly be a phone there.

She checked both directions, didn't see anyone, and got up. Teeth chattering, she walked casually away from the car she'd been hiding behind, buttoning her too-thin blazer, trying to blend in, look like a local—not that there were any locals out in this weather. Only when she was out of sight did she quicken her pace, tucking her freezing hands beneath her arms. After several minutes, she figured she might be somewhere in the vicinity of the hotel Carillo had recommended.

A frigid gust sent a flurry of snow into Sydney's face. She closed her eyes against the sting. When she opened them again, she turned, saw a dark figure racing toward her. She didn't stop to see if he was after her, or just someone in a hurry. She ran, darted around the first corner. And ended up on a street with a few windows lit by neon lights. The red-light district. The street appeared nearly deserted, the snow came down faster. She pounded on the first door she came to.

The window was lit, but the curtain drawn.

No answer. Syd tried the door, found it locked. She moved to the next door. And then the next. As she pounded on the fourth door, she looked up, saw a dark-haired woman, dressed only in a white lace bra and thong underwear, staring down at her. Sydney waved, beckoning her to answer the door.

She waited, turned back to the street, hearing a boat's engine echoing down the canal. Through the blur of snow, she saw a low-slung barge chugging her way. As peaceful as the boats moored in the canal appeared, she had completely overlooked that the water might be an avenue of danger.

In desperation she turned, pounded on the door again. "Hello? Anyone there?"

The door opened slightly and the woman who'd been watching her from the window peered out, looking amused. "My customers are usually male." Her accent was thick.

Sydney looked over her shoulder, heard the boat engine nearing, then someone shouting. She turned back to the door. "I need help. Please."

11

One hour later
December 5
Amsterdam, The Netherlands

Griffin parked his car around the corner, then ap-
proached Petra's house, squinting against the snow, which
was falling in near whiteout conditions. He'd heard through
Tex that Detective Van der Lans had called to say that he was
going to be delayed. Tex thought it might be a good chance
for Griffin to drop in, see the sketch before Van der Lans
returned. Griffin only hoped he could get in there without
Sydney asking questions about a case that he wasn't ready
to talk about. He'd heard that she'd nearly declined to do the
sketch. And though he didn't think Sydney was the sort to
hold a grudge, he wondered if her reticence had to do with
him failing to show up for Thanksgiving.

He tried to ignore the fact that if he'd simply called her,
things might be different. But the anniversary of his wife's
death had taken a larger emotional toll than he'd expected.
Explaining the reason he'd dropped off the grid was not
something he was ready to do either then or now, he thought,
as he took the porch steps two at a time, about to reach for

the brass knocker. His hand froze midair. The door was slightly ajar.

He listened. Heard absolutely nothing. Drawing his gun, he pushed the door open with his foot. He stepped in, eyed the hallway, then the staircase. Empty. Tex would have called if they'd finished. He would've sent a copy of the sketch to his cell phone. Or at the very least mentioned that it was on its way to the police station. Whatever was going on, he didn't like it.

The first door on the left was open. He stopped at the threshold, gun at the ready. After a quick glance down the hall, still empty, he entered the room. Saw the sketchbook on the table. The woman's body on the floor, a fallen chair in front of it, blocking his view. And next to the body, a black canvas case, its contents dumped out, scattered. He recognized Sydney's bag and the coat lying beside it.

He entered, scanned the room, saw the paneled door that had been kicked in. He walked toward the body. His pulse thundered as he pulled the chair away from it to see the face.

It wasn't Sydney . . .

They had murdered Petra. A bullet between her eyes. He turned back to the room, looked around. His gaze landed on the sketchbook. He flipped through a few of the pages. No drawing.

He examined the splintered panel door. Walked down the short hallway. Saw the bathroom at the end, the open window. He checked the rest of the house and was descending the stairs when his cell phone vibrated.

It was Tex.

"Whatever it is," Griffin said, "I don't have time. Petra's dead and Sydney's missing."

"I've already heard. It's partly why I'm calling. You've been burned. Blacklisted. Your operational status has been pulled. And if you don't get the hell out of there soon, they're likely to add murder to the charges. The police are en route to your location, because they've heard you've gone there to kill Petra."

Griffin stopped in his tracks. He shouldn't have been surprised, especially since the man he was sure was responsible for Faas's murder had tried to pin it on Griffin at the scene. If not for Petra decrying his innocence, Griffin wouldn't have escaped the mob from the tram. And now Petra—the only one who saw the man's face—was dead. Griffin reached down, scooped up Sydney's things, piling them onto the table on top of her sketchbook. "How long do I have?"

"Less time than you think."

"I've got to find Sydney."

"She's fine. She called me at the *Recorder.* She thinks she was followed, but managed to lose them. I'm about to send a team in after her."

"I need her, Tex. You know what this means to me."

"Can't do it, Griff."

"The sketch is missing. I only saw the guy from across the street, and not even his face. If she finished it, she may be the only person alive who knows what he looks like."

Tex didn't answer right away.

Griffin heard sirens in the distance. "Tex?"

"She's in the red-light district." He read off the address. "I'll give you fifteen minutes' lead time."

"Thank you." He grabbed Sydney's things, shoved them into her bag, then picked up her coat.

"Look, Griff. You don't get her to an airport ASAP, that entire country will be crawling with operatives looking for you. McNiel won't be happy if he has to explain to the Bureau how it is we lost an FBI agent in the Netherlands, before we even got approval to bring her there—and at this rate, I don't see them green-lighting this. It'll be one more nail in your coffin. I don't know who it is, but they're out to get you on this. That case was closed two years ago, and you were told to leave it alone."

"I did leave it alone. For two years."

"Like hell you did."

Now wasn't the time to waste in a useless argument. The last thing Griffin needed was to be on the wrong side of the jailhouse door with no way out. "You promised me fifteen minutes. Gotta go."

* * *

Griffin was halfway down the block when the first patrol car, siren blaring, zipped around the corner, its wheels sliding on the icy paving stones. Grateful for the snow that covered his escape, Griffin continued at a brisk pace to his car. His eye on the mirror, he drove a circuitous route in hopes of avoiding any possibility of surveillance. It took him minutes longer than he would have liked, but with an international warrant, he couldn't take any chances. The snow was coming down heavily when he finally knocked on the door, trying to imagine how it was that Sydney came to be holed up in a prostitute's house. Many of the windows on the street were dark, the street itself empty.

Someone pulled a curtain aside from the above window. A moment later, the door opened. Sydney stood there, a sight for sore eyes. "Petra. She—"

"I know," he said, stepping into the doorway, closing the door behind him. He handed Sydney her coat, but kept her bag slung over his shoulder. "We need to go. Now."

"As friendly as ever. This is Ivana," Sydney said as she put her coat on. "I think you should pay her for her time. She's lost business taking me in."

He looked past her, saw a young woman dressed in a thin robe, sitting on a cot-sized bed in a small narrow room just beyond the entryway. She was in the process of lighting a cigarette. And though he doubted that all but the most desperate would come out in this weather, Griffin pulled out his wallet, dropped a hundred euros on the table just inside her room. That done, he opened the door, saw two men walking in their direction, then shut the door again. "I don't suppose you have a back way out of here?"

Ivana rose from her seat, picked up the money. "Down the hall, third door on the right. The door next to the stairwell. But it leads only to a common garden."

He handed her another hundred euros. "If someone comes looking for us, take your time answering the door."

She smiled. "I can be *very* slow."

Griffin grabbed Sydney by the hand, led her down the

hallway to the back of the house. When he reached the stair-well, he stopped. "Plan B," he said. "We're going up."

"Up? I thought you wanted to get out of here."

"I do. But first I need to know if we're being followed."

The staircase was narrow, steep. He took the stairs two at a time, and heard Sydney keeping pace behind him.

"I don't suppose you want to tell me what's going on?"

"I'm trying to figure it out myself," he said. "What happened back at the house? Did you finish the sketch?"

"Only one. Of the woman. Someone came in while I was in the bathroom. I got out through the window right after they shot Petra."

"So you think you can reproduce it?"

"The sketch? Not perfectly, but close enough."

"Good. I'll need you to do that. Soon."

"After you tell me what's going on."

"When I can," he said, pausing, holding his hand out for Sydney to stop, listen. He heard nothing. Yet.

"Hurry," he said, and they continued up to the fourth floor, where a skylight, currently covered with snow, provided access to the roof. Griffin unfastened the latch, shoved the window open. "Stay here," he said, handing Sydney her bag before he climbed out. A small table and chair stood to one side of the rooftop balcony, which was currently buried in about a foot of snow. He waded through it to the railing at the front of the house, looked down, saw the two men standing in the doorway of the establishment next door. Farther down at the opposite end of the street, two more men approached another door.

Griffin backed up, took out his phone, called Tex. "Tell me those are your men searching this street and not the thugs who killed Petra?"

"They are."

"What the hell happened to the fifteen minutes you promised?"

"Apparently someone had the bright idea to track your cell phone. Basics, Griff. How am I supposed to fight that?"

"I'll be in touch." Griffin hung up, stared at the phone. He should've pulled its battery. He hadn't for the simple reason that until he found Sydney, he wanted to make sure Tex could reach him with any updates. He returned to the skylight. Sydney had climbed out, was standing next to it. "I'll have to get back to you on that drawing," he told her. "The men downstairs have been sent here to extract us. They're here to protect you. They know about Petra."

"That's good, then."

"Yeah. About that . . ." He removed the battery from his phone, dropped both pieces in his pocket, then took her hand in his. Her fingers were warm, soft. "Those men out there. They tracked my cell. If you could stall them. Give me a bit of a head start."

"A head start? What the hell is going on?"

He looked down, realized he was still holding her hand, and reluctantly let go. "I have to leave," he said as she glanced back at the stairwell at the sound of someone knocking on the door below, the sound carrying all the way up.

He took a step back, then another, distancing himself. He figured he had maybe two, three minutes before they converged on this rooftop. "I'm sorry. For everything. For not calling you at Thanksgiving to say I couldn't make it. For dragging you into this."

"Dragging me— What are you talking about?"

"I wish I could tell you, Syd."

And then he turned, started across the rooftop, and didn't look back.

12

December 5
Washington, D.C.

Miles Cavanaugh got up from his desk and crossed the room to the liquor cabinet. Just one drink, he thought, eyeing the bottle of vodka when his aide, Stephen Severin, interrupted him. "A slight problem, sir."

"What sort of problem?" he asked, pouring himself a glass of water instead.

"The package we were hoping to recover is not there."

"Not there?" Miles turned, faced his aide. Severin, a slight man with brown hair, stood in the doorway, looking far too calm for a person who knew the consequences if they failed to recover the package. Of course, that was precisely why he'd hired the man, wasn't it? His ability to remain calm in situations of crisis? "What do you mean it's not there? Where the hell is it?"

"It wasn't delivered to the office we thought it would be. By the time the mistake was realized, it had already been moved."

"Does Griffin have it?"

"We don't believe so, but we're keeping an eye out."

Miles looked at the bottle of vodka, thinking that one

small drink would go far toward soothing his frayed nerves. He walked away from the cabinet, took a seat at his desk, stared at the gleaming mahogany surface for several seconds. "This isn't happening."

His aide said nothing, merely waited for instruction. And what instruction could he give? All he'd wanted was one man out of the way. To be so close . . .

He leaned back in his chair, glanced over at the liquor cabinet. In that moment, he understood why certain highly placed individuals throughout history had succumbed to the temptation of taking their own lives. Getting into things that were complicated.

Getting caught.

That the very thought occurred to him right then told him he needed to slow down, think about this. Not do anything rash.

Rash.

That's how he'd ended up here, wasn't it?

But he was through with rash decisions and he reached for the phone.

"Who are you calling?" his aide asked.

"Bose."

"I don't think the CIA will appreciate that."

"It's their goddamned fault I'm in this mess, and he's in Amsterdam right now, which means he can be there within the hour."

Bose picked up on the third ring. "Yeah."

"It's me. The package has been lost."

"Sounds like a personal problem."

"And it'll be your personal problem if it's not recovered. So think of something clever that won't point to either of us and get it back. I do not want it falling into Zachary Griffin's hands."

13

December 7 (two days later)
Foreign Counterintelligence Office (FCI)
FBI Headquarters
Washington, D.C.

"Make yourself comfortable," the secretary told
Sydney, indicating she should sit in one of two chairs facing
the unoccupied desk of supervising special agent in charge
of the FCI squad, Brad Pearson. "He should be back in just
a moment."

"Thank you." Sydney settled in the right chair and focused
her attention on the framed print of J. Edgar Hoover, hoping
to empty her mind of the million thoughts swirling through
it. There was probably a perfectly logical explanation as to
why she'd been called into the FCI office, even though Foreign Counterintelligence was not a part of the Bureau she
had ever personally dealt with before. She, unfortunately,
couldn't think of one reason why she was here—unless it
had something to do with her trip to Amsterdam.

She'd been back two days, the whole time wondering what
had happened to Griffin. Whatever he was working was not
the normal case for him. But what the hell was it? Why had
he taken off before his team arrived to bring her in?

The ATLAS operatives who came to get her had been tight-lipped. Granted they'd treated her with fairness at the debriefing, trying to determine who had killed Petra and why. All she could tell them was that she didn't recognize the two men's voices, and yes, it appeared they were looking for something—what that might be she didn't know. What concerned her inquisitors the most was Griffin's involvement, and all she could tell them was that she had no idea what Griffin was about or where he'd taken off to, only that he seemed in a hurry to leave before they'd arrived.

Was there some other connection to ATLAS? She couldn't imagine one. When the ATLAS agents had debriefed her in Amsterdam, they had informed her that all aspects having to do with the sketch and Petra's murder were on a need-to-know basis—and no one at the Bureau needed to know. Her cover story, provided by ATLAS, was that she'd gone to Amsterdam for a simple sketch, because the reporter who'd witnessed a murder needed an artist who spoke English. It didn't matter that English was widely spoken throughout the entire Netherlands; this was the story they were sticking to. *Nothing* was to be revealed about her involvement with ATLAS to anyone outside the organization.

It seemed forever before SSA Pearson walked in. Tall, his salt-and-pepper hair shaved close, his requisite dark suit and tie favored by supervisors, he cut an impressive figure. His gray eyes took her in at a glance as she stood and they shook hands. "Sorry for the delay," he told her. "You can imagine how swamped we are after Senator Grogan's murder."

"I wasn't aware your office was investigating it," she said, taking her seat once more.

"We're assisting. He served on the Intelligence Committee about two years back and we did his background. Just checking to make sure there's nothing in the files that might have been overlooked. You know they caught the shooter."

"I'd heard."

"A schizophrenic who had been off his meds. Apparently he committed suicide in the jail."

This she hadn't heard. "He wasn't under a mental health watch?"

"He was. He made a noose out of his shirt and hung himself from the bed frame. It happens." Pearson walked around to his desk, sat, straightened his desk blotter, then leaned back in his chair. "Which brings me to why you're here. Your name came up through one of the intelligence agencies we share data with," he said. "An MI5 agent."

"A British agent?" she said, shocked. Then again, maybe this did have something to do with ATLAS. Pearson supervised the Spy vs. Spy branch of the Bureau, which shared intelligence with a number of agencies throughout the world in their fight against terrorism. She had assumed that ATLAS, being black ops and extremely covert, was not one of the agencies on their radar. Of course, some of what FCI did was so top secret, she couldn't be sure. Not knowing how to respond, she folded her hands in her lap, and said, "My name? Why?"

"That's precisely what we hope to find out. What I'm about to tell you is confidential. Apparently MI5 has been monitoring chatter from a group believed to be involved in the attempted assassination of one of their politicians from the House of Commons. They think it may be tied to the same group who killed Senator Grogan."

"Senator Grogan?" Sydney stared a moment, waiting for some sort of explanation. "I thought he was killed by a schizophrenic. I don't get it."

"Neither do we. Which is why you're here. MI5 would like to know what sort of involvement you've had with the senator in the past."

"I've never even met him," she said. "The only involvement, if one could call it that, is the coincidence of my doing a surveillance on the same day as his murder. A botched surveillance at that. So unless someone set up the whole thing to divert attention, I can't say."

"We are looking into that angle, but at this point we don't think they're in any way connected."

"Are you sure it was me they were talking about? Fitzpatrick is probably more common over there."

"Positive."

"In what context was my name used?"

"That you were an FBI agent working out of Quantico."

Which pretty much narrowed it down. Rattled, but trying not to show it, she said, "I have no idea what this is about."

"So you understand why, in light of the circumstances, we're concerned for your safety."

"Thank you. I'll be careful."

He slid a sheet of paper across the desk.

She picked it up. Saw it was a vacation request, filled out, lacking only her signature. "I don't understand."

"We think it best that you took time off until we sort through this."

"But—"

"Sign the paper, Fitzpatrick. When it comes to promotions, vacation leave looks far better than administrative leave."

She stared at the document, anger and frustration surging through her. This was Griffin's fault. ATLAS's fault.

Take a deep breath, Syd, she told herself, trying to work past the feeling of utter helplessness. Forced vacation leave because she'd been kind enough to assist an outside agency? What next? Suddenly she wondered about this report from MI5, and what it meant to her career.

"Do you need a pen?"

She nodded once, abruptly.

He handed the pen to her and she signed her name, then left, trying to decide what to do next. If her name was linked to a murdered senator, and she was forced to take leave, what exactly did that mean? That someone thought she was involved?

None of this made sense, she told herself, getting on the elevator and hitting the ground floor button. She knew nothing about the senator or his politics. But she knew someone who did. Her ex, Mr. Fast Track to the Top, Scott Ryan.

And that was enough for her. She got off on Scotty's floor instead. He was digging through a file box on his desk, pulling out manila folders, flipping through the documents.

"Hey," she said. "Shouldn't you be at lunch?"

"Eating in," he replied. "Too much going on trying to sort through all the files on Grogan before I send them up to FCI."

"FCI?" she said, casually. "Any idea why they're involved?"

"Hard to say with those guys. You realize Grogan's was the first background I ever did when I took this position?"

"No."

Scotty held up some document. "I remember the day I interviewed his wife. Nice woman. She actually baked cookies for me. Sort of spoiled me for every other background since."

Sydney glanced at the paper, figuring it was the transcript of his interview with her. "Are you going to Senator Grogan's funeral?"

"No. It's in Rhode Island. There's a memorial service here in D.C. this afternoon for him, though. And a reception at the house."

Just where she needed to be. "You should go. At least to the reception. Pay your condolences before she leaves for Rhode Island. I'd go with you if you want."

"I appreciate it, but there's the files to read. Too much to do."

"Yeah," she said, leaning against the door. "Probably best. Besides, it's not really my scene. *All* those politicians . . ."

He stopped what he was doing and looked up at her. "Maybe I should go. Pay my respects."

Scotty, so predictable. "Your car or mine?"

Senator Grogan's widow, Olivia, a fine-boned woman with dark gray hair cut in a page boy, sat in the formal living room of her Washington, D.C., condo, surrounded by several family members. She rose when she saw Scotty enter, Sydney at her side.

"Of course I remember Special Agent Ryan," she said, taking Scotty's hand in both of hers, after the woman who'd answered the door introduced them.

Sydney, thinking the widow was rather dry-eyed, recalled there being a rumor of an affair between the senator and his secretary, and figured the woman must have known about it. Smiling, Syd glanced into the dining room, saw the table filled with food items brought by other visitors. She held up the pink bakery box she'd insisted Scotty bring, filled to the brim with fresh cookies. "I'll just put these on the table," Sydney said to no one in particular, then backed out of the living room into the dining room. She made herself as unobtrusive as possible, listening with one ear while Mrs. Grogan reminisced about her encounter with Scotty during his background interview of her husband.

In truth, Sydney wasn't sure what she expected to find or even learn. But the moment she turned around and saw Tex walking in the front door, she knew her instincts in coming were right on the money.

It wasn't long before Tex found his way over to her. "So what brings you here?" he asked, looking down at the table as though interested in the food, not her.

"My name came up in the same sentence as MI5, never mind the senator's murder investigation. You wouldn't know anything about that, would you?"

"Why do you think I'm here, darlin'?" He picked up a cracker with salmon spread, popped it into his mouth, then took a second. "I just wasn't aware you knew about it yet."

"I got called up to FCI this morning."

"Good old Pearson. What did he have to say about it?"

"He wanted to know if I knew the senator. I don't. I've never even met him."

"No, but you've met Griffin, who was very much involved in the senator's doings. It's the only reason I can think of to connect you."

"Maybe if I knew why the senator was killed?"

Tex looked around to make sure they weren't overheard. "You've heard of LockeStarr Management?"

"Scotty mentioned that Grogan was going to be bringing up LockeStarr during his speech."

"They were one of the companies being looked at to manage the U.S. shipping ports. Someone leaked info that they were being investigated. Apparently Grogan took that as a sign to come out publicly against them."

"Who's investigating them?"

"We are."

"*You* didn't have him killed, did you?"

He gave her a look. "If we were in the business of hits on public figures, it sure as hell wouldn't look like one. No, what I think it has to do with is this mess Griffin's involved in. You happen to finish that sketch for him?"

"Yes. I actually have my briefcase in the car if you want to see it."

"I do."

Sydney glanced over, saw Scotty still involved in conversation with the circle in the living room. "Meet me out front."

She walked up to Scotty, saying, "I need to get some aspirin from my briefcase."

He dug the keys from his pocket, handing them to her, "I'm almost done here."

"Take your time."

Tex was waiting by her car when she walked outside. She unlocked the vehicle's door, then opened it. "You realize the sketch I have is of your subject's girlfriend, not the man Griffin saw?"

"We'll take what we can get."

Her case was beneath the front passenger seat, and she pulled it out, then removed a manila folder from within. It contained a copy of her reproduction. She handed it to Tex.

"What the . . . ?" Tex gaped at it for several seconds, then, his voice almost a whisper, he asked, "How sure are you about this looking like her?"

"Pretty sure, considering that one of the gunmen said it was a dead ringer for the boss's girlfriend."

"It's also a dead ringer for Griffin's dead wife."

Sydney stared at Tex in disbelief. His expression never wavered. She looked at the sketch, recalling that moment in Italy when Griffin told her of his wife's murder. "Griffin was there when she was killed," she said. "He wouldn't make that kind of mistake."

Tex returned the sketch to the folder, then handed it back to her. "I've known that woman for fifteen years. Hell. I was there when she broke her nose. Other than the short hair, it's her."

"It could be someone who looks like her."

"It could be, but my gut tells me otherwise," he said, then glanced over at Scotty, saw him watching them through the window. "Not a good place to talk. Meet me at Jumping Java at three," he said.

After he left, she opened the folder, looking at the sketch, trying to make sense of what Tex had said.

Griffin's wife was dead. He wouldn't lie about something like that.

So who the hell was this?

14

December 7
Washington, D.C.

The first thing FBI Special Agent Tony Carillo did was
order up a copy of the blood panel from the shooter's arrest,
and with that in hand, walked it to the FBI's own lab. Aside
from the PCP, there was one drug listed that Carillo didn't
recognize.

The doctor at the FBI lab read over the report. "Nothing
outstanding. This drug is used to treat hypothyroidism."

"The guy was schizophrenic. Went off his meds. So this
would be normal?"

"Depends. Went off his meds for how long?"

"I'm not sure anyone said. Why?"

"Might help to know why and when he went off. Because
he didn't like the way he felt on them? Or was it because
his symptoms weren't under control and that fed into his
delusional fears?"

Carillo finished his coffee, then tossed the cup in the trash,
saying, "Mind you I don't know jack about psychiatry, but
if he was paranoid and went off his meds because of a delusional fear, why would he still be taking his hypothyroid
medicine?"

"Good question. Then again, if he was having thyroid issues, those symptoms can sometimes mimic schizophrenia. So can PCP."

"Psychiatrist's report confirmed the schizophrenia."

"Did he know about the thyroid?"

"There wasn't any mention of it in his report."

"You might check. Could be a factor."

"Thanks, Doc."

"Anytime."

Next step for Carillo was calling the investigator at Metropolitan Police. He spoke with Kristofer Jones. "I seem to be missing a section of the report on the interviews on who knew the shooter. He have any relatives in the area? Coworkers? Friends?"

"Talk about your perfect loner," Jones said. "Couldn't find a thing on him. The closest we came was the girl who lived across from Hollis at his apartment complex, and the manager. The info should have been in the supplemental report."

Carillo thumbed through the papers in his folder. "Seems to be missing from my copy. Either of them have anything to add?"

"The usual. Quiet guy. Nice. But then, maybe we just didn't ask the right questions." He gave Carillo the address.

The neighbor, Lisa Reed, answered the door on the first knock. She did not invite Carillo in, however, choosing instead to step out onto the porch. "Baby's morning nap," she said, pointing inside to a blanket on the floor where her infant was sleeping. "I hope you don't mind."

"Not at all. I'm here about your former neighbor."

"Hollis," she said, closing the door, though not tightly.

"Right."

"Like I told the officers who were here, I didn't really know him. He was, I don't know. Odd. Quiet, nice, but odd. Most would probably dismiss it because of his profession. He wrote computer programs. I'd heard he was obsessed with computers." She crossed her arms, shivering in the cold air. "I was seven months pregnant when I moved in, so I suppose that might be why I didn't really get to know him. We said hi, but that was it."

"He ever have anyone over?"

"Truthfully I didn't pay attention. I do know he was up very, very late at night, only because you could see his light on at all hours."

"Any of your other neighbors know the guy?"

"Hard to say. They all pretty much keep to themselves. Most are older. Fifties, sixties. Wish I could tell you more, but that's really all I know about him."

"I appreciate your time," he said. As she opened the door, he caught a glimpse of the baby again. "You said you were seven months pregnant when you moved in? How old is the baby now?"

"Four weeks."

"So you haven't lived here all that long?"

"Almost three months."

"Any idea who lived here before you?"

"As a matter of fact, I do. Her mail still comes occasionally. Someone named Madeline Boucher."

Carillo got the particulars on Ms. Boucher from the FBI office and drove straight there. Learned from a neighbor that she went by the name Maddie, and worked at a clothing boutique nearby, where he found her straightening the hangers of dresses on a display rack. She might have been all of eighteen, tall, blond hair, and blue eyes, wearing blue jeans and a pullover sweater.

Carillo identified himself, and saw her expression turn to one of resignation. "I was hoping no one would make the connection," she said.

"What connection?"

"As the girl who used to be friends with the guy who murdered the senator?"

"Regular ice breaker at parties."

"Yeah. To say the least."

"What can you tell me about him?"

"Same as everyone else? The clichéd he was so quiet, I would have never suspected?"

"Except for his mental illness?"

"That part I didn't know. I mean, mostly we were just friends. We lived in the same apartment complex, and, well, during that time he was fine. It was the last couple months that I started noticing changes. It was odd. These weird little bursts of paranoia, talking to himself, the delusions that he was being followed."

"By who?"

She shrugged. "God only knows. At one time it was aliens. Another it was aliens from Atlantis. I mean, really out there. That if he didn't do something, they were going to kill everyone."

"Aliens from Atlantis?" Aliens he'd expect to pop up in the conversation of a mentally ill patient. Even Atlantis, he supposed. He just didn't expect them in the same sentence. "Anyone else witness this behavior?"

"The entire world. He devoted his Web site to it."

Another fact that hadn't been mentioned in the police report. His computer, yes, having a Web site, no. The computer hadn't yielded much information, because every file on it was deleted, so any Web sites he'd visited in the past were unknown, but the investigators had attributed the deleted files to the paranoid tendencies of being watched. "What was the name of the Web site?"

"Above Atlantis NWO." When Carillo raised his brows in question, she added, "That stands for New World Order."

Carillo jotted the name into his notebook. "And one more thing. About when did he start using PCP?"

"Excuse me?"

"The drug PCP."

"No way. That guy was so squeaky clean, he wouldn't have *ever* used anything. He barely drank. His brain was a temple—his words, I kid you not—and he wasn't about to pollute it with anything. Except coffee. He *definitely* drank coffee."

"He had PCP in his system at the time of the shooting."

"I have a hard time believing it. As weird as he was, I really liked him." Maddie moved from the dresses to a table with scarves artfully tossed about on it, and she pulled one up, fluffed it out a little, as though that arrangement was far superior. Carillo said nothing, merely waited, his experience always having been that it's best to let people talk, fill in the silence, and after a moment, she paused in her ministrations, looking up at him. "Not just weird. Brainy weird, you know? And very into conspiracy theory."

"What sort of conspiracy theory?"

"The typical. Corrupt government. Major corporations funding politicians to further their own interests. I mean, no one took him seriously. At least not at first. But then he sort of became obsessed."

"Over what?"

She gave a cynical laugh. "He hacked into the server of some company with some program his friend helped him write and said the evidence was right there. Don't ask me what it was, because I have no idea." She picked up another scarf, running it through her fingers, before laying it across the table. "Look. I'm sorry the senator was killed, and I'd really like to help, but when Hollis started saying that they were going to implant him with some mind-controlling device, that was when I started distancing myself. A little too sci-fi for me, you know?"

"You know the name of this friend who helped him write the program?"

"Izzy."

"Izzy what?"

"That's it. Just Izzy."

"Any idea where I can find him?"

"Sorry. The only time I ever met him was at Hollis's place. He was always working on Hollis's computer. Almost like a fixture there, if you know what I mean."

A woman walked in, and Maddie gave Carillo a tentative smile hinting that she hoped he was done with the conversation. He slipped his card on the counter. "If you think of anything else, give me a call."

"Sure thing."

Outside, Carillo went over his notes, wondering at the possibility that Hollis's symptoms of paranoid schizophrenia were brought on by PCP usage. Who else would bring up aliens from Atlantis? And brain implants? He could see why the guy would be dismissed as a nutcase. But a couple of things bothered Carillo, the hacking into the server for one. According to the police, the guy's hard drive was clean, but maybe a tad too clean. And now there was this mysterious friend, Izzy, who might have helped him program his computer.

Maybe it was nothing.

Then again, maybe it was something, and he picked up the phone and called an old friend in the FBI's Computer Analysis department. "Any chance you guys can do some deep forensic work on a PC?"

15

December 7
Washington, D.C.

Tex was ordering as Sydney walked into the coffee
shop, and so she was forced to wait for answers about her
sketch and the woman's identity until they were alone. He
handed a cup to her, then walked over to the condiments.
"You take anything in it?"

"I'm surprised you don't have that written down somewhere along with everything else you know about me."

"Tastes change."

"Half and half."

He poured a splash into her cup and she put the top on
before following him out. They stood on the sidewalk next
to a row of coin-operated newspaper stands, both of them
watching the traffic, not talking at first. Sydney figured
that Tex would tell her what he wanted and after several
moments, with no sign that he was in any hurry, she said,
"What's going on?"

"I'm not even sure where to begin."

"How about we start with Griffin's wife? If she's dead,
who's the woman in the sketch?"

"Honestly? I don't know. The building they were in exploded. He was rescued, she wasn't. Or so we thought."

"So you *thought*? Was there a body? DNA?"

"Charred beyond recognition. We were told the body was positively identified by DNA."

"Okay, either it was a sloppy investigation, or there's some other logical answer. After all, Griffin was a witness, you've got a dead body buried in his wife's grave and an alleged DNA test stating it's her."

"Look who you're talking to Sydney. It's not like someone couldn't have gone to great pains to fake a DNA test. And knowing all the players involved and what it could mean, I'm not about to ask to have the body exhumed."

Sydney wrapped both hands around her coffee cup, trying to keep warm. "Meaning what?"

"Meaning I have no idea what it means yet. I'm willing to concede that she very well could be dead, and this is just a huge coincidence. Except like I said, my gut's telling me otherwise. It's also telling me that this isn't something I can bring up at the next team meeting. Not if I want to help Griffin. I'm not even sure I can go to her boss about this."

"Her boss?"

"She didn't work for us. She was CIA," he said. "Jesus. I'm breaking about a dozen rules just talking to you about this stuff." He kicked at the dirty slush pile near the curb, knocking a piece loose, then crushing it underfoot. Finally he looked at her, said, "Bottom line? Griffin's in trouble."

Her first thought was that guys like Griffin were always in trouble. The word should be tattooed across his forehead. Tex meant something else. He had to have meant something else. But when she recalled how Griffin had acted when he'd left her on that rooftop in Amsterdam, sketch or no sketch, she knew this was different. "What sort of trouble?"

"He's been burned. Set up for a murder he didn't commit. His only hope is to let us bring him in, clear his name before he's found by anyone else. I don't think he's going to let us do that."

She stared at her coffee cup, watching the thin vapor of steam rise from the vent in the lid, thinking that had she refused to go out on that drawing, she'd be sitting in her office, doing what she was meant to do, with none of this touching her in any way. "You're about to tell me something I don't want to hear, aren't you?"

"Afraid so. Right now, Griffin is completely in the cold. He's got no one, and if he's not careful, the trumped-up murder charge will end up being real."

"Real? How?"

"He's after the man who murdered his wife. And if I know Griffin, he won't rest until he's killed him."

Sydney well remembered the pain in Griffin's voice when he'd told her about his wife and how she died. "Okay," she said. "Let's say this woman in this sketch *is* someone else. That means Becca really is dead, and some might think he'd be doing a service. Taking his wife's killer off the street."

"Except I think the suspected killer is a key player in this LockeStarr investigation right now, and I need him alive."

"Why? What's so important about LockeStarr?"

"We believe they're a front company for the Network. Recent intelligence came in that they're behind the recruitment of Dr. Fedorov, a Russian Vector scientist known for his work on chimera viruses, viruses that are fused from more than one type, in this case for bioweapons. We've heard that they're about to or already have tested one such weapon."

"Tested where?"

"That's the million-dollar question. Right now, every allied agency is scrambling to investigate any unconfirmed rumors of large-scale deaths, whether it's fish, birds, or suspected group suicides of splinter religious sects. We don't even know what the weapon's supposed to do. Poison the air? The water? Viral? Bacterial? If it really is Fedorov involved, we're guessing viral. Whatever it is, we've heard that it works and they're already lining up buyers. That means in order to find this weapon, I need this guy that Griffin's hunting down, and I need him alive, Sydney. And to keep him that way, I have to know who he is, who he was working with, and where this stuff is being manufactured, and your sketch might be the only tie we have to find him."

Sydney sipped at her coffee, ignoring the voice of reason

in her head that said she needed to discontinue this conversation, walk away, and not look back. What she did instead was ask, "Why are you telling me this?"

"A couple reasons. One, I need you. Griffin's got one objective. Kill the guy he thinks killed her, and he won't come in until he's achieved it. He knows damned well that if I show up, it'll be to stop him. You might be the only one in the world who could safely get close enough to him."

"And the other reason?"

"Right now he's considered a rogue spy, one we're under orders to bring in. Let's just say that there are a few agencies, including here in the U.S., that might not be so understanding should they run into him. And if this really is Griffin's wife involved in all this, there's something a lot bigger going on than even I know about. Someone went to a lot of trouble to make her look dead, and more recently to burn Griffin. The question is who? And why?"

"You've got to have some idea."

"The strongest being that when he started looking into his wife's murder, he stirred up a hornet's nest." He pulled off the lid from his cup, then dumped the coffee into the snow at his feet, the hot brown liquid cutting into the ice like acid. "The thing about hornets, you get stung by too many, you die."

Sydney tossed her half-full cup into the trash, having lost her taste for the beverage. "As much as I'd love to help, my office is never going to let me go. They forced me to take vacation leave."

"Maybe with good reason."

She looked up at him. "Pearson knows . . . ? God. How did I not see that coming?"

"There's a lot going on here and not enough time to go into it. So how about it?"

"Backroom politics aside, you think I'm just going to be able to jet off to Europe and find a man who doesn't want to be found?"

"I do, because you have something he wants. The sketch. He has no idea who it's of, but I damned well know he wants it."

"How do I know you're not using me as a way to find him?"

"I am using you. To help him."

Sydney shoved her hands into her pockets. "Look, Tex, I want to help Griffin. But the last time I ran out there for you, someone was murdered, and the killers came after me. That seems to be a theme with your group. I'm not sure I'm the right person for it," she said, taking a step back, and then another. Her mother wanted her home for Christmas. It was a promise she intended to keep. "I'm sorry."

She started to walk away.

"He needs you."

Sydney stopped in her tracks. Tried not to think about the history she and Griffin had together. The operation they'd worked in Italy. The time he'd come back for her, saved her life at risk to his own. It wasn't that she wasn't grateful. She was. It was that Griffin and his ilk were world-class spies. They were highly trained for that sort of work. She might be able to shoot with the best of them, handle herself in a fight, run an investigation. But she was not a spy. And now her job was on the line. "I need to think about it. It's the best I can do."

It was well after six by the time Sydney returned to her office, then drove home, telling herself that if she were smart, she'd stay far away from Tex and Griffin and anyone else involved with ATLAS. She was *not* getting involved. Griffin might be in trouble, but he was well equipped to deal with it, no matter what Tex said. And probably the last thing Griffin wanted was for her to be in his way.

Besides, what could she possibly do to help? He wanted the drawing, and she could send that electronically, assuming she even knew where to send it. And then what? If, as Tex said, it looked just like Griffin's wife, how would he react when he saw it? If it really *was* she, his quest for revenge was over. Still, there was bound to be a lot of pent-up anger, never mind unanswered questions that were going to cause a whole new set of problems, and she wasn't sure she wanted to be around when he found out.

Pressing the remote for the gate to her apartment complex, she drove in, and not seeing any vacant spaces at the perimeter of her building, pulled into the underground garage and parked. Her footsteps echoed across the cement floor as she walked to the elevator, pushed the button, and stepped on. Her apartment was on the fifth floor, down a long carpeted hallway and around the corner—in other words, about as far from the elevator as one could get. A good thing if one wanted peace and quiet. A bad thing if one was carrying groceries.

When she inserted her key into the lock, the door pushed open. She hadn't even turned the key yet.

Sydney stepped back, drew her gun, then shoved the door open the rest of the way with her foot. The apartment was dark. Reaching in, she flicked on the light switch, did a cursory search, saw the living room was empty, as was the kitchen. The hallway to the bedrooms and the one bathroom was to the right. She angled out, stepped to the side until she could see down the hall. Both bedroom doors were open, just as she'd left them. They were empty. The bathroom was empty. And there was no one in the closets.

She holstered her gun and walked back out to the living room. Nothing looked disturbed.

And though she was fairly meticulous about making sure her door was locked, she had been in a hurry this morning to make that appointment with Pearson at FCI . . .

"Oh, you are home."

Sydney glanced over at her front door, still standing open. Her neighbor from across the hall, Tina, stood there looking in, bundled up in a coat, scarf, and gloves, while her black Labrador, Storm, pulled at his leash, trying to get into Sydney's apartment. "Just got home. Why?"

"I think Storm scared off the two electricians who came to your door."

"Electricians?"

"From the utility company. Storm was growling at my door, and when I looked out the peephole, I saw them standing in front of your place. When I opened up to tell them you weren't home, Storm lunged at them. He's not usually a barker, but man. He sort of went nuts. Good thing I had him by the collar."

Sydney's gaze flicked to the door, then back down at the dog, who seemed inordinately interested in the scent on her threshold. She walked up, bent over, and scratched Storm behind his ears. "Good dog." Then to Tina, asked, "They say anything?"

"Not really. Just wanted to know when you'd be home. That was maybe a half hour ago? The one guy said he'd leave a card, and that was it. They took off."

"I wonder what they wanted." Sydney shrugged, acted as if it were no big deal. "Thanks, Tina."

"No problem. Storm, come," she said, tugging on his leash when he didn't immediately follow her down the hall toward the elevator. Once Tina was out of sight, Sydney examined her front door, but couldn't tell if it had been picked. Seeing no sign of a business card, she closed and locked the door, then called the utility company, asking if they'd sent anyone by. They hadn't.

Next call was to Tex. "You guys dispatch someone by my place disguised as utility workers?"

"Not us, darlin'."

"I was afraid you were going to say that." Tucking her cell beneath her ear, she told him what happened, while she grabbed her small, soft-sided suitcase, then started rummaging her drawers for clothes, wondering if three days' worth would be enough. "It seems my neighbor interrupted them before they got in. But my door was unlocked, which means they were that close to entering."

"What are your plans?"

"I figure I have two choices. Scotty's or a hotel."

"Or catch a flight to Europe."

"No way. This mess is clearly a result from my last trip there."

"And you think staying in a hotel is going to make them go away?"

She glanced toward the window, suddenly wondering if they *had* actually left. "Hold on," she said, turning off her light. She strode across the room, parted the curtain, looked out to the lot below, and saw a vehicle that stood out, mostly because it was backed into the space. "There's a white van parked with a view of the entry gate and the drive leading into the garage."

"You ever seen it there before?"

"No." And the coincidence of its presence right after the sighting of the false utility workers was enough to set her alarm bells ringing. Tex was right. It didn't matter where she went, or whom she stayed with. If they'd found her apartment this easily, they'd have no trouble tracking her down through her friends, maybe even her family. It was that last thought that spurred her to action. The farther away from them she was, the safer they'd be. "How soon can you be here?"

"Give me ten minutes."

She dropped the curtain, disconnected, then turned the light on to finish her packing. That done, she put her suitcase by the dining room table, turned a chair so that it faced the door, then sat there with her gun in one hand.

16

December 7
Washington, D.C.

Tex finally called. "I'm parked in front of the lobby doors. You want me to come up?"

"I'll meet you down there."

She grabbed her bag and keys, tucked her gun in her coat pocket. She did not turn off the light, in case they were watching her window from outside. Checking the hallway in both directions before stepping out, she locked the door behind her, then walked to the elevator, her hand in her pocket, finger on the trigger guard. Healthy paranoia seemed the wisest of courses right now, and before she even pressed the down button, the elevator bell signaled its arrival on her floor. She stepped to the side, her concealed gun aimed directly at the door. Tina and Storm stepped off.

Syd slipped her hand from her pistol, smiling in greeting as Tina asked, "Where you off to this time?"

"Business trip," Sydney replied, taking the moment to pat Storm.

"Must be fun doing what you do. All that travel and stuff."

"Trust me, Tina," she said, moving past her onto the elevator. "A little downtime would be welcome right now." She put her foot in front of the door to keep it from sliding shut. "Do me a favor? If you see anyone lurking around my place, call the cops? I phoned the utility company and they didn't send anyone."

"You think they were there to rip you off?"

An understatement to say the least. Even so, she felt it in Tina's best interest to instill a good dose of self-awareness, in hopes the girl didn't stumble into anything she shouldn't. "Burglars are pretty sophisticated nowadays," she said, nodding at the dog. "I'd pay attention to Storm's instincts."

Tina, looking slightly alarmed, pulled Storm next to her leg. "I will," she said, patting the Labrador's flank.

Sydney moved her foot, allowing the elevator door to slide closed. Tex awaited her downstairs. Apparently so did two men dressed in the utility company's uniforms, probably sent there to kill her. She only hoped she could get into the car and out of the parking lot before they succeeded.

The van followed them out of the apartment complex. "Definitely not one of ours," Tex said, eyeing it in his rearview mirror. "We'd at least come up with a real utility truck."

"That's comforting to know. How are you going to lose them?"

Tex hit the gas, made a quick right, doubling back around the complex. "I may not lose them. As long as I keep them at bay long enough to get you to where you're going."

"And where am I going?"

He glanced over at her, but said nothing as he returned his attention to the road. Not that he needed to say a word. She'd already come to the realization that there was nowhere she could go that wouldn't bring danger to those she loved. Back home to San Francisco was out of the question. They'd have no problem following a simple trail to her mother's home, thereby endangering everyone there, including her young sister and her stepfather. Scotty's was out for the same reason, even though he, technically, could fend for himself. Until she found out what was going on, who was after her, and why, she wouldn't be able to rest. She gave an exaggerated sigh of exasperation, because she knew that Tex would realize her primary goal would be to keep her family safe, which meant the farther she was from them, the better. "Which airport did you have in mind?"

"Dulles. There's a packet for you in the glove box. Your ticket, documents, money, and a credit card. And while you're at it," he said, as Sydney opened the glove compartment, pulling out a thick manila envelope, "you might want to leave your gun with me. Avoid some of the headaches if you take it into the airport."

"And if they follow me in?"

"I'm hoping to lose them before they realize that's where we're going. But that's the beauty of our pain-in-the-butt post–9/11 security measures. They're gonna have a hard time getting past the security checkpoint without a ticket."

"Last I heard, those checkpoints weren't exactly bullet-proof."

She opened the envelope, looked at her ticket and the passport, both in the name of Cindy Kirkpatrick, an AKA she'd used on a previous ATLAS operation, then eyed the thick stack of euros, all hundreds, as well as a credit card. "That's a lot of money."

"The spy business doesn't come cheap. Especially when you don't want to be using your own credit card. That one's cold and prepaid. There's about ten thousand euros on it. I'll refill it if needed."

"Who's funding this venture?"

"ATLAS has a rainy day fund, you could say," he replied, whipping the wheel over and switching lanes. "Which is why you need to keep your name out of it. Do not pull rank anywhere in that airport, because I can guarantee that your real name is flagged and the first computer check will shut us down. If it gets back, my boss will have my ass, yours will be handed to you by yours, and Griffin really will be on his own. There are a lot of agents working for ATLAS out in the field whose safety depends on this remaining under the radar, Sydney."

She removed her ID from her purse, along with anything else that might identify her. "Why would they connect me to this?"

"They're goddamned secret agents, Syd. They know you know me."

"Next time a secret agent walks into my office, I am *so* ignoring him."

"Good luck with that."

By the time they neared the airport, they'd lost sight of the van, and hoped they'd lost it. Tex stopped his car in front of the glass doors, as the warning announcement about unattended vehicles being towed aired over the loudspeakers. Sydney got out, opened the back door, and was pulling out her bag when she saw the van from her peripheral vision driving into the passenger drop-off zone. "They're here."

Tex drew his gun, held it low. "It'd really help if you could get in there without being ID'd. *Or* shot."

"I'd definitely like to avoid the latter, thank you." She looked around, saw three uniformed police officers standing about twenty feet away from the terminal entrance, eyeing the incoming passengers. Under normal circumstances, she'd pull out her credentials, then inform them there were two armed men in the van.

These were not normal circumstances.

Think. She needed the suspects distracted long enough for her to safely get inside, past security.

She grabbed her bag, slung it over her shoulder. Doing her best to look less like a federal agent and more like a frightened woman, she ran over to the officers. "Thank God! Some woman just stopped me and said that van's been following her all night," Sydney told them, pointing at the approaching vehicle. "She saw guns."

The officers looked in that direction, one radioing about possible armed subjects. Within seconds several more officers came running out the terminal doors as the van rolled up. The police drew their weapons, aimed at the vehicle. Pedestrians screamed, some ducking behind cars, others running into the terminal. Sydney, quickly forgotten in the general chaos, ran through the doors. She glanced back, saw the van speeding off, officers jumping into their patrol cars to follow, and she quickened her pace toward security, losing herself in the crowd.

Forty-five minutes later, she sat on the plane and had just slid her purse under the seat, then remembered to shut off her phone. She flipped it open and saw she had missed a call. She didn't recognize the number. She did recognize the country code, the Netherlands, and she hit redial, listening to it ring.

Someone picked up on the other end, but didn't speak.

"Hello?" she said, hearing faint static, but nothing else. Was it Griffin? Had to be. Just in case, she kept it vague. "If you're there, I'm coming out. I have something for you. I just need to know where to go."

No answer.

"Are you there?"

The static ended and she heard absolute silence.

"I'm sorry, ma'am," the flight attendant said, stopping by Sydney's seat as she made her preflight inspection round. "You'll have to turn off your phone."

Sydney hit the power button, then dropped the phone into her purse. If it wasn't Griffin, she didn't want to imagine who might be waiting for her when she stepped off that plane.

And if it was Griffin? She thought of the sketch, the resemblance to his wife. She wasn't so sure she wanted to be the one to show it to him.

17

December 7
Washington, D.C.

Right after the shooting, Izzy had been half tempted to get a room at the Hilton. God knew he had access to enough credit card numbers to book a room online, but then there was that whole ID issue—they always asked for it—and he only had the one with his real name. That left this place that took cash and asked no questions, with its pink neon sign with the T and the L burned out of the word *MOTEL*. At least the rooms were clean, two beds, a table with two chairs, and there didn't seem to be any bugs. It smelled of cigarettes, even though he'd asked for nonsmoking. The clerk sort of laughed, shoved the key toward him, and said, "Enjoy your stay."

Right. He'd slept fitfully every night since, waking each time he heard a car drive past on the street. He kept his trips outside to a minimum, and only for food. Tonight, after a quick run to the store to get some bottled water, snacks, and then dinner at McDonald's, he was back in the room, the TV on for company.

He sat at the faux wood table, eating his hamburger, while

playing solitaire on his laptop. With everything that had happened, his brain wasn't functioning, and he didn't dare connect to the Internet and chance he'd make a sloppy mistake, like the one he'd made the other day when he was trying to erase his tracks from Hollis's computer.

The TV droned in the background, and he paid little interest until he heard the TV newscaster say, "The suspect in the murder of Senator Grogan, twenty-three-year-old Hollis Kane, appears to have committed suicide this morning while in police custody at a mental health facility, where he was being evaluated. An anonymous source within the police department states that Hollis Kane was believed to have been a mental health patient, and had apparently stopped taking his medications, which may have led to the shooting and his eventual suicide. The matter is still under investigation. And in other news, the president states that the bill to beef up security in our nation's ports is his top priority, now that . . ."

Izzy nearly choked on his hamburger. Coughing, he guzzled half the soda, trying to clear his throat, as he switched channels, trying to find further updates. There were none. He pushed his half-eaten dinner aside as the realization hit. No way Hollis committed suicide. Besides, he wasn't on any meds that Izzy knew of. Somebody needed him out of the way. Maybe the guys in the white van, who came after Izzy . . . He tried to think who else might be in danger. What else was on Hollis's computer, and the first thing he remembered was the desktop background, the pictures of Maddie. The thought sent a wave of panic through him and suddenly the hamburger felt like a lead weight in his gut.

Hollis was already dead. And if Izzy didn't find Maddie, warn her, she was likely to be next.

The clothing store was dark, and there was only one car left in the parking lot. Izzy thought it might be Maddie's. He didn't dare approach until he was sure it was she, and he waited in the shadows near the car, until he saw her emerge from the side door, then cross the parking lot. He stepped into view.

She jumped on seeing him, dropping her key ring. "Oh my God, Izzy," she said, putting her hand on her chest. "You scared me half to death."

"I'm sorry. I didn't think it was, you know, a good idea to go inside."

"Why are you here?"

"I need to talk to you. It's important."

She seemed to think about it for a second, then said, "There's a Chinese food restaurant about a half mile up the road. Meet me there."

"I sort of parked a couple blocks away . . ."

Maddie stared at him for several seconds, and he wondered if it had been a bad idea to even come here. But then she picked up her keys from the ground, saying, "It's cold. I'll give you a ride."

She pressed the remote that unlocked her car, then got in. Izzy climbed into the passenger seat, shivering, and grateful when she blasted the heater, even though there was only icy air at first. He'd been waiting for at least fifteen minutes, and he hadn't bothered bringing gloves, primarily because he hadn't thought to grab them when he rushed from the motel.

"Which way?" she asked, after she pulled out.

He pointed. "There's some retirement home up there. In their parking lot."

"This is about Hollis, isn't it?"

He didn't reply.

"The FBI was here asking about him."

"What'd you tell them?"

"What could I tell them? Hollis was acting weird. Face it, he went off the deep end."

"He wasn't crazy."

"Oh my God, Izzy! Have you seen his Web site? He rambled on forever about Atlantis and aliens and Nazis and whatever else was on there, like the senator was behind it all or something. He killed the senator, and then he killed himself. He was nuts."

"I don't think he did it."

"There were *witnesses*, Izzy, that actually saw him with the gun."

"He wouldn't kill himself. And he definitely wasn't crazy."

Maddie turned into the retirement home parking lot. "I know you two were friends, Izzy. And I'm sorry. But Hollis sort of brought this on himself. He got too wrapped up in all that stuff."

"You have to understand what he saw. It's not what you think."

"Then what is it? Explain it to me."

"I think you could be in danger."

"Not you, too."

"I'm serious."

"Fine. If I'm in danger, we go to the police."

"And what?" he said, unable to keep the frustration from his voice. "Ask them to protect us? They couldn't even protect Hollis and he was in custody!" He stared out the windshield, trying to think what might convince her. "I was on his computer the other day, like maybe minutes after the shooting, and someone else was there."

"At his house?"

"Maybe. I wasn't at his house."

"How do you get on his computer—"

"Remotely. You don't even have to be there. But they were on it, and that means it wasn't the police. They hadn't even arrested him yet. Whoever it was, I think they were waiting for all this to go down before they deleted the files. And it didn't take them long to figure out who I was and come after me."

"They came after you. Fine. But I'm not involved in any of this. Why would they come after me?"

"Because your name was the only other one on Hollis's computer. He didn't know anyone else."

"Okay, so my name was on there."

"And your picture."

"Nobody has my address. I moved to a different city to get away from Hollis. I'm not even listed in the phone book."

"The FBI agent found you."

"He's like a cop. They're supposed to be able to do that."

"*I* found you."

And that apparently got her attention. Because she had most definitely not given her address to Izzy. Even so,

Maddie insisted on returning to her apartment to see if anyone had been there.

"Tomorrow," Izzy said. "We'll go there tomorrow in the daylight. It'll be safer."

"And where am I supposed to spend the night?"

"I have a motel room."

"Oh, right."

"Look. I'm not trying to hit on you. It has two beds. And it's clean. Just one night. And then we'll go by your place tomorrow. If it turns out I'm wrong, then no harm, no foul, okay?"

Of course, that was assuming Izzy hadn't been followed, and he looked around, wondering if it was possible that they had let him get away just to get to Maddie . . .

The following morning, Izzy kept a sharp watch as he drove up the street and into the drive of Maddie's apartment complex.

"Which place is yours?" he asked.

"The one with the open curtain in the living room window. See, it's fine. There's no one there."

And he wondered if maybe he was overreacting by thinking they'd come after Maddie. Maybe they weren't even after him. In the back of his mind was the thought that he'd jumped out his bedroom window at the sight of the van, only *hearing* someone knocking on his door. After all, it could have been coincidence. Maybe a neighbor asking to borrow something, and the van wasn't even there for him. But he didn't think so, and something told him it would be a bad idea to go inside. "Are you friends with any of your neighbors? Is there someone you could phone to double check?"

"Rhonda lives across the breezeway. Her front door faces mine."

"Call her."

The parking lot formed a giant U, with driveways at both ends, buildings on the exterior, and a pool and the office in the center. He drove past her apartment, continuing on around, parking in front of the pool in one of the visitor spaces, which gave them a line of sight through the wrought-iron fence to the other side of the drive as well as her apartment. "What do I say?" she asked, fishing through her purse for her phone.

"Make up something."

She put the phone to her ear, covering the receiver as she said, "Answering machine . . ." Then, directly into the phone, "Hey, Rhonda. It's Maddie . . . Um, give me a call when you get in?"

Across the way, a white van drove into the parking lot, its side emblazoned with a large "Florist" sign.

"Look," Izzy told her. "That's the same van."

"A florist van was at your place?"

"*And* at the store."

The van stopped in front of her building and a man in coveralls got out, opened up the side door, removing a bouquet of flowers. It didn't look like a deliveryman's uniform, Izzy thought. It looked more industrial. Like the uniforms that the utility company guys wore, except they weren't the same color.

"Those are real flowers," she said. Her voice wavered slightly as though unsure, and they watched the man walk up to her door and knock. "They could be real, couldn't they? A real delivery?"

"You have a boyfriend? Any other reason you'd get flowers?"

She shook her head. "What should I do?"

"You can't go home. Call your boss this morning. Maybe tell them your aunt is sick, dying, and you're going up to Maine to visit her?"

"What is it these guys are after? Why are they doing this?"

"I think they wanted to stop Senator Grogan, and Hollis found out about it."

"Who wanted to stop him?"

"I don't know." Right now he was hoping they could stay alive long enough to figure it out.

"We should go to the FBI," Maddie told Izzy as he drove from the complex. "Ask for that agent who came to see me."

"We can't go to the FBI. You ever hear of Robert Hanssen? He was an FBI agent who went to jail for the rest of his life for being a traitor. They even made a movie about it."

"For God's sake, Izzy!" she said, slinking down in her seat, to avoid being seen should the two men look that direction. "This isn't one of your video games. Besides, if that FBI agent was in on it, he would have killed me right then. Why waste a good opportunity?"

"Yeah? Well, how are they going to believe us if *you* don't? They're telling the news that the case is closed and they got their man, who's dead." Izzy glanced in his rearview mirror as he turned into the street. So far the van hadn't moved. "What we need is proof. Then the FBI will *have* to believe us."

"Let me ask you this, Mr. Gonna Save the World. If these guys are as dangerous as you say they are, how are you going to get that proof and not get killed yourself?"

"Easy. *You* send me an e-mail saying we're gonna meet somewhere. They show up, and we know who they are. We get this FBI agent to go with us so he can see."

"An e-mail? How is that going to do anything?"

"Because I have a feeling that they got into my computer with the same program that Hollis used when he hacked into their system."

"How do you know it will work? I mean, what if you send it and they don't come and then—"

"They'll come. I know just the place. But first we need to set you up with a fake e-mail."

They drove to an Internet café, where Izzy paid to use a computer, purchasing fifteen minutes. "Do you have Webbased mail?" he asked Maddie.

"How should I know? I just turn on my computer, and it's there."

"That's okay. We shouldn't use your real e-mail anyway. We'll make a new account. It's not like they'll notice." He quickly pulled up a free online e-mail site and made her an address. "What should we use for a screen name? Girls always have cutesy names with a number."

"How about Maddiebear23?"

"Maddiebear." He typed in the number, created a new account. "So what should we say? We want it to sound like it's a continuing conversation. Maybe one that started on the phone to explain why you're only just sending it?"

"I don't know. Maybe: 'I got your voice mail. Meet me at the—' Where did you want to meet?"

"Central Café."

" 'At Central Café tomorrow at two o'clock.' "

"No one writes *o'clock*. We'll just say *two*." He read over the message, his finger hovering above the mouse. "Well?"

"Wait. Maybe we shouldn't put the location until you answer it."

"Good point." He removed the location and hit send. "Guess we'll find out."

"Shouldn't you check yours and see if it got there?"

"Not yet. I'm sure they have my password, and are probably watching my account. If I open it too soon, it'll seem obvious. I'll open it tonight or early in the morning."

"What if they're watching the place early and they see us come in?"

"Don't worry. I have a plan."

Please let it work, he thought.

Because if it didn't, they were both dead.

18

December 8
Rijksmuseum
Amsterdam, The Netherlands

Zachary Griffin opened up his guidebook, adjusted his clear tortoiseshell-framed glasses as he pretended to read the information before looking up at the massive painting of Rembrandt's *Night Watch*. He stood there admiring it for what he felt was an appropriate time before moving on. He'd been at the museum for two hours, waiting. He'd been here yesterday and the day before, different guises both times, casing the place. Of course, the beautiful thing about museums, he thought, making his way back to the sculpture of Minerva and Cupid, was that they were filled with benches and seats. No one thought twice about seeing someone sitting there doing nothing but looking at works of art for interminably long periods.

A museum docent watched him as he entered the room, the same man who had been there earlier this morning. The docent looked away, his body language relaxed, unconcerned, and Griffin took a seat on a bench that gave him a clear view of the sculpture and the room at large. For several minutes he sat studying his guidebook, his peripheral vision picking up the movement around him. Just as he wondered how much longer he could afford to stay, Sydney finally walked in, and he suddenly recalled that moment he thought it was she lying there on Petra's floor—and then the relief when he'd learned otherwise.

He'd only dared the one call, and then, when she'd called back, he couldn't answer, and so sent a text message on where to meet. She had a background in fine art, and he knew she'd be able to read between the lines. This was the one place he could think of that would allow him to wait for any length of time unnoticed.

And now she was here.

He watched as she glanced over at the sculpture, gave a slight smile, then looked around the room, finally noticing him.

She walked over, took a seat. "Minerva? Goddess of wisdom and war?"

"Virgin goddess."

"So it's a metaphorical treasure that the two griffin at her feet are protecting, not the usual hoards of gold?"

"A nice touch, I thought."

"You would."

"It was good of you to come."

"I didn't really have a choice," she replied, her attention fixed on the statue, as though that was what they were discussing. "Whoever killed Petra sent someone to the States after me. Whether it was to stop me from reproducing that sketch, or just the usual trying-to-clean-up-any-loose-ends thing, I have no idea. Either way, if I'm going to be killed, I'd like to know why." She turned toward him, her look piercing.

"I can't tell you."

"Did I mention the two hit men after me?"

He hesitated. Wondered what harm could it do at this point to inform her? She was already risking her job just being here, never mind her life. He glanced around the museum. No one seemed to be paying them the least attention. "You brought the sketch?"

"Yes."

He nodded, looked down at his guidebook, not really seeing it. "Petra's uncle, an old informant, had contacted me, asking if I was still interested in looking into my wife's death. He arranged through his niece to have me contact him. He was afraid to do it himself."

"Petra was a spy?"

"No. Faas was. Why he decided to go through her, I'm not sure. Nor do I know if the information Faas intended to pass on really came from him. I suspect that someone set him up, was trying to set me up, especially after the assassination of Senator Grogan."

"What does the senator have to do with this?"

Griffin looked around, made sure there was no one within hearing distance. "Grogan wanted to open a new investigation into LockeStarr Management. The same company my wife and I were investigating two years ago when she was killed."

"I heard the man who killed Grogan was a schizophrenic who had been off his meds and somehow got hold of a gun."

"So maybe Grogan's murder had nothing to do with this. Or maybe someone used it as a specific means to draw me out, make this information that Faas thought he was handing over look even better."

"And what if it was a trap? Maybe they wanted you out of the picture. Or occupied with something."

"Then they knew the one thing that would do it. Becca's murder."

She looked away, stared for several seconds at the statue of Minerva. Then, in a voice almost too soft to hear, she said, "I think they succeeded."

"You know something." When she didn't answer right away, he whispered, "Damn it, Sydney. What do you know?"

She reached into her coat pocket and pulled out a folded piece of paper, handed it to him. "It's just a photocopy. The re-creation of the sketch of the woman Petra saw."

He took it, opened it, and the first thing he thought was the short hair was all wrong. She should have long hair. Long, dark brown—

He felt as if he'd been punched in the gut. This couldn't be . . . It couldn't . . . "Is this someone's idea of a joke?"

"This is who Petra saw with the man on the corner."

"That's impossible."

"I only drew what Petra directed."

"My wife's dead."

"Then it's someone who looks like her."

Griffin examined the drawing, the structure of her face, her eyes, her nose . . . He ran his fingers over the bridge. She'd broken it during an operation with Tex. She'd come home with two black eyes . . .

"Maybe it's not her," Sydney said.

"And what if it is?" His words came out harsher than he'd intended, the loud whisper seeming to echo off the museum walls, and he folded the drawing, pressing the creases in frustration. He stood. "I need some time to think about this. I need to be alone."

"*No*," she said, her voice low, but firm, as she stood, moving into his space, nearly chest to chest, her gaze narrowed. "You do *not* get to *think* about this. Someone's trying to kill me because I did this goddamned drawing, and like it or not, we are in this. *Together*."

Griffin shoved the drawing in his pocket as he looked around. Two women glanced over at them before turning their attention back to the display case on the wall. "Fine," Griffin said. "You have any ideas on where we look next? Because I'm fresh out. Being thrown for a loop does that to me."

"What do they want?"

"I'm sure killing me would be preferable. But barring that outcome, muzzled is the next best thing. And they've done that."

"So burning you solved part of their objective. They wanted you out of the way. You're out. Something must be going down. Something with LockeStarr?"

"Maybe. Like I said, Becca and I were working a case on LockeStarr when she— The last time I—" Hell. He'd been so wrapped up in avenging Becca's death that he'd failed to see how effectively he'd allowed his hands to be tied. How easily he'd been trapped. "Faas was supposedly giving me info on who killed Becca. I came here to find out where he got his info. And now?"

"You mean if she's not dead?"

"All the more reason to see if we can find out what Faas was up to before he was killed. There may be something here in his office."

"You think it would be here where he worked and not at his house?"

"I already checked his house. And he was killed leaving here."

She looked around the room, then turned to him, whispering, "Please tell me we are *not* breaking into this museum in the middle of the night. They have guards. With guns."

He looked at his watch. It was almost noon. "I was thinking more like this afternoon. And we won't be breaking in anywhere. They'll be letting us in." He glanced over at her. "As soon as we think of a reason why."

19

Carillo walked into Pearson's office, looking around, trying to figure out why anyone in the Bureau would be interested in working this spy stuff full-time. Beat the hell out of him, he thought, taking a seat in one of two chairs that faced Pearson's desk.

Pearson looked up from his paperwork. "I'll be right with you."

Carillo didn't answer. He knew Pearson's type. A little of that holier-than-thou attitude, even if the guy did earn it. Carillo sure as hell couldn't do what Pearson did. Put up with the administrative crap not only in the Bureau, but also all the other government agencies they dealt with. Too damned many asses to kiss.

Pearson signed the document he'd been reading, then slid it into a routing envelope, before turning his attention to Carillo. "How's the investigation coming?"

"It's coming," Carillo said.

Pearson leaned back in his chair, his expression one of annoyance. "And?"

"And I don't know enough about it one way or another to make a determination—never mind I don't trust anyone, including you."

"You're close to insubordination."

"I tend to do that when my bullshit meter's going off. And in this case, it started going off the moment two Company guys showed up at my favorite Taco Bell telling me I should turn down this job that you hadn't yet offered me—because they, and anyone else who did the least bit of background on me, are smart enough to know I would have turned it down had it come through the normal channels. So I have to ask myself why the CIA cares, and how they knew you'd ask me. Which means you all sat around and discussed who to pick for the investigation. And that tells me that this is a hell of a lot bigger than some schmuck senator who was offed by a schizophrenic who was conveniently placed in a cell with a blind spot so he could off himself. Not to mention why the hell does a foreign intelligence agency even care about an investigation run by the Bureau?"

"Anything else?"

"As a matter of fact, yes. Why me?"

"Your *sterling* reputation."

"Ding, ding, ding."

"Fine. Your tarnished reputation."

"As what? The bumbling detective who has no hope of realizing he's only running a façade investigation?"

"Hardly. We needed someone who would be overlooked as any sort of threat. You came highly recommended by the CIA due to a past case they'd had involving Fitzpatrick's father. They seemed to think that your unorthodox approach to work would be beneficial."

"I'm guessing that's not a compliment."

"You did have one admirer—in a backhanded way. Your former boss, Dave Dixon. He said that if we were looking for someone who would be underestimated, even dismissed, you were the man."

"Good old Dave."

"He also said you were effective. As long as we didn't examine your methods too close."

"So at what point were you going to tell me?"

"When we found out that, A, the senator's murder was more than what it appeared on the surface, and, B, when it became absolutely necessary, since this entire matter is on a need-to-know basis for national security reasons. If there was nothing to the senator's murder, it was as it appeared, you close out your case and go home none the wiser. If there was something to it, then you'd be in the perfect place to help Fitzpatrick."

"What about Fitzpatrick?" he asked, not wanting to get her in trouble, should Pearson merely be fishing for info.

"I'm aware that a report surfaced from MI5 with Fitzpatrick's name linked to the senator's. It wasn't a stretch to connect the dots to other OGAs, one of which doesn't even exist on paper," he said, obviously referring to that other governmental agency known as ATLAS. "That aside, should anyone inquire, what you're involved in is a simple murder investigation. You will report to me about the murder. Anything beyond that . . ." He opened his top desk drawer, taking out a business card for the *Washington Recorder*, and handing it to Carillo. "Your contact on who to give the information."

"James Dalton . . . ?" Carillo said, reading the name.

"I believe you may know him as Tex."

"Got it."

"Other than that, I have no immediate knowledge of Fitzpatrick's whereabouts or actions. As far as I know, she's taken some personal time off, and I will testify to that fact if required to do so."

Which told Carillo that they were all in big trouble if this went south. "Anything else I should know? Like the name of a good attorney if the shit hits the fan?"

"If that happens, call me. We'll both need one."

"Not a problem. I only have one concern about all this. No one's going to try to use this as a way to move me into supervision or anything?"

Pearson smiled. A first. "No worries there. Your strong disrespect for the supervisory role is well-known." His smile faded, and he was back to boss mode. "That limits who we can trust, and the less I know about what anyone does in their *free* time, the better. You are, in essence, Fitzpatrick's lifeline."

Pearson's parting statement echoed in Carillo's ears long after he left FCI to go pick up the forensic report on the shooter's computer. It was one thing for Sydney to go out and do some sketch for Griffin. Quite another when she was out there needing a lifeline to survive. Not when it involved the likes of ATLAS, an OGA that played for much higher stakes than anything the typical FBI agent was used to dealing with.

As he walked to the Computer Analysis unit, he consoled himself with the thought that it didn't matter that Sydney's name was linked with Grogan's, or that there was any big undercover investigation. She'd worked with ATLAS once before in Italy and came out fine. At least that was what he thought until he picked up the forensic report he'd ordered on the computer.

He didn't understand a lot of what he was reading, because they'd apparently only recovered partial files from the erasure. His instincts, however, told him that Sydney's problems were only a small part of the equation, and he called ATLAS right away to say he was bringing the paperwork over.

If any of this stuff was true, a lot of people were going to die.

20

Tex reread the latest report on the AUV investiga-
tion. On the off chance it was related, ATLAS had already
dispatched a ship to do some forensic salvaging in the area
where the college students had reported their boat was
blown up by the pirates. Marc di Luca was heading out
there in the next day or two, even though they had yet to
find anything unusual. This latest report, however, had Tex
worried. Although their suspicions were that LockeStarr had
to be involved in the theft of the AUV somehow, they hadn't
been able to make the connection, because the company that
had managed the port where the theft occurred was above
reproach—until an investigator decided to run a past check
to see what their record was in other ports.

And that was when he'd apparently discovered that this
above-reproach company had taken over the management of
that port only six months before the theft. It was the *previous* six months that made Tex sit up and take notice, even
though the record during that time was spotless. The com-

pany? LockeStarr. He called McNiel. "You read this report from MI5?"

"I did," McNiel said. "And I just got a call about something that wasn't in the report. Dr. Fedorov was definitely seen in the area right before the theft of the AUV. So if Fedorov is working for LockeStarr, that confirms our suspicions that LockeStarr's responsible for the missing AUV."

"But what the hell are they doing with it?" Tex asked, as his secretary knocked on his door.

"There's an FBI agent in the lobby to see you. A Tony Carillo," she said.

"I'll be right there," he told her. Then to Marc, he said, "Carillo's here now. Let me see if he's turned up anything on Grogan's murder."

"Keep me informed."

When Tex stepped off the elevator into the lobby of the *Washington Recorder*, he saw a man, late thirties, dark hair, dark eyes, wearing a charcoal suit, white shirt, and a necktie loosened at the collar. He stood there reading one of the *Recorder*'s faux articles on the wall. "Tony Carillo?" Tex asked.

"You must be Tex." Carillo turned, shook hands with him.

"Pearson mentioned you might be stopping by. We can talk in my office."

Carillo grabbed his overcoat and a leather portfolio from one of the chairs, then followed Tex to the elevator. "You guys really write those articles?" Carillo asked when they got off on Tex's floor.

"We actually have a couple agents on staff who have talent."

"You one of them?"

Tex laughed as he directed Carillo into his office, then closed the door. "Let's just say if I really was working as a journalist, I'd have been fired a long time ago. I'm lucky I can write a competent report."

"Nice," Carillo said, looking around. "We get cubicles at the Bureau."

Tex eyed the industrial gray tile floor and the rather battered wood desk and matching credenza that he'd acquired from the government surplus warehouse. His only concession to luxury was the small fridge, which he had bought himself. "It's not the most luxurious of digs, but it works."

"Anything with a goddamned door is luxurious where I work." Carillo tossed his coat onto one of the two chairs by Tex's desk, then sat in the other. "So, I take it from everything that's going on, this mess with Grogan's murder is the tip of some iceberg?"

"We believe so. We just haven't figured out which iceberg. You discover anything?"

"Depends. I have a list of phone numbers received from his office, and identified all but one in the few days before he was murdered."

"What's the number?"

Carillo handed over a sheet of paper from his portfolio. "It's the one underlined in red, second to the last, came in just before the senator left for his speech. His secretary didn't recognize the number, but she said no one unusual called. Just his wife. I might try interviewing the secretary later. She was, uh, overly distraught. I gathered she and the senator were having a fling while the Mrs. was holding down the fort back in his home state."

"Frankly, I could use something a little more solid than a phone number that can't be cross-referenced."

"Maybe this'll help." Carillo opened up his portfolio once more, this time pulling out a manila folder, and sliding it across the desk. "It's a report from our computer forensics about your shooter's hard drive. Read this, and you're gonna wonder what're the chances your suspect, Hollis, hangs himself all on his own in the one exact spot that is out of view of the camera."

Tex opened the folder, flipped through the pages and pages of printouts. "You mind giving me the *Reader's Digest* version?"

"I'm sure one of the Bureau's computer geeks could say it better, but our shooting suspect liked to dabble in computer viruses. Even though the computer was wiped, we were able to bring up bits and pieces of e-mails he stockpiled from various computer systems he'd hacked into. I'll let you read what they recovered, but it sort of mirrors this whole nano-chimera-virus-looking-for-Atlantis thing that showed up on his Web site."

"Chimera virus?" Tex said, turning through the pages with renewed interest.

"He was a conspiracy-theory freak. It's like he was basing the crap on his Web site from what he found on these e-mails."

"So you think someone killed him because of these e-mails?"

"Unless you can think of a better reason. Someone went to a lot of trouble to erase this stuff through several layers, which made it difficult to retrieve anything."

"You look at this, the guy seems like a nutcase. What's your take on it?"

"The likely scenario? Whoever he hacked must have discovered the security breach, probably set him up to open a loaded e-mail and traced it back to him. Assuming this stuff is as incriminatory as I think, I'm guessing the hackee saw their stuff on the hacker's computer, probably found his Web site, and saw the connection to the e-mails from their own system. Your shooter was a fairly competent hacker. Unfortunately for him, he didn't realize anyone would notice."

"Apparently they did."

"Yeah. I'm guessing he probably figured that out right around the time someone strung him from those holding cell bars."

"You think he shot the senator?"

"Put it this way. The cocktail of drugs found in his system was almost too convenient. And from our background on him, he's got no real experience with a firearm to aim that well, even on a good day. And how the hell'd he get the gun past security into the community college where the speech took place? My opinion? Highly possible that someone was behind him, shot the senator, then placed the gun in his hand. He was so delusional when they picked him up, he wouldn't have remembered what happened. Perfect patsy."

"You want a cup?" Tex asked, pushing his chair back, getting up, then walking over to the coffeepot on the credenza beneath the window.

"Thought you'd never ask," Carillo said. "Black."

Tex opened the cabinet below, pulled out a mug, filled it and his own, then brought both back over to the desk. He handed Carillo a cup, then sat. "Okay, let's say we discount the kid as the shooter. You got any ideas on who would want Grogan dead?"

"Since I don't know what he was involved in, I can't say. But the obvious? Someone wanted to shut him up."

Tex wasn't even sure where to begin reading. "Any of these e-mails prove it?"

"Let's just say they're what brought me here. At first glance, most of what they recovered was pretty harmless. Clearly the suspect was out there poking around in several systems, seeing what he could come up with. But this conspiracy stuff? He forwards one of them to another e-mail address. The e-mail he forwarded wasn't recovered, but he writes in the body of his e-mail, 'Bio lab, France. I was right. Danger . . .'"

"Right about what?"

"Don't know. But in another e-mail, he talks about how many people will die from the chimera viruses and needing a stem cell of viruses, whatever the hell that is. Then you go to his Web site and it gets weirder. That's when you get into the aliens and Atlantis and chimera viruses being manufactured to take over the world. Frankly it reads like a science fiction computer game."

"Except the kid's dead."

"Exactly."

"Who'd he send the e-mail to?"

"That would be one of the missing links. We've got the address, but it's Web-based and the name attached to it is apparently fabricated."

Tex flipped through the documents, his eye catching on the printout of the kid's Web site, thinking of that stolen AUV, and the possibility of a bioweapon. Sure, it sounded bad, but there was nothing to say it wasn't a hoax or some

Web site fantasy with nothing to it. God knew there were a million others just like it on the Internet. But then he read the traces recovered from that last e-mail. One word in particular, actually only a partial word: *dorov*.

Fedorov?

Tex wondered if he would have caught it had he and McNiel not just finished a conversation about the guy a few minutes ago. "Jesus," he said, picking up the phone, calling his boss. "McNiel? I just got a report from the FBI. I think you better get in here."

21

December 8
Amsterdam, The Netherlands

A ruse to gain entry into the private offices of the Rijksmuseum was not going to be easy. Then again, Sydney had learned one very important lesson during her years in the FBI. One didn't need to know all the answers. One just needed to know where to find them. Her go-to man was Michael "Doc" Schermer, an agent working out of the San Francisco field office. If anyone could think of a ruse that would work, Doc Schermer could. Lucky for her, he didn't get too bent out of shape about receiving calls around three in the morning, especially if it involved looking up obscure pieces of trivia that might help solve a case, even if it wasn't necessarily sanctioned by the Bureau—or any other government entity.

"Doc? It's Syd. Sorry to wake you, but I need a favor."

"This something I might serve jail time for?"

"Not you specifically, but my chances are pretty good. Here's what I need." She described the museum, the murder, and their need to get into the victim's office. He took notes, told her he'd call her back. She and Griffin used the downtime for a quick shopping trip on the Fifth Avenue of Amsterdam

for proper attire, after which Sydney procured a hotel room.
She took a shower, a quick nap, and finally got a call from Doc
Schermer with their plan of action.

"I have two possible scenarios," he said. "One, you could
pose as a representative from the Gardner Museum in
Boston, saying you were following up a lead from Faas that
had to do with Rembrandt's *The Storm on the Sea of Galilee*,
stolen about twenty years ago. That would get you in the
door from the curiosity factor alone."

"How so?"

"My feeling? Any director of a museum carrying Rembrandt's work would give their eyeteeth for even a glimmer
of a chance to be the first to see the recovered painting and
be the one to tell the world."

"Might be a little overkill. What's your other scenario?"

"Every October, the Rijksmuseum celebrates something
called National Archive Day. Sort of like an *Antiques Road-
show* thing, where someone can bring in a piece of artwork,
like a painting, print, or even a letter from a famous artist
to learn more about it. And though they say they don't give
official statements regarding the authenticity of the piece,
they'll make an assessment as to it being a reproduction or
an authentic work."

"You realize it's December?"

"Like anyone could miss the Christmas decorations up
since the day after Halloween?" he quipped. "Yes. But
they also clearly state that it will take *several* weeks for an
answer. So you show up there, saying you spoke with this
Faas guy back in October about some piece of art, and he
only just asked you to come back because he'd written up
something. It does two things. It gets you in the door, and if
you're lucky, you get to follow someone to his office while
they look for said missing report."

"I'm liking the stolen Rembrandt idea better."

"Then make it the best of both worlds. Have it be a letter
from Rembrandt. That would have value to a museum that
carries Rembrandts, but not as monumental as the possibility
of finding a stolen masterpiece."

"Thanks, Doc. Let me talk it over with Griffin. See what he thinks."

"I'll see what I can dig up for a letter that might work. Send it via e-mail."

"You are amazing. I owe you."

"You ever run across the winning lotto ticket, remember you said that."

She and Griffin decided on the letter from Rembrandt and, as promised, Doc sent out a good facsimile of an aged-looking document that he assured them would whet the appetite of any expert on Rembrandt. "The beauty about this," Doc told her, "is that you can walk in with a copy—not original."

"Always appreciated."

After a little further research on the Internet to verify a few details, then the use of the hotel's business center to print out the necessary documents, they had what they needed for their operation. Donning their new clothes, Sydney in a double-breasted navy business suit, her hair swept up in a bun at the nape of her neck, and Griffin, charcoal suit, with a burgundy and gray striped tie, they left Griffin's car behind, instead calling for a cab to take them to the front entrance of the Rijksmuseum, part of which was under construction. Upon entering, they walked to the information desk, where Griffin, positioned a foot behind Sydney, stood silently by while she asked the woman for Faas Meijer.

The woman's mouth opened, then closed, her flustered look growing, when Sydney added, "We flew in from Boston. We were supposed to meet last week, but I had to reschedule. He should be expecting us."

"I— Can you wait here one moment?"

"Of course."

The woman moved to the other end of the counter, picked up a phone, and turning her back, said something too soft for Sydney to hear. A moment later, she returned. "Geert Jansen, the assistant director, will be right out."

"Thank you."

About three minutes later, a man in a dark suit walked up,

spoke to the woman behind the counter, then faced Sydney and Griffin. "How do you do? I am Geert Jansen." His Dutch accent was thick, but his English impeccable. "You are from the Gardner?"

"Cindy Carillo," Sydney said, holding out her hand. "And this is Greg Zachary, insurance adjuster for the Gardner Museum," she said, indicating Griffin, who held out a card, which the man took. "I'm sure you must know about the Rembrandt letter that Faas Meijer was researching for us?"

"I—no. I do not. I would think he would have mentioned it."

"Unfortunately our calls to him have gone unanswered, and you can imagine our concern over not hearing from him. It goes without saying that this letter is very valuable."

"Yes. Well, I'm sorry to have to tell you, but he was killed not too long ago."

"Oh dear God," she said, looking at Griffin, covering her mouth with her fingers in what she hoped was a suitable impression of utter shock. "That's why he hasn't returned our calls. I—I'm so very sorry to hear this."

"Yes," Geert Jansen said. "We're all very shocked."

"I feel terrible even asking about it," she replied, placing her hand over her heart. "But the Rembrandt letter. Do you know if he finished examining it? We're all very nervous about the results."

"I must admit that I wasn't even aware he was working on it."

"That was part of our agreement. Until we were certain it was authentic, we were not about to let it be known that it even existed. Faas agreed to these terms."

Jansen clasped his hands as he eyed the briefcase that Griffin held. "I don't even know where such a piece might be."

"Perhaps locked in his office?" Griffin suggested.

"Yes. That would make sense." He patted his pockets, and said, "Let me get my keys."

"And Mr. Jansen?" Sydney gave a pleading smile. "You can understand our need for the utmost discretion. Should something happen to this item, we would not want to publicly embarrass either the Gardner or the Rijksmuseum.

Until we find Faas's report, we are . . . not even sure what we are dealing with."

"Of course." He left them, and Sydney glanced over at Griffin, who gave the slightest tilt of his head as if to say, *You're on track.*

Geert Jansen returned shortly thereafter, directing them to follow him. At that same moment, Sydney's phone vibrated in her purse, and she slid the bag from her shoulder, dug the phone out of the front pocket as she walked. It was Doc Schermer. "Fitz? A slight problem with that scenario I concocted. It won't fly."

A soft ping indicated the arrival of the elevator and they stepped on. The doors were closing as she said, "Why not?"

"Faas knows nothing about paintings or even Rembrandt. His expertise was in small antiques."

Before she could reply, the elevator descended and the signal was lost. They rode to the bottom floor, followed the museum director out, then down a long hallway. He stopped in front of an office door, unlocked it, then stepped aside so they could enter. The compact office was sparsely furnished with only a desk, a file cabinet, a computer on a separate stand, and not a piece of paper in sight. If there was anything, the police had probably boxed it all up, and taken it back to their office as evidence. Even the small cooler on the chair by the door was empty, the sort that might be used to pack a lunch in. The only thing that appeared untouched were the numerous books on the shelves that covered the back wall, each volume on antiques, and she hoped that Griffin noticed, because they were . . . screwed. No other way to put it, she thought.

And just when she was about to signal to Griffin that they needed to leave, that Geert Jansen probably had called the cops when he went back for his "keys," she noticed the blinking light on Faas's phone. That meant they had not yet shut off his voice mail. Even better, one of the speed dial buttons was marked, "Voice Mail," with the number 66793 written beside it. Either Faas was too busy to remember his code, or the police had jotted it down, after acquiring the code through their investigation. She refused to entertain the idea that the set of numbers belonged to anything else. "Mr. Jansen, do you mind if I use the phone? My associate in San Francisco was trying to reach me with some extremely important information, but the signal dropped."

"Please. Help yourself," he said, smiling far too brightly, she thought.

Sydney picked up the phone, hit the voice mail button, listened to the prompt, which was in Dutch, and figuring it worked the same way as most voice mailboxes, keyed in the code. Bingo. The newest message was, of course, in Dutch. "Hi," she said, over the recording. "This is Cindy Carillo. We're at the museum now . . . Yes. He's right here. Hold on." She held the phone to her chest, so that Jansen wouldn't be able to hear the recording. "Mr. Zachary?" she said to Griffin. "The director wants to speak with you."

Griffin hesitated, apparently reluctant to give up a position of advantage with a view down the hallway. Even so, he moved into the room, took the phone from her and put it up to his ear, as she whispered, "He knows."

"Hello," he said into the receiver.

Sydney walked around the desk, until she was right next to Jansen, noticing the sheen of perspiration on his upper lip. "Is something wrong, Mr. Jansen?"

"No. No. Everything is fine."

"You seem nervous."

"Nervous? No." Jansen shook his head, his glance straying to the door, which confirmed in her mind that he was waiting for someone.

She looked over at Griffin, tapped her watch to tell him time was up, but he gave a slight shake of his head, which told her whatever he was listening to took precedence. She decided it was time to change tactics, gamble. She turned back to the director. "Mr. Jansen, I have a confession to make. We are not really from the Gardner Museum. We're friends of Faas's. Private investigators hired to find out who killed him."

"Investigators?"

"Faas had information that he intended to pass on to my associate, but he was killed before he could do so."

"*Hemeltje*," Jansen said, then visibly relaxed. "I am very relieved. Detective Van Meter told me I should call if anyone came by asking about Faas. He said there were art thieves looking to steal something that Faas had purchased."

"Van Meter?" Sydney replied. "The detective in charge of the case was Van der Lans."

"No, no," Jansen said. "Van Meter. He came by after the police finished searching this office and left me his card. He insisted I call his mobile directly, day or night, if anyone showed up asking for Faas. I called him upstairs. When you didn't know what sort of art Faas dealt with, I—I assumed you were the thieves he warned me of."

"You called him?"

"Right after you arrived. He said he and another officer would arrive within ten minutes, and that I should wait with you in Faas's office."

Griffin dropped the phone into the cradle, then drew a gun from the back of his waist.

Jansen saw it, stumbled back into the desk, his eyes wide. "*Mijn God!*"

"Mr. Jansen," Griffin said, carefully moving past the man into the doorway. "I may not know art, but I know cops. They'd ask you to call the station in an emergency, and they would *not* ask you to accompany suspects into isolated areas."

"But he gave me his card."

"Much like the card I gave you upstairs? It wasn't real. Call the police station and ask if they have a Detective Van Meter working the case. If they do not, have them send officers immediately."

"You aren't going to kill me, are you?"

"I won't need to. Your Detective Van Meter plans to kill all three of us."

22

December 8
Amsterdam, The Netherlands

Griffin remained in the doorway, his gun aimed toward the elevator. "The call?" he said to the museum director.

Jansen turned, picked up the phone, his hand trembling as he punched in the number. He spoke Dutch, his voice shaking as Griffin heard him mention the name Van Meter. Then with a hollow-sounding "*Bedankt*," he hung up. He looked at the two of them. "You are correct. There is no Van Meter working on the Faas case. I told them to send officers."

"How many exits are on this floor?" Griffin asked.

"There's a stairwell near the elevator and another down the hall, through the service doors of the storage area."

"Let's go. You're not safe here."

"But—"

"*Now.*"

Sydney urged Jansen out the door toward the storage area. Griffin followed. They reached the end of the hallway, where a set of double doors covered in stainless steel blocked their way. An electric keypad was mounted to the right. Jansen

started punching in a code, when Griffin heard the ping indicating the elevator had arrived.

He looked back, saw two men rounding the corner. The
men stopped in their tracks, as though surprised. Jansen hit
the last key. The door buzzed and he pulled it open.

"Hurry!" Griffin said.

A sharp crack echoed down the hallway. Plaster flew off
the wall by Sydney's head, and she dove to the side. Jansen
fell to his knees, cowering. Griffin fired back. The men retreated behind the wall. Sydney, safe for the moment, was
just a couple of feet from the door, and had a better angle
on the suspects. Unfortunately, from the side of the hall he
was standing on, no way they were making it into that door
unless Sydney could cover them.

"Syd!" When she looked over at him, he slid the weapon
across the hallway floor.

She picked it up and aimed. "Go!" she said. Griffin
grabbed Jansen by his collar, then ran to the door as she
fired. The moment they were in, she took several more shots
as she sidestepped into the hall and into the door. Griffin
pulled it shut behind her, and she handed him the weapon.
He released the magazine, saw he had two rounds left. "Cutting it close."

"I live for danger. Now let's get the hell out of here," she
replied.

The hallway was long, wide, lit by a single row of fluorescent lights overhead. Their footsteps echoed down the con-
crete corridor as they ran toward the far end. Behind them,
someone pounded on the metal doors.

"Will those doors hold?" Griffin asked as they ran.

"According to the installers . . . even . . . withstand gunfire," Jansen said. The hallway ended in a T intersection,
with another set of double doors right before them, as well as
down another hallway to the left and to the right, and when
they reached it, Jansen bent over, his hands on his knees,
taking deep breaths. "Some . . . of the pieces stored . . . down
here . . . are worth millions."

"Which way?" Griffin asked.

Jansen pointed. "Exit . . . at the loading dock."

Griffin gave a final look back, listened. The pounding had stopped. "How long would it take them to get here from upstairs?"

"They would have to run . . . all the way around the museum . . . Unless they acquired a key code."

"Let's go." Griffin holstered his weapon, and the three continued to the last set of double doors. Jansen punched in a code, and the door buzzed. He pulled it open, and they stepped into a cavernous room filled with crates, some large, flat, leaning upright, probably containing paintings, others bulky and square and stacked several crates high. The space smelled of dust, and Sydney sneezed twice as they briskly worked their way around the maze of stored goods.

"Faas's voice mail?" Sydney asked Griffin.

"Someone telephoned Faas, saying they know he received the package and they wanted it back. They were going to send someone by and he was to meet them outside the museum at six." It was, Griffin noted, the same time he was to meet Faas, which meant he'd been set up—whether by Faas or someone else, he didn't know.

"A package?" Jansen said. "Faas received one the day before he was killed . . . A new clerk delivered it to my office by mistake. It was postmarked from Paris."

"You told this to the police?" Sydney asked.

"No. I didn't think he was murdered because of something to do with the museum. But the police must have heard the voice mail. They were in his office long enough."

"Any idea what was in the package?" Griffin said. "Or what was so special about it?"

"I wasn't there when he opened it, but when I asked about it, he showed me. A letter opener. Ebony and gold. With Faas's background, I assumed it was an antique, especially considering the size of the package in comparison to the piece. It must have had a lot of packing." Undoubtedly what Faas had been stabbed with, Griffin thought, recalling the moment the knife fell from his grasp into the snow.

To which Sydney said, "They were looking for something when they killed Petra. Maybe that was it?"

Perhaps the police hadn't found it. They had to go back for it, he thought, just as Jansen stopped in his tracks, a horrified expression on his face. "Do you . . . think those men will come after me?"

"The faster we get out of here," Griffin replied, "the safer you'll be."

"This way," Jansen said, winding his way around a few more dusty crates, pushing through another door that opened to a freight elevator. Beside it was a stairwell, and Jansen led them up two flights. The door led to the interior courtyard of the main entrance. Several police officers were running through it, and Griffin and Sydney stopped.

Griffin held his arm out to prevent Jansen from going any farther. "Is there another way?" Griffin asked.

"Won't the police protect us?"

"If we hope to find Faas's killer, it's imperative we get out without anyone knowing we were here."

Jansen looked at each in turn, then, as though coming to a decision, nodded. "The basement storage. It will take us to the entrance for the bus tours." He led them back down the stairwell, stopping on the floor with the freight elevator. They took it down a couple more floors into the bowels of the museum, and then through a series of twists and turns, until they finally emerged into an underground parking garage, where several buses were lined up, one loading with passengers. "There," Jansen said. "Follow the ramp up past the tour buses."

Sydney and Griffin walked toward a group of tourists who stood waiting for the second bus when a police car cruised down the winding ramp. Jansen ran into the road, waved for it to pull over.

"Blend into the crowd," Griffin said.

She glanced back, saw Jansen talking animatedly to the officer, then pointing in their direction.

Griffin grabbed Sydney's hand as the first bus started off. They sprinted toward it, and Griffin hit the side. The driver stopped, opened the door, and Griffin said, "Thanks. We almost got on the wrong one."

He climbed up the steps and Sydney followed. The vehicle accelerated as they walked toward the back row of seats, and she saw the officer getting out of his patrol car, calling something in on his portable radio as he and Jansen walked toward the group of waiting passengers, clearly looking for them.

"How long till they figure we're here, not out there?" Syd asked.

"A few minutes at the most," he said, as the bus drove up the winding ramp into the daylight, allowing them to see a number of police cars moving into the area. "If we don't come up with a viable plan, we'll be sitting in a jail cell within the hour. And that I can't afford. I need to get back to that museum. And soon."

"Are you nuts?" she whispered. "That place is crawling with cops."

"That letter opener this Van Meter is looking for? If the police didn't find it, I know exactly where it is."

"And then what?"

"France to find out where the letter opener came from, and what the hell is so important about it. Assuming we come up with a plausible reason for the driver to stop."

"That I can do," she said. "Let me know when and where."

From his vantage point on the bus, Griffin saw the patrol cars converging in and around the *museumplein*. If possible, he wanted a little more distance between them and the Rijksmuseum. But then he heard static from the radio, saw the driver reaching for his mike. "Now," he said to Sydney. "Before he answers that call."

She stood, screamed, "Oh my God! Stop the bus!" She ran toward the front. "Please, stop the bus!"

The driver looked in his rearview mirror, put his hand back on the steering wheel, ignoring the radio dispatch call. "What's wrong?"

"My husband's heart medication," she said, her hands clutched to her throat, her tone pleading. "I left it at the museum!"

Passengers stared, some complaining. Even so, the driver pulled the bus over, and Griffin, having followed Sydney to the front of the bus, relaxed slightly as the door opened, allowing them to exit. "My apologies," he said to the driver, handing him several euros just before he stepped off.

On the sidewalk, they rushed back in the direction of the museum, and once the bus passed they flagged down a taxi, got in, took it to the central train station, then walked inside the crowded terminal. The instant Griffin saw the taxi depart with a new passenger, he bought two tram tickets, and he and Sydney took the very next tram that arrived, then exited when it was apparent the route would take them too far to the south. They walked the remainder of the way to the hotel beneath a leaden sky that threatened more snow. For the moment, several bicyclists were out and about, taking advantage of the break in the weather, and Griffin pulled Sydney to a halt when she almost stepped in the bike lane, the shrill bell of the cyclist warning them off. He looked at her, gave a grim smile. "You're actually pretty good at this."

"Almost getting run over by bicyclists?"

"Falling into a role. Back there at the museum."

"Thanks."

"The histrionics on the bus, however . . ." he said, holding up his hand, waving it to indicate her part was only so-so.

"It got the damned thing stopped, didn't it?"

"Guess it did."

They walked for a few minutes in silence, and then she asked, "So now what?"

"Now we go back for the knife."

"Knife? I thought it was a letter opener?"

"Murder weapon, then."

Sydney looked up at him, her head tilted. "Why didn't the killer take it after he stabbed Faas?"

"It was dark. Maybe he didn't realize it was *the* knife/letter opener they wanted. Or maybe he did, but when Petra and I showed up unexpectedly, we scared him off. He fled and had to leave the knife behind. I'm not sure it was intentional—its use as a weapon. After listening to that voice mail, I have to assume that Faas was smuggling it out of the museum to bring it to the caller as requested, or to bring it to me in hopes of avoiding the caller."

A woman and child approached from the opposite direction, both bundled up in thick coats, scarves, and woolen hats. The little girl, tufts of blond curls escaping her hat, waved at them, and Sydney smiled, waved back. Once they were out of hearing range, Sydney asked, "And the cops didn't recover the murder weapon?"

"Assuming this is what the killers were after, if they had, you think anyone would've bothered coming after Petra, asking if she had it? It snowed so much that night, and since. Unless one knew exactly where to look, they'd never find it."

"And you do?"

He pictured the arch, the garden entrance to the Rijksmuseum, the moment he saw Faas stumbling toward them, his hand against his chest, holding the knife . . . "Yeah. I think I do."

"We're probably on the top-ten-most-wanted list by now, never mind the area is probably crawling with cops."

"This time we wait for dark."

23

December 9
National Counterterrorism Center (NCTC)
Washington, D.C.

"We received a report that there was a woman in the
museum with Zachary Griffin. Anyone in this room care
to tell me who she was?" The bearer of said tidings, Roy
Santiago, assistant deputy director of national intelligence,
looked none too happy as he addressed those present.

It was the first that Tex had heard of Griffin's whereabouts
since he'd dropped Sydney off at the airport, and he was
careful to keep his expression neutral, not react to the news
he'd been so desperate to hear. There were too many sets of
eyes watching everyone else in the room, each, Tex noted,
connected to so many acronyms one almost needed an index
to sort them out. The CIA's NCS and SAD, the FBI's FCI,
ATLAS, NSA, DIA, as well as the White House contingent,
including Miles Cavanaugh, and no fewer than two generals.

Under normal circumstances, this was the last place Tex
should have been, but McNiel insisted on his and Marc di
Luca's presence, to show that ATLAS was fully cooperating
in the search for Griffin. Marc, however, was deploying that

afternoon to Jamaica, and Tex envied him since it meant the job of bringing in Griffin fell squarely on his own shoulders. An unenviable position, he thought as Santiago's gaze landed on their boss, McNiel.

"Yours?" Santiago asked.

"Definitely not one of my agents," McNiel said.

"But Zachary Griffin is. What the hell is he doing out there?"

"My understanding is that he is following up a lead on who killed his wife."

Tex, standing at the back of the room with the few other operatives who didn't rate a seat at the table, saw the National Clandestine Service director glance over at the Special Activities Division director. Since both the NCS and SAD were divisions in the CIA, it was, he figured, a look worthy of notice. Especially if it turned out that Griffin's wife, a CIA agent, wasn't as dead as everyone had been led to believe. It wouldn't be the first time a case agent was killed in action, then miraculously brought to life once the mission was over. That was assuming that, A, she wasn't really dead, and, B, it was the CIA who had facilitated her "death" because there could always be a C, that she had done this herself for reasons he couldn't even begin to fathom.

"His *wife*?" Santiago asked. "Would someone care to explain?"

CIA's SAD director, Ian Thorndike, said, "Becca Price. One of our case agents. She was killed working a joint operation with ATLAS two years ago on the LockeStarr matter."

Alan Adams, Santiago's aide, leaned toward Santiago, whispered something in his ear. Santiago cleared his throat, looked down at the papers in front of him as though searching for something in particular. "And where are we on the murder investigation of Senator Grogan?" he asked Adams in a low voice.

To which Adams said, "Schizophrenic who went off his meds. Tragic incident all the way around."

Santiago nodded, then glanced at Pearson. "Has the FBI confirmed this?"

"We've only just begun the investigation," Pearson said.

"But the initial information appears correct. As soon as we have something definitive, I'll let you know."

"Thank you. Back to the more immediate matter?" He looked right at McNiel. "How do you intend to bring in Zachary Griffin?"

McNiel, in turn, pinned his gaze on Thorndike. "If certain other entities who had information on Griffin's whereabouts were to pass that on to us, we might make more progress."

Santiago checked his notes, then looked at the CIA director. "Thorndike?"

"We had reason to believe that Special Agent Griffin might return to the Rijksmuseum to retrieve a package that had been sent to this informant who was murdered."

"What package?"

"We don't yet know what was in it."

And Santiago said, "The same informant that Griffin is alleged to have murdered?"

"The same," Thorndike said.

In two steps Tex was at the table. "There is—"

Marc grabbed him by the arm, pulling him back. "Now is not the time, *amico*," he said.

Tex clamped his mouth shut as McNiel raised his hand, saying calmly, "Assuming you're willing to believe the black propaganda that's being spread about my operative."

"Black propaganda?" Santiago repeated, looking around the room. "You're accusing some entity of spreading disinformation about your operative?"

"I am," McNiel said, and Tex resisted the urge to cheer. "This informant's niece witnessed his murder, and in no way implicated my case agent to the police."

"The same niece who was also killed, allegedly by your case agent?"

"Again, untrue."

"When you find out who is responsible for the dissemination of this black propaganda campaign, let me know. In the meantime, I'd suggest you bring in Griffin before someone else does. They might not be as careful. Now that we have that taken care of, let's start on the security plans for the upcoming global summit."

Tex watched both CIA directors, noting that neither had looked up during the time Griffin was under discussion. Ever since the formation of ATLAS, CIA's paramilitary SAD acted as though the two groups were in a pissing match, probably because McNiel had been handpicked from SAD to run ATLAS and had poached a few of his best men to come over with him, including both Tex and Griffin. The question remained, though. Would the CIA go after Griffin just over a turf war? Or was there something else going on here that neither he nor McNiel could see?

Hell. Of course there was. Tex had a photocopy of Syd's damned sketch. The one that told him there was definitely something more going on. The drawing he couldn't pull out at the moment without implicating himself and Sydney in this whole mess. And, taking a much needed calming breath, he stepped back against the wall, making sure he did not speak unless spoken to, and then only to give the vaguest answers on what Griffin might try or where he might go.

After the meeting, he, Marc, and McNiel were walking down the hallway, about to get on the elevator, when Pearson of the FBI caught up to them. Without turning or giving any indication that they were even having a conversation, Pearson said, "You let anything happen to my agent, and I will personally assist the CIA in blasting your little kingdom from here to eternity. Are we clear?"

"Very," McNiel said.

The four got onto the elevator and rode it in silence. On the ground floor, Pearson exited first, strode off without looking back.

McNiel put his hand on Tex's arm, stopping him. "You had better be right about Griffin's matter tying into Locke-Starr."

"Griffin just needs some time."

"That's something we're running out of. And fast."

24

December 9
National Counterterrorism Center (NCTC)
Washington, D.C.

Even before the meeting was over, Miles Cavanaugh
realized that he needed to salvage things before they got out
of hand. Thorndike was still in his camp, or rather Thorndike
thought Miles was in the CIA camp. Either way, it needed
to stay that way. Miles couldn't afford anyone looking at
him too closely. Not now, when there was so much at stake,
he thought, striding toward the elevator, then hesitating
when he saw that the ATLAS director, his two agents, and
the FBI's Pearson had beat him out the door. He slowed his
pace, waited for them to step on the elevator, then he took
the next down. By the time he made it to the ground floor, he
saw the ATLAS agents talking as Pearson stormed off. And
as desperately as he wanted to hear what they were saying,
he wasn't about to put himself in a position that left him
alone with either. He didn't trust them. He didn't trust that
they wouldn't be able to see right through him and know that
his career, hell, his life, hung on their investigation.

Squaring his shoulders, he stepped off the elevator, walked

past them, not stopping until he hit the street corner. And then all energy fled and he stood there, not moving.

He had to pull it together. He did not claw his way this far up to lose it because some agent had never gotten over his dead wife. Good God. He'd heard that at the time of the explosion, Griffin's wife was in the process of divorcing him, and the man *still* couldn't let it go.

Miles hailed a cab, not even bothering to wait for his driver. He had it drop him off outside the restaurant he frequented for lunch, dismayed to see that his hands were shaking. He needed a drink and he needed it now. He walked in, barely able to see in the dim light as he made his way to the bar, and sat at the counter. "Vodka martini, please."

The bartender, a red-haired man in his mid-twenties, nodded, then proceeded to make the drink. Miles watched, envious of the man's job, wondering where he'd be if he hadn't had his own political aspirations . . .

"A bit early to be drinking, isn't it?"

Miles stiffened at the voice. He looked into the mirror over the bar, saw the shiny bald head of Chet Somera looking back at him. "If you'd left the meeting I just left, you'd be drinking too."

The bartender dropped an olive in the martini glass, then slid it over to Miles, who dug some money out of his pocket to pay for it. He took the drink and walked to a table far from the bar, Chet following. "What are you doing here?" Miles asked.

"I followed you from the meeting."

Miles acted as though this didn't bother him. "Worried I wouldn't show?"

"Just following orders," Chet said. "The boss wants to talk to you." He held out a cell phone.

Miles took it, noting that the call had already been placed. He didn't like that he was being followed, and said so into the phone.

"You are one of my best investments, Mr. Cavanaugh. I don't want anything to happen to you. But if the pressure is too much . . ."

"I'm fine."

"Then tell me what transpired at the meeting."

"A woman was seen helping Griffin. They want to know who she is."

"And does anyone know?"

"If they do, they're not saying."

"Could it be the FBI agent your men lost at the airport?"

"Could be," he said, growing more uncomfortable with each question. "But if it was, she flew out of the U.S. under a different name."

"Any mention of Grogan's murder?"

"I know the FBI's brought in some agent from San Francisco."

"Who?"

"Some guy named Carillo. I don't think we need to worry about him too much. At least from what Thorndike said the other day."

"Why is that?"

"The way Thorndike put it, if the guy put as much effort into working his cases as he does trying to get out of working them, he'd be a top-notch agent. I'm still trying to figure out how it is that the CIA managed to get any input into *who* the FBI put on it."

"Do not underestimate Thorndike. He did not get where he is by being careless."

"Thorndike is too wrapped up in finding Griffin. Trust me."

"So no rumblings about appointing Senator Grogan's replacement until the special election?"

"It's business as usual. I really don't think they're looking beyond the immediate murder, due to the suspect's mental health—certainly not about appointing a replacement. Unless of course you've heard something from the governor's office?"

"They've tossed a few names out, but want to wait until after the funeral before saying anything publicly. In the meantime, keep me informed. I want to know what this San Francisco FBI agent finds—if anything—on his investigation."

The boss disconnected, and Miles handed the phone back to Chet, saying, "Tell me you found this Izzy from the electronics store."

Chet dropped the phone in his pocket. "Not yet. But we

may have found another friend. The girl whose picture was on the computer."

"May have?"

"Missed her the first time around, but we've got something in the works. Apparently she's been in touch with this Izzy, which makes it convenient for us. Take them both out at the same time." He grabbed a handful of peanuts and stood. "Having second thoughts?"

Miles took a deep breath, but said nothing. He didn't dare.

Chet gave a shrewd smile. "That's what happens when you sell your soul to the devil, eh?"

Miles watched him go, thinking that was exactly what he'd done, sold his soul. And he had no way out. No way at all. With a sigh of resignation, he finished his martini, then promptly ordered another.

25

December 10
Washington, D.C.

Izzy waited until the next afternoon to open Mad-die's e-mail from his laptop, then sent her a response: "Meet me at Central Café at 2." Once that was done, they drove straight there, even though the meeting wasn't scheduled for another two hours. The café location was across the street. Izzy and Maddie were viewing it from the second floor window of a bookstore and coffee house that had an entrance to the shopping area on the opposite side of the block. This way, he figured, he could be sure of the area, then contact this FBI agent to meet them before the bad guys showed.

Izzy bought a couple of magazines from the bookstore, and he and Maddie sat there, drinking coffee, pretending to read, just to be sure the area would work. Deciding it would, he was just about to ask Maddie for the FBI agent's number when he noticed a white van drive by on the street below. It was marked "Ander's Catering," but looked an awful lot like the florist van. Izzy researched the name on his laptop, while Maddie kept watch. No such company in the area. It circled the block twice. There were other white vans, but none drove past more than once. A few minutes later, they saw two men walking down the street, nothing notable about them, except when they got to the coffee shop, one man walked in, while the other stayed outside the door.

"You think that's them?" Maddie asked.

"Yeah. I think it is. We should make that call now."

Maddie pulled the business card out from her pocket, handing it to Izzy. "The agent wrote his cell number on the back."

Izzy took out his phone, eyed the card, saw the agent worked out of San Francisco. The cell phone also had a San Francisco prefix. Since anybody could have a card printed up and write his own cell number, he verified the San Francisco office main number from the Internet and called that instead. Someone answered, "FBI. San Francisco. How may I direct your call?"

"Yeah, hi," he said, his gaze out the window on the coffee shop across the street, and the man standing in the front. "I was wondering if you have an Agent . . ." He glanced at the card. "Tony Carillo."

"He's away from the office."

"Is he working in Washington, D.C.?"

"Please hold."

Elevator music played. He turned the phone onto speaker, then set it on the table, saying, "They're checking."

Maddie kept watch out the window. Suddenly she reached over, grabbed his hand, her face turning white. "I think they see us."

He peered out across the street, saw the man in front of the store, looking up. "Oh my God . . ."

Too late. The man turned into the shop, called out to someone, then pointed. Maddie put her cell phone up to the glass. "Maddie! What are you doing?"

"You wanted proof? I'm getting it."

Izzy watched the two men dart across the street. "They're coming! We have to go!"

He grabbed his laptop and backpack, then Maddie's hand. It wasn't until they reached the stairwell that he realized he'd left his phone and the card for the FBI agent on the table. He glanced back, decided it wasn't worth the risk, then hurried Maddie down the back stairs on the opposite side of the building, hoping like hell the two men would not split up to cover both exits.

26

December 10
FBI Headquarters
Washington, D.C.

Carillo had just typed in his password unlocking his computer when his cell rang.

It was Doc Schermer. "Any chance you're looking for a Maddie?"

Carillo stopped on hearing the name. "Maddie Boucher? She called?"

"Not exactly. One of the secretaries said some guy called the main office line, asking if you were working in D.C. She knew you were out there on some hush-hush thing, so she transferred him to my line."

"He leave a name?"

"Never got a chance to talk to him. It sounded like something happened, because he called out her name. And then he said, 'They're coming. We have to go.' The line stayed open for quite some time."

"You hear anything else?"

"After about a minute of nothing, I hung up. Unfortunately the number comes back to a prepaid phone. I checked, because the guy definitely sounded scared."

"With good reason."

"Any idea who it was?"

"If I had to guess, my missing link. Izzy. I better find out what's going on." He disconnected, called MPDC, identifying himself and asking for Records. Amber Jacobsen answered. "Any chance you can run a moniker check for me?"

"Sure. What's the name?"

"I-Z-Z-Y. That's what it sounds like. Not sure if that's how it's spelled.

"That it?"

"That's all I got. Wait. He's into computers. Maybe hacking."

"Hacking? I'll see what I can dig up."

"Thanks. I'll be in the field."

He left his number, disconnected. She called back a few minutes later. "I found a possibility," she said. "If it's the same Izzy, he was arrested as a juvenile for ripping off some computer cables about five years ago. His real name is Alvin Isenhart."

She gave him the address, and he drove straight there. No one answered his knock. The front door was locked, and he walked around the unit, finding a gate to a patio door, which was also locked. No broken windows, but some interesting tracks in the snow behind the apartment, right below a bedroom window. He inquired with a neighbor, found out that Izzy worked at an electronics superstore a few miles up the road; he drove there, checking with the manager.

"Izzy?" the manager said, when Carillo gave him a spiel about running a background check. "Not really sure what happened to him. Left here suddenly the other day. Looked like he was gonna hurl, and asked to go home. One of the clerks up front thought maybe he was having relationship problems, because someone tried to deliver flowers here to him."

"Flowers? When was this?"

"A few minutes after he went home sick. It was right after the senator got shot. On every TV in the place, so it wasn't like you could've missed it."

"You don't by chance happen to have the kid's cell phone number, do you?"

"Got it right here." He pulled a Rolodex from his desk, flipped through until he found the numbers. Carillo jotted both his cell and home number in his notebook.

"I appreciate your time," Carillo said, giving him his card. Calling his office, he put out a BOLO on both Izzy and Maddie and made sure it was forwarded to all the surrounding agencies.

In the car, Carillo checked with Doc, found out the cell number was the same.

Not that it did him any good, since no one was answering it. He didn't leave a voice mail, and thought about the coincidence of the kid taking off right after the senator's murder. Add to that the call that Doc overheard, and it meant one thing.

They needed to find this kid before someone else did.

27

Griffin had been extremely quiet since their initial return from the museum, and Sydney assumed his thoughts were consumed by the sketch of the woman Petra had described. Amazing he could even function after seeing it, she thought, as they walked the few blocks of residential streets toward the museum. He hadn't dared park any closer, even if he could have done so. This at least gave them the advantage of looking as if they belonged in the neighborhood, dressed as they were in jeans and casual coats, Griffin again sporting his tortoiseshell-framed glasses.

She glanced over at him, saw him keeping a sharp eye on their surroundings. Snow drifted down, but not enough to keep anyone indoors, and there were a number of pedestrians walking down Hobbemastraat. Lights shone from several windows of the houses they passed, a suffused golden glow illuminating tiny snowflakes that danced and twirled about the glass panes. Sydney imagined the residents sitting down to dinner with their families in rooms warmed by a fire, reminding her how much she missed her own family, even her mother's overprotectiveness. It did, however, make her wonder about Griffin, where his family was, and she realized how very little she knew about him.

"Over there," he said as they walked down the street, then stopped about a half block away. "That arch leads into the garden entrance to the Rijksmuseum."

She surveyed the scene, noting it was a fairly busy intersection, what with the tram stop situated on the corner and the multitude of windows from the residences and businesses that faced the museum on the other corners. Not one conducive to a hit. "Where was he when he was killed?"

"About midway between the entrance of the museum and the arch. Someone waited for him in the garden after he exited the museum. He staggered from there toward the arch," he said as a patrol car cruised by, its wipers moving swiftly to clear the snow from the windshield. The vehicle slowed as it neared the murder scene, then cruised on. Griffin, however, remained rooted to the spot. "We have to assume the entire area is under surveillance, which means we need a plan."

"I like the plan where we leave."

She nearly jumped when he linked his arm through hers. "My plan's better," he said, leaning over, whispering into her ear, his lips brushing her lobe. A shiver swept through her. "Lovers."

"Your *plan* sucks," she said, trying to pull her arm free, but he held tight. "Come up with a better one."

He looked at her, smiled. "Payback for Italy. For every time I tried to get you on that plane home and you refused."

A car approached, its headlights blinding her, and she smiled back at him, reaching up to caress his cheek for effect, her fingertips scraping the day's growth of whiskers. When she saw his smile fade at her touch, she said, "Don't forget that payback's a bitch. Because I am so paying you back for this."

Once the car passed, they continued on, arm in arm across the street, toward the arch that was flanked on either side by massive-trunked trees, the bare branches towering into the dark sky. A wrought-iron fence surrounded the museum property, but the gate was open and they walked through beneath the grand arch, where just beyond it on either side, a bench was placed so that one could sit and view the vast landscape, at this moment beautiful, cold, and lonely. Trim paths meandered around formal beds framed by snow-covered boxwood hedges interspersed with tall, conical topiaries. No matter where Sydney looked, everything was masked with a soft blanket of white, hiding the imperfections, the shadows, the secrets, muffling her footfall, even on the gravel.

To the right, about twenty yards beyond the archway, a statuette of a lion stood sentinel. "That's where he fell," Griffin said, nodding toward the sculpture.

She examined the lion bust, followed a visual path from there to where Griffin said he'd been stabbed, and she realized that the snow at the top of one of the bushes nearest the bust seemed . . . less perfect, as though it had been disturbed.

"Wait here," Griffin told her. He walked toward the statue, then stopped, bent down, felt around, and stood, both hands filled with snow. "It's not there," he said, forming a snowball, then throwing it at her.

Sydney brushed the white crystals from her coat. "Taking out your frustrations?"

"Surveillance?" he said. "And look like you're having fun."

"You are so going to get it." Sydney bent down, scraped up a handful of icy slush, trying her best to look happy. She lobbed her snowball, not at him, but the bush where she saw the dip in the snow. "How about over there? See the dip in the hedge, like someone hit it and knocked the snow from the top?" She gave a loud laugh, quickly formed a couple more snowballs, then ran toward him. Hit him square in the chest. Before he could move, she hit him again. "Ha!"

He shook his head, grinning as he moved back, working his way toward the bush. "There's such a thing as overkill."

"You wish," she said, scraping together several more snowballs, then throwing them at him as he ducked.

He started forming his own, tossing the occasional one for effect. She kept up her assault, when suddenly he stood, called out, "Truce. I give!" And then he began to meticulously brush the snow from his pants, all the way down to the cuff. He found it, she thought, just as they heard a vehicle engine start up from across the street. They both froze momentarily, until Griffin gathered two handfuls of snow, forming it into a tight ball. And then he stalked toward her.

"You said truce," she pointed out.

"I lied." He tossed the snowball into the air, neatly caught it, a devilish look in his eye. "Unless you can think of a better way to get out of here?"

She shook her head, backing up, then turned, ran beneath the arch to the gate, saw the headlights as the vehicle pulled out of its space. She stopped in her tracks, turned toward Griffin just as the snowball hit her in the leg. "They're coming."

"They're going to see what they want to see." He lunged toward her, picked her up, spun with her in a circle, stopping finally when she faced the street. "Let's make sure it's what we want," he said his mouth to her ear, his breath against her skin. "You have visual?"

"Yes."

"Keep your face close to mine. I doubt they'll recognize you, but they might know me."

Holding Sydney tight, he backed her to the arch, until she felt the cold of the mortar seeping through her coat in sharp contrast to the warmth of him against her.

She leaned her head on his shoulder, saw the vehicle cruising toward them. Moving too slow for her comfort, she thought. It neared, and she saw the silhouette of a man's head, the movement of him turning, watching them.

She looked up at Griffin. "Definitely interested in us."

"Showtime."

And he lowered his mouth to hers.

His lips were cold, but then quickly warmed. She hadn't expected she'd notice that. But then neither had she expected that he'd kiss her as part of their cover, and she tried to relax, telling herself that this was the sort of thing spies did. Pretended to be something they weren't. Lovers in the park, throwing snowballs, then ending their play with a kiss.

The entire episode meant nothing. The fact that he held her, one hand at her head, fingers splayed in her hair, the other hand sliding down her back, pulling her closer until she felt him tight against her. It meant nothing.

Her breath caught, not because of his mouth on hers, but because the headlights of the approaching car surrounded them in light.

Her pulse quickened, not because he held her a second or two longer than required, but because of the danger.

And when the vehicle finally passed from view, its occupants perhaps dismissing them as the lovers they pretended to be, Griffin let her go. Cold air rushed between them, and he stepped back, not looking at her, but at their surroundings, giving her the moment she needed to catch her breath, compose herself. Then he linked his arm through hers, and they continued their walk, as though this had merely been an impromptu stop on their way. They leaned in to each other, talked about the buildings, holding their hands up to catch snowflakes, saying nothing of import.

All an act.

Unfortunately her heart, still rapidly beating, didn't know the difference, and it was quite some time before it slowed to a normal pace.

They sauntered up Hobbemastraat, then circled back around to the car. Once there, Griffin pulled the item he'd found from his pocket and held it for her to see.

"That's definitely *not* a knife," she said, eyeing the sealed Ziploc bag. Inside was a clear plastic tube about an inch in diameter, containing yet another smaller vial filled with a yellowish medium that she hoped was very much frozen. Knowing the things Griffin and his kind were involved with, it was bound to be deadly. Very deadly.

And then she eyed the droplets on the outside of the bag. "Please tell me that's melted snow and that it isn't leaking . . . ?"

28

December 10
Washington, D.C.

Miles Cavanaugh paced the floor in his office, wait-ing for the damned phone to ring. Bose should have called by now, saying the matter had been handled. What the hell was taking him so damned long? The multi-agency task force to bring in Griffin had been a fiasco. Nothing had gone right. And then there was McNiel, that damned director from ATLAS, who seemed to walk on water. Someone should have ordered him to turn over all the records on Griffin. Worse yet, Miles had heard they'd nearly caught Griffin twice, and *still* he'd managed to slip through.

How? Every allied agency had Griffin's name on their list. His passports under every AKA he'd ever used were now worthless, his credit and bank accounts were no longer accessible. He was completely, utterly in the cold. So how the hell had he eluded their every safeguard?

The phone rang. Miles tore across the room, picked it up. "Yes?"

"I found them. Griffin and the woman."

"Where are they?"

"Driving. I'm following them now."

"To where?"

"Not sure yet. Southeast is all I can tell."

"I want that package found."

"Well, judging from their actions, I'm guessing they found it. They stopped at a store and bought a small ice chest and there wasn't a six-pack in sight. Unfortunately, I was on the other side of the canal or I would've had them by now."

"Good. When you get them, clean it up. I don't want Griffin or this woman around in the end."

29

December 10
Two hours outside Amsterdam
En route to Winterswijk

Moonlight cast its pale glow across the countryside,
the vast snow-covered fields, with the occasional village
seen in the distance. They'd been on the road for almost an
hour, and Griffin checked his rearview mirror. The car was
still firmly on their tail, had been since they left Amsterdam.
Not hard to miss, since one of its headlights was slightly out
of adjustment.

At the moment, there were no other vehicles on the road,
which was sort of a good news–bad news thing. Good in that
it allowed Griffin to verify that they were definitely being
followed, which meant he needed to lose the tail before he
led them right to his contact's door. Bad in that no witnesses
and lots of wide, open space left plenty of opportunity for
whoever was on their tail to make an attack.

If there was going to be one, Griffin wanted it on his terms.
He braked hard, and the car backed off momentarily, but not
for long. It soon sped up, trying to jockey for position along-
side them, undoubtedly trying to ram their fender, which
would send them spinning. He'd seen the move, used it him-

self. Griffin hit the gas, pulled ahead, heard the screeching of tires as the other car followed. "Syd."

He reached over, tapped her on the thigh. She opened her eyes, looked around sleepily. "What?"

"I can't drive and shoot at the same time." Griffin swerved slightly, braking, then stabbed the gas, hoping the car behind him would back way off.

"Can't a girl catch a nap around here?" she said, opening the glove box, removing the weapon.

"Take out his tire, then you can sleep."

Sydney rolled down her window, the icy wind whipping at her hair as she shifted in her seat. Unfortunately, he realized, it meant she'd be shooting weak-handed, never mind against the glare of the headlights, but that couldn't be helped. He'd seen her on the range and in the field. She was a damned good marksman. When she was in position, he said, "Get ready."

"I'm ready."

The roadway straightened, and he looked in the mirror, saw the vehicle's headlights. He let his foot off the gas. The car jerked suddenly as he hit a pothole.

"Not helping," Sydney shouted.

"Sorry." He focused on the road, tried to keep his driving smooth. She fired a shot. And missed.

Come on, he pleaded silently. *Make it*. She fired twice more in succession.

He heard the sound of metal scraping metal, and he looked in his rearview mirror, saw the car skidding off the road, the beams from its headlights bouncing, then finally coming to rest, at a downward tilt as though the car had landed in a shallow ditch. From the corner of his eye, he saw Sydney scooting back into position, raking her hair out of her face with one hand, as she lowered the Glock to her lap, then rolled up the window.

"Nice job."

"Yeah. Mind if I finish my nap now?"

Somehow he doubted she was going to be able to sleep. Even so, he smiled, relaxing for the first time since they'd left Amsterdam.

* * *

About a half hour later, with no indication that they were being followed, Sydney looked up, reading the sign on the expressway. "Exactly where are we going?"

"Winterswijk. I have contacts there who can get me a decent passport. I need ID. Until I get some, we can't go anywhere."

"I thought spies had stacks of passports, one for every day of the week."

"Until you get burned."

The drive to Winterswijk, a small village on the eastern border near Germany, took an additional hour, and Sydney dozed for the latter part of the trip, waking as Griffin stopped, then made a turn down a long road. To the right, a thicket of trees, branches bare, stretched as far as the eye could see. Griffin drove past the village filled with quaint storybook houses, some with thatched roofs, all with windows glowing gold against the night. Eventually he turned down a street that led away from the village, and into a forest, his eye constantly on his rearview mirror as they wound their way down a single lane road that eventually led to a large white farmhouse.

Griffin parked in the drive, behind a gray Volvo wagon and a brown pickup truck. "We're here," he said. "Hope you like dogs. Dirk has a couple of Hungarian vizslas. They're friendly as long as he's around."

They got out and walked up the snow-covered path to the door, which opened before they even knocked. Light spilled onto the walkway. A large russet-colored dog bounded down the porch steps, nearly bowling Griffin over in its enthusiasm to greet him.

"Chip," a deep voice called out from the porch. The dog stopped in its tracks, its tail wagging. Just behind it, a man, tall as the doorway, stood there, and the dog returned to his side as he waited for them to enter the house.

"Zach," Dirk said, clasping Griffin's outstretched hand with both of his. "You made good time." He stepped out onto the porch, looked around, his gaze sharp.

"The weather held," Griffin replied, stomping the snow from his shoes before entering. "How have you been?"

Before he could answer, a woman walked up. Sydney figured she was somewhere between forty and fifty, a head shorter than Sydney, with brown wavy hair that framed a pretty face and blue eyes that lit up the moment she saw Griffin. "Zachary!" she said, rushing forward, her hands outstretched.

"Monique. You still look the same. As beautiful as ever," he said, having to bend to accept her greeting, cheek to cheek, three times.

She turned to Sydney, a look of curiosity in her gaze. "And who is this?"

Griffin made the introductions.

"How long can you stay?" Monique asked.

"Only until morning."

"Sometime you must come when you can stay longer," she replied, taking their coats. She led them through the front parlor past a piano to a room that opened up on the right just before the kitchen. A small sofa and chairs faced the hearth where a fire crackled within.

"Now sit. Drink, while I cook dinner." She left the room.

Dirk poured wine and handed them each a glass. "Surely you didn't make this trip just for a passport."

"You're right." Griffin gave him a brief history of the last week's events, culminating with finding the sealed vial at the museum. "Two people are dead, and someone followed us here. I have a feeling they're after what's in that cooler."

"What do you think it is?"

"In my line of work? Things that are frozen in cryo tubes, then placed in another vial and then in an airtight plastic bag usually have deadly consequences. The question is, why would someone send it to Faas?"

"Faas's niece didn't mention anything about this to you?"

"No. Just that Faas had recently received something I'd be interested in that might answer the who and why. Specifically something I'd want to see in person, because I'd been looking for it for the last couple years. I assumed, naturally, that he meant information on who killed my wife. Not a frozen biological sample."

Dirk poured more wine into his glass. "Maybe there's something else. Something about where it came from?"

Sydney, recalling what the curator told them at the museum, said, "Faas received a knife from France. Possibly the knife he was killed with."

"What sort of knife?" Dirk asked her.

"The curator thought it was an antique, because that's what Faas dealt with. Originally that's what we thought we were searching for."

"Only because Faas seemed to be handing the knife to me when we approached him." Griffin repeated Faas's dying declaration. "At first, I thought he was asking me not to let them get the knife. That he dropped it and I needed to find it before they killed everyone."

"A logical conclusion, considering the circumstances," Dirk said.

"It was what he uttered at the end, 'from Atlant,' that didn't make sense."

"He was dying," Dirk pointed out. "Hard to say if he was even talking to you."

"Looking back, Faas was obviously telling me he'd dropped the vial and that's what I should be looking for. The knife may have been a ruse to make sure the package had a purpose to get it to Faas without question."

"Unless we're overlooking the obvious. What if there was something significant about the knife? Something that might be a clue as to where the vial came from?" Dirk asked.

Griffin rubbed at his temple, the day taking its toll on him. "The pattern on the hilt maybe. Distinctive. Black and gold. Other than that, it didn't look like anything more than a convenient murder weapon."

"Short of recovering the box it was mailed in, it may be your best lead. What sort of pattern? Maybe it was an antique specific to somewhere in France?" Dirk took a pad of paper and a pencil from an end table drawer, handing both to Griffin.

He sketched out the design. "Mind you, art is Sydney's strong suit, not mine, but I think it's fairly accurate."

Dirk eyed the rough drawing of the knife and the pattern on its handle that resembled a string of tulips placed end to end. "This I have seen before . . ."

"Where?" Griffin asked.

"Something makes me think at my wife's office." He glanced at Sydney, saying, "She's a doctor, so maybe it is medical . . . Mo?"

Monique stepped out of the kitchen to see what he wanted, her fingertips slightly dusty from flour. He held up the knife drawing. "This pattern. Where have I seen it recently?"

"Very likely when you met me for lunch, and we walked past the lab at the hospital. Well, the individual portion of the pattern," she said, covering up all but one of the tulip-shaped symbols. "It's the Greek letter psi. Or rather a string of them. In virology it represents a viral packaging signal."

"Packaging signal?" Sydney echoed. "As in that thing in our cooler contains a virus?"

At once they all looked at Griffin, and Dirk said, "Any chance we're dealing with a nice *mild* virus? Swine flu?"

"Is Lisette in the area?" Monique asked. "This is, after all, her specialty," she said, referring to another ATLAS agent, Dr. Lisette Perrault.

"I have no idea where she is."

"Well, then . . ." Monique smiled, her eyes sparkling as

she turned toward the kitchen. "If we all come down with sore throats in the next couple days, we'll know if we should worry, yes? In the meantime, let's hope they used proper care and handling when they packaged it for transport."

"Cheery thought," Sydney replied.

And Dirk said, "Monique is ever the optimist." He looked at Griffin. "What do you plan to do with it?"

"We can't very well cart it around Europe if it is a deadly virus," he replied. "Especially if this is what Faas and Petra were killed for. Because it means they're hoping to recover it and that puts anyone who has it in danger."

"Can one of your teams come pick it up?"

"That's clearly the best option," Griffin replied. "Let's hope they don't try to bring me in with it. After we eat, Sydney can phone Carillo and make arrangements."

Sydney heard the clang of pots and pans, and water running, followed a few minutes later by the loud sizzle and tantalizing scent of frying fish. Only then did she realize she was starving and hadn't eaten a thing since morning.

"Dinner!" Monique called out, and they moved into the kitchen, sitting at a round table in the very center. Monique set out a large platter of fried fish, the likes of which Sydney had never seen. It was very thin, and she watched a moment, saw Griffin pick up his fork, scraping the flat fish from the bone. Sydney followed suit, and found it light, crispy, and mouthwatering.

Unfortunately there was little time to relax after dinner, because she needed to make that call to Carillo.

"So how's Europe?" Carillo asked her.

"Cold. And a few too many people who are using us for target practice. I don't suppose Tex is with you? I have some information he needs to pass on to HQ. Preferably Dr. Lisette Perrault."

"I'm meeting Tex later this afternoon. He's supposed to follow up on some promising leads as to where to find Griffin."

"He having any luck with that?" Syd asked.

"Zilch. Secret agents these days, ya know? What's up?"

She briefed him on the discovery of the vial, and their suspicions of its contents, and the importance of getting someone out to secure it from them at once.

"And you're sure it couldn't be some other biological sample? Like maybe this Faas guy was on his way to a sperm bank?"

"Unless he was carrying around Einstein's potential progeny, I don't see that worth killing for." She glanced at the drawing Griffin made of the knife, the pattern on the hilt. "There was a symbol on the murder weapon that could possibly have been some sort of a warning. Griffin sketched it out. One of his contacts said it is actually a repeat of the Greek letter psi, which is also the symbol used in virology packaging."

"So you can recognize it on the grocery store shelves? Tell it apart from the bacon?"

"In the labs. Like biohazard symbols. We're heading to France since that's where the package originated from. I'll send a picture of his sketch over the phone. Maybe you or someone there can see if there's something else about the pattern that we're missing."

"I'll give it to Tex once he gets out of his meeting. They're all up in arms about this stolen AUV. They think it's tied into the senator's murder, even though *publicly* everyone's sticking to the theory that a lone gunman was responsible. A tragic isolated incident. Can you spell conspiracy theory?"

"What's an AUV?"

"Automated underwater vehicle. Sort of a robot submarine drone thing. I think they're worried that a terrorist could strap some nukes to it and send it into a busy port would be my guess. Apparently there was a sighting somewhere between Jamaica and the Cayman Islands, so they've sent a ship out to see if it's connected. Your friend from Italy's there now. Marc di Luca."

"Lucky Marc. Any chance he needs backup? Jamaica sounds a hell of a lot warmer than here."

"I'll put in a good word for you, should there be an opening. In the meantime, keep in touch. Oh, and that pattern on the knife hilt?"

"What about it?"

"If it really is something to do with virology, you might want to pay special attention. Double up on the gloves."

"Thanks Carillo. Always a help."

She hung up, then looked over, saw Griffin staring into the fire as he sipped at his wine. He was quiet, too quiet, and Sydney wondered how much it hurt him to be placed in this situation, seemingly alone and abandoned, where he had to go through middlemen to contact his own agency.

That wasn't, however, what occupied her mind after they retired for the night, sharing a spare room with twin beds. In fact, she thought about what happened out there at the museum. The kiss. Wondered if he had contemplated it at all, thought about her.

But when she looked over, saw him in the moonlight, his back to her, she knew what caused his silence. It wasn't his job. It wasn't the kiss. It wasn't her at all.

He was studying the sketch she'd drawn. The one of his wife.

She told herself it didn't bother her. She was not, however, a good liar—at least not to herself.

A chill swept through the room, and she turned her thoughts to Marc in Jamaica. Clearly he had the better assignment.

30

December 10
Off the coast of the Cayman Islands

Marc di Luca stood on the deck of the *Desdemona*, a 270-foot medium endurance cutter, watching the forensic divers enter the water. One team was assigned to recover the remains of the victims, if any; another would recover what might be left of the *Random Act* and the students' belongings. Both teams would attempt to determine, if possible, why that location might have drawn someone to explore it with an AUV.

It wasn't the worst assignment he'd been on, even though he'd been none too happy about it. It was more that ever since he'd left his home in Italy to work for ATLAS U.S. full-time, it seemed he was anywhere *but* in the U.S. Today was no exception, he thought, as he scanned the horizon. No other boats in sight. Water calm, skies sunny. All in all a beautiful day, as long as one ignored the bank of dark clouds on the horizon that foretold a coming storm.

Marc left the deck and returned to the control center where the lieutenant oversaw the personnel monitoring the cutter's radars, closed circuit televisions, electronic surveillance, navigation and communication systems. The lieutenant's attention was fixed on the monitor closest to him, where grayish-green images of the divers were visible as they swam near the ocean floor, the bubbles from their air tanks rising to the surface. The cutter had been here several days and still the crew had yet to find anything noteworthy, at least in the location where the two witnesses had claimed to be when the explosion occurred. "Any sign of an older shipwreck?" Marc asked, eyeing the monitors as well. "Something where a treasure might have been an issue?"

"Been a couple storms. Could be buried under silt."

The morning had passed with no significant finds when Director McNiel called, asking if there was anything to report. "Not much," Marc replied. "Unless you count the underwater ruins, which on further inspection appear to be a sunken ship."

"Is it possible that these pirates were that far off? That they were after the ship, and whatever was buried there?"

"Anything is possible, sir, except that your two witnesses said the pirates never ventured toward the shipwreck."

"What about biological agents?"

Marc's gaze flicked to the monitors, trying to determine the significance of that statement. "Sir?"

"I'm sure Tex informed you that he received confirmation on the Russian scientist, Dr. Fedorov? He was last seen in the area of that stolen AUV. He was a researcher for Vector," he added, referring to the heavily guarded Siberian laboratory. "Marburg, Ebola, that sort of thing. Add to that, a source at the FBI recovered some partial computer files from the shooter's computer which supports our suspicions on a possible biological agent."

"Viruses? In the middle of the ocean? Is that even possible?"

"I have no idea. Which is why I'm sending in a team that has that expertise. Lisette's heading it up. They should be arriving within the hour."

"Any word on Griffin?" Marc asked.

To which McNiel said, "Let me know when the team arrives." Apparently he wasn't free to speak, since he didn't even acknowledge the inquiry on Griffin. After McNiel disconnected, Marc stood there a moment, staring at the monitors, watching the divers. Even if Griffin hadn't gone AWOL to search for his wife's killer, Marc doubted there was much for him to do here. Of course, that was exactly why McNiel had assigned Griffin to the cutter. Keep him out of the way while the rest of them worked the LockeStarr case.

A lot of good that did.

An hour later, Marc watched as Lisette Perrault hopped off the helicopter, her dark hair assaulting her face as she ducked below the rotors. Two men and one other woman followed: Lisette's partner, Rafiq, the only one of the four who wasn't a scientist, then Dr. Raj Balraj and Dr. Patricia Zemke. After their equipment was unloaded, the chopper took off, leaving the four standing on the helipad as Marc walked up to greet them. He hadn't seen Lisette since their last operation in Tunisia, the location and destruction of a suspected Black Network bioweapons lab. Even that short time with Lisette had taken its toll on his emotions. He'd known better than to get involved with a fellow agent who was assigned long-term to another country—hadn't he seen the disaster of Griffin and Becca's marriage and impending divorce just before she'd been killed? Griffin had never fully recovered from it, and Marc suspected that was part of the reason for his own difficulties, things not working out between him and Lisette. The fear of failure. He just hadn't expected the sight of Lisette last month in Tunisia, after all that time away, would remind him how much he'd missed her—feelings Lisette hadn't seemed to reciprocate, he thought as she held out her hand, saying, "It's good to see you."

"You too," he said, shaking her hand, ignoring the pull of emotions, then greeting the others. He turned his attention back to Lisette. "Director McNiel said that there were some biological concerns?"

"Yes," she replied, attempting to comb her fingers through her hair, only to have the wind whip it right back into her face. "Of what magnitude, we're not sure. At this point, it is only speculation, based on some recovered partial computer files, and the sighting of the Russian scientist near *Amphitrite* when there was no valid reason for him to be there." She reached down, picked up one of the boxes. "Is there a spot we can set up a lab?"

"They're giving you use of the wardroom." He helped carry the equipment to the officers' lounge, then led her up to the control center, because she wanted to see the area where the AUV might have descended.

She watched the divers on the screen, then eyed the map that someone had tacked up. A red pin had been placed on their current location in the Atlantic.

"What are they expecting?" Marc asked. "For you to take samples of the water here to see if they're planting a virus? Isn't the ocean too vast for that?"

"I would think so. If you were going to spread a water-borne virus, I'd think you'd want a smaller body of water. And you wouldn't need an AUV for that, so I'm not sure that this intel Director McNiel received is accurate."

"It may not be accurate, but whatever the actual purpose for that AUV, someone went to a lot of trouble to make sure there were no witnesses."

31

December 10
Washington, D.C.

"Do you believe me now?" Izzy asked, several hours later.

Maddie leaned against the wall. She nodded. "I believe you."

Izzy wished he felt a sense of relief at her answer. All he felt was scared. This had spun out of control faster than he'd realized, and he didn't know how to fix it. "I left that FBI agent's card back there with my phone."

At the moment they were holed up in an alley across the street from the back entrance of the building they'd fled earlier that morning. He thought he'd been so clever picking that building for their setup. Easy in, easy out.

And it would have worked, had they not been seen.

"We don't need the number," she said. "We could go to the FBI office."

"But we didn't get the proof. They're not gonna believe us."

"Then you have to make them believe us. Besides, I have the picture on my phone."

"We can't get to the FBI," he replied, "if we can't get to the car." Unfortunately the exit they had used was on the opposite side from the parking garage where he'd left his car.

"Maybe they're gone. Go see."

He didn't want to go see. He didn't want to do anything but go home and pretend that none of this ever happened. Then again, if it hadn't happened, he wouldn't be standing here so close to Maddie.

"Go on," she said, giving him a little push.

Izzy looked back at her, saw her nod in encouragement, and he realized that for her he was willing to pretend bravery—up until the point he saw a white van drive past. He jumped back, his heart beating fast. He liked Maddie. Just not enough to die for her. "We need to think of something else."

Down the alley in the opposite direction, he saw only thick traffic. That way took them farther from his car, but if it worked out right, they could double back and avoid being seen. "Keep close to the wall. Maybe the Dumpster will cover us."

He hoped.

They'd nearly reached the street when he heard the screech of tires. He looked behind him, saw the van speeding down the alley. "Run!" he said, pulling her by the hand. The alley intersected into a one-way street, the traffic coming from the right. He guided Maddie toward the oncoming cars, figuring the van would have to stop to make a turn. They raced down the block, and he glanced back, saw someone bailing out from the van's passenger door.

He and Maddie reached the corner, turned to the right again, and he threw his hand up, praying for a taxi as they stepped off the sidewalk between the line of parked cars, not daring to stop. The first taxi passed. And then another. And just as their pursuer turned the corner, a cab stopped. Izzy yanked the door open, pushing Maddie in. He jumped in after her, slammed the door. "Take us . . . to the FBI office," he said, trying to catch his breath, as the driver pulled out into traffic.

Izzy swiveled around, saw the man racing toward them, finally giving up as the cab gained speed. He leaned against the seat, trying to slow his breathing. Maddie reached over, grasped his hand, her eyes closed, whether from relief or the desire to forget any of this happened, he wasn't sure.

The meter ticked up with each mile, before the cab finally stopped in front of the FBI office. It took all of Izzy's money, and five more dollars from Maddie. That left about four dollars for dinner. Not a lot of choices, he thought as they walked to the metal detector in the lobby. He put his backpack on the conveyer belt, along with his laptop, and Maddie her purse. Once through, they walked up to the receptionist who sat behind a thick glass window, undoubtedly bulletproof. Made him wish he was on that side of it.

"Hi," Izzy said to the woman. "I was wondering if you know where I can find Agent Carillo? He works out of the San Francisco office. He's supposed to be here on a case."

The woman typed something into her computer as two men walked in, one a uniformed police officer, another a man in a suit, both talking about the Redskins game. The receptionist saw the agent, saying, "Bradshaw. You know if there's a Carillo working here from the San Francisco field office?"

"Not that I know of."

"Then can we speak to someone else?" Maddie asked. "It's important."

"I'll take it, Suzie," the man in the suit said. "Special Agent Bradshaw," he told them. "What seems to be the problem?"

Izzy hesitated, only because he knew what the agent's reaction was going to be. Then again, what choice did he have? "We're being chased. These guys came to my apartment and to hers, and they're trying to kill us, because we knew the guy who was arrested for killing the senator."

The agent glanced at the officer, then back at them, his expression one of disbelief, if Izzy was any judge. "Senator Grogan?"

"Yeah. We have a picture of the guy. Show him, Maddie."

She took out her phone, brought up the picture.

"This guy was chasing you?"

"Yeah. We sent an e-mail to my computer, saying we were going to meet at the coffee shop. And then we waited across the street, and when they got there, they saw us and Maddie took their picture. And that's when they chased us."

"Right . . ." This last was drawn out, as the agent reached back, rubbed his neck. "Because you knew the guy who killed the senator. I'm not sure I understand."

"Oh my God," Maddie said. "You're right, Izzy. They're not going to believe us."

The agent looked at her, his gaze narrowed. "What'd you call him?"

Maddie froze, worry clouding her eyes.

"No, you're not in trouble," the agent said.

"Izzy . . . ?" she repeated.

He turned to the receptionist asking, "Can you get the names on that BOLO that came out on this?"

She typed something in the computer. "Madeline Boucher and Alvin Isenhart, AKA Izzy. If found, contact SA Carillo. He's apparently working out of HQ."

The agent looked at them, asking, "That you?"

Izzy and Maddie nodded.

"Contact HQ," he told the receptionist. "Let Carillo know we have those two subjects at the field office."

32

December 10
Washington, D.C.

If Carillo thought using his red lights and sirens would have gotten him to the field office any faster, he would've used them. Unfortunately some minor fender bender had had the entire street backed up, while everyone craned their heads to see what was going on, turning a ten-minute drive into twenty. When he finally made it, he found the two witnesses in an interview room, waiting.

Maddie smiled when she saw him, probably glad to see a familiar face. The kid, Izzy, didn't look so hot. "You okay?" Carillo asked him, taking a seat at the table.

"Just wondering if we're wasting our time."

"You tell me."

"Well, you're not writing anything down."

"One, I haven't asked you anything yet. Two, I want to hear what you say. Trust me, you'll be telling this so many times before we're through, it'll make your head spin."

"No one else believes us."

"Well, they don't know what I know. So lay it on me."

And the kid couldn't shut up after that. Everything seemed to check out just as Carillo thought it would. Until Carillo said, "Tell me about the computer."

"Hollis's computer?"

From what Carillo had read in the reports, Hollis, the alleged shooter, had been the one dabbling in the dark arts of Internet hacking. Which made him wonder why Izzy would even question which computer. "Is there another computer we should be looking at?"

Izzy swallowed. "Mine? I, um, erased everything. Or tried to."

"Why is that?"

"I didn't want to be in trouble?"

"For what?"

The kid wiped the sweat from his upper lip, took a deep breath, then stared at his lap, saying, "Because it might be partly my fault the senator's dead?"

Now this Carillo hadn't expected. "Maybe you better start at the beginning," he said, this time careful to take copious notes.

"It was just a hobby," Izzy explained. "For me, it was all about the challenge. I'd hack into these Web sites, then notify the companies that they had a security flaw. You know, sort of doing them a favor so they could fix it."

"I'm sure they were real appreciative."

"Some were. I mean, we were the good guys, right? Better us than the black hats."

"Go on," Carillo prodded.

"For me, I was in and out pretty quick. You know, covered my tracks. Connect into a chain of computers remotely, so if someone tried to find me, well, that wasn't about to happen."

"So how does this tie into the senator's murder?"

"Hollis would play these games. We all did it sometimes. You know. Like open the newspaper, read a random article about something, like a company, then see how long it took to hack into that company's computer? I swear, I just thought he was in it for fun. It was this game and his Web site that started it."

"How?"

"About two months back, he's reading an article on the Web. And then he starts going off about how all these pharmaceutical companies are working behind the scenes to create these viruses just so they can come up with medicines and vaccines to make money. You know, like hanta, bird flu, swine flu. They're all manmade, he says, and he can prove it. So he hacks into this company in San Francisco, and that leads to this U.S. lab in France and then an e-mail talking about manufacturing something called a chimera virus and they're getting funding for it, by saying it's for vaccines, but they're looking for the stem cell of viruses."

"Stem cell of viruses?" Carillo repeated. "From a lab in France?"

"They weren't *real* stem cells. It was a term they used. Like finding what started life. And then it gets even weirder. They're talking about finding them near Atlantis. I mean, they weren't talking about finding Atlantis, all woo-woo, space aliens and historical stuff. It was like, someone mentioned it in the e-mail, like they were dubbing it this name. You know, like Project Atlantis."

Project Atlantis aside, Carillo was alarmed at what he was hearing. Especially after his conversation with Sydney. Too many linked parallels to what she was working on, namely France and viruses, which, in his opinion, moved everything this kid was saying from the highly improbable category to the better-sit-up-and-notice category. What he didn't get was why this whole Atlantis thing was bugging him . . . "Hold on a sec," he said, flipping through his notes, distinctly remembering Syd saying something about this guy Faas and what he uttered before he was murdered . . . finding something before everyone was killed. Carillo located it in his notes. The word *Atlant* . . .

Atlantis?

"Jesus . . ." He flipped to a blank page, poised his pen over the paper. "Anything else?"

"Not much more to tell, other than Hollis starts to go crazy, saying he knew it all the time. He showed me the e-mail. I mean, it didn't make any sense to me, this stem cell stuff, but he was pretty adamant they were talking about us over here, not in France."

Carillo looked up from his notebook. "Why do you think that?"

"Because one of them reads, 'What about Grogan?' and the response is 'Don't worry. It's being dealt with.' And Hollis is obsessed with this. He's like, 'They're going to kill the senator.'"

What they had was a convoluted mess, and Carillo wondered if this stuff was so vague that he was reading things into it himself, including the connection to Sydney. As it was, he understood why no one believed the kid. Carillo wasn't even sure *he* believed him. Except for the gut feeling that Hollis did not kill himself and there was something about the senator's murder they were all missing. He went back through his notes. "Okay, so if I get this straight, you guys backdoor into this lab's computer in France that is making something called a chimera virus, and somewhere along the line, it points back to Senator Grogan? Here in the States?"

"Yeah. And that's why I thought Hollis was going to see Grogan. To warn him. But I think by that time they must have gotten to him. Because he was acting all strange that day. Delusional. I mean, he was always a little out there. Just ask Maddie." She nodded, and he continued, saying, "But this was different. Like they gave him something. You know, that made him act weird. I wanted to take him to the hospital, but I didn't. I should've, but I didn't . . ."

"Hey, kid," Carillo said, seeing him start to tear up. "It was out of your hands. You couldn't have known."

"You think so?"

"Yeah. I do."

Izzy nodded, took a breath, then continued. "He kept saying he had to stop Grogan and find the ship."

"What ship?"

"I have no idea. But they were going to hijack it and Hollis was saying this proved everything."

If what this kid was saying was true, then this case was

way beyond Carillo's expertise. "You mind sitting tight while I make a phone call?"

Maddie stirred herself, saying, "Can I use the bathroom?"

"Me too," Izzy said. "And maybe get something to drink?"

Carillo got an agent to escort the two to the restroom, then buy them a soda, while he called Tex. "You remember that missing link I was telling you about? He's sitting in an interview room here at HQ, spouting off things like hijacked freighters and pharmaceutical labs in France." Carillo gave him the rundown from his notes.

"Any chance that lab in France was Hilliard and Sons Pharmaceutical?"

"Not sure. I didn't ask."

"Well, do. It's a U.S.–based corporation used for viral research."

"Part of the LockeStarr conglomerate, I take it?"

"We've suspected so, but haven't been able to prove it," Tex replied. "I don't like the timing of this. Not with Griff and Syd headed for France. Right now, the more info we can get, the better."

"I'll check." Carillo returned to the interview room where Izzy and Maddie sat waiting, both drinking canned sodas.

Izzy was certain that Hilliard was the name of the company, and Carillo repeated the info to Tex, who asked, "You think this computer kid is legit?"

"I'd have to say yes."

"Can he get into Hilliard's system?"

Carillo lowered the phone. "Any chance you can hack into this lab again? Recover any of that data?"

"Depends," Izzy said. "The lab patched their security flaws and added a few more safety measures. Hollis tried. Couldn't get in a second time."

"You hear that?" Carillo asked Tex.

"Yeah." He was silent for a moment, then, "Ask him how hard it would be if someone had access to the actual computer *inside* the lab."

Carillo asked Izzy. "Piece of cake, he says." And then Carillo realized what Tex was after. "Please tell me you're not thinking of sending Sydney and Griffin in there?"

"Right now, it's only a glimmer of an idea, since I don't have authorization for an unsanctioned black op. I'll get back to you after the task force meeting."

He disconnected and Carillo relaxed for all of three seconds, when it occurred to him that just about everything they were doing was unsanctioned. That thought did little to comfort him, and he hoped like hell that Sydney was okay.

33

December 10
National Counterterrorism Center (NCTC)
Washington, D.C.

Bose called Miles precisely five minutes before the
task force meeting started. "I got an update, but you're not
going to like it. I lost them."

"What do you mean you lost them? Do you have any idea
what this will do to me?"

"You think I care?"

Miles pictured the view from his White House office, reminding him of all he had at stake. "You had better care. If
you want to be paid."

"It might help if you tell me where they're headed."

"I have no goddamned idea where."

"I'm the brawn, you're the brains. They have the item,
where would they take it?"

"*You* were the one following them."

"Yeah, well, that was before they shot out my tire. And
now they've got a day's head start on me."

Miles glanced at his watch. "I have to go. I'll get back to
you." He disconnected, then ran down the hall to the conference room, where the security task force meeting had

already started. Lucky for him the men sitting around the table were too wrapped up in their conversation to notice his tardiness and he relaxed—until he heard the subject matter.

"So what is this team in France planning to do?" Roy Santiago asked. "Walk inside and get this information?"

"They're waiting for our direction," McNiel said. "We haven't yet figured out how to proceed."

Miles reached for the pitcher of water and poured himself a glass, trying not to appear too interested, as Thorndike said, "What makes them so sure this lab in France is involved?"

"We have an informant who apparently tapped into the lab's computer."

Miles's hand shook, knocking the pitcher into his glass. "Sorry," he said, setting the pitcher down, worried he might dump water over the entire table.

Thorndike glanced at him, then turned back to McNiel, asking, "How do you know the information is valid?"

"We won't know until we check it out. But our informant mentioned the stolen freighter, stating that it was hijacked for the specific purpose of testing this new virus."

To which Miles said, "That freighter has been on every news channel since it went missing however many weeks ago. Anyone could take that and twist it. The *Enquirer* already said it was stolen by space aliens in the Bermuda Triangle, for God's sake."

"He's right," Thorndike said. "It's not that much of a stretch to concoct some strange story about viruses."

"Except," McNiel said, "we just received a report from the navy saying a freighter was seen off the coast of Brazil with fifteen dead."

Miles had also seen the report. He just hadn't expected them to link it to the lab's virus so quickly. His mouth grew dry, and he eyed his glass of water, wondering if he even dared pick it up.

"And what," Santiago asked McNiel, "is being done with this information? I'm assuming *someone* is going to determine what is on this freighter?"

"We have a team not too far from it, just off the Cayman Islands," McNiel said. "We'll send them out to assist. It's possible that none of it is related, but we want to discount any terrorist threat."

"Agreed," Santiago replied. "Apprise me the moment you know anything. I'd like to know we're on top of any terrorist activity, especially in light of the upcoming global summit. Hard to brag to the attending countries that terrorism is our top priority when we don't even know what's going on near our own backyard."

Miles felt his stomach clench with each passing minute, and by the conclusion of the meeting he couldn't get out of there fast enough. He rushed back to his office. When he stepped through the door, his cell phone rang, and he pulled it out, thinking he didn't have time to deal with the bullshit of Washington right now. Not when he had a bigger problem to handle, he thought, answering the call, fully expecting to hear his secretary droning on about some trivial matter that needed attention. "Hello?"

"We seem to be having a bit of a communication problem, Mr. Cavanaugh."

Miles froze on hearing the voice. It took him a moment to recover. "No. No problem."

"Then why hasn't this matter with Zachary Griffin been handled?"

"A momentary setback. He'll be dealt with soon. In fact, he and the woman with him are probably headed toward the lab in Paris right now." He related the information he'd learned at the meeting, concluding with "I intend to send Bose there to cut them off."

"Tell Bose he is no longer needed."

"Why?"

"We already have someone in France who can deal with them, which means it is time to redirect attention by pointing out that the CIA is *facilitating* a double agent. One who is currently feeding information to the Black Network."

Miles sat mute for several seconds. "Thorndike? Running a double agent? Are you sure we can get away with this?"

"If it's handled correctly, Mr. Cavanaugh, Thorndike and his CIA agents will be scrambling to pick up the pieces. In fact every agency involved in this mess will have to reevaluate their own positions. I expect it will cause quite a stir."

"How will this help us?"

"Because it's a win-win situation."

"So that you can discover the identity of this CIA agent working in France to kill him?"

"No. So when several ATLAS agents end up dead, they'll attribute it to the act of espionage by this alleged double agent. We learn who he is when they are forced to make an arrest for espionage, they remove him from our midst, and no one is the wiser."

Miles leaned back in his chair, relaxing for the first time that day.

"And Mr. Cavanaugh? These sorts of opportunities come few and far between. If you value your position, handle this matter with great care. I really don't want to have to find a new deputy security adviser."

The sudden dial tone on the other end echoed in his head. He put the phone down, then stared at it for several seconds. The threat wasn't lost on him. If he didn't succeed, he'd be found dead. Either by his own hand or theirs. He'd be just another White House statistic. No one ever investigated those deaths beyond the obvious clues conveniently left behind. Something that might titillate the Internet for a few weeks, listed on some conspiracy Web site, then forgotten. The out-and-out murders made to look like suicides were quickly swept under the rug, if for no other reason than to ensure the public that their policymakers weren't being run by groups no better than the common Mafia.

Hell if he'd become victim to that. Miles was not going to let Griffin live. Or anyone helping him, either. He needed his own ace in the hole. He'd plant Bose near that lab to make sure Griffin didn't escape. First, however, he needed to handle the Thorndike matter, so he started scrolling through the numbers on his phone until he found the reporter he'd slipped anonymous information to in the past, Merideth Garrett. He called, saying, "Merideth? It's me. I have something I wanted to let you know in the utmost confidence. It's about the deaths on board the *Zenobia* and a CIA agent in France who is working as a double agent. If you want the story, however, there are conditions."

"Such as?" Merideth replied, and he was certain he could hear her salivating.

"You protect your source, for one."

"That goes without saying. Let me get a fresh pad of paper."

34

December 11 (the following day)
Washington, D.C.

"A double agent?" Thorndike shouted, slamming the
newspaper on the table. "It's bad enough we had to go to the
extremes we did to avoid someone leaking the existence of
this agent to the press, now I have to contend with the lies
that I'm allowing a double agent to operate in the CIA? This
is bullshit!"

Thorndike looked around the room, his face red, the vessel
in his temple beating so hard it looked ready to burst. Every
other security chief and director shifted in his seat, and Miles
imagined that each was trying to think what sort of information might have been compromised.

The only thing that would make Miles any happier in that
one moment would be to hear that Griffin was dead. Soon,
he told himself. Aloud, he said, "I'm sure it isn't as bad as
it seems." He reached for the newspaper, careful to keep
his expression from reflecting how he truly felt. Not that he
needed to read the article. He'd practically dictated it. "After
all, it doesn't state any names. That's something."

"Unless," Thorndike said, "you're the goddamned agent
sitting out there deep undercover and the people you're

moving with begin to put two and two together. This is an unmitigated disaster for us, for the agent, for everyone."

"Pull the plug on the operation," Miles said. "Cut your losses and walk away. It's only money."

"For God's sake, are you insane? There are countless lives at issue. I want to know who leaked this information, because if anything happens to my agent, we won't need to wait for a special investigation. I'll personally put a bullet through the bastard's head."

Roy Santiago steepled his fingers as he looked Thorndike directly in the eye. "You aren't accusing someone in this room, are you?"

"Tell me who else knew about it?"

"Does anyone even know who the agent is?" Santiago shot back. "Or even the nature of the operation?"

"*Someone* knew the op was in France. How the hell did that happen?"

Santiago took a deep breath, leaning back in his chair as his gaze swept the room, then landed on Miles. "He's right. Someone obviously leaked this to the press. Contact DOJ. I want an investigation started. You'll report to me with your preliminary findings, and since Pearson is here, we can save the DOJ the extra step of contacting the FBI to provide the investigators."

Miles grew increasingly hot beneath the man's scrutiny. "But no name was ever mentioned. There's no violation of the Intelligence Identities Protection Act."

To which Pearson said, "There's still been a breach of national security. If it gets nipped in the bud now, we save this administration from a major scandal later."

"I agree," Santiago said. "If you don't feel comfortable taking this on, Miles, then we'll wait for Phillip," he said, naming the other deputy security adviser. "He has experience with this sort of thing, and you're already assigned to the security detail for the global summit."

"No," Miles said. "I'll get started at once."

"Thank you. And if there's nothing further, gentlemen? I have an appointment that can't wait."

Santiago stood, and everyone else followed suit, except

Pearson, who remained seated, watching Miles as the others filed out of the room. "You seem uncomfortable," Pearson said.

This was not spinning in the direction Miles had hoped. "I am uncomfortable. There's speculation of a double agent, and no one else seems too concerned over that fact. I don't like that it's in the paper any more than you do. But regardless of where this information came from, what if the real national security breach is that one of our own CIA agents is feeding information to the enemy? Who's looking into that?"

"Good point," Pearson said, sliding his chair back. He stood, gathered up his notepapers from the tabletop. "If you happen to know of any firsthand knowledge of information being passed on illegally, I'd like to hear about it."

Miles nodded. "I'll contact DOJ right away."

Pearson left. Miles didn't move for several seconds, not wanting to give away how much the last few minutes had actually shaken him. It seemed the only thing going in his favor at the moment was that the federal government, no matter which branch, operated slowly. Any ensuing investigation was bound to take weeks, even months. That meant there was time for some damage control. And the first thing he needed to control was making sure the reporter didn't reveal her source. Ever.

35

December 11
FBI Headquarters
Washington, D.C.

"You can't go in there!"

"The hell I can't," Carillo said, pushing past Pearson's secretary to throw open the office door, that morning's paper clutched in his hand.

Pearson, the phone pressed to his ear, eyed Carillo as he stormed into the room. "I'll get back to you," he told his caller, then dropped the phone into the cradle. "Shut the door," he told Carillo.

Carillo reached back, pushed the door closed. "You saw this?"

"The article on the double agent in France? I'm pretty sure everyone in D.C. saw it."

"And?"

"And what?"

"And Sydney is heading to France. Is she walking into a trap?"

Pearson eyed him, as though contemplating what, if anything, he should reveal. Finally, he said, "I'm not entirely sure."

"Not entirely sure? Is that supposed to make me feel better?"

"The CIA has been running a covert infiltration operation in France for the past two years that may link the lab in Paris to LockeStarr. In addition, Senator Grogan had sat on the committee involved in the investigation of LockeStarr, at least until it stalled with the death of a CIA operative. And as I'm sure you've heard, the senator was discussing reopening the investigation just prior to his murder."

"None of which is new, except it puts someone associated with LockeStarr at the top of the list of suspects."

"Until we received information that the senator was actually *part* of LockeStarr. What he didn't know was that he was the focus of the investigation."

Carillo opened his mouth, but closed it again as he digested Pearson's last sentence. *"Grogan* was part of Locke-Starr? *Senator* Grogan?"

"Per the CIA."

"And he didn't know they were investigating him?"

Pearson nodded at the paper Carillo held. "Correct."

"Thorndike thinks the double CIA agent was working for Grogan?"

"As much as Thorndike won't want to admit it," Pearson said, "it looks like his undercover operative may have been feeding information to the senator. There's no other explanation as to why the senator was suddenly fired up to *open* a new investigation right around the time we were actually about to move into high gear. Had we not suspected him, he could very well have sat on that committee knowing every move we were about to make."

"Double agents on both ends."

"Exactly. The fact someone recently leaked information about an infiltrated agent that very few people even knew existed tells me this leak is somewhere high up."

"So what are you doing about this?"

"What can I do? I just sat through a meeting this morning, knowing that one of my own agents may be in danger, and I couldn't say a damned thing. But I can tell you what I would be doing if I was on this investigation. I'd be questioning this damned reporter to find out who her source is."

"I'll head there next. In the meantime, what do you want me to tell Fitzpatrick?"

Pearson picked up his coffee cup, took a sip, then looked in. It was empty. He set it back down on his desk in frustration. "In light of the article, and this morning's meeting, I think it's time we stepped back. Get ahold of Fitzpatrick. I want her to terminate the operation. Her life is more important."

"I'll let her know."

"I mean it, Carillo. I want her on the first plane out of there."

Carillo reached up, massaged the back of his neck. "Yeah. About that. You realize she's not exactly the best at following rules these days?"

"Tell her to get on that plane if she wants to keep her job."

Carillo walked out, then called Sydney's cell phone and left a voice mail. "FYI, an article came out in the paper today about a double agent in France. No names. More that the timing of its release is suspect. Call me," he added. "I have a bad feeling about this, never mind Pearson wants you off the case."

He tossed his phone on the car seat, realizing it wouldn't matter what he told Sydney. Too damned stubborn for her own good. A commendable trait at times. Unfortunately, one that could get her killed.

36

December 11
Off the coast of Brazil

Marc di Luca felt like a space alien in the full hazmat
suit. He stood just out of hearing from several World Health
Organization doctors sent to investigate the possibility that
some unknown virus had stricken the crew of the *Zenobia*,
after the freighter was found floating in the middle of the
Atlantic by a passing naval boat. All aboard were dead, and
at first it was believed that pirates were responsible. After
all, the ship had been missing for weeks with no word. It
was the sight of several corpses in the cabin, their skin un-
naturally dark, dried blood crusted around their eyes, noses,
and mouths, that made the authorities doubt that pirates were
involved at all with the ship's disappearance, and think that
the real culprit was some unidentified illness. They quickly
backed off without exploring further. Once word of the illness reached the WHO, then the National Institute of Virology in Johannesburg, South Africa, it wasn't long before a
full investigation was started.

Of course WHO knew only part of the story. They had
no knowledge that Director McNiel had pulled Marc and
Lisette from the *Desdemona* and flew them south off the

coast of Brazil to pose as two of the several WHO doctors who were dispatched to the *Zenobia*. Even though Marc had no medical training besides basic first aid, HQ insisted that he accompany Lisette because of the possibility of terrorist action, and he found himself wondering if their assignment together bothered her as much as it did him.

Then again, maybe she was over him. Marc had a way to go yet, and he tried to put her from his mind, telephoning ATLAS headquarters as soon as they'd seen enough to report back. When their boss answered, Marc told him what the initial findings were. "No signs that any violence occurred. No signs of weapons. No signs of pirates. And definitely no AUV on board. Which is not to say it wasn't here."

Director McNiel was quiet a moment, then, "Any chance this was natural, and not part of some terrorist action?"

"Lisette tells me we really won't know until further tests are run. In the meantime, they're treating the scene as a biohazard. She wants to take a more thorough look without drawing attention."

"Check back with me when you know more."

Marc disconnected, finished suiting up, then waited with Lisette and the other doctors to board the ship. Once on deck, he and Lisette broke off from the main group. Their goal was to search places that might have been overlooked, and they started in the mess hall, since, if pirates or even terrorists had been on board, they would have had to eat, like the rest of the men. Lisette began examining the tables, while he started in the kitchen.

"Over here," Lisette called out. He returned to the mess hall to where Lisette stood near one of the smaller tables in the far corner of the room. There were only two chairs set around it, as opposed to the larger table in the center, which seated twelve.

"What is it?" he asked.

"Small bits of broken glass." She pointed to the floor in the corner.

He took a closer look, saw thin, curved clear pieces as though from a vial.

They moved the chairs, then lifted the table away from the

wall. Lisette crouched down, not the easiest thing to do in their hazmat suits with the breathing apparatus. She opened her small equipment bag, found a wooden tongue depressor to scoop the bits of glass into a plastic tube, and used it. Once the tiny shards were safely contained, she dropped the tongue depressor in with them and was about to cap it shut when someone walked into the room. They both looked up, unable to see who it was because he also wore a biohazard suit and mask.

But then they weren't looking at his face.

They were looking at the gun he pointed at them.

Marc stood, shielding Lisette. "Who are you?"

"You may call me Daron. Not that it matters." His accent was thick. Somewhere from South America, Marc thought. "What does is why you two would be interested in trivial things." He waved with his gun. "Step away from the table, so that I can see what you find so interesting."

Marc remained where he was.

The man leveled his weapon. "You would die for your friend?"

"Yes," Marc said.

"No," Lisette interjected, moving from behind Marc. He felt her brushing up against him as she took her place on his right.

"And what is it you found?" the man asked.

"Broken glass."

"Give it to me."

She placed the cap on the tube, held it out, and Marc could see the wooden tongue depressor inside it.

The man took it, lifted it to the light, then gave it a shake. "Now the three of us are going to walk out of here, then off this ship, without alerting anyone as to what you've discovered."

"And if we don't go?"

"A lot of people will die between here and the shore. So if you care to see their executions, try to make a break. If you would like to save many lives, cooperate."

Marc and Lisette both had weapons, but they were secured beneath their hazmat suits, rendering them useless. It was, unfortunately, a necessity, as they were there undercover, hoping not to alert anyone who might be watching the boat that they suspected something more. Apparently their efforts had failed. Or someone had been forewarned they'd be there.

"We'll cooperate," Marc said.

"I thought so. You first," he told Marc. "Dr. Perrault and I will follow, as though she were ill. If anything happens, she will be the first to go."

Marc focused on Lisette, saw her give the slightest of nods. He turned, walked up the few short steps out of the mess hall onto the deck. Outside, he glanced back, saw their captor with one arm around Lisette as though physically assisting her to walk. One of the other doctors approached, and Marc said, "Dr. Perrault doesn't feel well. We're taking her back to shore."

"Do you need help?"

"No. We'll be fine."

The others went about their business, paying the three of them little attention as Marc climbed down into the waiting boat—not a simple task dressed as he was. There they found a second man, dark hair, weathered face, wearing a hazmat suit without the breathing apparatus or hood. He was also armed. The twenty-foot sport boat was not the same one they came in on, and Marc wondered how it was that no one seemed to notice when it pulled up to the ship. Daron directed Marc to take a seat next to him, then had Lisette sit directly opposite in the U-shaped seating area at the back of the boat. As the vessel set off, their captor removed his hood and facemask, then his gloves.

"Are you sure that's wise without being decontaminated?" Lisette called out over the roar of the boat's motor.

"There is nothing on board the *Zenobia* that can harm you. The virus is long dead."

Lisette removed her headgear, then set it on the seat next to her. "Hemorrhagic filovirus?"

"Not exactly."

"Not exactly? What does that mean?"

"You ask too many questions, Doctor." He faced the front of the boat as it sped away from the *Zenobia*.

Marc wasn't about to be dissuaded from learning what he needed to know, and he pulled off his own hood and respirator, the wind whipping through his hair as they picked up speed. "What's so important about that broken vial?"

Daron looked at him, the expression on his tanned face one of annoyance. "Unfortunately it was lost at the time the virus was released. We wouldn't want anyone to believe that what happened on the *Zenobia* was not the result of some natural transmission." He gave a leering smile, adding, "But the two of you can rest assured, you'll have a firsthand look at what causes the virus when we reach the compound."

Which explained why the man had demanded that Lisette pretend to be ill. If she and Marc were found dead of the virus, wherever they happened to dump their bodies, who would question it? Their captors sure as hell weren't going to let the two of them loose, not with the knowledge they held.

He glanced at the driver of the boat, who seemed intent on steering toward the shoreline, which from their position appeared to be nothing more than endless jungle. Both men were armed. The driver wore his gun holstered, while Daron held his pointed at Marc, probably determining that he was the greater threat. Marc glanced at Lisette in her hazmat suit, thinking no way could he or Lisette get to their Glocks.

It was time to even the odds.

He waited for Lisette to look at him. When she did, the fear in her eyes was replaced by determination as he massaged the web of his hand, then tilted his head toward the driver. She reached up, touched the corner of her right eye, then swept her finger back to her ear, rubbing the lobe. It was a signal they'd used before, a cue that she would follow his lead. Several minutes passed and they were nearing shore.

Marc presumed there were armed associates waiting for them, but a specific opportunity failed to present itself as Daron kept his gun pointed at Marc. Finally, though, Daron seemed to be growing tired, his arm lowering slightly with each jar of the boat. Not low enough, Marc thought, as they sped closer to land, where he was now able to discern specific vegetation. Time was running out. And then, finally, Daron dropped his arm, resting it on his thigh, the barrel aimed toward the bottom of the boat.

Now or never, Marc thought.

He dove across the seat, pushing Daron's leg into the gun while grabbing the barrel, trying to keep it down.

From the corner of his eye, he saw the driver turn, reach for his own weapon. Lisette swung her face mask up into his jaw. The unexpected force knocked the man back into the steering column. The boat veered wildly, throwing Marc off balance. Daron pressed the gun to Marc's chest, his finger on the trigger. If Marc's grip on the slide failed, he was dead. He tried to twist the gun away, but the vessel bounced across the whitecaps. He and Daron fell to the bottom, still fighting for the weapon. He heard a shout, saw something large flying overboard.

Lisette . . .

He felt the slide of the gun slipping in his sweaty palm, felt it cutting his hand. He was going to die, and all he could think of was he had to save Lisette. And then he saw a flash of red hurtling toward his face as the boat jumped one last time, then crashed on the shore.

37

December 11
Washington, D.C.

Carillo drove to the newspaper office, hoping to speak to Merideth Garrett, the reporter who'd written the article about the double agent. Though he'd identified himself, the receptionist at the desk told him that Ms. Garrett had been inundated with calls and wasn't taking any. "Not even the FBI?" he asked.

"You name the alphabet agency, they've been here," she said. "And reporters, too. She's asked to be left alone. But if she changes her mind, I'll put you in line."

"Thanks," he said, not leaving a card. He returned to his office at HQ and ran a full computer check on the reporter. Apparently this wasn't the first big Washington scoop she'd run. Judging from past entries, she had a source pretty high up. Though he doubted she was going to come out and reveal it, when it came to someone's life being on the line, in his mind, it was worth trying, and he intended to pay a visit to her during the evening when she got off work. Since he had plenty of time to kill, hours in fact, he pulled out that report on the recovered files from the shooter's computer.

After reading it again, he looked at the photo of the pattern on the murder weapon that Sydney had sent, then drove out to the history department at the University of Virginia to speak with Professor Denise Woods, who taught conspiracy theory as part of her coursework. They'd used her before on Fitzpatrick's last case, and Carillo figured she might be able to clarify a few issues with the case for him. Granted it was a lengthy trip, but he liked her work. And her, if truth be told.

Carillo knocked, then opened the office door. Professor Woods, a striking, petite blond dressed in a cream-colored turtleneck and dark slacks, was seated at her desk. Her look on seeing him was one of mild amusement, and he wasn't sure if he should be offended. "Professor. Good to see you again."

"A long way to drive just to visit. What brings the FBI to our hallowed halls this time?"

"I was hoping you might have some information on a symbol in history."

"It doesn't involve any of my students, does it?"

"Not this time. Since you're one of the few experts on conspiracy theory that I know of, you were the only one I could think who might help. We're drawing blanks here."

"Then by all means . . ."

He crossed the small office and handed her the copy of the knife hilt sketch that Sydney had forwarded to him. "This was the pattern from an antique shipped to a museum in the Netherlands. The murder weapon."

"I must admit," she said, eyeing the photo, "your cases, at least what I've seen of them, are interesting. Anything in particular you're looking for?"

"The *Reader's Digest* version? On the one side we've got the guy who shot the senator. Ran a Web site on conspiracy theory, which goes into Atlantis, Nazis, aliens, the gamut. On the other side, I've got this knife and a guy who made a cryptic remark about it just before he died. 'From Atlant.' Me, I'm thinking that the shooter's obsession with Atlantis might be connected to this dead guy's last breath, telling them 'from Atlant.' As in from Atlantis. He also mentioned dropping something. But the other guys were thinking he was referring to the knife which was lost at the murder scene, and when they go looking for it, what they find instead is a vial with a suspected virus inside. You with me so far?"

"So far," she said, looking intrigued.

"On the surface, neither case seems connected, except that a certain branch of the government that doesn't exist on paper is involved with both. And they're thinking that the pattern on this knife handle might help them pinpoint where the virus might have originated." He tapped the photo of the sketch detailing the pattern. "One source thought these symbols were like the Greek letter psi, or the symbol used on virology packaging. In other words, I was hoping you might be able to provide some insight into a conspiracy, because right now, frankly, we've got nothing."

"Your source is right," Professor Woods told him, examining the sketch. "The pattern appears to be the Greek letter psi, repeated. There are a lot of possibilities, I'm afraid. The Web site and the symbol on the letter opener could be a reference to past attempts to connect the lost city of Atlantis to an alien race that perished when the island sank beneath the ocean. Atlant—assuming it is only a partial word—could refer to Atlantis, which still fits into the symbol on your knife hilt, since the Greek letter psi shares the characteristics of Poseidon's trident. And, believe it or not, we can even throw in the Nazis for good measure."

"No offense, Professor, but I'm not sure how you got from point A to point B here. The Nazis connected to Atlantis?"

She gave him a patient smile, saying, "The Nazis actually sent an expedition to Tibet, allegedly to find and therefore prove the existence of the Aryan/Atlantean roots of their so-called superior race."

Carillo looked at the sketch of the knife hilt. "Discounting the Nazi angle, what sort of Atlantis conspiracies are out there?"

"A lot. What I can tell you is that according to some historians, if one looks hard enough, all roads lead not to Rome, but to Atlantis. There are quite a bit of cross-cultural references to historical and religious similarities that are attributed to the ancient Atlanteans, including the great flood that some attribute to Noah and his ark."

She typed something into her computer, then pointed to the screen, showing photos of Egyptian pyramids and tombs. "Some believe that the Atlanteans were far more technologically advanced than anyone else from their time, as evidenced by the hieroglyphics found in certain ancient Egyptian ruins that resemble spaceships. Flying vehicles would have come in handy to view the vast array of ancient art visible only from the sky, such as that found in Peru, for instance."

"I'm pretty sure we can discount the space angle, too. What I want to know is if this dead guy's reference about from Atlant could really be Atlantis?"

"Sure. The question is, Atlantis the lost city, or evidence of the inhabitants?"

"I'd have to go with the lost city. The kid who dug up this info seems to think Atlantis was really only a reference name, maybe based on rumored location." Carillo saw a world map on the wall. "You happen to have a theory that might narrow down *where* to find it?"

"The locations are as numerous and as varied as the number of legends told. Anywhere from the Arctic to the Antarctic. The most popular theory is somewhere in the midst of the Atlantic, causing many to believe the ocean was named after the lost city."

Carillo studied the map and the Atlantic's vast area. "Forget popular, and let's shoot for logical."

"According to the Greek philosopher Plato, Poseidon brought two springs of water to Atlantis. One hot, one cold. A hot spring is usually caused by geothermal activity, which supports the theory that an earthquake or volcanic activity destroyed Atlantis. If so, then it would place it somewhere along the tectonic plates of the Atlantic, or locations where there is known underwater volcanic activity. Anywhere from Iceland to the Bahamas, all the way down to the African continent."

"Any chance you can narrow it down even further?"

"From everything I've ever read, my favorite location is here." She tapped the map in the Caribbean basin, then ran her finger in a circle that encompassed Cuba, Haiti, and Jamaica.

The very area where ATLAS was searching for the missing AUV.

38

December 11
ATLAS Headquarters
Washington, D.C.

Tex walked into the director's office, where McNiel
sat at his desk, his fingers pressed to his temples. He looked
up, saw Tex, and said, "Tell me you have some good news?"

"Some. We picked up the vial from Griffin's contact in
Winterswijk. It's on its way to Germany for testing. Griffin was long gone by the time our agents got there. And I
got a call from the captain of the *Desdemona*. They found
the missing AUV on the ocean floor in the general vicinity
of where the students saw the freighter. They're recovering
it now. The big news? Carillo called. He just left Professor
Woods's office."

"Woods?"

"She teaches conspiracy theory as part of her coursework
at UVA. She's a good source when you're looking for the
obscure. Carillo and Fitzpatrick used her for information on
that Vatican operation last month."

"And this has what to do with our case?"

"The coincidence of location." Tex briefed him on what
Carillo had learned.

McNiel sat there in silence for several seconds when he'd finished, staring at the pin map on the wall showing the location where the college students had first sighted the pirated freighter, as well as its final location where Marc and Lisette were currently assisting the WHO doctors to determine the crew's cause of death. "Atlantis? What are the chances . . ."

"Exactly. And according to Carillo, it gets even more skewed if you start linking this whole conspiracy to the death investigation on the senator."

"You've lost me."

"The suspected shooter's obsession with aliens from Atlantis. He ran a Web site called Above Atlantis NWO. As in New World Order."

"Please tell me you're kidding. I thought this was a case of simple hacking into the wrong server."

Tex nodded at McNiel's computer. "It gets even better, if you want to look it up. Especially when you start reading his crap on viruses and the coming end of the world if they find Atlantis."

McNiel typed something on his keyboard, then focused on the computer screen. "It looks like every other conspiracy Web site. Oddly fascinating if you're into that stuff. But there's not enough to go on here."

"Unless you add in Griffin's angle. Faas's dying statement. From Atlant. Carillo thinks he was about to say *Atlantis*, and that it was Faas's attempt to let us know this virus he'd hidden in the snow was connected to the murders of those students off the coast of the Cayman Islands."

"Connected, how?"

"By location. The professor puts Atlantis right about in that same area where the missing AUV was found, which isn't too far from where the students were killed."

McNiel looked back at the pin map. "Call Marc to let him know. Coincidence or not, this virus connection has me worried."

Tex called. It went straight to voice mail. "Either Marc's phone is off or he's out of range."

"Try Lisette."

Tex did, with the same result.

"I don't like it," McNiel said. "I spoke to Marc this morning. Unless someone started up that freighter and moved it out of range, there shouldn't be any communication problems." He walked over to the desk and found the number for the lead contact from WHO for the freighter investigation, and called it. "We're trying to reach Dr. Perrault and her partner . . ." McNiel listened, thanked the man, then hung up the phone. "Marc and Lisette were seen leaving on a boat headed toward the coast after Lisette took ill."

"Leaving? With whom?" Tex asked, taking a seat in the chair opposite McNiel's desk.

"A doctor. Assuming he was a doctor," McNiel said, looking up at a map on the wall. A red pin indicated the last location of the freighter, just off the coast of Brazil.

Tex eyed the map. "At least Marc has experience in the Amazon. He worked that operation out there about two years ago when they were searching for the Network's compound."

"That's what I don't like. The proximity of this compound we've never been able to find, along with this phantom virus-laden freighter."

"And now two missing agents."

McNiel took a frustrated breath. "Marc and Lisette are highly experienced. I have a hard time believing that someone could just walk on that ship and take them off without some planning."

"Who knew they were out there?"

"Everyone at that security task force meeting."

They exchanged glances, and McNiel swore.

"I think we can move a suspected leak to definite," Tex said.

"But from where? Every director in that room could be taking the information back to his office with the best of intentions. The leak could be anywhere."

"It's supposed to be eyes-only. What about Thorndike? He's still angry over me and Griffin leaving CIA."

McNiel tapped his fingers in his desktop, as though contemplating the thought of Thorndike being involved in espionage. "I can't see him going to that extreme. Even so, we can't trust our information is private. As of this moment, ATLAS is going into a full-scale covert action operation."

"Is that any different from what we were doing?"

"Let's just say I won't be announcing our further activities to the security task force. I now have two missing agents. And that doesn't count the mess that started with Griffin. My guess? Someone in this government is compromising the safety of my agents. I want them brought down," he said, his voice taking on an icy calm. "Do I make myself clear?"

"Very."

In other words, Tex had just been given a green light to do whatever it took to get McNiel his answers. Even if it meant running a black op on his own government.

And the first person he intended to recruit was Griffin.

39

December 11
Amazon, coast of Brazil

Marc opened his eyes, finding Daron unmoving, his face crushed. The gun had flown from Marc's hand on impact, and he looked around for it, saw it several feet away next to a red and white fire extinguisher, blood smeared across the surface.

He started to scramble for it.

"There's no one else here."

Marc froze at the sound of Lisette's voice. He turned, shielded his eyes from the sun to see her standing over him. "You're okay?"

"Who do you think hit the bastard with the fire extinguisher?" she said, reaching down to help him to his feet. "You looked like you could use some assistance."

"The driver?"

She pointed out to sea. "I think he's history."

"Guess I owe you one." Marc looked offshore, saw the man floating facedown, then turned back to Lisette. "Are you hurt?"

"A few bruises. You?"

"Fine," he said, kneeling next to Daron, feeling for his pulse. There was none. He stood.

"Now what?" Lisette asked. "We have no cell phone signal. I checked."

Marc scanned the area. There was nothing but jungle on either side of them as far as the eye could see, and behind them, endless ocean. The *Zenobia* was no longer in sight. There was no beach to speak of. The ocean water lapped into the tree line, creating a swamp at the edge of the jungle. "They must have a compound around here," he said, going up to look at all the boat's gauges. The sun beat down on them and he could feel the sweat dripping off his back. "Couldn't be too far. There isn't much gas." He was about to hop out of the boat to see if they could push it back in the water, when he saw the crack in the hull and the water seeping in near the front of the boat. "Looks like we're walking."

"Please tell me there are no snakes in this part of the world."

"Hardly any," he lied.

"Can we at least strip out of this gear?"

"Better wait until we get through the swamp. The boots will help keep our feet dry, and we can hide everything in the jungle. No sense hanging out a flag that there are two of us."

Lisette pulled at the front of her hazmat suit, and he did the same, feeling the welcome offshore breeze enter his neckline, cooling his sweat-soaked shirt. Beneath their suits, they both wore black T-shirts and black BDU pants tucked into military boots. Not exactly the best color to blend in during the day, but then they weren't thinking of traipsing through a jungle when they dressed this morning.

Even though the suits were hot, difficult to move around in, Marc and Lisette got to work, searching the boat to see what they could salvage. He found a canvas bag filled with tools, the majority of which he dumped. Lisette rummaged through the front of the boat and found binoculars and a first aid kit as well as some other items she tossed into the bag. Marc pulled open Daron's hazmat suit and went through his pockets. A cell phone, cigarettes, and a lighter, but no wallet or ID. The phone was on, but no signal. He left the phone, but took the lighter. "I don't suppose you found any water."

"Not a drop," she said.

"My kingdom for a canteen, even an empty one."

"What would you give for some clean biohazard tubes?" She patted the pockets of her hazmat suit.

"Better than nothing. What about the one with the glass found on the ship?"

"I have no idea where it is. But if their sole purpose was to take it and us to prevent anyone from suspecting that this virus was manmade, they failed."

"Unless of course we die out here. Then they've succeeded."

"McNiel will send someone for us."

"Only if he knows where to look."

He searched the horizon, seeing nothing. Just endless ocean, and he glanced up to the sky, saw clouds moving in. If it was humid in that jungle now, it would be even more so once the rain came and went. He gripped the side of the boat, saw a small anaconda swim past, maybe five feet in length. Thankfully Lisette didn't notice. He hopped off the port side into the shallow water. When he reached up to help Lisette, they heard someone shouting in the jungle on the starboard side. Lisette grabbed the canvas bag, jumped down next to Marc. Both ducked, just as two men in camouflage fatigues armed with M4s came bursting from the trees, their boots splashing in the swamp.

Marc put his finger to his lips, then pointed into the jungle, indicating that Lisette should head in first and he'd cover her. He drew his Glock, held it ready. When she was in the trees, he felt the boat move as someone started to climb on board. A shout followed, something about a body in the water. He heard splashing and assumed that they were wading into the ocean to retrieve the driver's corpse. Marc glanced back, saw Lisette in the shadows, her gun drawn. Now or never. He crouched down, backed into the trees, keeping the boat between him and the open sea.

When he reached Lisette's side, he said, "Did you see how many?"

"Only two."

"Good odds."

The men were speaking, their voices drifting toward them on the wind.

"French," Lisette said. "With the occasional Portuguese scattered throughout."

"We were heading due south when they took us from the boat. I'd say that puts us in French Guiana or Amapá."

"Quiet." Lisette closed her eyes, apparently trying to listen. Like Marc, she was fluent in several languages, her specialty being Russian. Neither of them spoke Portuguese. But French was Lisette's native language, and she was better able than he to translate the mix. After a moment, she looked at him, smiling slightly. "They seem to think that the boat crashed and that is what killed the two men. They surmise that the driver fell out and drowned after the crash. They think the hostages met the same fate."

"I like their reasoning."

"They are going back to the compound."

"Stay here or follow?"

"What are the chances we'll be found if we stay?"

Marc glanced out to the horizon, then at the boat and the surrounding jungle growing right up to the water, thinking the wreckage would be next to impossible to spot from the air or the sea. "Our best bet is to get out of these hazmat suits and follow."

Lisette gave a sigh of resignation. "I had a feeling you were going to say that."

The dense jungle teemed with insects, buzzing and biting. Marc and Lisette could do little more than brush them away from their skin as they tracked the two men, staying far enough back to avoid being seen, but still keeping the men in sight. Both searched for movement in the leaves above, leaves that canopied what appeared to be a definite trail leading from the swampy coastland to the dense interior of the rainforest. They would never have been able to find the path on their own.

If they were in Amapá as he suspected, they sure as hell weren't heading toward any metropolitan areas. The

Amazon rainforest dominated more than ninety percent of Amapá, and seventy percent of that forest was unexplored, knowledge he'd learned from a previous ATLAS operation that took him into the area a couple of years ago in search of a splinter terrorist group suspected of working some sort of bio lab for the Black Network. ATLAS had not been successful in their search back then. The jungle was too dense, and the canopy of broad-leafed trees and vines prevented them from locating the compound from the air.

And now it seemed that he and Lisette were on the trail of someone who had sent two people specifically to the freighter. Whether because they knew ATLAS had agents there or to determine if anyone suspected the deaths on board were possibly due to a terrorist action, Marc didn't know. At this time, it mattered little.

There was no doubt in his mind that they were dealing with the same group. Which meant that they could very well discover what had eluded them before. Of course, if they found the compound, Marc wasn't sure of the next step. He hadn't quite gotten that far in his plans. He only knew that they couldn't survive on the edge of that swamp hoping that someone might pass by and find them, which meant walking into the lion's den was their next best option to stay alive.

Up ahead, the movement on the path stopped, and Marc held out his hand in warning. Lisette stilled behind him. He pointed into the dense foliage; she nodded, then carefully threaded her way within, crouching out of sight behind a large, broadleaf plant. Marc did the same on the opposite side of the path, and moments later, as a mosquito landed on his face, and he fought the urge to slap it, or move at all as he held his Glock at the ready, he heard the heavy steps of someone on the trail. One of the guerrillas, his M4 held in front of him, lumbered past, checking from side to side. He continued on another twenty feet, then stopped, retraced his steps even more slowly on the return, checking behind the bushes and trees that grew close to the trail. Marc saw him approaching Lisette's spot. If the man gave it any more than a cursory glance, he'd see her. And Marc would have to kill him, which would bring the other running.

He could take them both. That wasn't the issue. What concerned him was that after hours of following them on this trail, he didn't know how close they were to the compound. The last thing he needed was for a couple of gunshots to bring out reinforcements.

The jungle floor was covered in damp and rotting leaves, no rocks anywhere for him to toss. And just when Marc decided that he was going to have to shoot, to hell with the noise, he heard a rustling, snapping, static sound coming from high up in the canopy of trees. The rain, he realized, just as the front man called out. The rear gunman turned, hurried away down the path, as the warm precipitation eventually found its way through the dense leaves, the large drops splashing down to the forest floor.

Neither Marc nor Lisette dared move for the longest time, and it took every ounce of concentration to ignore the itching from the mosquitoes' continuous bites. Marc turned his face upward, but not much of the rain made it down, at least not yet, and he took a deep breath, trying to fill his lungs with the hot, humid air. Lisette made a soft click, and he clicked back, signaling that he agreed it appeared clear. Lisette stood, her gun pointing up the trail as she crossed over to where Marc waited.

"That was closer than I cared for," he said quietly.

"Too close."

They stepped out, started down the path until several minutes later, they could no longer tell which direction the two men had taken. When the sun had been out, Marc knew they were heading due west. Now, with the rain obscuring the sun, the direction was no longer obvious. Their makeshift tour guides were long gone, and that meant that Marc and Lisette would be navigating the trails—if they ever found them again—on their own. Their odds were diminishing with each passing minute, and Marc stood there trying to decide which trail to take, none of them looking thoroughly traveled. Finally he picked one, and a few feet down he came to a couple of important realizations.

First, they were thoroughly lost without a way to contact anyone.

Second, there was a trip wire across the trail in front of them.

One wrong step and they were dead.

"We're damned lucky we didn't blow ourselves up long before now," Marc said as he and Lisette attempted to navigate the paths, which were turning wet and slippery from the rain. Undoubtedly the closer they got to the compound, the more traps they'd have to contend with. They'd relied on the two gunmen to get them through. Now they were on their own, and an hour later, his head ached and his shoulder and neck muscles protested from the constant looking down, making sure they weren't tripping land mines.

They'd located five more trip wires, two in the last hundred yards, and so it wasn't surprising that they'd covered very little distance. Even so, he hoped the increasing frequency of the booby traps was a good sign—assuming this alleged Network compound even existed, and they weren't walking into some drug cartel by mistake. Not that one wasn't as dangerous as the other. At the moment, he and Lisette were tired and hungry, and he was regretting his decision to follow the two gunmen.

The sound of the rain did little to muffle the constant birds' chirping and insects' buzzing. What it did do was remind him that he was damned thirsty. Eventually water started seeping down the long vines twisting around tree trunks, some of it pooling into the bases of plants, and Lisette took out her clean biohazard tubes and found a plant with sword-shaped leaves, using it to direct the water into her tubes. Marc did the same. It wasn't much, but it helped. The tubes filled, they both drank, and Lisette used some of the water to wash her face.

"No canteens," she said, looking up into the bright green canopy.

"What are you talking about?"

"The two men. Neither carried any water. You don't do that out here unless you are very sure of where you're going."

She was right. That meant that the two had to have access to a nearby water source. The logical explanation was that the compound was very close. Unfortunately it did neither of them any good. Even if there was a clear trail, with the danger of the trip wires, they couldn't go any faster.

They rested about ten minutes, then started out again when they heard the sound of someone moving up ahead. Lisette and Marc stopped in their tracks, then stepped back into the jungle, listening.

Signaling to Lisette to stay where she was, Marc moved closer, and through a break in the leaves, could just make out an armed sentry on his rounds. Marc quickly assessed the location. The trail opened to a clearing of low-lying plants, but no trees for at least a hundred yards. And beyond that, he saw a razor-topped chain-link fence. Inside the fence's perimeter, however, the trees created a thick canopy over the several buildings within, and in a few places, the shallow roots had grown beneath the chain link, lifting it. Apparently they weren't too worried about discovery in this remote a location with such good camouflage. The low shrubs allowed the sentries to see anyone approaching the compound on foot from the jungle, yet effectively camouflaged the area from above, where air patrols might notice a cleared jungle floor or rooftops of a building.

The guards, like the two men who had found them on the beach, were carrying M4s, the Cadillac of guns compared to the usual cast-off weapons smuggled in from other countries that usually ended up with the drug cartels. In Marc's mind that meant money, organization, and the means to put it all to good use.

This was bigger than the average drug runner.

His gut told him they had found the hidden South American compound for the Black Network. Quite possibly the location where this deadly hemorrhagic virus was located.

And they had no way to warn anyone.

He and Lisette retreated back into the forest, far off the trail into a shelter of vines that had crept across the branches of several trees.

Intending to wait for nightfall, they found a wide tree with strangler roots shooting out from the sides, which created a cradle of thick, smooth branches. Not exactly the softest of beds, but much drier than the damp forest floor. The jungle's oppressive humidity after the rainstorm sapped Marc's strength. At the moment they were seated at right angles, their shoulders touching as they leaned against the smooth and twisted trunk. They napped the best they could, each taking a shift as sentry. When it was his turn, he crept out to the forest's edge near the clearing and watched the guards, making note of their patrol patterns and the compound layout, at least what he could see from his vantage point.

When he returned, Lisette was awake—assuming she'd even slept. They were hungry, bitten by more bugs than Marc could count, and when Lisette pulled out two granola bars, his stomach rumbled. "Where did you get these?"

"The boat. In the same compartment as the first aid kit. They're probably ancient, but I'm fairly certain granola has the same half-life as radioactive waste."

He wanted to kiss her. Hell, he would have had she given him the slightest sign that she was still interested, and he wondered—not for the first time—if she was seeing someone else. Or was it, as she said, that their job as ATLAS agents made it too difficult to maintain a relationship, especially when they were constantly being deployed to foreign countries, with their various operations keeping them apart for weeks at a time.

"Do you ever think about us?" he asked, after he'd finished his granola bar and the last of his water.

"Snake."

"What?"

He looked over at her, saw her pointing to somewhere beyond the veil of vines, then focused that direction. At first glance it appeared as though he were looking at a tree limb mottled in shadows maybe eight inches in diameter. On closer inspection he realized the limb was moving, and he reached for his knife, as the twelve-foot-long anaconda coiled and uncoiled around the tree limb, its movement slow and lumbering as it lowered itself to the ground. He relaxed somewhat at the sight of the large bulge in the snake's middle. Unless the reptile was looking for an after-dinner snack, it wasn't hungry. And sure enough, when its head made contact with the ground, it slithered off in the opposite direction, undoubtedly toward the water and more desirable habitat. "No worries," he said.

"The answer is yes."

Marc glanced at Lisette, but she was still watching the anaconda. "Yes?" he echoed.

"Do I think of us. I do." Her answer caught him off guard, and just when he was wondering how to respond, that this was surely a positive step, she said, "But I also think of Becca and Griffin and how he suffers, even two years later."

"Their marriage was over long before she was killed."

"But it changed things," she said, leaning her head back against the tree roots.

"Why?" he asked, even though he felt certain he knew the answer.

"Because I realized I could never live that way, wondering every time you leave on an operation, if you will be coming back . . ."

He didn't tell her that he shared the same fears about her—even to this day. What he did say was "I wonder if things would have been different if we were accountants not spies."

"We are not."

"If we get out of here, I could always go back to school."

She smiled, her dark eyes lighting up with humor as she reached out, grasped his hand, and gave it a quick squeeze, her palm, like his, hot and sticky with sweat. When she let go, her expression turned serious. "I am hoping you have been thinking of our next move, instead of what might have been."

"I have. But I figured if a snake was going to eat us, it was time to open up."

"You opened up, as you called it, before I saw the snake."

"Maybe I'm psychic."

"What you are is incorrigible. Your plan?"

"Our only option is to break into the compound and find a way to communicate with the *Desdemona* or HQ to give them our location." He nodded in the direction of the compound. "I've been watching the sentries. They pass by in fifteen-minute shifts. One of them was leaning on the fence, which tells me it isn't wired. I don't imagine they're going to have the grounds lit up like a beacon, not when they're worried about aerial surveillance, which means our best chance is after nightfall."

"Are you sure you wouldn't like to get started on that accounting degree immediately?"

"You afraid of crawling on your belly through the jungle?"

"You did see the size of that snake?"

"It was full."

"It probably has relatives. Hungry relatives."

Marc looked at his watch, determining that they might have another hour before it was fully dark. "I think the snakes are the least of our worries."

"At least the snakes without legs." She sighed, leaning her head back into the tree, no doubt figuring that there was nothing left to do but rest until the appointed time. Marc tried to concentrate on Lisette's breathing instead of the buzz of insects and the rustle of leaves. A primal scream cut through the night. An answering cry caused the hairs on Marc's neck to prickle, and he rested his hand on the butt of his Glock, unable to tell what sort of animal it was or how near or how far. Very soon the jungle sounds closed in, the air grew suffocating, and the dark surrounded them completely.

40

December 11
Paris, France

"Griff? I think we found that connection on Locke-
Starr."

"Hold on." Griffin pulled Sydney's cell phone from his
ear, looked for the button to turn the volume up, so that he
could hear Tex over the music coming from the café next
door to the restaurant where he and Sydney were eating
dinner. "Shoot."

"I need you to run a black op. Unsanctioned. According
to our intel, in order to get what we want from the outlying
lab, we need access to the main computer in the Hilliard and
Sons Montparnasse office." He told Griffin about the digital
virus that would give them access to the lab's computer to
retrieve what they needed. "Only problem is we're shorthanded."

"We've worked under worse conditions," Griffin said.
Tex was holding something back; he was sure of it. "What
gives?"

"The information—which we believe is legit—may have
been . . . compromised."

"Compromised? How?"

"We're not yet sure. Marc and Lisette are both missing. They were last seen on that hijacked freighter found floating off the coast of Brazil. Entire crew was dead from some unknown hemorrhagic virus, which we think could be connected to this lab."

"They're missing?" The information hit Griffin like a ton of bricks. He should have been there for them. McNiel had assigned Griffin to accompany Marc on that mission. Had Griffin not gone AWOL, searching for his wife's killer, he would have been there. He could have helped them . . .

"We think it has something to do with the article in the paper about a French double agent in the CIA employ, and—"

"You're thinking this article refers to my wife?" Sydney had mentioned the article after Carillo had left her a voice mail, and Griffin had looked it up on the Internet. He turned his back, not wanting to face Sydney during this conversation. Lowering his voice, he said, "*If* she's alive, there is no way she'd be guilty of espionage, so if anyone's thinking of using this as a witch hunt—"

"I have no idea if she's alive, Griff. All I'm saying is the timing's suspect and we could use some help getting into that lab."

"And what? You think I'm going to be able to walk in there and get it? By myself?"

"I hear Dumas is in town."

"That's the best you can do?"

"You could always turn yourself in and I could send a real team, once we have one available."

"Give me Dumas's number."

"Thought you'd see it my way."

"Only because I have a few questions for him myself." Two years ago, Father Emile Dumas, a Vatican spy, had been there right after the explosion that Griffin had *believed* had killed his wife, Becca.

But he thought about the fact that no one had yet seen Becca alive. Who's to say that Petra really saw her? This whole thing could be an elaborate trap, a setup, and he wondered if that had also been the case for Marc and Lisette?

That they were targeted? Tex was right. The timing of it all was suspect and he knew in his gut they were related.

Even worse was the realization that had he not been self-ish, had he gone with Marc as ordered instead of on this one-man quest for revenge, Marc and Lisette would not be missing. "I'll call Dumas," he told Tex, "and I'll give him our location."

Father Emile Dumas, dressed in the black garb and crisp white clerical collar of his faith, briefcase in hand, walked into the Paris hotel room he'd procured for Sydney and Griffin. Griffin had mixed emotions about working with the man, and not just because Dumas was somehow linked to Becca's death, as it were. Dumas had an unshakable faith in God, the Catholic Church, the pope, and the free world, in that order. Griffin had no such faith, especially after his wife's death. Unlike the other agents Griffin was used to working with, Dumas did not carry a weapon. Even so, he was highly trained, one of a small number of priests handpicked by the last pope to assist the allied agencies in investigations that might cross paths with the church. And since terrorist threats often affected the church, Griffin and Dumas ran into each other at regular intervals.

"You seem troubled," Dumas said, eyeing Griffin in return.

"You've undoubtedly heard the rumors about my wife?"

"Tex informed me."

"And?"

"I know what you know. Nothing more. Like you, I believed she was killed."

Griffin saw no sign of subterfuge in the priest's steady gaze. But then, the man was as skilled as any spy Griffin knew. Even so, Griffin had to be content. He needed Dumas if he was to succeed with this latest assignment. "What can you tell us about this lab?"

"The main office is located in the Montparnasse district. The building was used as a makeshift hospital during World War II, first by the French, then later by the Germans during the occupation, and in the last two years was under extensive remodeling."

Dumas took out the plans as well as a map of the city, showing them to both Griffin and Sydney. "I drove by there this morning. Armed security guards man the reception area in the lobby. There is also an armed guard at the rear entrance."

Griffin studied the map. "Short of blasting through the back and storming the front, what do you suggest?"

"If you had the time, underground via the catacombs—and that's assuming you could find the way. As I said, the Germans occupied this building during the war, and there are bunkers below in the tunnels that they entered from inside the building. I can check with some contacts to see if there is a tunnel rat who knows the area, but to my knowledge, most of these tunnels have been blocked off by the authorities to prevent unauthorized access."

"You mean there is authorized access?"

"To some tunnels, yes. Such as the Cimetière du Montparnasse, where most of the tourists visit to view the many bones. But kilometers of these tunnels are not mapped, and there are many areas not even the authorities go into."

To which Sydney asked, "What do you mean, *if* we had time?"

"Because the only access to some of these catacombs is from the outskirts of the city. A ten-hour walk below ground, due to the many twists and turns. And that is only if you know the way. If you do not, you are lost in an endless maze down there and your bones will join with the millions of others."

"What is it with spies and tunnels and bones?" Sydney asked.

Griffin ignored her, saying, "So if not underground, then how?"

"There is the rooftop," Dumas replied. He opened up his laptop, punched in the address, and brought the building up via satellite map, showing a rooftop garden with tables and potted plants around the perimeter, clearly taken during the spring or summer. "Of course, we'll need real-time satellite for a more current picture, but as you can see, entry can be made from here," he said, pointing to the garden area. "Your initial access can be the adjoining building, an apartment building that has been converted to business offices above this brasserie. I dined there for lunch this afternoon to case it. The restroom is at the rear. Just beyond it, a staircase and the elevator to the upper floors, but the door at the top is locked with a keyless entry. The door appears to be used by the office workers when they come down for lunch to eat at the brasserie, which is owned by the same corporation."

"Alarmed?"

"Yes. A fairly new and sophisticated system. I expect they arm it after everyone leaves the building, and since, at the end of the day, most would leave via the front entrance, not through the brasserie, it is probably armed when the main entrance is armed."

"And a gamble if it turns out it isn't."

"One can only hope you make it to the rooftop garden before the gendarmes arrive. Although they would be preferable to the Network's own armed security. The building is four stories high. You should be able to make it. And the plus is that the brasserie is open late. That allows you entry to the building."

Griffin sat back, watching Dumas go over the plans, thinking that a few days ago he'd come to Europe, knowing full well that there had to be a link between his wife's murder and the old LockeStarr investigation.

And now he was this close to finding out . . .

Griffin went over the plans one last time, confirming their roles. Real-time satellite photos showed that though there were guards at both the front and the back of the building, there were none on the rooftop. Initial access would be made via the restaurant, primarily because any alarms and locks in that building were bound to be less sophisticated than anything the Hilliard labs might have. Dumas would act as the lookout up until the point they entered from the rooftop. After he and Sydney broke in and planted the computer virus, they'd meet up at the designated rendezvous point where Dumas would be waiting.

"Any questions?" Griffin asked. No one had any. Dumas

left to warm up his car. Sydney checked her weapon, holstered it, then waited while Griffin did the same, then sheathed his knife in his boot. Like Sydney, he was dressed all in black.

He looked over at her. "It's not too late to walk out."

"Someone's got to look after you."

He smiled slightly, took a step toward her, reaching out, placing his hand on her shoulder, feeling the warmth of her seeping through her sweater. He had so many conflicting emotions going through his head on this case, about Sydney, about his wife, that she might be alive. He wasn't sure what to think . . .

Except that Sydney was here, now.

Dumas knocked on the door. Griffin let go, opened the door, and the priest said, "I forgot my gloves."

"We should go," Sydney said.

They followed Dumas to his blue Peugeot, then rode in silence to the Brasserie Chez Ettore. Dumas dropped them off in front, then drove to the rendezvous. Inside the brasserie, the laughter and chatter provided a perfect cover as they stepped on the lift, which lurched its creaky course upward inside its antique brass cage. When at last they arrived at the top floor, Griffin disabled the alarm, then picked the lock on the solid oak door with a discreet plaque that read "Martin et Bernard, Consultants."

They walked through the elegantly appointed office space to a door that opened to a long roof garden. Embedded into the mansard roof, it was well hidden from the sidewalk below, and they wouldn't have known it existed had it not been for the satellite photo that Dumas had shown them. Unlike the image on the computer, however, the garden was currently enshrouded with snow, lending it a ghostly look, accentuated by the tall, bare rose trees that stood sentinel at equal intervals around the periphery of the garden, each tree encased in a plastic sheath to keep it from freezing during the winter.

At the end of the garden opposite them, a high wall with a locked door divided the rooftop space between the Martin et Bernard and Hilliard. A blast of northern air hit them as

Griffin held the door open, and Sydney stepped onto the hitherto virgin snow. To their left, he saw the great Cemetery of Montparnasse. The bare dark branches of its trees were the only indication of the cemetery's long intersecting avenues, lined by a multitude of silent statues and sepulchral monuments—row upon row of houses for the dead, all sleeping peacefully under a soft, thick blanket of snow.

Above them, silhouetted against the light of the moon, were the numerous chimney pots, an unlikely cover should anyone chance to be looking up. He picked the lock of the door that led to Hilliard's side of the rooftop, a twin of the garden that they had just left, except on this side there were no roses.

According to Dumas, they had five minutes before the watchmen changed shifts. While he went to work on the Hilliard rooftop building entrance, Sydney walked to the balustrade and looked down to the street below. It seemed an eternity before she raised her hand, signaling that one guard was entering and the other exiting. He opened the door. She hurried over, being careful not to slip, stepped in, and he followed, pulling the door shut. They waited, not moving until they were certain no one was rushing up the stairs to come after them. If so, they figured they had a better chance to escape via the roof rather than be trapped in a staircase.

Finally, when their sight had adjusted and they felt certain no alarm had been tripped, he said, "Let's go."

He flicked his light on, then off, giving them a quick view of the staircase, narrow, steep. Guns drawn, they descended slowly, pausing to listen every now and then. The office they needed was accessed on the ground floor, and when they reached that level, Griffin held out his hand, stopping her to listen for the guards.

According to Dumas's intel, the office with the computer access was three doors down and to the left. It was locked. They didn't dare use a flashlight, not here on the ground floor on the same level as the guards, and so they moved slow, Sydney running her hand along the wall undoubtedly to keep her balance and perspective. When they reached the third door, they stopped, and Griffin holstered his gun.

While Sydney stood guard, her weapon trained toward the front, Griffin examined the door, using a tiny LED light, no bigger than a half dollar, checking for a secondary alarm system, before turning his attention to the bright brass dead bolt. LED in one hand, he took his lock pick set from his pocket, flipped it open. He used his thumb to slide up the picks he needed, pulling them out the rest of the way with his mouth, handing the case to Sydney. She shoved it in her pocket, then held his light for him.

It took him a couple of minutes to work the pick, teasing it until it unlocked, because the lock was new, more difficult. He slid the picks he'd used in his top pocket, then drew his gun, before opening the door. They stepped in and he locked it from the inside.

The room had no windows, an advantage to avoid being seen from the outside, but not so good from the inside. Any significant light would show beneath the door, giving them away, and he made a quick survey of the room, seeing a jacket hanging from the back of a chair. He pulled it off, then shoved it into the base of the door to keep the light from shining through to the outside. Flicking on the wall switch, he tucked the LED in his pocket, then immediately moved to the computer at the desk, while Sydney started searching the file cabinet, flipping through countless file folders.

He inserted the thumb drive into the USB port, then woke the computer. It was locked with a password. Unfortunately, no one had anticipated this most basic of operations.

Sydney turned her attention to the calendar on the desk, pointing. " 'Dispersal P/DC.' Whatever they're dispersing it's listed for tomorrow."

And before either of them had a chance to ponder the significance of what P/DC might mean, or come up with a viable password for the computer, they heard heavy foot-steps outside the door, then the sound of someone inserting a key into the lock.

Griffin drew his weapon, aiming it toward the door as it swung open. A moment later the room was flooded with a light so bright it blinded him. He squinted, tried to see past it.

"Put down your gun," came a deep voice with its cultured French accent. "There is no escape. My men are carrying high-powered automatic rifles. Your weapons on the floor, *s'il vous plaît*, then slide them over."

Griffin glanced at Sydney, then slowly bent down, placing his gun on the linoleum tiles. Sydney did the same.

They had no choice. Better this than instant death, and he used his foot to slide his weapon toward the doorway.

"Search them."

Two armed guards entered, both carrying semiautos, as well as long guns strapped to their backs. The shorter of the two kept his gun pointed at them, while the other kicked both weapons out the door, then approached Griffin, patting him down first before doing the same to Sydney. He removed Griffin's lock pick set from Sydney's pocket, opened it, then tossed it on the desk. "No weapons," he said in French.

The blinding light was shut off, and a man Griffin recognized from intel reports, Luc Montel, stepped into view. He was tall, with gray hair, dressed in a suit, the shirt collar open. He eyed the monitor, then the flash drive in the computer tower. "I presume that is the reason for your presence?" he asked. "What were you looking for?"

"It's not ours."

Luc took a gun from one of the guards and aimed it at Griffin. "*What* were you looking for?"

Griffin said nothing.

Luc pointed the gun toward Sydney, while keeping his gaze on Griffin.

And Sydney said, "Proof. Computer files."

"Proof of what?" When neither answered, Luc nodded toward the guard, whose gun he took. "See what they've got, Arnaud."

The guard stepped forward, typed something on the keyboard, undoubtedly the password Griffin had needed. He prayed the guard wouldn't recognize the file.

Griffin kept his gaze on Luc, hoping to keep his attention fixed, saying, "There's nothing on there."

"Indeed. Arnaud?"

"It contains a file."

"Open it."

He heard two clicks as the guard maneuvered the mouse to access the flash drive. "It doesn't open."

Griffin glanced at the screen, saw nothing happening. They'd failed. Even so, he wasn't about to announce their attempt at downloading the virus to Hilliard's computer. "As I said, there was nothing on there. We didn't have the password to copy any files."

"Apparently our security efforts work," Luc said. "Now what to do with the two of you . . ."

The guard who searched them said in French, "It will be difficult to smuggle two bodies. And DNA if we kill them here."

"True," Luc said. "What do you suggest?"

"To make it seem as though they came and went. Tie them up, and toss them below. Shoot them down there. It will be years before they are found, and their bones will be lost amongst the others."

"Take care of it." Luc looked at his watch. "Unfortunately, I have an important meeting I am expected at in a few hours."

"What are you planning to do?" Griffin asked in English. No sense letting on that he understood every word.

"Is this that moment you get me to confess as a delaying tactic?" Luc gave an exaggerated sigh. "You realize this entire operation was a setup?" The words struck Griffin like a blow to his gut. His instinct had told him as much. Someone was using his dead wife to get to him. And Luc smiled, saying, "If truth be told, you're much better off dying a slow death in the bunker. Now if you'll excuse me, I must leave." He returned the gun to the guard, then walked out of the room.

The first guard took out plastic ties often used by law enforcement for handcuffs. He walked up to Griffin first, saying, "Hands behind your back." Anger surged through Griffin as he felt the cuffs being pulled tight.

The guard moved to Sydney, cuffed her, then pushed them both toward the door. Griffin stepped out into the hallway, quickly taking in the situation. Everything Luc said was true. They would've been killed before they ever made it out, he realized, as the guard gripped his arm, directing him down the hallway past the two other guards with automatic weapons standing on either side of the door.

One of the four guards led the way, another took up the rear, the remaining two each taking custody of Griffin and Sydney, guiding them down a back staircase. The lead guard unlocked the door at the bottom, holding it open so that everyone could pass through. It led into a long hallway that ran the length of the building, dimly lit overhead by a row of fluorescent lights that wavered in intensity as though about to burn out. The floor was tiled in dull gray linoleum, and their footsteps echoed as they walked toward a steel door at the end, its huge rivets testifying to its solid state. When they reached it, one of the guards took out a large key, the sort used in very old jails, and Griffin wondered if the door wasn't a relic from World War II, opening to the underground bunker Luc had mentioned.

Griffin was half correct. The construction was definitely from that era, but it led to another staircase, again leading down. At the bottom, beneath a lone light bulb housed in a steel cage, was another door, the same construction as the last. The guards halted them at the top, and the lead guard descended alone, using the large key to unlock, then open the door at the bottom. It creaked as he pushed it flush to the wall, before returning to the top of the steps. "Take them into the bunker," he said.

Griffin's guard grabbed his arm, then Sydney's, forcing them side-by-side down the staircase. At the bottom, he pulled them to a stop, saying, "Don't move."

The weak light spilled out into the cavern casting their shadows over more steps that descended about four feet into the darkness. Sydney stood stock-still beside him, her mouth hanging open as she viewed the cavern. "Oh my God . . ."

As Griffin's eyes grew adjusted to the dark, a musty smell wafting in on the cool air, he realized there were thousands and thousands of skulls and bones stretching out at least eight feet in front of him, before dropping off into the blackness beyond. They were looking at part of the underground cemetery, the bone-filled catacombs, undoubtedly that part not accessed by the public on their tours.

Griffin craned his neck around, trying to see who was behind them.

"I said, don't move," the guard shouted.

Like hell. He looked at Sydney, mouthed the word *jump*. She looked down at the stairs, the chaos of bones, then nodded.

"Now!"

They flew out the door into the pitch black. Air rushed through his hair, and he landed with a clatter on his feet, then fell back, rolling to his side as he bumped and jarred his way down an avalanche of skeletons that echoed and rattled in his eardrums. His mouth and nostrils filled with dust as the bones continued to fall on top of him.

"Shoot them!" a guard called out in French.

The sound of automatic gunfire filled the cavern, sharp deafening cracks bouncing off the cavern walls.

"Are they dead?"

"There's no light down there. How do I find them?"

"You idiot. Arnaud, get a light. Close that door. Do not give them the advantage."

"What if they escape?"

"To where?" the other guard replied. "Those tunnels were closed off a long time ago. Hurry with that light. I want those two killed."

Griffin heard the door slam with a loud clang that echoed down the tunnel walls.

And then dark and absolute silence.

41

December 11
Washington, D.C.

Carillo and Tex took a seat in the back of the room, while Izzy sat at the computer, all waiting for the moment when Griffin's access to the lab's computer system opened the door. Izzy's fingers danced across the keyboard, his gaze glued to the screen. The only time he paused was to sip from a mug filled with black coffee and four sugars. Too sweet for Carillo's taste, and the guy was already on his third cup. "Firewall's still up," Izzy said, tapping the cursor down the screen.

"Give 'em time," Tex replied, looking at the clock. "Maybe they haven't found the right room."

"What if they can't get to the computer?" Carillo asked.

Maddie, who was seated at a table near them, her head resting on her arms, eyes closed, looked up long enough to say, "Trust me. I've seen Izzy work. He could get in without them."

"Maybe," Izzy said. "After hours and hours. This way makes it easier. All we need is for someone to double click that file . . ."

"Let's hope it doesn't take hours," Carillo replied, then

nodded his head toward the far side of the room so that he and Tex could talk without being overheard. "What're you planning on doing with these two when they're done?"

"Safe house until we conclude the case."

Carillo glanced at Maddie, who appeared to be dozing again. Her only fault was in having her picture on the wrong guy's computer. Not that he had time to worry. There were too many facets to this case to feel sorry for any one person at the moment. "How about the reporter that ran that article in this morning's paper?"

"Other than she seems to get the inside scoop on more stories than every reporter this side of the White House?" Tex replied.

"My thoughts exactly."

"Actually, I—"

"We're in!" Izzy said. "Yeah!" He tapped away at the keys, his foot, his whole body bouncing as he worked. Apparently the caffeine was kicking in. "I was worried they wouldn't be able to get into a computer to open the file and execute it. But they must have found one."

Carillo walked over to the monitor to watch Izzy, while Tex pressed the button on his Bluetooth ear piece, opening a communication with Dumas. "They planted the computer virus," he told Dumas. "So far so good . . ."

"You find anything, yet?" Carillo asked Izzy.

"Need a couple seconds to get around."

Carillo waited, trying to follow, but Izzy opened and closed computer windows so fast, Carillo couldn't keep up. He looked over at Tex. "Any word from Griffin yet?"

"Still too early. They're not supposed to meet up with Dumas for another thirty. Clearly they succeeded."

Carillo eyed the clock. He didn't like waiting on this side of the action, not with Sydney out there facing things like double agents and viruses—the noncomputer type. She was competent, but some of this stuff was beyond her expertise and training. Hell, it was way beyond his, and he wasn't sure he'd be out there doing the same thing. After about ten minutes, he realized he couldn't stand the waiting. He had to do something besides watching Izzy clack away at the computer. "Any reason you need me to stick around? I was thinking of running a little background on that reporter."

"Go ahead," Tex said, apparently distracted. "I'll be taking off as soon as I get someone up here to watch these two."

Carillo left. If he wanted to get the goods on this reporter—because he damned well knew that something was up with her—he was going to have to see her personally.

42

December 11
Alexandria, Virginia

Tex pulled in behind a minivan parked on the street,
which gave him a view of the reporter's house. Merideth
Garrett lived in a middle-class neighborhood of Alexandria,
where Christmas lights sparkled along a number of rooflines
of the mostly two-story, brick-fronted homes. No Christmas
lights were on at her place. No lights at all.

He checked his watch. His contact at the paper said she
had left her office about fifteen minutes ago, which meant
he had plenty of time to wait. Just about to settle in, he saw
another car parked farther down and someone seated within
it—something he might not have noticed had another vehicle not backed out of the driveway across the street, its white
reverse lights shining just enough to allow Tex to make out
the top of the guy's head.

Tex exited his car, its cab light having already been disconnected, and he left the vehicle door slightly ajar to avoid
any noise. He crouched below the eye level of the vehicles
parked between him and the other car, nearly slipping in a
patch of snow that hadn't been cleared from the sidewalk. As
he neared the last vehicle, he drew his gun, held it against his
leg, then made his final approach.

He walked up to the car's passenger window and saw the driver watching him, a gun pointed in his direction.

"Jesus effing Christ, Tex," the driver said. "I almost shot your ass."

"Carillo? You said you were doing *background* work on her. Not *coming* here."

"I like the personal touch. Get in the damned car so I can roll up the window. It's cold out there."

Tex got in.

"Was I that obvious?" Carillo asked.

"Only because someone backed out across from you," Tex replied. "Driveway's empty now, so I'm thinking you're good."

"Aren't you a little out of your jurisdiction? Like the wrong country?"

"You're thinking CIA. ATLAS sort of works in the gray area."

"That area I know well. What the hell you doing here?"

"Got tired of twiddling my thumbs waiting for Sydney and Griff to come up for air."

"Any word on them yet?"

"No. And frankly I'm worried," Tex said. "With Marc and Lisette missing, and the timing of this article, I've got a really bad feeling it's all connected. Figured I'd pay this reporter a call to see if she'll consider revealing her source in the interest of national security."

"You allowed to beat confessions out of reporters?"

"Technically not. But placing bugs in their houses when one goes in to politely ask questions tends to be overlooked."

"Unless one ends up in court."

"And that's where plausible deniability comes in," Tex replied. "If you don't know I'm planting them, you can't testify to it."

"Glad you're not telling me, and saves me the trouble of coming up with a better idea. Figured you guys would've had her phone tapped by now."

"Already tried that on her landline. She uses her cell phone almost exclusively."

Carillo leaned back and gave a sigh. "Remember the good old days before cell phones were all the rage?"

"Gathering intel was a helluva lot easier back then."

Headlights from an approaching car lit up the dark street. The vehicle slowed, then turned into the driveway of the reporter's house. "That her?" Carillo asked.

Tex watched as she got out of her car, then walked up the drive to a side door. "It's her."

"You think if we both show up, it'll be a bit of overkill?"

"I think—" Tex stared at the upper story, the movement he saw in the darkened window. "There's someone in that house."

"The hell . . . you think it's CIA?"

"No way. As pissed off as Thorndike was this morning, he probably peppered this place with bugs the moment she left for work. In and out. Which means this can't be good."

They flew from the car, raced across the street to the closest house, keeping tight against the snow-covered shrubs, crouching below the window line, their weapons drawn. Tex signaled to Carillo to take the corner of the house, giving him the vantage point down two sides. When Carillo was in position, Tex moved to the side door, checked the knob, found it unlocked. He waved, and Carillo ran up. They stood on either side of the door.

"Ready?" he whispered.

Carillo nodded.

Tex pushed the door open with his foot, aimed his weapon. The place was still dark.

Most people turned the lights on when they came home.

Tex glanced around, saw the light switch in the up position. He pointed. Carillo nodded in understanding. Seemed that either her light had burned out, or it had a little help. Tex was betting on the latter, and he and Carillo entered the kitchen. They began their search on the bottom floor, room by room, when they heard a sound coming from the front of the house. They moved toward the stairs. Tex took one step and almost tripped.

He looked down, saw a body on the floor.

"It's the reporter, Merideth," Tex whispered. He crouched beside her, put his fingertips to her neck. No pulse.

A floorboard creaked at the back of the house.

Her killer was still there.

Tex motioned for Carillo to follow him. As they neared the rear of the house, they heard a door slam. A dark figure raced past the window. Tex and Carillo ran back through the kitchen, out the side door. They heard a car engine starting, the rev of a motor, then the screech of tires. The car was gone by the time they got to the sidewalk.

"Son of a bitch," Tex said, watching the taillights disappear around the corner.

He and Carillo returned to the darkened house. "She dead?" Carillo asked.

"Real dead."

"Guess we don't need to plant those bugs."

"A bit of a waste at this point." Tex rubbed the tension from his neck. "You touch anything in there?"

"Just the door on the way out."

"Let's get rid of our prints, then get the hell out of here before someone calls the police."

They met up at Tex's office at the *Recorder* about a half hour later. Carillo stood in the hall as Tex unlocked the door, turned on the light, then threw his coat on the extra chair. "You want a drink, while we wait on word from Griffin?"

"What'dya got?" Carillo asked, shrugging out of his own coat.

"Whiskey." Tex poured two glasses, then handed one to Carillo.

Carillo lifted his in toast, then took a sip. Very smooth. He looked over at the bottle, saw it was twenty-five-year-old Scotch whiskey. No wonder. "You think CIA hit her?"

"The reporter? Hell no," Tex said. "Thorndike would've been first in line to find out who her source was."

"Unless he knew who the source was."

"Any reason the FBI would want her dead?"

"None whatsoever—never mind we tend to avoid that sort of thing. What other alphabet agencies we need to consider?"

Tex stared at his glass, swirling the amber liquid. "Maybe it's not one of ours."

"Then who would it be?"

"I'm guessing whoever is after Griffin. Probably the Network."

"The Network? What are they? A renegade TV station?"

"International cabal of crooks is probably the easiest explanation."

"And what, like they infiltrated the government?"

"Some of them *are* the government."

"Always a comfort to hear."

Tex put his feet up on his desk, drained his whiskey glass, then looked Carillo in the eye. "So maybe it depends on your interpretation of the government. These guys have some heavy-duty movers and shakers who fund their favorite politicians."

"Like Grogan?"

"Like Grogan."

"So they're behind burning this CIA agent in France? And burning Griffin?"

"I'd bet my retirement on it."

"Maybe even this Atlantis conspiracy?"

"Whatever that is, exactly, yeah," he said as his cell phone rang. "Tex." He listened, then suddenly sat up, putting his glass on the desk. "You're sure . . . ? Goddamn— Uh, sorry, Father, but goddamn it to hell . . . Yeah . . . Keep me informed." He disconnected, looking at Carillo. "That was Dumas. He says Griffin and Syd didn't make the rendezvous."

Carillo looked at his watch. "They were due a little over thirty minutes ago."

"It's possible Griffin found something, maybe needed to backtrack. Happens all the time. But Dumas can't get a hold of him by cell."

"What about Sydney's cell?"

"They wouldn't have used it on a black op. Too big an identifier."

Carillo should have known, and the thought sobered him. Suddenly he lost all taste for the expensive whiskey, and he set his unfinished drink on the desk, thinking that he had to do something to help. After a moment, he said, "We find who killed this reporter, we find this Network mole?"

"That'd be my guess."

"Where do we start?"

Tex pulled a sheet of paper from his desk. "My feeling? Someone who's been involved in this from the beginning knows something. Here's the list of names present at each of the security task force meetings ever since Griffin was burned." He slid over a sheet of paper.

Carillo picked it up, looked at it. "Who are you liking as a suspect?"

"Anyone who's not me."

"That narrows it down."

"Unfortunately it could be any of them."

"Then we've got a lot of bugs to plant. I vote we go alphabetical."

"That puts Cavanaugh at the top," Tex replied. "Good place to start, now that I think about it. He's said a couple things that just seemed off. Besides that, I'm not really sure how he got where he is."

"Meaning what?"

"Meaning you can usually trace the smashed fingers of those left behind on the ladder of success as others have climbed their way up. Cavanaugh? He sort of came out of nowhere."

"So even if he isn't guilty of espionage, he's guilty of something? How do you want to go about this?"

Tex reached over, grabbed the bottle of whiskey, topped off Carillo's glass, then refilled his own. "Not get caught, for starters. It could lead to a prison sentence."

Carillo held up his glass. "I'm all about the gray areas."

"Yeah, this might be beyond the gray areas. Just so you know."

"Put it this way, Tex. My wife's divorcing me for everything I've got, and then some. In other words, my pants are already down, so it's not like throwing me in jail and taking away my pension's gonna do much more than she's already doing."

"Makes me glad I'm not married."

43

The air smelled of moldy, damp earth. Lying on her
side, Sydney tried to free her hands. No such luck, and she
remained motionless for several seconds while she took
stock of herself. Nothing felt broken. A little banged up,
definitely bruised, but she could live with that. She could
even live with the fact her face was pressed into something
smooth and round, about the size of a human skull. What she
couldn't live with was the total Stygian blackness. She hated
the dark. Hell, she was afraid of it. Her one phobia. "Griff?"
she whispered.

"Over here."

Somewhere behind her. She tried to roll over, sit up, but
with her hands behind her back, the motion sent her sliding down even farther, like being on a mountain of ceramic
Lincoln Logs. A much preferable vision to the reality, she
thought, aware of the dust in her mouth, grateful it had no
taste. She scooted toward the sound of Griffin's voice, feeling herself sliding again, using the motion to roll in his direction. A few seconds later, her feet touched a more level
surface. "This is the point where you tell me that you have

a secret tracking device activated and your guys will come rushing to the rescue any second, right?"

"I knew I forgot something when I dressed this morning."

She heard him moving below her, as though he were shifting around in a bunch of hollow blocks. "What are you doing?"

"Trying to get to the knife in my boot."

"A knife? For God's sake, I thought we were going to die down here."

"We still might die down here. You ever try to get a knife from your boot with your hands tied behind your back?"

"Maybe I can get it."

He cursed as he slid farther from her. When the pile of bones stopped moving, he said, "I'm putting my foot toward you. You should be able to feel the hilt at the top of the boot. Slide it straight out."

She heard something clunk down beside her, a skull, no doubt, and she reached back toward him with her cuffed hands. "Can you move a bit closer?"

"I'm upside down. It's not as easy as you think."

Sydney snaked toward him, felt the top of the boot. Just a little bit farther, and she had the knife, slipping it out, grasping it tightly in her hand. "Got it."

"Let's get to the bottom of this pile. If we drop it, at least we have a chance of finding it."

Holding tight to the knife, she maneuvered her way down the pile of bones until her feet touched the cave floor. They worked their way to a sitting position, back to back. Sydney opened the knife. And even though she worried he'd slice his wrist, he managed to slide one tie over the blade and cut free. From there, it was short work to remove hers, and he pulled her to her feet. She lost her footing, slipping on a long bone, and he caught her.

"Thank you," she said, her face against his chest. She could hear his heart beating.

"We're not out of here yet," he said, righting her.

And though she wanted nothing more in that moment than to have him continue holding her, erasing the chill of being there bound and helpless, she stepped back. "Any bright ideas?"

"Let's take a look."

He pulled his small LED from his pocket. "Guard missed it," he explained, as he shone it around, lighting up the piles and piles of bones, with the skulls staring out at them.

"I think I liked it better in the dark."

"Over there." Griffin aimed the light, and she saw iron bars blocking off the part of the tunnel they were in—a dead end if there ever was one. If there was any hope, it was on the other side of the wrought-iron gate, locked with a thick chain. Griffin pulled on it, as though determining its strength. "If I had to guess, it's to keep people out, probably away from the bones."

"Lucky for us." She eyed the lock. "Can you pick it?"

He examined the lock. "The pick I need is back in that office."

Griffin shone his light up. Sydney noticed another bunker door, probably belonging to the adjoining building, the steps having crumbled away a long time ago, leaving no access, even if they could somehow open it from the outside. Their best bet was climbing over the top of the cage that closed them off from the tunnel beyond. It stood about ten feet high, the top of the cavern several feet higher. On the other side, it would be next to impossible to get up without a ladder. On this side, they had the advantage of about six feet of bones piled against it.

"Our best bet," Griffin said.

Griffin helped Sydney up the bone pile, which lost a couple of feet in height as they shifted and moved. He lifted Sydney higher. She was able to grab on to the top bar, pulling her foot over to straddle the frame. Griffin flashed his light, and she looked down, thinking that ten feet was an awful long way.

Suddenly the cavern lit up as the guards opened the bunker door.

"Where are they, you fools?"

"Over there! They're getting away."

Two guards started down the steps, then fell as they hit the mountain of bones.

Griffin jumped up, swung over, and was down the bars almost before Sydney had reached the bottom. He took her hand, dragged her away, just as the guards fired at them.

Griffin heard the shouting behind him. He didn't turn to look. Any delay could mean death. Instead he pressed his thumb on the tiny switch for his LED, the blue light reflecting off the rough-hewn ground of the limestone tunnel for a quick second before he let go. Several more shots sounded in succession, the sharp cracks echoing through the cavern. About ten feet ahead he'd seen a tunnel leading off to the left, and several feet farther up a larger tunnel leading to the right. He left the light off, not wanting to give them a clue, just in case they'd gotten through the locked gate. Holding Sydney's hand, he counted the paces, then quickly flashed the light, saw the opening to the left. He pulled her in, then stopped, listened. He heard them talking, their voices carrying through the tunnel, then the sound of heavy footsteps. Apparently they'd shot the lock.

"What now?" Sydney whispered.

"We need a couple weapons before we go farther."

"You're not thinking of going back?"

"Not without firepower."

He turned on his light, took a quick look at the keyhole-shaped tunnel they'd entered, the top rounded, the bottom narrow down the center, and rock benches carved along the length, probably part of the shelter from the war. Perfect for what he had planned. They stepped up onto the ledge, their backs pressed against the wall. The bench placed them a little over two feet above the ground, and Griffin watched the main tunnel, saw the light bouncing on the cave floor as one of the guards called out, "There are two tunnels up ahead. Which way? To the left or right?"

"To the right!" the other said. "The manhole."

Griffin waited for the first guard to pass, saw him shine the light into their tunnel, its beam hitting the opposite wall as he continued straight, leaving Sydney and Griffin in the dark. The second guard walked up, his flashlight beam also hitting the opposite side. As he walked past without looking, Griffin jumped. He wrapped his left arm around the man's neck, cutting off his circulation, pulling him backward off balance. The guard reached up with both hands, clawing at Griffin's arm.

Griffin grabbed the rifle as it swung from the guard's shoulder strap. The moment the first guard turned toward him and aimed, Griffin pulled the trigger, the sharp report cracking off the walls. The first guard slumped to the ground. Griffin dropped the rifle, brought his arm up, applying pressure to the guard's carotid. The man jerked a few times, then went limp.

Griffin lowered him to the ground, fished through his pockets, finding the plastic cuff ties. He secured the man's wrists behind his back. "Wait here," he told Sydney, handing her the man's rifle and handgun. "I'm going to get the other weapons."

He stopped at the edge of the tunnel, listened, heard nothing. Using the guard's flashlight, he checked in both directions, then ran down the passageway, retrieving the first guard's gun. As he reached down to pull the rifle strap from the dead man's shoulder, he noticed a tattoo on the man's forearm. A black scorpion. Something he'd seen on other operatives for the Network.

That answered the question about who these men were working for. Now all he and Sydney had to do was get out of here. One of the guards had said something about a manhole being the only way out. So be it. He only hoped the other two guards who hadn't followed them through the tunnels weren't waiting at the top.

Sydney stopped, thinking she heard a distant echo coming from the direction of the dead guard. She aimed her pistol.

Griffin stopped with her. The only sound now was their breathing. He tapped her on her shoulder, indicating they should continue on, and she reached up, adjusted the strap of the long gun hanging at her back, its unfamiliar weight making her shoulder ache after their endless minutes traips-

ing through this last tunnel. According to Griffin, the one
guard had said the tunnel to the right led out, but as of yet,
Syd hadn't seen any indication that they were getting any
closer to escaping.

"It ends," Griffin said, pointing.

His pale blue light bounced off a very solid-looking limestone wall, and her heart sank. "Maybe there was more than
one tunnel to the right."

And then Griffin shone the light upward. "There."

She saw a dark hole about four feet in diameter at the top
of the cave, and as he moved the light about, it reflected off
the bottom rung of an iron ladder affixed to the wall of the
narrow tunnel, before it disappeared into darkness higher up.
It was undoubtedly the manhole the guard spoke of. Unfortunately, the opening was ten feet above the ground and they
had no way to get to it.

"What now?" she whispered.

"I'm thinking."

A shout from the main tunnel brought them up short,
someone crying, "*Ici!*"

"You better think fast," Sydney said, aiming her gun that
direction. "No doubt someone found the dead guard."

A moment later, an answering shout told her she was correct. It was only a matter of minutes before they were discovered, maybe less, and situated where they were at the end
of the tunnel, they were the proverbial sitting ducks.

"Get up on my shoulders," Griffin said.

"I'm not leaving you down here."

"You have a better idea?" he said, aiming the light upward
once more.

She eyed the bottom rung, so tauntingly close that she
could almost touch it with the barrel of her rifle . . . "Actually, I do," she said, tucking her handgun in her waistband,
then slipping the rifle from her back to see if her idea held
merit. "You think these shoulder straps would hold your
weight?"

Griffin reached down, pulled on the strap of his rifle.
"You're brilliant."

"Yeah," she said, first ejecting the magazine from her long

gun, before ejecting the round from the chamber. "Remember that the next time you're mad at me." She shoved the magazine in her back pocket, then slung the gun across her back again.

"Take the light," he said, handing it to her. She put it in her front pocket, and he said, "Ready?"

He put his hands on her waist, she gripped his shoulders, and they stood there, an infinitesimal moment in the dark, the heat of his chest next to hers, and his breath on her cheek. "Ready," she said, and the warmth vanished as he lifted her.

She slid one knee onto his shoulder, then the other. He shifted, stepping to the side, and she gripped the hair on his head to keep from falling.

"Try to save me a few strands," he said.

"Hold still and you won't have to worry." She reached up with her hand, feeling around for the tunnel opening and the rung of the ladder, its rough metal surface cold against her hand. "Got it," she said, as the sound of heavy footfall echoed through the tunnel.

"They're getting closer."

"Thank you, Dr. Obvious." She hooked one arm around that lowest rung, then grabbed the rifle slung across her back, slipped it off, unhooked and threaded it so that it was hanging downward. "Done. You think we should hang the other one from this to make it lower?"

"*Cette voie!*" someone shouted.

"No time," he said. "Climb up and shine that light down so I can see."

Sydney ascended so that she was several rungs higher, before reaching into her pocket and retrieving the light. She turned it on, aimed it downward. Griffin stood there, looking up, the rifle about a foot above his head.

He jumped. The strap held as he grasped the long barrel, swinging in the air. A gunshot rang out, its echo cracking down the tunnel. "Go!" he said. And her last sight of Griffin before she shut off the light was him attempting to hoist himself up the length of the rifle.

44

December 11
Washington, D.C.

Miles Cavanaugh lived in a downtown apartment in an upscale area of D.C. No doorman at the front, Carillo noted from the passenger seat of the utility truck Tex drove. He and Tex both wore Pepco Electric jackets over their street clothes, on the off chance anyone looked too close. The white truck, with its blue and green Pepco logo, looked like the real thing, the only difference being the additional equipment inside, everything from plastic explosives to an array of electronic gadgets and listening devices that no utility company had access to. "I take it you guys do this a lot," Carillo said.

"Not sure I can legally answer that," Tex replied, pulling up about two doors down from the building. "But I have been flagged down by a few citizens demanding to know when their power would be restored."

Carillo got out, placed the orange cones on the street, while Tex opened the back of the truck and took out the equipment box.

They approached the complex, moving around to the back of the building to access the telephone from Cavanaugh's unit. Carillo kept watch while Tex tapped into the trunk line, waiting for Cavanaugh's number to come up on his monitor. "Shouldn't we be wearing phone company uniforms?" Carillo asked.

"Probably. But this is all I could get at this hour. Trust me. No one will pay attention, long as they see the official signs."

As soon as Tex finished, he disconnected, closed the box, then motioned for Carillo to follow him into the condo.

Cavanaugh wasn't home. It took Tex less than a minute to bypass the security system, then break into the house. Once inside the flat, Tex placed several devices, while Carillo looked around, hoping to find some sign of Cavanaugh's activities. The place was clean—unless one counted the unusual number of gold ingots found in the false bottom of his dresser drawer.

"Wonder how much this is worth?" Carillo called out to him.

Tex walked in, looked into the drawer, picked up one of the ingots, rubbing the face of it with his gloved fingers. "Feels real."

"Quite the stash on a government salary."

Tex replaced the ingot, then the false drawer bottom. "Guess our instincts were right," he said, as he and Carillo left. "Gold is one of the Network's favored payment plans. No paper trail."

Tex reset the alarm, locked the door, then shut it tight, while Carillo stood guard at the end of the hall, watching the elevator. "Let's go," Tex said.

Carillo pressed the button. The elevator door opened. Thorndike and another agent stood there, guns out, pointed at them.

"Step in, boys," Thorndike said. "And don't make any sudden moves."

Thorndike holding a gun on them . . . Definitely the last person Carillo would ever have expected to see, and he wondered how the CIA director was going to spin this. The four men rode the elevator to the ground floor. Outside, the street was deserted. Thorndike directed them to the left. They walked for a block, when Thorndike said, "See that van up there? I want you both to get in when the door opens, then have a seat. And shut up."

The van was much larger than the truck Tex and Carillo had used. As the back door opened, Carillo saw a man in black standing guard just inside. Tex hopped up, followed by Carillo. The guard patted first one, then the other, looking for backup weapons. The interior of the surveillance van contained monitoring equipment with two chairs at the console, both empty.

Tex sat in the first chair, Carillo the second. Thorndike stepped in, pulling the door closed.

Tex glanced at the monitors, then back at Thorndike. "Why are you here, Thorndike? Trying to get some dirt on your buddy Cavanaugh to keep him in your pocket?"

"Trying to find out if my agent's in danger."

"Which agent would that be?"

"Covert. That's all you need to know."

"I'd think you'd save this local surveillance work for your minions. You're operating out of your jurisdiction."

"You think I'm worried about spending time in jail?"

"I think you're worried about something, or you wouldn't personally be here."

Thorndike stared at Tex, his jaw clenching. He nodded toward the door, telling his men, "Leave us alone for a few." The two CIA agents exited. Thorndike never took his eyes off Tex. "What do you think you know?"

"You were the one who burned Griffin trying to get him out of Europe."

"And why would I do that?"

"After this morning's paper, I'm guessing to protect a certain agent in France."

"This is interesting. Go on."

Carillo said, "Might as well show him."

Tex pulled the copy of Sydney's drawing from his pocket, unfolded it, then held it out. "This was the sketch from a description by our now dead witness, who said *this* woman was with the guy who killed Faas."

Thorndike looked at the drawing, then sank into the chair at the monitor console. "It's true then."

"What's true?" Tex asked.

"She's turned."

Tex looked as if he were going to be sick. "So it is Griffin's wife?"

Thorndike nodded. "That's why I approved Griffin's burn notice. I couldn't take the chance he might run into her. It was too dangerous."

"And what? You thought he'd hop on the first plane home after his contact was stabbed? He *thought* he was getting information on who killed Becca."

"And now it seems she's the one behind the murders."

"I don't believe that."

"Who do you think started this mess to lure Griffin out there?"

"You're saying Becca is trying to kill her own husband?"

"What other explanation is there? It was her idea to fake her own death."

"Jesus."

"Exactly." Thorndike glanced at the monitors, then back at Tex. "She'd been working as a double agent that entire time, and she needed a safe out to move over to LockeStarr. She knew that Griffin would never allow her to go."

"If she's working as a double agent, maybe—"

"Don't you get it? She *lured* Griffin out there. She alone knew the name of the contact, Faas. Not her handler. Not anyone. Why the hell else would she do it, if not to draw him over there?"

"And why would she?" Tex said, his voice rising.

"Because we were about to reopen the investigation into LockeStarr. And look what's happened as a result. Every one of us has been spinning our wheels looking for Griffin and trying to salvage my operation over there. And what do we have to show for it?"

"Depends," Carillo said. "You kill the reporter?"

"What the hell are you talking about?"

"Murdered."

"My men saw her leave her office," Thorndike said. "She was very much alive this evening."

"And we saw her lying on her dining room floor, very much dead."

Thorndike got up, opened the back door of the van, looked at the man who'd been sitting at one of the monitors when they'd first walked in. "Get Lawley on the phone. I want to know what's going on with that reporter."

Tex must have decided Thorndike's reaction was legit, that he wasn't behind the homicide, because he added, "Carillo's telling you the truth, Thorndike. Someone killed her."

And Carillo said, "Broke her neck in the time it took us to walk across the street to her side yard. Whoever it was, they were in and out."

"Professional hit?"

"Definitely," Tex said. "I have a feeling that the only reason they didn't have time to stage it as an accident was because we showed up. So I'll ask you again. Why are you here?"

"Cavanaugh knew that I was running a double agent. He's the only one who could have leaked that info."

"He knows Becca's alive?"

"No. Only I do. He only knew I was against Griffin going to investigate his wife's death because I was worried it would compromise my operation. I never mentioned her name. To anyone."

"And what?" Carillo said. "It didn't occur to you that he might want Griffin burned for nefarious purposes himself? You realize he had about a million bucks in gold stashed away up there?"

"Oh my God. He's the leak. Someone's been paying him, and I've been handing him information the whole time . . ."

"Clearly the Network got to him," Tex said. "Question is, how'd you get roped into it?"

"I wanted to expose LockeStarr."

"I get why you wanted that. But Cavanaugh?"

"Miles wanted it for the political gain. Renew the investigation, reap the glory. At least, that's how he explained it to me." Thorndike took a defeated breath. "And since it went hand in hand with my goal, why not? And then Griffin stepped into the mix. I'm sure that rattled Miles, but not for the same reasons. I was too busy trying to protect my asset in the field to realize what was going on. For me, if Griffin recovered this package and exposed our mole inside Locke-Starr, all hell would break loose."

"What package?" Tex asked.

"A biological agent shipped to and stolen from a lab in France, that we believe was intended to be sold to terrorists. That and the proof we needed to shut down LockeStarr."

Carillo doubted that Tex was about to mention that they'd recovered the suspected vial. Not until he knew more and could inform McNiel. "What sort of biological agent?" Tex asked.

"Manufactured. Specifically for a bioweapon. Beyond that, I don't have a clue."

To which Carillo said, "And that was *before* you discovered that your double agent was two-timing you?"

"Yes. So as you can see—"

"Thanks to our very own double agent right here?"

"What?" Thorndike said.

"Cavanaugh." Carillo nodded at the monitor, showing two men standing in the front of the apartment building. "He's home. And he's brought a friend."

Carillo watched Cavanaugh on the display talking to some man wearing a ball cap. Unfortunately they couldn't see his face. "Anybody know this guy?" Carillo asked.

No one did, and Tex said, "Time to make some hard and fast decisions, Thorndike."

Thorndike stared at the monitor, his gaze fixed on Cavanaugh. "Fine," Thorndike said. "You two follow whoever this other person is. We'll stay on Cavanaugh, since we're already set up."

"We're on it," Tex said.

"Soon as we get our guns back," Carillo added. Thorndike nodded to the guard at the door, who returned the weapons to the two men. Carillo holstered his, saying, "Been nice. But let's not do this again anytime soon." He jumped out, then waited for Tex.

They crossed the street, not wanting to walk up directly in front of Cavanaugh's apartment building. "How do you want to work this?" Tex asked.

"Since neither man probably knows me, I'll move up on foot. You be ready with the truck, just in case."

"Be careful. If they're from the Network, they're pretty sophisticated."

"A bullet's a bullet," Carillo said. "One hits you, doesn't matter who's wielding the weapon."

"Except these guys don't often miss. I'll get the truck. Call me if they move."

Carillo started that direction, then stopped, saying, "You think Thorndike's on the up and up?"

"I don't always agree with his methods, but yeah, I think he is."

"That's all I need to know."

Tex left and Carillo started toward the apartment, wondering exactly what Miles Cavanaugh's involvement in all this was. Normally a guy like Thorndike would be far removed from a case such as this, but then normal cases didn't usually involve deputy security advisers to the president. The thought of what Cavanaugh had access to was frightening, but not as frightening as whom he might be passing it on to.

About a block down, Carillo crossed over so that he was on the same side as Cavanaugh. As he neared, he could hear the two men speaking. Cavanaugh faced Carillo, though he wasn't looking at him. His attention was clearly focused on the man whose back was to Carillo. Carillo eyed the stranger, thinking that for this neighborhood, he seemed . . . out of place. Definitely out of place in comparison to Miles Cavanaugh's suit, tie, and camel overcoat. In contrast, the man wore jeans, tennis shoes, a leather jacket, and a ball cap, not that any of those would be out of place for a young upwardly mobile sort out for a casual stroll. But this was clearly no casual stroll, and the ball cap bothered the heck out of Carillo.

There were certain places that hats screamed, *Look at*

me, banks being one of them. Carillo had lost count over the years on how many guys wearing ball caps had robbed banks. They did it to hide their features from security cameras placed above eye level. Like cameras in banks. And security cameras out in front of posh apartment complexes.

Carillo slowed his pace, alarm bells ringing in his head as Cavanaugh's eyes widened, and he took a step back, saying, "What are you doing?"

Two shots and Cavanaugh crumpled to the ground.

Carillo was reaching for his gun when the suspect turned, fired at him.

Carillo dove behind a car at the curb. When he came up the suspect was halfway down the block. Carillo ran after him, saw Cavanaugh on the ground. He raced past, figured someone would call the cops. More important to catch the shooter. Then he heard a screech of tires as a vehicle sped down the street. Thank God, he thought. Tex.

But it wasn't Tex. It was a smaller white van—probably the same one that Izzy and Maddie had described. It stopped at the far corner, and the shooter got into the passenger seat. It sped away and Carillo ran after it, hoping to see a license plate. There was none.

By the time Tex made it to Carillo's location with the Pepco truck, the shooter was long gone. They made a quick search of the area, then returned to brief the CIA operatives who'd been monitoring the complex. Thorndike was livid as he stared down at the body of Miles. "What the hell did you get yourself into, you goddamned son of a bitch?"

"Just a thought," Carillo said. "But you shoulda asked him yesterday."

The CIA surveillance vehicle pulled up, stopped outside the apartment complex.

Thorndike stiffened. "Get that van out of here. Everyone get the hell out of here before we're connected to this mess."

Carillo shrugged out of his utility jacket, then looked up at the security camera. "Before you go, you might want to confiscate that video if you don't want the cops to have it."

Thorndike nodded at one of his men. "Get the damned camera recording first."

Carillo pulled out his phone.

"What are you doing?" Thorndike said.

"Reporting the shooting," Carillo said. "Since I'm working the senator's murder, it's not a big stretch that I'd be out here."

Thorndike nodded. "Everyone else, move."

When the CIA guys left, Tex took stock of the situation, then said, "I think I'll park the truck a couple blocks from here. Might be hard to explain."

"Any chance you can bring my overcoat back with you? It's flipping cold out here."

Tex left, then returned a few minutes later with Carillo's coat.

"You sure you want to be here?" Carillo asked him.

Tex held up his press pass. "Reporter for the *Washington Recorder.*"

"Forgot about that cover. Convenient." He leaned down, patted Cavanaugh's pockets, pulling out a cell phone. "The way I see it, he won't be needing this anymore, and the cops will just tie it up in evidence for weeks."

Tex grinned. "You realize that's not exactly by the book?"

"Like I said, all about the gray."

The cops took Cavanaugh's murder as an attempted robbery, and Carillo didn't bother to correct them. He did, however, give a description of the shooter, admitting that he was just a few feet away when it occurred. By the time they finished questioning Carillo and he was allowed to return to his hotel, he was dead on his feet. The moment he sat on the bed, Tex called.

"Griffin's back, they're safe. Figure that's worth finishing the bottle over. I can bring it to the hotel. It'll save me the commute home. I'm beat."

"The extra bed's yours. What happened in France?"

"Apparently they had a bit of a run-in with the lab owner."

"What'd Griffin have to say?"

"Haven't talked to him yet. Dumas called me right after he dropped them off at their hotel. Griffin lost his phone in the op. Give 'em a few, and they should be up to their room.

Maybe you could give Sydney a call, find out what's up. And tell Griffin I'm glad he's okay."

"Sure thing."

"See you in a bit."

Carillo called Sydney's number on speed dial. "You need anything out there?" he asked when she answered. "A shipment of arms? A ticket home?"

"All of the above?" Sydney replied.

"How you doing?"

"There are some places in Europe I'd rather watch on the Travel Channel."

"Like?"

"Every place in which someone's trying to kill me, which pretty much covers the entire continent these days. I take it you heard about our operation?"

"Only that you were missing and now you're found. Figured you would have called by now."

"Sorry, but I was in imminent need of a shower. A little too much bone dust for my taste." She briefed him on what happened and their near escape.

"Pearson won't be too thrilled when he hears," Carillo said when she'd finished. "He's already threatened to terminate you if you don't leave there now."

"Last I checked, he's the one who signed my vacation papers. What's got him all fired up?"

"Besides a couple murders and some intel that the CIA was running a covert action operation in the very country you're visiting?"

"France is a big country. There's bound to be more than one covert action running out here."

"Except it's only now coming out that their undercover operative is actually a double agent, who has apparently been feeding info to the Black Network. You did get my message about it breaking in the newspaper?"

"That makes no sense. If the Network is handling this double agent, why would they leak the info to the press? That's the last thing they'd want to do."

"Maybe it has nothing to do with them. Maybe it's simple down-home politics. Someone discovered some dirty laundry and is airing it as a way to divert attention. What didn't come out in the paper is that Grogan might have been working both sides himself."

"Grogan?"

"They think he wanted to open up the investigation into LockeStarr as a way to keep tabs on what the good guys were doing so he could give the info to the bad guys."

"Then who killed him?"

"That, Pollyanna, is the million-dollar question. The more I dig into the shooter's background, the more I'm beginning to believe in conspiracy theory. And while you two are running around sightseeing in Europe, your ATLAS friends are out here searching for the source of a mysterious virus that killed everyone on board a pirated freighter found floating off the coast of Brazil. You'll never guess where that freighter was seen just days before everyone ended up dead."

"I'm stumped."

"Atlantis."

"Atlantis?"

"As in the lost city. Under water."

"You're serious."

"As a heart attack. One location of this legendary city is believed to be off the coast of the Cayman Islands, which is where a bunch of college kids were shot when said freighter was passing by days before it was found with everyone on board dead from the virus."

"The virus *we'd* been carting around?"

"We're thinking they're probably one and the same."

"My brain's starting to hurt from even contemplating all this."

"Tell me about it. Right now though, ATLAS is missing two agents who went to the ship to investigate." He told her about Marc and Lisette's mission.

"What does all this have to do with running a double agent over here?"

"Because every time someone ran an operation to expose LockeStarr, it blew up in their faces. Figuratively and literally. The case with Griffin's wife being the first. The fact you were caught being next. Which brings me to my next point. The identity of the double agent. You in a place we can talk?"

"Hold on a sec." He heard what sounded like a door opening, then closing, and he guessed that Sydney had moved somewhere she couldn't be overheard. "Just what the hell are you trying to tell me?" she asked, her voice lower, sounding on edge.

"That double agent? It's supposed to be Griffin's wife."

"Please say she was working for us."

"Afraid not, Pollyanna. According to her boss at the CIA, she's working against us. Allegedly she stole the virus and sent it to Faas, using him as a way to lure Griffin into the open."

"Faas was in on it?"

"Hard to say, since he's conveniently dead. Which is the long way of saying watch your back."

45

Predawn
December 12
Paris, France

Sydney stood there shivering in her pajamas on the
narrow snow-covered balcony. The damned thing wasn't
more than twelve inches wide, meant for decorative potted
plants rather than people, and she wondered if the wrought-
iron balustrade would hold her weight if she fell against it.
She'd moved there the moment Carillo started talking about
Griffin's wife, then told her everything Thorndike had to say,
and as cold as it was, she could only stare out at the darkened
buildings across the street, the brasseries and cafés that were
now closed, the dim streetlight shining down on the trodden
snow on the ground below.

She had to figure out a way to break it to Griffin. But how?

*Hey, that wife you thought was dead, but isn't? It gets even
better. Looks like she's working for the Network as a double
agent . . .*

An icy blast of wind brought her to her senses, and she
opened the balcony door, returned inside. She glanced at the
sliver of light beneath the bathroom door, heard the water
running. Griffin was in there showering, and she could well

imagine that his thoughts were also on his wife. But Sydney doubted they were running in the same direction as her own.

She considered what Carillo said, that Pearson wanted her to return to the States, and right now she was more than ready.

The water shut off, and Griffin, dressed only in his sweat-pants, exited the bathroom a couple of minutes later, drying his face with a towel. She tossed the phone on her bed, and he said, "Who was that?"

"Carillo."

"What'd he want?"

"Besides finding out about our operation? Update on the Grogan investigation among other things . . . You know, I could really use a drink," she said, grabbing her toothbrush from her bag, then returning to the bathroom.

"Same here," he replied, walking to the bar.

Even though she'd rinsed her mouth out in the shower, she felt as if there was still a film of bone grit and limestone on her teeth and she brushed longer than normal. She didn't notice that he'd walked up to the bathroom door, stood there watching her, until she dropped her brush into the glass on the sink, then turned around. He held a drink out for her, and she took it, sipping, thinking the brandy tasted odd after the toothpaste. What she didn't expect was for him to step in even closer, so that she had nowhere to turn. Setting the glass down, she looked at him, wanting to tell him that there were things they needed to discuss. But when she opened her mouth to speak, no words came. They'd narrowly es-caped death this night and she had a feeling that he needed the same thing she did, to feel close to someone, safe, alive. She looked up at him, the questioning in his eyes, and she took a breath, reached up, drew him to her, tasted the brandy on his lips.

His kiss was swift, sure, much more intense than that one they shared outside the museum. And when she felt him slip his hand inside the shoulder of her pajama top, felt his mouth on her neck, trailing kisses on her bare skin, lower and lower, she took a deep breath, saying, "We have to talk."

He hesitated, his mouth lingering on her chest, his lips

burning a hole right through to her heart, fittingly, she thought, considering what she was about to do. Slowly he straightened, looked at her, stroking her face with his thumb. "This is not a good conversation, is it?"

She shook her head.

"Is it about the case or us?"

"Both?"

"Are either one of us in danger at the moment?"

"No."

"Then it can wait."

He kissed her again, and she let him, knowing it was entirely selfish on her part. She wanted him. Now. His hands swept beneath her flannel top, across her back, his skin smooth against hers, and just when her knees felt as though they were about to give out, he lifted her, carried her to the bed. He laid her upon it, then lowered himself on top of her, kissing her neck, leaving her helpless, unable to move.

And then her phone rang. She wanted to ignore it, but it was there on the bed beside her, ringing in her ear. Griffin raised up on one elbow as she reached blindly for the phone, answered it.

"Whoever it is, make them go away," he whispered in her ear.

It was Carillo. "Forgot one thing, Pollyanna," he said.

"What's that?" she asked as Griffin traced a finger down her neckline, then started working at the buttons.

"You okay? You sound a little out of breath."

"Only because I had to run to answer the phone."

"It's about Miles Cavanaugh."

"What about him?"

"He's dead." He told her his suspicions about the murders and the significance to Griffin.

"Oh God," she said, her voice barely a whisper.

"Yeah," Carillo said. "Figured you should know. Call me when you have some definitive plans or plausible lies so I can figure out what I'm going to tell Pearson."

"I will." She disconnected, then dropped the phone, only vaguely aware that Griffin had moved to the side, was watching her closely. "Cavanaugh's dead," she said.

"I never liked the guy."

"Carillo thinks he's the one who outed your wife to the newspaper."

"What are you talking about? What does Cavanaugh know about my wife?"

"The newspaper article. The reporter who ran it was killed, and so was Cavanaugh." She stopped, realizing she couldn't go on, couldn't tell him what Carillo had said. Not after everything they'd been through tonight. Pure selfishness on her part, she knew, but she wanted him, and informing him would ruin everything.

"That's it? That's what was so important that he had to call you in the middle of the night? "

"He thought you should know," she finished lamely.

"Damn it, Sydney. What aren't you telling me?"

There was no good way to continue, and waiting until tomorrow would only make it worse. "Thorndike thinks Becca is working for the Network and that she was the one who lured you out here."

He said nothing for the longest time, and then he got up out of bed, pulled on his pants, then his shirt.

"Griffin. We need to talk about this."

"There's nothing to say," he said, putting on his shoes, then grabbing his coat. "Carillo's wrong. They're all wrong. And whoever killed Cavanaugh saved me the trouble."

He walked out, slamming the door behind him.

Great. She stared at the ceiling, then took a deep breath, thinking that all too often, it seemed, doing the right thing sucked. Big time.

Sydney sat up, wanting to hurl her phone across the room. And she might have, except that it was her only lifeline to Carillo and she needed it and him. Instead, phone gripped in her hand, she got out of bed, walked to the balcony window, pulled the curtain aside, wondering if Griffin was really going to drive off and leave her, or just go for a walk and cool down.

She eyed the snow-covered street, looking for their car parked about a half block down on the opposite side, figuring that Griffin would be walking out the front doors any moment. And sure enough, there he was. He didn't even look up. His hands shoved in the pockets of his overcoat, he strode with purpose across the street, then stopped suddenly when he reached the other side. He changed his mind, she thought. Changed his mind and he was coming back.

But he stood there, not moving, and she knew something was wrong.

Her heart thudded when she saw him slowly hold his hands out to his sides, away from his body. A man walked up, holding a gun on Griffin. He reached beneath Griffin's overcoat, and took his weapon from him.

A second of indecision, then she dropped the curtain, ran to her suitcase, pulled out pants and a sweater, threw them on, and then her socks and shoes. Her hand was shaking as she dug through Griffin's backpack, searching for his backup weapon. She found a knife, but no gun. Where the hell was it? They'd taken two pistols from the guards.

In the car. Griffin had put the extra gun in his glove box.

She took the knife, turned her phone to vibrate mode, shoved it in her pocket, then grabbed her coat, bag, and gloves, then the car keys, and ran to the door, opened it. The hallway was clear in both directions. But then she heard the ping of the elevator, and she had no idea if Griffin and the gunman would be on it or if it was someone else. And what if they took the stairs? Left with no choice, she stepped back in, closed the door, looked around.

She needed an escape route and fast.

46

Predawn
December 12
Paris, France

Griffin balked at the open elevator door, angry that he'd let his emotions get the better of him. And because of it, he'd walked right into an ambush with the goddamned son of a bitch who'd been chasing them since Amsterdam. "How'd you find me?"

"Easy. I followed the priest from the lab. Figured it was only a matter of time before he hooked back up with you."

"Which begs the question of how you found out we'd be there?" Griffin asked, since he knew damned well they hadn't been followed after they'd shot out his tires when they'd fled to Winterswijk.

"Shut up and get on the elevator," the man said, shoving the nose of his gun in Griffin's side. "Talk to anyone without my okay, they die first, and then you."

"To where?"

"Your room."

The last place Griffin wanted to go. Not with Sydney up there. But he had no choice except to continue on, his only hope that opportunity would present itself before he got there.

Fate decided otherwise.

The man holding him at gunpoint was a pro, making sure he kept just to the back and side of Griffin, his gun hidden in the pocket of his overcoat when they'd entered the hotel lobby a minute ago. And when they arrived at the desk the clerk hadn't even bothered to look at Griffin when he had asked for the spare key, having left the other one in the room with Sydney. The clerk barely glanced up from his book, grabbed the key from the slot, then shoved it across the counter, before turning his attention back to whatever riveting page he'd been on.

If only they'd taken the stairs, Griffin might have been able to get to the knife in his boot. A pretend stumble, then draw. But his captor had directed him to the elevator.

And now, here they were. Griffin pressed the third floor button, dismayed to see that he was too close to the wall to get to the knife. As the door slid shut, he started formulating a plan to take the gun. One sidestep, a strike with his elbow—

A sharp jab of a needle in his thigh told him he'd underestimated this man. The injection, intramuscular, meant Griffin had about a minute, maybe two, before he started feeling the effects—and that was assuming it was a drug, not a poison. A fight would send it through his system faster. He needed to remain calm. Formulate a backup plan . . .

There was a knife in his backpack, just inside the hotel room door at the bar. All he had to do was take one step to the side, pretend to stumble, grab it, then turn and kill him.

The elevator door opened, and he had no choice but to step off, start down the hallway, his heart thudding with each step, every pump sending the drug into his veins. He started to feel lightheaded, woozy. He thought of Sydney. On the bed. Vulnerable. And now he was bringing danger her way.

Had to warn her . . .

"Open the door."

"So you can kill me?" He tried to speak loud enough for

her to hear. His tongue felt thick, heavy, and he was having trouble fitting the key in the lock, turning it. Fine motor skills failing fast. He was running out of time. The door swung open. He looked over. Attempted to focus. Felt a rush running through him.

Backpack . . . on the bed . . . too far . . .

Sydney . . .

47

Sydney peered through the window from the bal-
cony outside. The slit in the curtains was just enough to make
out the interior of her hotel room, the door as it opened. She
saw Griffin standing there, the suspect behind him. Griffin took a step in, stumbled. He caught himself on the wall,
stood there a moment, then took three more faltering steps
and fell to the ground.

Sydney clamped her mouth shut. Her pulse raced. The
suspect closed the door, walked over, nudged Griffin with
his foot. *Please let Griffin be faking it. Reach out, grab the*
guy, pull him down.

But Griffin never moved.

A million thoughts raced through her head, but the one
she kept coming back to was that he'd been shot. With her
limited view, she couldn't see any blood, but what other explanation was there?

Any doubts that he might recover faded when she saw
the suspect holster his gun, step over Griffin's body, pick up
the bottle of brandy from the bar, pull off the top, then take

a swig. He moved to the edge of the bed, sat, drank some more, looking around the room. And then he took out his phone, pressed a button, and held it to his ear.

Syd tried to listen, heard nothing but the pounding of her pulse. When she looked again, he'd set his phone on the bedside stand, put the brandy bottle next to it, then walked over to Griffin, dragging his body between the two beds so that he was no longer in sight. When he'd finished, he sat back on the bed, picked up the TV remote and the brandy bottle, then settled against the headboard, flicking through the TV channels as though he had all the time in the world.

She needed that gun from the car. Stepping away from the window to the side of the balcony, she pressed herself against a potted topiary, which stood between her and the balcony next door. In order to get to the other side, she was going to have to scale the building from the outside of the balcony, hanging over the street. She gripped the wrought iron with her gloved hands, tested it against her weight, swung one leg over, then the other. Foot by foot, hand by hand, she started moving to her left, hoping that the iron was firmly attached. She glanced down. Three stories seemed a hell of a lot higher from this side of the balustrade, she thought, and she sent up a prayer that she'd find a balcony window unlocked.

48

December 11
Washington, D.C.

Carillo and Tex, having finished the bottle of Scotch, had fallen asleep on their respective beds. And so it was that when Carillo heard a faint beep, he didn't immediately stir. But there it was again. "You hear that?"

"What?" Tex asked.

It suddenly occurred to Carillo where the noise came from. He pulled out Miles Cavanaugh's cell phone from his pocket, looked at the screen. "Looks like someone didn't realize Cavanaugh's dead." And Carillo smiled in the dark. "He's got mail."

49

Predawn
December 12
Paris, France

Sydney used the knife to jimmy open the third bal-cony window, and found the room empty. Putting her ear to the hallway door, she listened, heard nothing, then stepped out. She was going to have to walk by her own room to get to the stairs, because there was no way she was chancing the elevator, and as she passed by her door, she slowed, heard the drone of the TV but nothing else. By the time she made it to the stairwell, her hands were shaking, her knees weak.

She gripped the railing, descended as quickly and quietly as she could. At the bottom of the stairs she hesitated, saw the clerk buried in a novel, prayed he wouldn't notice her and ask for her key. She didn't want any attention brought to herself, and as she exited to the lobby, she looked straight ahead.

The clerk turned a page in his book, and Syd hurried out the door into the night. Instead of crossing the street in front of the hotel and chancing that the suspect might be watching from the window, she kept close to the building, until she was certain she wouldn't be noticed. The car was where they'd left it, and she looked around, tried to see if there might be someone else keeping it under surveillance. If there was, they weren't close enough for her to spot them, and she unlocked it, got in, locked the door, then sat there, momentary relief flooding through her as she realized just how narrow her escape had been.

Shaking herself, she reached over, unlocked the glove box, pulled out the gun and placed it in her lap. If she'd had the weapon with her, she would have shot the bastard from where she stood on the balcony. Unfortunately that wasn't the case, and she looked over toward the hotel, wishing she'd thought to somehow prop open the door to the room she'd climbed into to escape.

Her cell phone vibrated against her pocket, and she nearly jumped, not expecting to feel it. She wanted to cry when she heard Carillo's voice. "Griffin," she said. "I think he's dead."

"He's fine."

"What do you mean he's fine?" she said, too worried to keep her voice down. "I saw him fall. He didn't move, not even when—"

"What do you mean you saw? Where are you?"

"In the car outside the hotel. I got out through the balcony."

"Okay. Look. The guy who's got Griffin is called Bose. He just left a voice mail on Cavanaugh's phone, letting him know he's got Griffin drugged and handcuffed—"

"Oh my God—"

"—*and* he's waiting for you to come back to the hotel room. He's thinking he's going to make it look like a murder-suicide as soon as his associate gets there."

Sydney's gaze shot to the hotel, the window on the third floor. *Griffin was alive.*

And she'd left him there alone.

"I've got to go get him."

"Slow down there, Pollyanna. There's a team en route."

"An ATLAS team? And if they arrest Griffin on that trumped-up warrant?"

"Better than Griffin dying. You know if there was any other way, Tex would have found it."

A small price to pay if they got him out alive, and she
looked up at the curtained window, tried to imagine what
might happen if she waited for a team to arrive. Miles Cavanaugh, who it seemed had been involved in this mess from
the beginning, was dead because someone else wanted him
out of the way. And now she was supposed to sit back while
some unknown entity brought Griffin in and booked him on
charges that probably originated with whatever backroom
deal Cavanaugh had been running with the Network? Not a
chance. And what if this associate of Bose's got there first?
"An hour is a long time," she told Carillo. "What if it's too
late?"

"Pearson will have my ass, and I *swear* I'll kick yours if
you go in there and try to play hero."

"I promise I won't go in and play hero," she said, staring
up at the hotel room. In fact, the idea forming in her head
was anything but heroic.

50

December 12
Brazil

The jungle never slept. The sound of toads and birds continued on into the night, and Marc was grateful, since it helped mask some of their movement. Marc and Lisette waited for the sentry to pass, then crawled through the low-lying shrubs to the fence. Lifting the bottom, Marc allowed Lisette to slither through, before he followed. On the other side, they hid for a few minutes in the shadows, their black clothing helping to conceal them. As Marc had suspected, there were no outdoor lights on the compound grounds, lights which could be seen by anyone flying overhead should they be looking. And in South America, someone was always looking for jungle compounds in the hunt for drug smugglers.

Marc watched the area for a few minutes, checking his watch. By his estimation, the next sentry was due in about ten minutes. Most of the activity, from what he'd seen earlier, and even now at night, seemed to be occurring at the other end of the building. People came and went through what Marc presumed were the main doors. A guard stood just outside, which meant they'd need to find another way in. There were other doors closer to them, with the nearby windows dark, leading Marc to believe that the rooms were unoccupied. "I might have a lock pick in my wallet," he told Lisette. "Or, we could see about climbing up onto the balcony and finding something up there."

"Maybe we should first check the door to see if it's unlocked."

"Why would they keep it unlocked?"

"Because the place is surrounded by miles of swamp, anacondas as large as a house, and guards with big guns. If they aren't worried about tree roots displacing fences so that someone could crawl beneath, they must feel secure that any threat will come from a different direction."

She had a point, and, when he was certain that the guard near the front wasn't looking their way, he sidled against the building, tried the knob. It turned and he opened the door so that it was slightly ajar. All inside was dark and he heard nothing to indicate anyone was within. He waved her over. Together, they stood pressed against the building, Marc watching the guard up front, before opening the door. They slipped inside, and she whispered, "What was it you wanted to mention?"

"I hate it when you're right."

"You must hate it an awful lot. Now let's find a phone to call home."

He flicked on the lighter he'd taken from the boat driver, discovering that the door was merely a hallway that led to another door, this one locked. "Ha!" he said. "You're only half right."

"Are we keeping score now?" she said, her gun out, trained on the door they'd just entered.

He moved down the short hall, holding up the lighter looking for any sign of an alarm system. Seeing none, he used his knife, sliding the blade into the jamb, circumventing the basic lock. He pocketed the lighter, kept his knife in his right hand, his gun in his left. The knife would be their first choice, the gun their last resort. "Ready?"

"Ready."

Another hall, this one appearing to lead to the main area

of the complex. This end was dark, apparently not occupied at night. There were several doors on either side, each one unlocked. They were empty, which confirmed that this wing wasn't being used. And then they came to a door that not only was locked, but also was emblazoned with a biohazard sign on it.

"We have to go in," Lisette whispered.

"Our priority is the phone."

"We have a boat filled with dead people and a mysterious virus that they alluded to being kept here when we were kidnapped. I need to see in there."

"Your hazmat suit is buried in the swamp."

"We open the door and I make an assessment."

"An assessment of what? That they're practicing safe virus containment? When do you determine that? When you figure out what the incubation period is, as you start bleeding from every orifice?"

Lisette took a deep breath, her tone filled with exasperation. "Why must you be so dramatic? Just open the damned door and let me take a look. I don't need to go in. If there are viruses floating around, we are dead anyway. There is no seal on the bottom of this door."

"Fine." He holstered his gun, then used his knife to bypass the lock. Unfortunately the lock was of a better quality, no doubt because of the biohazard danger, and he was forced to dig out his pick from his wallet. It took longer than he liked, Lisette holding the lighter for him as he slid the instrument into the locking mechanism, teasing each of the pins into place. He opened it, and Lisette, with the lighter, stood on the threshold looking in, while he kept watch. As he was thinking that she was taking her damned time, he heard the shuffling of feet, a loud laugh, then the sound of keys unlocking the very door they'd used to enter the hallway. Someone was coming. Two someones, by the sound of the voices. The sentries were about to walk in on them.

Marc pushed Lisette into the biohazard room, stepped in after her, and shut the door as quickly and quietly as possible.

"Shh," he said into her ear. She let the lighter extinguish, and the two of them stood there in the dark, while the sound of booted feet traipsed up the hallway past them. He relaxed slightly as the two men continued their conversation in a language he couldn't understand, Portuguese, he thought, their laughter telling him that they were relaxed and going about their routine, never realizing there were any intruders. Still, he and Lisette didn't move for a minute, maybe more, on the off chance that any other guards might pass by in the opposite direction.

When they heard no more sounds, she flicked on the lighter again, saying, "We are well and truly in the frying pan, we might as well make use of our time here."

He looked around, seeing an office that was plainly furnished. The drop ceiling was paneled with large acoustic tiles, and a few overhead fluorescent lamps, which they didn't dare turn on. Against one wall he saw two desks, industrial gray, that looked as though they'd been bought in a surplus warehouse, their surfaces covered with papers. To the right he saw a large window set next to another door, and on the other side, a working lab filled with beakers and vials and petri dishes, as well as some stainless steel equipment including what he thought might be a cryogenic freezer.

He knew next to nothing about chemistry or anything related. That was Lisette's expertise, and he trusted that she knew what or where she could search. That at least gave him some relief that they weren't going to die from walking in. Lisette saw a box of latex gloves on one of the desks, pulled two out, hitting a container of empty vials next to it. She moved the vials away from the edge of the desk, put on the gloves, then started going through the papers, handing the lighter to Marc, while she searched.

"What would you like me to do?" he asked.

"Stand guard. This search could take a while."

He liked that idea. Less chance to pick up any stray diseases that might crawl beneath that lab door, which, he noted, also wasn't sealed. Lisette shuffled through files in the desk drawer, while he stood sentry. When he looked over at her, she was reading something.

"This is Dr. Fedorov's paperwork," Lisette said, flipping

through the documents. "This is why they stole the AUV. Why the kids were murdered on that boat. They weren't pirates searching for gold. They weren't even *looking* in the same area. They just didn't want any witnesses to the *actual* location, which was much farther out, much deeper."

"Witnesses to what?"

"To them lowering that AUV down to the world's deepest hydrothermal vent . . ." She was scanning each document, excited, talking more to herself than him. "This makes perfect sense. If one wanted to search for new, as of yet undiscovered viruses, perhaps to genetically alter current viruses, one would want to look where life first formed."

"The primordial soup theory?"

"Not quite. The new theory is that life *began* at hydrothermal vents on the ocean floor. To put it simply, a chemical reaction which produces a form of energy that can be harnessed by other processes," she said, even though he had no idea what she was talking about. "They're taking viruses emerging from the mouth of the vent where temperatures exceed six hundred degrees Fahrenheit . . ."

"With an AUV? How does it survive temps that high?"

"They don't need to get that close. They follow the vent stream up. The very fact the viruses can exist in such extreme temperature changes as it leaves the vent, then cools . . ." She folded the set of documents, handed them to him, then started digging through the desk again, this time reaching beneath the desktop, then inside the drawers, looking, undoubtedly, for something that might be hidden. "I think," she said, getting down on her knees to peer into the drawers, "Fedorov was combining these with known weapons viruses to withstand heat, to better control them."

And that he did understand. A virus that could survive extreme heat sources was far more effective as a bioweapon than any known virus that had been used for weaponization thus far. "Combining? How?"

"Fedorov's specialty was chimera viruses," she said, pushing aside several file folders, then shoving her hand beneath them. She found something and pulled it out. A small black book.

Mark peered over her shoulder as she opened it and saw its pages were filled with handwriting in both blue and black ink. He recognized a few Russian words, but wasn't as fluent as Lisette. "Fedorov's journal?"

"I believe so . . ." She turned the page. "I'm hoping to find his own notes on chimera viruses, something he may not have documented specifically in his research papers. I suspect it's what killed the men on the *Zenobia*. Their outward symptoms appeared to be blackpox."

"Like smallpox?"

"Only worse. Deadlier. A recombinant virus made from smallpox spliced with Ebola. Something the Vector scientists in Russia cooked up a couple decades ago."

"I thought they killed that program? Too dangerous?"

"It is, which is why I'm trying to find more on what happened. No one, even Fedorov, would want to unleash something that deadly and uncontrollable onto the world. Not unless you had some safeguards built in, which, now that I think about it, our captors alluded to . . ." She paused to read further, turned several pages in rapid succession. "Apparently creating a deadlier strain wasn't his intent. He hoped to harness the viruses found at the mouth of the vent where life began . . ." She ran her finger across one of the lines, narrowing her gaze, as though trying to translate the Russian. "Normally you'd make a DNA copy from the one, and graft it into the other. The RNA of the—"

"Remember who you're talking to, here."

"The virus from the vent is like a master key, with more than one place to insert genetic code, allowing him to manipulate the viruses in ways he couldn't do if he was working with the originals, which would limit the amount of splicing. His goal was to create a virus that had its own shutoff switch, so that one could use it for a weapon, wait for the fallout, then move in safely without danger, like we did on the *Zenobia*. It was brilliant."

"Was?"

"He decided to destroy it."

That Marc didn't expect.

She ran her gloved finger along the page, then looked up

at him, before turning back to the book. "According to his notes, he was infected by his own virus . . . Dropped a beaker and cut his finger . . ." She paused, clearly absorbed in what she was reading. "Seventy-two hours until the onset of symptoms . . . He figured he had five days to destroy all of it before he . . . Oh my God . . . You *don't* want to die this way."

"I don't want to die period. What about the virus? *Did* he destroy it?"

"All but three vials, which went missing right before his accident. Well, two, actually. One of those three was tested on the ship, which is part of what made him change his mind . . . The devastation . . ." Her voice faded as she apparently absorbed the enormity of what she was reading. "He said it wasn't what he intended it for. He did not tell them he destroyed it. The pages run out. His notes, I mean. I assume because he died."

"So how did he destroy it?"

She got up from the desk, walked over to the windows that gave them a view into the actual lab, then pointed to a massive work bench that had instruments mounted across the surface, as well as within a metal box. "He used that. A high-intensity, ultrashort pulse titanium-sapphire laser."

He recognized that some of the instruments were used to direct laser beams. "Way too *Star Trek* for me," he said, then stilled when he thought he heard a sound in the hall. He put his finger to his lips, handed her the papers she'd given him earlier, then stepped softly toward the door. Opening it slightly, he peeked out, saw nothing. "We should really get the hell out of here."

She slipped Fedorov's journal and the papers into the thigh pocket of her fatigues, gave one last look around, then stopped suddenly. "A telephone!"

He turned from the door, saw the phone on the wall. Something about its placement bothered him. A compound this far out in the jungle probably wasn't going to have phone lines strung up somewhere. Anything beyond that would require a sat phone. He was an idiot to think they could march in here, pick up some extension on a desk, and call HQ. And the moment that thought crossed his mind, Lisette grabbed the receiver, put it to her ear, then slammed it home, recognition of what she'd done written on her face. "They answered the line," she said.

"Time to leave." Marc looked at the door to the hall. They were outmanned and outgunned, and he didn't like the odds. The other door led straight to the lab, where countless vials and beakers reminded him of the men who had bled to death from some as of yet unknown hemorrhagic virus. He didn't like those odds any better. He figured they might have a minute, maybe two. He pulled open the office door a slit, peered out, then quickly closed it. "We need to think of something and fast."

Lisette checked the lab door, found it unlocked, then took a quick visual of the room. Marc glanced in, saw several UV light units mounted on the walls. Aside from the cryogenic freezer, and the workbench with the laser, there was a stainless steel worktable and on the wall above it, glass cabinets that held even more lab equipment. Lisette closed the door, saying, "You remember that operation we worked in Morocco?"

He looked up at the drop ceiling, the large acoustic tiles, then back at her. "The one where I broke my arm?"

"At least it was your left arm."

Marc climbed up onto the desk, removed one of the tiles. "Couldn't you think of an operation where I didn't get hurt?"

No sooner had he gotten into position, the lab office door burst open, slammed into the wall, then bounced back into the side of the guard who entered first. He was quickly followed by three other men, all carrying M4s. They stopped, their guns swinging around as they checked the room. "There's no one here," the first guard said. Unlike the other guards Marc had overheard, this one spoke clear French, no Portuguese thrown in, making it easier for Marc to understand.

"Check the lab," the second guard said.

The first guard walked over, glanced into the window. He did not open the door. "There's no one there."

"Someone picked up that phone."

The first guard turned, looked at the phone, then noticed

the desk, the papers that seemed askew. He looked up, saw one of the tiles displaced slightly, swung his gun upward. "There. In the ceiling."

Marc watched the guard push the tile aside with his gun, then pop his head in after. Classic mistake. Perfect opportunity to take a head shot—had Marc actually been up there. The guard ducked, then jumped off the desk. "They must have escaped through the ceiling."

"Where does it go to?"

"The entire complex. Entrance could be made into any room."

"Entrance? Escape, you mean. We check them all."

"What about the lab? What about the virus?"

The first guard looked over. "Who would be stupid enough to go in there? If they did, it will kill them. Alvaro, you stand guard here in case they return. We'll check the other rooms."

Alvaro, the shortest of the three men looked around. "I don't like this place. Too dangerous."

"Then stand outside the door, you coward," he said, then walked out with the other guard.

Marc crouched behind the closed lab door, watching the guards in the reflection of the glass enclosed cabinets over the laboratory worktable. Alvaro waited for the other two to leave, then turned, gave the room one last look, before following them out. He did not close the door completely. Marc stood for a better view, and saw the heel of the guard's military boot just outside the office door, his position telling Marc that he was faced outward.

Marc waited several seconds, hearing nothing but the loud hum of the equipment in the lab, something he was grateful for, since it masked any movement they might have made. He motioned to Lisette, who was lying on the floor beneath the window that separated the lab from the office. Had any of them given the lab more than a cursory glance, they would've been caught. "They're gone," he whispered. "One's standing guard in the hallway."

She scooted up into a kneeling position, still keeping below the window. "I see your arm survived."

"Only because they weren't about to enter anywhere the virus might be." His arm had been broken in Morocco when they'd used the drop ceiling ruse there and he'd hidden behind a door that was kicked open. That man had died the moment he stepped in the room.

"I don't suppose you have any brilliant ideas?"

"Other than maybe coming in here to find a phone was not the best plan of action?"

She smiled. "I'll deal with armed men over snakes any day."

His return smile faded as he thought about their situation. "What we need is transportation out of here. And a bargaining chip to ensure our safety."

"As far as they know, we have a freezer *full* of bargaining chips. The virus. They have no idea he destroyed it—"

"Neither do we—"

"It doesn't do us any good if someone shoots us before we can assert our position . . ."

Marc looked over at her, then up at the glass cabinets, catching the reflection of the door where the guard stood sentinel. "Time to turn the tables," Marc said.

51

December 12
Network Compound
Brazil

Marc and Lisette waited until the sounds of the
other guards searching the rooms had faded enough to tell
them they were not an immediate threat. Marc signaled to
Lisette, then opened the lab door just enough to slip into the
outer office. His Glock in hand, he moved toward the office's
hallway door, where the one guard stood just outside. Marc
quickly sidled up to the wall, then behind the partially open
office door. When he was in position, he nodded to Lisette,
who was back in the lab watching him from the reflection of
the glass cabinets. She tossed a pen, and it clattered across
the floor. The guard shifted in the hall, but apparently didn't
hear it. Marc saw his shadow in the doorway, guessed he
might be looking into the office. Hearing no other sounds,
Marc signaled again, and this time Lisette knocked on the
wall down low. As expected the guard stepped into the room
to investigate, walking toward the lab, his M4 pointed at the
closed lab door. The moment the guard passed him, Marc
stepped out, shoved his gun in the man's back, and said in
French, "Don't move or you die."

* * *

The guard, undressed, gagged, and hands tied behind his back, was seated inside the lab, right below the window, his back to the wall. Lisette walked into the office area, while Marc, now dressed in the guard's clothes, stood watch over the man, a gun pointed at his chest. Lisette returned a moment later, purple gloves on each hand. She took a small stainless steel container that resembled a narrow propane tank, put a rack of vials inside, then closed the top.

"What are you doing?" Marc asked.

"Getting an insurance policy." Her back to them, she turned around, holding up an open vial filled with white powder. She tossed Marc a bio mask, then pulled one on herself. "Put your knees together," she told the man in French.

He shook his head no, his brown eyes narrowing with hatred.

She waved the vial in front of his face. "Do you know what this is? The same virus that killed fifteen men on that ship, men who died the same bloody and painful death that killed Dr. Fedorov. I can pour it on your face and we solve the problem. Or you can cooperate and save yourself. Now put your knees together. If you move and the powder drops, you will breathe it in and die from the virus. Do you understand?" She moved the vial closer to his face. His eyes widened. He quickly brought his knees together, and she placed the vial between them. When she let go of the glass tube, he pressed his legs together even tighter. She and Marc left the room, closing the lab door behind them. Lisette pulled off her mask and tossed it on the desk. Marc pulled off his own mask, then peered into the lab's window. The guard hadn't moved, not even to see if they were gone. His knees, however, were starting to shake. Marc walked over to Lisette's side and whispered, "You sure we won't be exposed?"

She grabbed a vial from the box on the desk, the same vials he'd seen earlier. "This is what he's holding. I took it from here. The powder you saw inside is preservative, as is the one he's holding between his knees. If he drops it, he might hyperventilate from fear, but it's completely inert. Everything else has been destroyed."

"Assuming he was successful. Unless you're counting the two missing vials. It'd be nice to know how much damage they could do in the wild."

"The ship was isolated. But if it killed everyone on board that quick, think what one vial could do in a crowded space like an airport? A week later, they're dead."

"And what do you have in there?" he said, nodding to the portable cryofreezer.

"More of the same," she said, holding up one of the inert vials. "The actual virus was in a liquid medium. You don't think I'd chance carrying around the real deal, even if there was any to be found?"

Marc peeked out into the hallway. It was, so far, empty. They stepped out, closed the door behind them, and started walking toward the main compound area. "I liked this plan better when we were just coming in for food and a phone call."

"You'll be fine," Lisette said. "As long as no one here has actually seen the real virus."

"Fine. How do we know that we won't be exposed from being in there?"

"Like I said, there are no seals on the doors. If there was anything floating around, they wouldn't need any guards. Everyone would be dead within a week of exposure."

"I feel better already."

"According to what I read, the UV rays kill it. The UV laser just works faster."

Hence the UV lights mounted everywhere in the lab and down the hallways, he figured. Even their kidnapper had mentioned that what had killed those men on the boat was no longer active. Fedorov's so-called shutoff switch must have worked. He hoped.

They walked about twenty yards to a T intersection, heard the sound of booted feet echoing down the hallway to the right. Marc and Lisette stepped out, Marc with his gun pointed toward Lisette's back. When Marc saw the two guards who had entered the lab, he held up the portable freezer, saying in French, "I found her trying to steal the virus."

The first guard stepped forward. "Who are you?"

"Marco. I just started a few days ago. Alvaro's back in the lab, guarding it in case anyone else is there. I just came in from the perimeter and found her trying to get out the door."

The fact Marc knew Alvaro's name seemed to calm any suspicions, and the guard nodded, saying, "Bring her this way."

"What about the virus?" Marc asked, lifting the freezer unit.

"You carry it."

They followed the guards to a room near the front of the compound, where Marc saw a sat phone and radio communication equipment, TV monitors of the surrounding area, as well as a switchboard, which was undoubtedly where the call came in when Lisette had picked up the phone in the lab.

Two other armed men looked up, one standing as they entered. "What is this?" he asked, his tone telling Marc immediately that they were in the presence of the man in charge. If his voice wasn't enough, the stars on his collar were. Guerrillas with rank. This one was a general.

Marc closed the door behind him, then stepped slightly away from Lisette so that his M4 was clear of her. He held up his cryo canister. "She took some virus from here."

"What?" the man said, his gaze flicking from the canister to Marc. "Who are you?"

And Marc said, "The one who is going to save you from being killed. If she dies, the vial she is holding will fall and we'll all be dead."

Lisette held up the same vial she'd shown him in the office, her finger over the open top.

"Then take her out and kill her."

Lisette held the vial even higher. "Only if you want to die with me. If anyone makes a move, I release it. I'm not afraid to die. Are you?"

The general froze, looked her right in the eye as though trying to decide if she was bluffing. And then he waved at the men to lower their weapons. "What do you want?"

"Your cooperation," she said. "To communicate to our base, then safe passage out of here."

He eyed the vial, weighing his choices. "So," the general said, looking at Marc. "It was you who killed Daron?"

"*I* did," Lisette replied.

The general's gaze narrowed ever so slightly, as he turned his attention back to Lisette. "Bring her the sat phone."

One of his men brought it to her. She didn't reach for it, saying instead, "Place it on speakerphone." He did and she gave him the number to call. McNiel answered. "It's Perrault," she said, speaking English. "We were taken prisoner on the *Zenobia*. We're in an enemy compound where the virus is being stored off the coast of Amapá, south of the *Zenobia*'s current location. We are being monitored on a sat phone."

"Understood," McNiel said.

"I have a sample of the virus and we want to go home."

"We're picking up the coordinates from the sat phone now, and they're being transmitted to the navy as we speak. They have a battleship about ten minutes by air from your coordinates. And if anyone thinks of taking advantage of that time, or anything happens to either of you, a missile strike is a hell of a lot faster. Do they understand?"

Marc looked at the general, who apparently understood every word. The man took a deep breath, telling his men in French, "Put all your weapons on the floor. You will cooperate. That is an order."

And Marc breathed his first sigh of relief since they left the stolen freighter.

52

December 12
Paris, France

The desk clerk turned a bemused eye to Sydney. "I'm sorry, madame, but I do not understand. You have a very good room."

"And now I'd like another."

"Another?"

"Yes. My husband and I have had a fight."

He gave an annoyed sigh, turned to the computer, saying, "We are booked."

"There are empty rooms on either side of ours. You said so when we checked in. Privacy, you said."

"Yes, but tomorrow the rooms are all booked. There is a big convention and every hotel in the area is booked. "

"I only need it for the one night. I'm sure we'll be over our fight by tomorrow."

"You can promise this?" he asked.

"Absolutely."

Sydney paid him, took the key, then walked toward the staircase. Once she was out of sight of the clerk, she drew the handgun from her waistband. At the top floor, she trained the weapon toward her old room, sidestepping past it, before backing to the room she'd rented. Keeping her gun aimed, she glanced at the lock, inserted the key, opened the door, then slid in. The moment she bolted it shut, she leaned against the frame, taking a deep breath.

"You can do this," she whispered, then glanced over to the window she'd come through earlier. She crossed the room, parted the curtain, looked out to the street below. No one moved about at this late hour, and she tucked the gun back into her waistband, opened the window, then stepped out onto the balcony.

The cold air hit her face, and she stood there a moment, taking deep breaths, trying to steady her nerves.

You can do this . . . She took one last look around, willing herself to remain calm. Though she had every confidence that an ATLAS extraction team would be better equipped, the very thought that Griffin could be dying on that floor kept her from waiting. And what if this hit man decided to end Griffin's life right there? Or his associate showed up?

She couldn't risk it, and with that thought, she climbed over the balustrade, then started easing her way to the third room on the right. The wrought iron was cold beneath her bare hands. Her foot slid on a bit of icy snow. She caught herself, tried to slow her breathing as she hung there. Heartbeat racing, she gripped the vibrating iron railing with her arms. Just a few more feet. Righting herself, she started forward again, then stopped outside the window. She swung one leg over the balustrade, then the other, waiting for her pulse to slow.

The drone of the TV from her room covered any other noise and she took a step closer, peered through the same slit in the curtain. He was there, seated against the headboard, his gun gripped in his right hand, resting in his lap, its barrel aimed in her general direction. He appeared to be dozing, but she couldn't be sure. On the bedside table was the bottle of brandy, and she hoped like hell he'd finished it.

She took a step forward, reached out, pushed on the window. Heard something smash on the floor inside. A trap.

He opened his eyes, raised his gun. She flung herself into the topiary.

A shot shattered one of the panes.

Sydney aimed at the window, waited, waited . . . saw him pull aside the curtain. She fired twice. Heard him fall to the ground. And still she didn't move, kept her gun aimed into the room.

Finally she pushed herself out of the topiary, stood, reached into the broken window, keeping her weapon pointed within.

He was on the floor, bleeding against the marble tile, his gun lying about a foot away from his hand. Sydney unlocked the window, had to shove it open, moving his body as she did so. The glass he'd placed on the balcony door handles as an alarm had broken on the floor, and she used her foot to shove the shards aside before stepping in.

Bose. She remembered that Carillo had said his name was Bose, and she reached down, felt for a pulse. He'd taken a shot in the chest and the gut. If he wasn't dead, he would be soon, and she moved around him, picked up his gun, then went to find Griffin.

She saw him lying on his stomach between the bed and the wall nearest the bathroom, his face slack, his skin cold and clammy and his breathing slow and shallow. His hands were cuffed behind him, and his fingertips were looking blue, which meant either the cuffs were too tight, or he was overdosing. She assumed this Bose had a cuff key, and returned to the man's side, patted his pockets, found the key on a fob in his pocket. She unlocked the cuffs on Griffin, tried to rouse him, growing more worried by the second.

She phoned Carillo. "Is Tex still with you?"

"Right here."

"Put him on." He did, and she asked, "What's the French equivalent of nine-one-one?"

"Two-one-one. Why?"

"The good news? I have Griffin, but he's out like a light. The bad news, he's turning blue, I need to get him to a hospital, and there's a dead guy on the floor of our room . . ."

"Bose is dead?"

"Assuming that's who I shot." She paused, listened, heard sirens. "I think someone already called the police."

"Syd, if the cops show up, you could both be in jail for

days until we get this sorted out. Let them take Griffin to the hospital. You get out of there."

"And what if Bose's associate shows up? Or follows us? No way am I leaving Griffin." She looked around the room, took stock of everything, imagined what the French police would make of the broken windows, the dead body, and Griffin, out cold.

"What are you going to do?"

"I'm not sure," she said, as the sirens grew louder. "But whatever it is, I better think of it fast."

53

December 12
Paris, France

"How are you feeling, monsieur?"

Griffin opened his eyes, taking in the strange surroundings, the plain white walls, the sound of something beeping in the background. "What happened?"

"You were given another dose of naloxone. The first wore off and the morphine in your system took effect once more. Do you not remember what happened?"

He remembered waking up in the ambulance finding an IV in his arm, then arriving at the hospital, but his thoughts remained fragmented as he tried to recall how he had ended up here, escaped from the hit man who'd drugged him to begin with. He focused on the young nurse, her brown hair pulled back in a ponytail, her gray eyes regarding him kindly. "I don't remember."

"Your wife said that someone attacked you?"

"Where is she?" Griffin tried to sit up, nearly pulling the IV from his hand.

"She is waiting in the lobby, monsieur," the nurse said, pushing him back down, then checking the IV to make sure he hadn't dislodged it. She rubbed her fingers over the tape, then pressed a button on a remote, raising the bed so that Griffin was sitting up. "There is someone here to see you. A priest."

Griffin's brain seemed to be moving at a snail's pace. "A priest? Was I dying?"

"Had your wife not brought you in, you very well might have." She looked toward the door, saying, "Ah, here he is now. Shall I close the door, Monsignor?"

"Merci," the priest said. Father Dumas stood facing Griffin, his hands clasped in front of him, his expression peaceful, calm, and unassuming, and looking nothing like the Vatican spy that he was.

"Where the hell is Sydney?" Griffin demanded, once the nurse stepped out.

"Monsieur Griffin. You should not agitate yourself or you will send the doctors running when they see your blood pressure," he said, walking up to the equipment, peering at the numbers beeping on the screen. "And right now we need the time to come up with your cover story."

"Did you know?"

"Know?"

"What they said. About my wife."

Dumas leaned down, one brow raised in a sardonic arch, saying softly, "Which wife are we talking about? The woman posing as your wife in the lobby who *saved* your life or the other one?"

"My *real* wife, you god—"

"Tsk, tsk." Dumas reached out, tapped the monitor, shaking his head. "You must calm yourself, Monsieur Griffin. This is not good for your blood pressure." He pulled up a chair, taking a seat next to Griffin's bed. "As I explained before, up until the moment that Tex telephoned me, asking if I could assist you with this case, I knew what you knew. I saw what you saw. And I believed what you believed. My conversation with Tex was brief, and as of yet, I still don't know the particulars regarding Becca. Is she alive?"

Griffin stared into the priest's dark eyes, trying to determine if he was telling the truth. He didn't always trust

Dumas, but at the moment he had no reason not to believe him. "You said Sydney is in the lobby?"

"She is being questioned by the police. Which is why we must quickly talk. They will be coming in to question you as soon as the doctor allows it."

"Is she okay?"

"She is fine. But my contact in the French intelligence here tells me something is going to transpire at Monsieur Luc Montel's winery, the sale of the information we seek regarding Hilliard, and having you locked up could endanger countless lives."

"Sale of what?"

"We haven't the time to go into it now. Suffice it to say that your cover story, your recollection, must match Sydney's to avoid any delays or questions about your identities if the two of you hope to get out of here and continue with what you were doing. She gave them your alias on your passport that you picked up in Winterswijk. She also had to move some evidence around in order to get you to the hospital and not have either of you considered a suspect in any way or endanger your mission."

Griffin desperately tried to remember what happened, but everything after he entered the room was a blank. "I'm listening."

"You and your wife argued. She booked the room next door. While she packed her belongings, you went for a walk. This stranger, whom you have never seen before tonight, took you at gunpoint, forced you to your room to rob you. He did not expect to see your wife standing by the balcony window and he shot at her but missed. You and he struggled for the weapon and you managed to knock it from his hands, at which time he jabbed a syringe of some drug into . . . ?" Dumas looked at Griffin in question.

"My thigh."

"Your thigh. When he came after your wife with the syringe, she grabbed his weapon from the floor, fired twice, killing him. You fell to the ground unconscious, and remember nothing else."

"And what really happened?"

Dumas was about to tell him when there was a knock at the door. He quickly stood, placed his hand on Griffin's, then raising his other in the air, made the sign of the cross as the door opened, saying, "In the name of the Father, the Son, and the Holy Spirit. Amen."

A nurse stood in the door, next to a man in his late thirties, wearing a dark suit. The police inspector, undoubtedly. Griffin turned to Dumas, said, "Thank you for the prayer, Father."

"Bless you, my son." And Dumas and the nurse left, leaving Griffin with the investigator.

54

December 12
Paris, France

Sydney paced the small lobby area, waiting while the police questioned Griffin. This death investigation was her fault. She should have waited until morning to tell Griffin about his wife. Thank God for Father Dumas. The moment Sydney called him, told him what happened, he came straightaway.

And more importantly, he didn't judge her.

Looking down the hall, she saw the priest and the nurse approaching from Griffin's room. As expected, Dumas pretended not to know Sydney, saying, "Are you the wife?"

"Yes," she said, looking from him to the nurse. "Is he okay?"

The nurse smiled. "He is doing much better, madame."

"Then he will be released soon?"

The nurse's smile turned sympathetic. "Unfortunately, no. Once the naloxone wears off, it may need to be administered again to counteract the effects of the morphine. As such, your husband must remain under close observation."

And Dumas said, "Perhaps you would like to say a prayer for his continued improvement?"

"I would," Sydney said, and he took her hands in his, as the nurse excused herself and walked off.

When she was out of earshot, Dumas said, "He really is fine. How are you?"

"Worried."

"And I expect you have had no sleep?"

"None."

"A dangerous mix. Lack of sleep and trying to deal with the Network."

"Griffin doesn't believe she could be a double agent."

"Two years ago, he thought he buried his very patriotic wife, and if I understand the situation correctly, he only just learned she was alive," Dumas replied, holding his hand out, indicating that she should follow him down the corridor to the exit. "Asking him to change his mind about her loyalties in so short a time without benefit of seeing the evidence would be hard for anyone to accept. I think the bigger question we should be asking is whether or not she is truly alive or is this all an elaborate ruse?"

"From what this Luc said in the lab about our ambush being a setup, I'd guess the latter."

He waited until two nurses making their rounds passed them in the hall before answering. "So it would seem. In the meantime, Tex informs me that the CIA is now cooperating, and will be forwarding their case files on LockeStarr."

"Including the files on Griffin's wife?"

"That remains to be seen."

55

December 12
ATLAS Headquarters
Washington, D.C.

Early the next morning, Tex sat in his office reading the report on Miles Cavanaugh's cell phone records, trying to pinpoint specifically whom Cavanaugh had been in contact with. Tex never thought the man had orchestrated this entire witch hunt for Griffin on his own, and now that they had confirmation that LockeStarr, therefore the Network, was behind Cavanaugh, it would be nice to pinpoint some of the key players. But other than the one call received from Bose when he'd had Griffin drugged, the other numbers on Cavanaugh's phone came back to prepaid throwaway cell phones. They were monitoring those numbers now. Unfortunately there had been no further activity, and Tex figured they'd been abandoned the moment Cavanaugh was murdered, undoubtedly to avoid further scrutiny.

Someone knocked on his office door. "Come in," he said.

Tony Carillo walked in, carrying a file box. He kicked the door closed behind him, crossed the room, then dropped the box on Tex's desk. "In case you run out of reading material. You look like hell, by the way."

"Not so chipper yourself."

"Yeah. I was looking for an intravenous line for my cof-feepot, but they haven't invented one yet."

"I'm sure it will come as an app for your phone real soon. What's this?"

"My files on Grogan's homicide. Figured we could cross-reference them to your LockeStarr mess and Cavanaugh's records, maybe see what matches, what doesn't. You get the files from CIA?"

Tex nodded to the boxes in front of the credenza, wonder-ing how they were going to cover everything. "Might as well pour yourself a cup. We'll be here awhile."

"What'd your boss have to say about last night's activi-ties?" Carillo asked, walking over to the coffeepot.

"He wasn't too happy to find out Griffin had been am-bushed. We find who set him up, we probably find who's behind LockeStarr."

"I think we need more coffee," Carillo said, eyeing all the boxes. "Definitely more space. You got a conference room, something with a bigger table?"

"There's one down the hall."

After he and Carillo finished carting the files to the other room, they set to work sorting the paperwork, trying to find something that stood out.

Tex refilled his coffee cup, then opened another folder and started reading. What he discovered was that a lot of the doc-uments seemed to go over what they already knew. Overlap-ping but separate investigations run by different agencies on the same entity. "Nothing like a little mutual cooperation," Tex said. "Imagine what would happen if we all worked to-gether."

"Don't even get me started," Carillo said, pulling out sev-eral of the folders from the CIA box, and spreading them out on the table. "Then again, I'm impressed that Thorndike even turned these files over to us."

"You know damned well he redacted everything he thought was too far above us."

Carillo examined the folders, his eye catching on one in

the middle. He opened it and read the single sheet within.
"Either he's turned a new leaf, or he missed one."

"Thorndike?"

"See for yourself." Carillo slid the sheet toward Tex.
"That, my friend, is the contact info for a CIA handler."

"Handler for who?"

He pointed to the name at the bottom. "Griffin's wife."

56

December 12
Paris, France

Griffin felt out of it, as though he'd been at some drunken party the night before, tired as all get-out, and needing a shower. He looked around the room, trying to remember what had happened and where he was. Hospital. France. Drug injection. Police questioning.

He pressed the button for the nurse. A tall, brown-haired woman entered about two minutes later. Apparently a shift change. He didn't recognize her. Didn't care. "I'd like to leave now."

"The doctor has not yet released you."

"Regardless, I'm ready."

"But monsieur, you should remain here, rest."

"Where's my wife?"

"I heard her say something about a meeting. She would be back afterward."

Which meant Sydney was out investigating something she shouldn't. He flung the covers off, sat up.

"Monsieur, your IV. You must be careful."

"Will I die if you release me?"

"I will get the doctor immediately."

"Thank you." Only then did he sit back, deciding he could wait a few minutes more. But apparently the nurse's idea of immediate differed from his.

Almost an hour later, the doctor showed up, taking his time reading the chart, listening to Griffin's lungs, and checking the reaction of his pupils before deciding that he would allow Griffin to be released.

The only problem Griffin failed to foresee was that he had no transportation, and even if he did, he had no idea where he should go. The hotel had been compromised, for one, never mind it was probably off limits due to the police investigation.

He sat on the bed for several minutes after he showered and dressed, until he thought to check his belongings for his cell phone. Opening the plastic bag, he saw only his wallet and some change. He'd forgotten that the phone had been confiscated by the guards last night. It was disposable, pre-paid, no great loss, and he looked at the telephone by the side of the bed, trying to remember Sydney's number, feeling as though his brain was wrapped in a fog. He couldn't remember the number and had no choice but to wait.

Eventually the nurse appeared at the door, knocking, asking if he was dressed. He told her to come in. She opened the door, revealing a wheelchair, saying, "Your wife is here, monsieur. Waiting in the lobby."

Griffin refused the wheelchair, ignoring the nurse's protests as he left his room on his own two feet.

Sydney stood when he walked into the waiting area, holding up a large cup of coffee. "*You* are an expensive date," she said. "Do you realize how much your little jaunt last night racked up on my credit card?"

"Just be glad it's coming out of Tex's budget, not yours," he said, taking the coffee, grateful for the caffeine. When they were in the parking lot, he said, "Where have you been and where's Dumas?"

"Out and waiting elsewhere. We couldn't very well have

him hanging about if we aren't supposed to have met him. Hope you're feeling back to your old self."

He looked over at her, figured she knew something. "Why?"

"We're making a little side trip. Visiting your wife's handler."

57

December 12
ATLAS Headquarters
Washington, D.C.

Tex looked up from his paperwork as Carillo walked into the room, a box of donuts in one hand, a large coffee in the other. "How's the kid doing?" Tex asked. Another ATLAS agent had brought Izzy back to HQ this morning to continue working on the computer files he'd downloaded from the Paris lab computer, and Carillo had gone up to check on him after making a donut run.

"He's doing fine," Carillo said. "But for a computer nerd, he brought up a good point. Which, in my mind, means we've got a problem."

"Bigger than backtracking two years of investigation on LockeStarr because the left hand doesn't know what the right hand's doing?"

"How about the fact that Cavanaugh was in charge of overseeing the security for the global summit? Perfect place to mount a terrorist attack." Carillo dropped the pastry box on the table, and opened it. "Sure you don't want one?"

Tex ignored the donuts, thinking about the implications. The summit started in two days. The president was supposed to make an appearance and the vice president would be attending, along with the heads of state from a number of countries in the Western world.

Not only would chaos ensue should the heads of state of other countries perish while visiting the U.S., but the residual worldwide political upheaval was bound to have a dire impact on foreign relations. A number of visiting dignitaries were from countries at *tentative* peace with the U.S. Wobbler nations, Tex called them. Anything might set them off, and the loss of their leaders, combined with the current teetering global economy, the loss of jobs, the civil unrest, would certainly redirect that blame squarely on the shoulders of the United States. And that didn't count the countries that weren't wobbling, countries that were squarely against the U.S., and waiting like vultures for the first sign of weakness in order to strike a blow. Their joining forces with the wobbler nations would be devastating to the free world.

He called McNiel, who said, "I want you and Carillo to go over *everything* with this kid. A full report, and I want it and the kid ready to brief the security task force within the hour. Lisette's already on her way to brief them on what she and Marc found."

"We'll be ready," Tex said. He hung up the phone, looked outside, staring at the dull gray clouds, trying to gather his thoughts. A terrorist attack while the summit was in session could start a global crisis beyond anything that they'd ever imagined.

An hour later, McNiel was seated at the head of the room, Thorndike on one side, Pearson on another. Careful screening, with the knowledge that there might still be a mole even though Cavanaugh was dead, led to the inclusion of the Secret Service, as well as the military, all men handpicked by McNiel and Thorndike. Tex took a seat just as Lisette appeared in the doorway, sporting several red bumps on her face, undoubtedly mosquito bites left over from her trek in the jungle.

"Gentleman," McNiel said, as she walked into the room. "Dr. Lisette Perrault."

They all stood, and General Livingston said, "I'm assuming you can shed a little light on this virus situation?"

"I'll try," she replied, then took a seat next to McNiel. The others sat as well.

"How are you doing?" McNiel asked quietly.

"A little itchy," she said. She looked over at Tex, smiled, then turned her attention to the men at the table. "What we're dealing with, General, is a chimera virus. The WHO team have identified it as a cross between blackpox and an as yet unknown virus that was cultivated from the deep sea hydrothermal vent off the Cayman Trough. It's why the AUV was stolen."

"Why modify or cross them at all?" Thorndike asked. "Isn't blackpox already a modified virus?"

"To put it quite simply, stability, predictability and the all important dispersal methods when weaponized. Not that this virus is stable, but that's why the attempt was made." She opened a file folder, passed out sheets around the table. "As I'm sure most of you know, the majority of bioweapons have failed due to inadequate dispersal methods. For instance, the heat from a bomb would kill the virus, and render it useless. Or the sun's rays would neutralize the matter within hours before it could do much harm. Assuming this is what they used on the freighter to kill the crew, whatever they crossed this with, it allowed them to control its dispersal to the crew, then rendered it harmless after so many hours, once the host is dead. We're analyzing it in the lab and comparing the results with the vial recovered in Holland, and the remnants of the destroyed virus found at the compound."

"Forgive me if this sounds ignorant, Dr. Perrault," the general said. "But if we can't do anything about it, how the hell is this going to help us?"

"Because there's still a vial outstanding. This way at least we open our eyes to the increased threat, whether a dirty bomb, powder, aerosol, or something we haven't yet discovered. We should be watching for anything suspicious that could include any of these means. We don't know the method of dispersal on the *Zenobia*, since all we found is a vial, which was lost during the mission. Regardless, you should cancel the summit until the threat is resolved."

"And what happens," the general said, "if it's already been disbursed? How contagious is this, and how soon would we know?"

"Dr. Fedorov died within a week," Lisette replied. "If it's too late, quarantine may be our best option. What I do know from the research papers I was able to recover in Brazil, once the host is dead, after seventy-two hours having been exposed to air and sunlight, the virus in its current form dies and is no longer a threat. As mentioned, it's able to withstand high heat, which makes it a tempting choice for a bioweapon."

"Can it be reproduced?" the general asked.

"We don't know enough about it, as all Fedorov's work was stolen," she replied, and Tex could read the annoyance in her eyes over the question. Here she was, trying to save lives, while the general was looking to stock his arsenal of weapons. "Other than it is very dangerous to work with once it reaches room temperature and if it becomes airborne while it is viable."

Someone else said, "Better to quarantine everyone."

"That'll go over well," Pearson said. "Welcome to the U.S., and by the way, we need to lock you in the summit hotel in case you might be contagious before you die . . ."

"If Cavanaugh weren't already dead," the general said, "I'd kill him myself. This is a political nightmare."

"If we're going to quarantine everyone, we need to spin this in the best possible light," the security adviser said.

"The summit doesn't officially start for two days," Santiago told them. "Most of those on the premises are hotel personnel, security, or the volunteers staffing the conference. With the exception of a few who came early to see the sights, the majority of dignitaries haven't even arrived yet."

"This," the general said, "is what we call a no-brainer. We shut it down. Better to piss off a few people now than a few countries later."

There was a knock on the door, and the conversation halted when Carillo and the whiz kid, Izzy, dressed in faded jeans, tennis shoes, and a frayed sweatshirt, entered. "Is this bad timing?" Carillo asked.

"Come in," McNiel said.

Izzy halted in the doorway, undoubtedly noticing the imperious stares of the high-powered men sitting around the table, all dressed in suits with power ties or military uniforms loaded with medals. Izzy elbowed Carillo to get his attention, saying a tad too loud, "These guys look like they could use some donuts. We should've brought them some."

"Trust me, Izzy," Carillo replied. "Donuts will not make them any less grumpy." Carillo directed Izzy into the room, having him sit in an empty seat next to Tex before taking a seat himself. "Go ahead and tell them what you know."

Izzy shifted in his chair. "Should I like stand or something?"

"You're fine," Carillo said.

"Uh, yeah. Well, I'm Izzy, and I, like, used to sell computers until all this happened, the senator getting shot and all. My friend and I hacked into a computer from a lab in France and that was how it got started. And then Mr. Carillo found me and asked me to help get back into the computer—" He leaned toward Carillo, whispering, "Do I tell them about breaking into the lab in France and the, uh, computer virus we planted?"

"Better to leave that kind of stuff out," Carillo replied.

"Oh. Sorry. Well," he said, directing to the room at large, "once I analyzed what we'd downloaded from the computer, I discovered that there are these chimera viruses—uh, that'd be real viruses, not computer viruses—like the one they tested on that ship. But I guess you know about that, and uh, the other two vials from the lab in Paris. One was recovered, one's still missing, and a bunch of people are gonna be killed if we don't find it before they sell it."

Everyone broke out in conversation at once, all trying to be overheard.

"Let him finish!" The general's booming voice cut through the cacophony.

"Uh, I also read something about Senator Grogan's wife? Like she was going to be sacrificed same as her husband?"

"About the virus, boy!" the general demanded. "They didn't

say where this damned virus is or who's trying to buy it?"

"It's sort of confusing. They're selling something. Port security information. The buyer's coming to some winery in France. The seller is someone named Becca?"

The room went silent. Thorndike's face drained of color as he sat back in his chair, deflated. Tex felt his own stomach twist, wondering how Griffin would take this latest blow.

"You're sure about this?" McNiel asked.

"Yeah. But I'm not sure who it was being sold to. And, uh, why they might also be selling this still missing vial at the same time, because they don't really go together, you know? Port security and a virus? I'm still analyzing the recovered data."

"For God's sake, son," the general said. "Get back to analyzing."

Izzy looked at Carillo, who said, "I think we're done here."

The two stood, then walked toward the door. The moment they left, Thorndike said, "This is beyond a political disaster."

"Let me check into it," McNiel said. "He may have interpreted something wrong."

Thorndike nodded.

It was the general who broke the tension, when he said, "That kid was selling computers before he got here?"

"And TVs," Tex said.

"Somebody hand him an application, teach him how to speak properly, and hire his ass before Microsoft swoops him up."

"What are we going to do about Senator Grogan's widow?" Santiago asked. "This sacrifice he was telling us about. I'm assuming this is the same group who took out her husband?"

"So it would seem," McNiel said.

"Regardless of what her husband was allegedly involved in," the security adviser said, "we owe her a duty of protection. In fact if I'm not mistaken, she's giving some fundraiser late this afternoon, a tea of some sort, where she's going to announce her intention to run for her husband's office. If anyone was going to place a hit on her, that would be a prime location."

And Thorndike said, "We can't just assign anyone. There

are a lot of clearance issues that we want to avoid, since we're not done with the whole LockeStarr investigation. You heard what the kid said. We've got a virus to contend with. Something that can kill who knows how many people."

"As far as clearance, we can handle it," McNiel said. "Lisette could pose as FBI."

"What about her French accent?" Thorndike asked. "Since we don't know who's trying to kill Olivia Grogan, we don't want to make anyone suspicious, especially considering the parallel operation in France."

Lisette smiled, and in a perfectly cultured Boston accent said, "Would you prefer something from the New England area?"

And so it was agreed. Lisette would pose as an FBI agent, and the discussion centered on how many agents would be needed for backup at the fund-raiser. Far better that conversation than the one no one wanted to discuss. That Becca, a CIA agent, had the stolen security data on every U.S. port and was trying to sell it.

But sell it to whom?

58

December 12
Washington, D.C.

Olivia Grogan stood at the uppermost window of her townhouse in downtown Washington, D.C. The room had been her retreat during her late husband's political career. Four floors up, it completely muffled the noise from below. She seemed better able to concentrate, and that was something she very much needed to do right now. This afternoon was the pre-summit tea, where she would make an unofficial announcement of her intent to run for her husband's now-vacant office.

A knock interrupted her thoughts. "Come in." Olivia turned to see her aide, Gerard, standing in the doorway, watching her.

"Your father's here," Gerard said.

She glanced at the clock on the mantel. It wasn't quite eleven and the tea started at two. Her father was early. As usual. "I'll be right down."

He left, and she took the moment to compose herself before following him downstairs. Her father had one goal in mind. Returning the Network to the center of the U.S. government's operations instead of the fringes where it now sat.

Her husband almost ruined it with his trying to reopen the investigation into LockeStarr. A shame he had to be killed, as she did love him in her own way. But her father would never allow a thing like love to get in the way of his plans.

His one goal was to continue the work that had started generations before.

Olivia, her father, and his before him had been a part of the Network from before World War II even, chosen by the elite powers of the time, the political and corporate dynasties that ran America. Her gaze swung to a group photo of her and her father at camp in Martha's Vineyard, surrounded by some of those very families. She well remembered those glorious summers, getting to know the other children, making connections that would serve her for the rest of her life.

It was where she first met her husband.

He was in the same photo, standing next to his father, a congressman, and her gaze rested on her husband's boyish face among the dozens of other persons who had gathered for the annual group photo. He had been a mere seven at the time, and she had been six.

Her study wall was lined with photos from every summer since then, in which she'd attended camp with her father, up until she left for college. The memories served to remind her what the true purpose of her goal was. Her husband, however, did not appear in another photo. At the time, she had assumed it was because his family had moved to the West Coast, and she gave it no further thought. At least not until their chance meeting twenty-three years later, when they'd run into each other while attending the same political fundraiser. He had recognized her, something she had found extremely charming. Unfortunately, when they'd started dating, she hadn't realized the impact his absence in those photos would have on her life, her career. Her father only knew that the elder Grogan was a solid Network man, and therefore gave his blessing to the engagement that followed.

Her father would never have allowed it had he known the truth.

Unknown to any of them was that Grogan's mother had left the embrace of the Network after her husband died of

a heart attack twenty years before Olivia's engagement.
Twenty years of outsider influence. No one could have
foreseen that his mother's decision to maintain a quiet life,
raising her children outside the circle, would have such dire
consequences. After Grogan married Olivia, everyone assumed he would return to the fold. He did not. But when
Olivia's father had suggested a quiet divorce, he'd been
overruled by the Network hierarchy.

They would use Grogan without his knowledge.

And so it was that she'd made love to him and gained his
trust. She'd steered him where needed and reported on every
move he made when she couldn't sway him. She had the
inside knowledge on backroom deals that were outside their
circle. For the Network it had been close to the best of both
worlds.

For her it had been hell.

Somewhere along the way, unexpectedly pregnant with
her first child, she'd nearly strayed from the path as she'd
started to fall in love. She wanted out, wanted to raise her
children away from the political life. Grogan was ready to
walk away from everything for her and the baby.

Her father wouldn't allow it.

He'd told her that Grogan was a wild card, and any progeny of his created more risk than benefit. One, his genes
were flawed. Two, as evidenced by her current state of mind,
she wouldn't be able to make the hard decisions necessary if
children got in the way. She terminated the pregnancy, had
her tubes tied, informed her husband she'd had a miscar-
riage, and they would try again.

He never suspected a thing, even when no children were
produced. He enjoyed the sex up until Olivia's looks started
to fade, and then he began a series of affairs.

Olivia never objected.

She was the perfect political wife.

The Network came first.

"Daddy," she said, walking into the front parlor where her
father, gray-haired and in his early seventies, sat on the
couch, waiting for her. "You look well."

He stood, and she leaned over, allowing him to kiss her cheek. "How are you?"

"Fine," she said. "A bit tired."

"I'll make this short and you can nap before you have to get ready for this afternoon."

She took a seat in the chair opposite him. The same chair she'd been sitting in the day when she'd greeted those who'd come to pay their respects after her husband's murder. The same chair she'd been sitting in when her father had come to tell her that her husband had become a liability. She took a breath, sat up straight, and waited, even though this time, she knew what he had to say. After the events of today unfolded, everyone involved in the planning and security of the summit would be removed from office, and the Network could move in quickly, quietly, presumably to clean up the mess, taking over the vacated positions that would allow them one step closer to totally controlling the government.

"It's here," he said, opening a long, thin case. He lifted a strip of gray foam, revealing more of the same, and nestled within it, a thin vial containing a cloudy substance. She reached out to touch it, and he pulled the container back. "Careful. You could get frostbite. It was frozen with dry ice for shipping."

"Will it thaw in time?"

"It'll be ready. More important, are you ready?"

59

December 12
Washington, D.C.

Carillo looked up at the elegant brick townhouse.
Old money, he thought, walking up the steps. He knocked
on the door, waited, and was about to knock again when it
suddenly opened. Olivia Grogan stood there, looking at him,
her expression one of bland patience.

"Mrs. Grogan? I'm Special Agent Carillo, FBI," he said,
holding out his credentials so that she could see them, as
well as the badge. "I was the agent assigned to your husband's homicide."

She seemed somewhat taken aback, as though not expecting to come face-to-face with anyone on the case. "Would
you like to come in?"

"Thank you."

She led him inside and to the front room. "This is my
father, Brandon Godwin."

Agent Carillo stepped forward, shook her father's hand,
saying, "Nice to meet you."

"Have you learned something in the investigation?" Brandon asked.

"Truth is, I'm here about another matter entirely. There's

no real delicate way to say this, ma'am, but is there anyone you know who might have an interest in seeing you dead?"

Olivia looked at her father, before turning her attention back to Carillo. "I—I don't understand."

"All I can really say is that we're concerned enough to ask you not to attend this affair you have planned."

And her father said, "I'm sorry. That's not possible."

"This is your daughter's life we're talking about."

"And her career."

Olivia sank into an armchair, not saying anything.

"And what," her father continued, "is the Bureau's plan if she decides to attend?"

"If it can't be avoided, we do have agents who do dignitary protection."

"How credible is this threat?" he asked.

"Very. Without going into details that could compromise our investigation, I wouldn't be here if there wasn't a good reason."

"Allow me to talk to my daughter a moment. Privately."

"Of course," Carillo said.

"Olivia?"

Grogan's widow stood and followed her father to the patio, through a set of French doors, closing them behind her. Carillo could see them talking, quietly, urgently, and wished he could hear the conversation. When they emerged a few minutes later, he fully expected Olivia's father to take the reins.

He was wrong.

"This dignitary protection?" Olivia asked. "What does it entail?"

"We assign an agent to escort you around the next few days. Where you go, the agent goes. We will have someone sitting on your house, too."

"Who would escort me? You?"

"No, ma'am. We'd assign a female agent. She can, uh, go places I can't."

"And how will I explain this—what would you call her? A shadow?"

"She can pose as your aide. Arrive when you arrive, leave when you leave."

Olivia crossed her arms, closing her eyes for a moment, then looking straight at her father. "I think this will work out fine."

"She can meet you here or at the fund-raiser this afternoon," Carillo offered.

"Here is probably best. It starts at two. Say, one o'clock? It will give us time to familiarize ourselves with each other."

"I'll drop her off here at one."

"Thank you, Agent Carillo. I so look forward to meeting her."

60

December 12
Paris, France

Sydney wished Dumas had not left, but he had an appointment that he couldn't break, which meant she was alone with Griffin, en route to see his wife's CIA handler, Reggie Carter. It wasn't that she expected Griffin to act any differently, or lash out. She just wasn't sure how to phrase it—delicately or otherwise. Somehow saying Carter might be the only one who could verify whether Griffin's wife was actually dead or alive seemed, well, harsh. Instead she said, "Are you okay to drive?"

"More than fine," he replied, and she handed him the keys, then gave him the address.

The main roads, which had been cleared and salted, were beginning to take on a gray, gritty look from the afternoon traffic. In spite of the cold, the brasseries and cafés on the Boulevard du Montparnasse were doing a thriving business. As they drove past a gothic-styled church, she glimpsed a flurry of gaudy mufflers and snowcaps—children hard at battle in a snowball war in the open *place*. Eventually the cafés and restaurants vanished, being replaced by the elegant apartments, embassies, and ministries of the Seventh Arrondissement, as the wide street transformed into the Boulevard des Invalides.

Griffin turned the car into a narrow side street, which, probably because a government ministry occupied most of the block, had been cleared of snow. He turned another corner, then pulled up in front of a discreet iron gate that fronted the courtyard of a belle époque apartment with a steep mansard roof. There was no parking out front, but plenty around the corner. They walked back to the apartment, and Griffin opened the gate, its hinges squeaking as they stepped into a narrow courtyard, flanked by a staircase on either side. They took the stairs on the left, which led up to Carter's fourth floor flat.

"Is he expecting us?" Griffin asked.

"I'm pretty sure he's not," Sydney replied.

"All the better."

"Why?" she asked, thinking he was taking this very well, considering.

"To see his reaction. Get a feel for what's going on. If he's covering up something or not. If nothing else, he'll have the answers we need."

Made sense, she thought, as they stood outside Carter's door, painted robin's egg blue.

Griffin knocked.

No answer.

He knocked again. Nothing. He tried the handle, found it locked, started to turn away, then hesitated. "You hear something?"

Sydney listened. The sound barely carried through the door. A soft buzz. "Alarm clock?" she said.

He looked at his watch. "At three in the afternoon?"

In Sydney's mind, there was only one reason someone didn't shut off an alarm. Because one had set it and left, or something prevented one from reaching it.

Griffin motioned for her to move back. Neither of them had weapons, and normally, when one broke into an apartment, one would want a gun handy.

Sydney had a sinking feeling, however, that a weapon was totally unnecessary in this instance. And as Griffin kicked

the door open, and they stepped in, then walked to the bedroom, she saw her instinct was correct. Reggie Carter, the
handler, apparently had never made it out of bed. Hard to do
when one was missing half one's brain.

Griffin hoped to find some indication of his wife's existence,
even though he knew he'd find nothing. A good handler
would never keep evidence on the premises that might jeop-
ardize him or his covert operative. Even so, Griffin made a
quick search of the bedroom, riffling through the drawers,
hoping to find something. Anything.

He carefully ran his hand around the edge of the mat-
tress, looking for a slit where one might stash paperwork
that would be overlooked in an ordinary search. Coming up
empty-handed, he eyed the corpse, figuring the guy hadn't
been dead that long. Probably killed sometime in the night.
And if there was anything? Whoever killed him probably
took it.

A professionally staged suicide, with the gun just inches
from his right hand. Someone didn't want him talking, that
much was obvious. But talking about what? That Griffin's
wife was alive or that she wasn't? Or was there something
else he knew?

A distant siren cut his thoughts short. "We better get out of
here," Griffin said. "Careful not to touch anything. You don't
want your prints coming back to this scene."

Sydney nodded, started for the door, then stopped by the
dining table, looking at something that had fallen to the
floor, the corner of ivory paper just visible beneath an antique china cabinet. She bent down, picked it up. "An invitation," she said.

Before she had a chance to examine it, Griffin looked out
the window, "I think the police are coming up here. Let's go."

She shoved the card in her pocket, then followed him from
the room. They took the back stairs, wanting to avoid running into the responding officers, and Griffin didn't relax
until they were safely back in Dumas's hotel room. It could
have been coincidence the gendarmes were called right after
their arrival. Then again, maybe not.

Dumas walked in shortly after they did. "I have news about the police investigation on the shooting in your hotel last night," he said. "It turns out the deceased would-be robber is wanted for murder in Amsterdam . . . For Faas's niece."

"His true record, or a doctored record?" Griffin asked.

"His true record. Apparently he was a little sloppy when he climbed out the window after the murder. A pack of cigarettes fell out of his pocket onto the bathroom floor. Detective Van der Lans was able to lift a print off the cellophane."

"And where does that leave the investigation here?" Griffin asked Dumas.

"My contact at the police tells me they're taking the entire affair at face value—a good thing, since your precarious medical condition precluded the luxury of waiting for a cleanup crew to come out and sterilize the scene. Sydney did a good job of ridding the place of items that might raise questions beyond the robbery scenario she'd concocted. Had the Amsterdam murder case not come out, they might look deeper. As it is, they are not."

To which Sydney replied, "The second Amsterdam suspect must be the associate that Bose talked about in his call to Cavanaugh. I wonder if he's the one who killed Becca's handler."

"Her handler is dead?" Dumas asked.

Griffin told them what they'd discovered. That was when Sydney pulled out the card she'd found on the floor, saying, "What are the chances?" She handed the paper to Griffin. "Same date, same time as marked on the calendar in the lab. And in a dead CIA agent's apartment, no less."

Griffin examined the cream-colored card, an engraved invitation to the Château d'Montel Winery. "Buyer 9 P.M." was scrawled across the top. "Hope the two of you don't have plans for the night."

61

December 12
ATLAS Headquarters
Washington, D.C.

Tex leaned back in his chair, exhausted, ready for a nap even though it was only midmorning when McNiel walked in. "You heard Carillo got Olivia Grogan to agree to a dignitary escort?" Tex asked.

"Good," McNiel said. "What about Griffin? You have an update yet?"

"Sydney said he was out of the hospital, and they were going to follow up on a lead."

"What lead?"

"I gave Dumas the information on Becca's handler. They're going to pay him a visit, if they haven't already. That should at least verify if she really is a working asset and not a figment of someone's imagination, resurrected from the dead for the sole purpose of leading us like lambs to the slaughter."

"I hope not. Thorndike's last contact with her handler was that LockeStarr had lined up a buyer for their port security data that had been stolen. He was counting on Becca to recover it before it could be sold. Now he's wondering if even that information is suspect. If she really did steal that virus, it's hard to imagine she'd be procuring the port security data to bring to us."

"You think she was working a double deal? Procure the data and sell it *and* the virus to the same buyer?"

"I have no idea what to think. No one's seen or heard from her that we know of, and there's only Thorndike's word that she's alive, and even that has only been through her handler."

"What about the witness and the sketch?" Tex asked. "Petra's description was on the money."

"Petra? As far as we know, she was part of it and they killed her in case anyone got to her. Or maybe she merely saw someone who looks like Becca—a double they arranged to make it look good. Like the ambush at the French lab, this whole thing could be a setup."

"You believe that?"

"I'm not sure what to believe anymore." McNiel sat, leaning his head on the back of the chair, clearly as frustrated as Tex was about all this. "The one thought I keep coming back to is what if it is her?"

"That presents a whole new set of problems. I've run it every which way. Let's say she's innocent. On the one hand, she and Griffin were getting divorced, so it's not like she needed to ask Griff for permission to take on this assignment. On the other, playing dead without telling your spouse, even if it is for the good of your country—well, it's pretty damned low no matter how you spin it. But espionage? I just can't see her guilty of that. Not the Becca I knew."

"Thorndike and I both looked at the information Izzy culled from that computer," McNiel said. "It's pretty damning. If she is alive, Thorndike wants her brought in. He can't depend on her for recovering the port security data from Luc Montel before he sells it. And that's assuming she's even on our side."

Tex's phone rang. He picked it up. "*Washington Recorder.*"

"Tex?"

"Griff. Glad to hear you're okay," Tex said, dreading the conversation he knew was to come. "McNiel's here. I'm putting you on speakerphone." Tex pressed the button, then dropped the phone in the cradle.

"Griffin," McNiel said. "How are you feeling?"

"I've had better nights. I'll get right to the point. The CIA handler? He's dead." Griffin told them what they'd found, including the invitation. "It may have something to do with Becca."

McNiel was silent for several seconds, then, "Look, Griffin. There's no good way to tell you this. Thorndike gave the order to bring Becca in."

"She's alive then?"

"He has *no* idea. If she is, he wants her in custody. At all costs. There's evidence that she stole the virus from Hilliard's lab and sold it. We're not sure to whom, but it's pretty damning. I saw it myself."

"How can you believe that? Who would she even sell it to?"

"Possibly the same buyer to whom Luc intends on selling that port security data. It needs to be recovered at all costs. Thorndike's asked for our help on that."

"When's the sale supposed to take place?"

"Tonight. At Luc's estate in France."

"That would explain the invitation we found in the handler's apartment."

"Normally I wouldn't ask this, but we're out of options and time. I need you to run it. You're the closest agent and you know all the particulars."

There was a long pause on the other end.

And McNiel said, "It'll be hard, but I can send another team, Griffin. It doesn't have to be you."

"No."

"After last night, you have to consider this may be a setup."

"Can we take a chance that it isn't?"

"No." McNiel visibly relaxed, probably thinking that Griffin was taking this extremely well. Tex wasn't fooled. He knew Griffin. "How many men do you need? It may be tough to get anyone there, given the short time frame."

"Two should suffice. Between them, Dumas, and Fitzpatrick, we can pull this off."

"Fitzpatrick is out. Pearson wants her off the case and home."

"I'll let her know, but she tends to be stubborn about these sorts of things."

"You let anything happen to her and we'll be cleaning the latrines for Pearson over at HQ. You do *not* want to work for me if that happens. Are we clear?"

"Very."

"Fine." McNiel looked at his watch. "I'll let Thorndike know about his handler. Keep me informed. And I want updates to Tex every hour."

"Yes, sir."

Tex picked up the phone after McNiel left, saying, "Griff. I'm sorry about Becca. I mean, if it turns out— It's not like she knew you'd be going out on it, right?"

"What am I supposed to believe?"

"What I want to believe. That if she is alive, she's still one of us."

"I'll let you know if that holds true," he said, his voice terse. "Call you in an hour."

Griffin disconnected, and Tex listened to the dial tone, thinking—hoping like hell—that if Becca was alive, she had not crossed over. Because if she had, if anything happened to Griffin because of her being a double agent, he'd fly over there and kill her himself.

62

December 12
Washington, D.C.

Olivia tucked the tube of lip gloss into her clutch purse, heard it clink against the small bottle of perfume, then snapped it shut. She did not, however, immediately get up from the cushioned stool in front of the mirror, instead she remained there, staring at her reflection for several seconds, fingering her short locks of gray. She'd wanted to color it years ago, but her father insisted that gray hair on a woman of her stature and beauty would be translated as intelligence and wisdom. He'd been right, of course, but it didn't stem the small streak of vanity running through her, thinking that had she colored it back then, she might have a list of lovers as long as her late husband's had been. Then again, maybe not. She'd put the Network's needs above her own for so long, she wasn't sure she'd even know what to do if she had a strange man in her bed.

Though an hour away from the actual event, her father was downstairs, and insisted on remaining until after the FBI agent arrived. He hadn't been happy about the arrangements, but then, there was really nothing they could do.

If either of them wanted this plan to succeed, they had no choice but to cooperate.

Standing, she turned in front of the mirror, deciding that the knee-length black velvet gown with its white collar lent the right amount of sophistication and conservatism to someone who had only recently lost her husband, all without detracting from her looks. Satisfied, she left her dressing room and went downstairs to where her father waited.

He was smoking a cigar on the patio. She opened the French doors, the pungent scent of smoke wafting in with the cold air. "You seem calm."

"I am," he said. "I have every confidence you'll be able to pull this off."

"Even with an FBI agent trailing my every move?"

"That's what makes this plan so beautiful. She'll be so busy looking out for who might be trying to kill you, by the time she realizes what's going on, it'll be too late."

63

December 12
Paris, France

Sydney occupied herself watching TV after Dumas left to get intel on the dead CIA agent, even though what she wanted to do was talk to Griffin about his wife. Not that she dared broach the subject as he sat at the desk, working at the computer, trying to find something on the found invitation that might help them. And so she flicked through the TV channels, unable to understand a word of the rapid French, trying to be as inconspicuous as possible for Griffin's sake. He might not be showing any outward signs of turmoil, but this entire operation had to be tearing him up, as evidenced by last night when he'd stormed from the room on hearing of his wife's activities. And that was when Becca was only *suspected* of espionage. Now they'd moved beyond mere suspicion and wanted her brought in.

Emotional involvement was never a good mix with any sort of operation, and were she in charge of this, she would have removed Griffin from the team.

But Syd wasn't in charge. And all she could do was be here for him, much as he'd been there for her in Rome when she'd been trying to find out who'd killed her friend.

Besides, there was more to this case than met the eye, the most important fact being that no one they knew had actually *seen* Becca, and the one man who allegedly had was now dead. So who killed him? Becca to cover her tracks? Or someone else to cover that Becca was never present to begin with? Sydney turned on the bed, propping her head up on her hand, noting the determined look on Griffin's face as he concentrated on the computer screen. "I can't help thinking this is a setup. That she's not really going to be there."

He looked at her in the mirror over the desk. "I intend to find out."

She waited. He offered nothing further, and though she wanted to ask him what he'd do when—if—he saw her, she didn't have the guts. What did one say to the spouse you thought had been dead the past couple years? *You're looking good . . . by the way, you still want that divorce?*

And that brought up another thought, one she didn't want to look at too closely. Was Griffin still in love with Becca?

A selfish question, she knew, and one she was saved from examining when Griffin said, "I think we can stop wondering if this invitation is legit."

Sydney sat up as he turned the computer screen her way, reading the text.

"'Luc Montel, head of Hilliard and Sons Laboratories, Paris Division, will be present tonight at the Château d'Montel winery.' Apparently Luc owns the winery and is sponsoring the dinner. A gesture of goodwill among the movers and shakers who make viruses and vaccines. And with them, according to this list, will be a number of foreign and national dignitaries."

"We have one invitation and four agents. They're bound to check IDs at the door, Griffin."

"I'm sure they will, which means the invitation is useless, other than it confirms where we're going. With the dignitaries listed here, they'll undoubtedly be screening for weapons. But if a couple inept socialites can crash the White House, two spies have an equally good chance of crashing a ball."

"You realize I'm not a spy?"

He cocked an eyebrow at her. "We'll make one out of you yet."

"Before you start converting me, we've got to hit the stores if we're going to blend in with the haute couture."

Dumas returned right about the same time they did from their shopping trip. "I've checked with some of my sources about the dead CIA handler," he told Griffin as Sydney hung up her dress. "No one knew he was here, in an official capacity or otherwise, though his lease shows he'd been living in the flat for the last two years."

"Which fits with when my wife allegedly arrived in France."

"Perhaps," Dumas said. "But forgive me for voicing my concern in that he met his demise right after this article in the American papers came out about the double agent."

Several heartbeats passed while Sydney waited to hear Griffin's response.

"I know," was all Griffin said, and she actually breathed a sigh of relief. No storming from the room, no outward sign of anger.

Even so, as Sydney readied herself for the operation, she hoped this entire thing *had* been an elaborate setup to make Griffin think his wife was still alive. For all his calmness, she wasn't sure what he might do if he actually ran into her tonight and confirmed that she was a double agent.

They'd soon find out, she thought, as someone knocked on the hotel room door.

Dumas got up to answer it. "That should be the support team that Tex was able to round up." He slid back his chair, stood, then walked to the door, peering out the peephole before opening it. "Come in, gentlemen."

Giustino, an Italian *carabinieri* agent who often worked with ATLAS, and Donovan Archer, an American agent, walked in, both dressed in tuxedos. "Heard you might need a little assistance," Donovan said, slapping Griffin on the shoulder.

"They scrape the bottom of the barrel to bring you two here?" Griffin asked.

Donovan grinned. "I just finished an operation in Germany with Giustino when the call came in that you needed help." He looked over at Sydney. "Ah, the prodigal Sydney Fitzpatrick that Giustino has told me about," Donovan said, holding out his hand to her. "Donovan Archer."

"Nice to meet you," Sydney said, shaking hands. She turned her attention to Giustino. "It's good to see you again, Giustino. How are you?"

"*Molto bene, grazie,*" he said, walking up and giving her a kiss on both cheeks. "And you are even more beautiful than the last time. You must come back to Italy, yes?"

She smiled. "One day."

Griffin eyed the two men. "Aren't you a bit overdressed for being the support team?"

Giustino shrugged. "You were going to crack the safe yourself?"

"Good point." Griffin had cracked a few in his time, but Giustino was the expert. "If this is a setup of some sort, the faster we're in and out, the better. Right now, the biggest problem I foresee will be getting in with four weapons. The newspaper mentioned enhanced security because of the stature of some of the guests—though I have a feeling Luc may have invited them just to beef up security and not have it noticed. Especially if he'd always intended to make the sale there."

"So what do you suggest?" Giustino asked.

It was Dumas who came up with the answer. "The bakery supplying the dessert is right here in Paris. One of the oldest and most respected, and it closes very early, so there will be no one on the premises."

"And how will that help us?" Griffin said.

"A baker with access to the château's kitchen has a better chance of smuggling in weapons than gate crashers through the front door. And this bakery has several vans. They won't be using all of them tonight."

"What happened to 'Thou shalt not steal'?"

"Since you will be borrowing it for the greater good, when you have finished, an offering in the proper amount to the proper charity will help."

* * *

Stealing the van appeared to be the easy part. Dumas dropped them off at the back of the bakery, then waited just up the alley as a lookout. There were four parking spaces and three delivery vans. Griffin wasn't sure if that was good news or bad that maybe the fourth spot belonged to the van delivering the dessert to the winery. He only hoped it didn't return while they were still in the lot.

"Wait here," Griffin said. Sydney stood by the back door while he broke into the bakery, found a set of keys, one of three, hanging on a rack on the wall in the office. He started out, when his eye caught on the laundry room off the rear entrance. Just inside, he saw two bins, one filled with dirty towels, the other with white jackets and pants, all waiting for the laundry service. Griffin dug through the bin, found four fairly clean sets, then left.

Outside, he tossed Sydney the clothes, fumbled with the keys, hoping it was for the van on the far side, since that would be less obvious to anyone walking into the lot. Fate intervened. The keys belonged to the van closest to the door. He unlocked it, they got in, and he was just about to turn the key in the ignition when the fourth delivery van turned in.

"Duck," he said, reaching over, pulling her down.

From just over the top of the dash, he saw the van park, and the driver, dressed in the white uniform like those in the laundry room, got out. He walked up to the back door, using his key to get in. Griffin hoped he wasn't planning on staying long, because the last thing Griffin wanted to do was start up the van while the guy was inside. Thankfully, he was only inside about two minutes before he came out, pulling the door shut behind him. He did not, however, leave, but stood there on the back stoop, smoking a cigarette.

"Damn," Griffin whispered, drawing his gun.

"What's happening?" Sydney asked.

"He's smoking. I don't know if that means he's going back inside when he's done or what."

The man finished his cigarette, tossed it, then happened to glance down. Judging from the look of suspicion on his face, he undoubtedly noticed the footprints in the snow leading to the van Griffin and Sydney were hiding in. He stepped off the porch, started following the trail, at the same time pulling out a cell phone.

Griffin slid down even further. Too late.

"Hey! What are you doing in there?"

A car honked from the alley behind them, and Father Dumas called out, "Monsieur! Can you tell me how to get to Saint-Pierre-de-Montrouge?"

The bakery employee hesitated. Griffin threw open the door and hit him over the head with the butt of his gun.

"Was that necessary?" Dumas asked, getting out of the car to assist.

"A lot easier than trying to explain why we were *borrowing* his van. Help me tie him up and get him inside."

"This will probably take a larger donation," Dumas said, eyeing the man as they lifted him from the ground.

"If it goes by actions taken, Father, I owe a lot more than I'm worth."

64

December 12
ATLAS Headquarters
Washington, D.C.

"All right, listen up!" McNiel stood at the head of the room, waiting for the group of agents to quit talking. "In a few minutes, we'll start reviewing our dignitary protection for Senator Grogan's widow, Olivia. Tex has the op plans. Take a look, familiarize yourself with the players, then we'll get started."

Tex passed out the copies to the five ATLAS agents who were assigned to the operation, including Marc di Luca. When Lisette walked in wearing a blue dress that fit her curves to perfection, Marc's jaw seemed to drop, and Tex had to wave the op plan in front of Marc's face to get his attention. "Down, boy," Tex said.

"Where's she going to hide her gun?" Marc asked.

"We're working on it. Read your plan."

Tex took a seat next to Marc, and McNiel said, "If you notice, you have two packets. The first one is eyes-only, numbered, and needs to be returned before you exit. It's highly classified and we don't want anyone leaving it on their desks, in their cars or the men's room. Second packet has all your emergency contact numbers, call signs and op plans should this turn into a medical emergency. Eyes-only packet, second page, please."

Robert Ennis raised his hand. "Isn't this sort of overkill for a simple dignitary protection that one or two FBI agents could handle?"

"Under normal circumstances," McNiel replied, "it would be. If you follow along on the op plan, you'll see why we're taking this threat very seriously. Olivia Grogan's name came up as a potential victim by the same crew suspected of killing her husband."

"You mean LockeStarr?"

"Exactly. Since we don't have the available FBI agents with proper clearance, we're having Lisette Perrault pose as FBI Agent Lise Pera. Since she'll be wired, you'll be able to hear her when she's out of visual. Her emergency code phrase will be 'I can really use a drink,' and failing audio, she'll grab a glass of champagne. Any questions?"

"How long will we be watching Grogan's widow for?" Ennis asked. He was standing in the back of the room, leaning against the wall.

"For as many days as it takes to determine the threat and resolve it. After today, we'll be cutting down the number of required agents to two per shift. Any more questions?"

McNiel looked around the room. No one had any, and so he continued on, saying, "We've set up a security checkpoint at the entrance, a slight and unexpected inconvenience for the guests, but better a metal detector than a dead senator's dead wife. Stevens and Gerard will be stationed just outside the entrance. If someone suddenly decides they don't want to pass through the metal detector, I want that person stopped and detained. The remainder of you will be working inside, some as waiters, others as standard security. Any questions?"

"Basic security work," Ennis said. "Piece of cake."

65

December 12
Paris, France

Ten minutes later than they'd planned, they were on their way to the château at the winery, Griffin at the wheel, Sydney riding shotgun, Giustino and Donovan in the back of the catering van. They'd left the hapless employee tied and trussed beside the laundry bin at the bakery, which meant he'd be found by morning at the latest. Father Dumas had driven ahead. He'd remain on the perimeter of town, should they need him, and would call the police as a last resort—last, because not only were they supposed to take Becca into custody, should they find her, but there was still an international warrant for Griffin's arrest. Warrant or not, Griffin had no idea what they were heading into, but he'd decided it was far better for him to be arrested than for harm to come to the others.

After they'd been on the road for some time, they hit a patch of rough asphalt, and the two cases of whipped cream started rattling around. Griffin glanced back to make sure they hadn't tipped over. Giustino, however, had his arm across both boxes, keeping them safe. Beneath the cans, and hidden with a false cardboard bottom, were their weapons, two in each box, as well as all the cell phones, with the exception of Griffin's.

Sydney looked over at him. "You really think this whipped cream idea is going to fly? Not exactly gourmet, considering the reputation of the bakery."

"They're metal," he said. "At least that way if they're screening the kitchen help, the cans will cover the guns from a metal detector."

"Yeah. It's convincing them that we should all be allowed inside with cans of whip cream that has me concerned. We'd have the real deal, thick, decadent fresh cream in a pastry bag, not grocery store stuff. We're supposed to work for a bakery. One of the finest."

"Wing it, Fitzpatrick."

"Easy for you to say. At least you speak French."

Although a several-days accumulation of snow had settled onto the countryside, a touch of burnt orange peeked through the thick bank of clouds on the horizon with the setting sun. As the car sped along the corniche overlooking the Loire River, graced by Renaissance châteaus on the opposite bank, a brief flurry of tiny snowflakes whirled about, melting as soon as they hit the windshield, and, thankfully, the road.

A few minutes later, they crested the hill. Griffin caught sight of the château's roofline in the distance with its steep gables and turrets. He'd heard the turrets had been added within the past decade to give it a castlelike appearance to match the illustration on the winery's label. "There it is," he said, pointing.

"That's a mansion," Sydney said. "Not a château."

And Giustino said, "Delusions of grandeur, *si*?"

"You think we can pull this off?" Sydney asked Griffin.

"Getting in? Yes. Finding out what it is we need to find? That remains to be seen."

No one said a word after that, but he knew they were all thinking the same thing. Would they find any information on Becca and what had happened to her?

Part of him wanted her to be alive, the part that felt no one should die the way he believed she had, by explosion, burned beyond recognition. It was the darker part of him that he didn't want to examine too closely. The part that demanded answers for all the questions he had if she really was alive. The part that said if she'd turned on her country, on him, on everything they'd believed in, then she was better off dead. He was grateful when his cell phone rang, not wanting to continue the direction of his thoughts.

Father Dumas was on the other end. "You're not going to believe this. Luc just passed me on the road, going the opposite direction."

"Looks like he's not taking any chances, and he's picking up the buyer in person."

"That should make it easier for you to get into his office."

Griffin hoped. Of course there was always the possibility that Luc had taken the port security information with him, was going to sell it in person, but somehow he doubted it. Too dangerous. "We're almost there. If you don't hear from us in two hours, call the police."

They crossed the bridge, then drove along a narrow road that meandered through rolling hills covered with acres of barren grapevines dusted with snow, and Sydney was glad the trip was nearly over. Griffin slowed the van at the entrance, where two men stood guard at the gatehouse. He conversed with them in rapid French, making Sydney wish she had mastered languages in college in addition to criminal justice. The gate opened, and the guard waved them through.

"What'd you tell him?" Sydney asked.

"There was a problem with the dessert, and we were there to inspect it."

"What was the problem you came up with?"

"He didn't ask, I didn't say."

Good enough for her, she thought, as Griffin continued down the hill toward the château, where lights blazed from the tall windows of the *première étage*.

Griffin pulled around to the service entrance, which was located in one of the turreted additions, parking far enough from the building to allow them some concealment in the van. He handed his cell phone to Giustino, who hid it in the false bottom of the box beneath the whipped cream. "You both understand," Griffin said, "that if anything happens, if anything goes wrong, your first priority is to get Sydney out. That's an order."

"Understood, *amico mio*," Giustino replied, and Donovan nodded. Everyone but Donovan got out, since he'd be waiting at the wheel, ready to take off at a moment's notice should they need a quick getaway. Griffin and Giustino each carried one of the boxes, and Sydney followed them across the drive to the pseudo-gothic entrance. The men wore their dress clothes beneath the white catering uniforms, their polished black shoes looking as out of place as Sydney's Prada heels did beneath hers. She only hoped her dress wouldn't be too wrinkled after being stuffed beneath the white smock and pants. The guard didn't seem to notice their shoes or her bulky uniform, merely glancing at their identity papers, which assured him that they had indeed come from Le Pâtisserie de la Cité, one of Paris's most notable confectioners.

Again, Sydney wasn't able to understand the conversation. She was, however, able to see that getting inside wasn't going to be as easy as getting through the gate. "What's wrong?" she asked Griffin in a low voice.

"The guard said we're not on the list. Giustino is telling him that it was an oversight, as we are supposed to fix the dessert, due to a mistake."

Giustino set his box of whipped cream down, still arguing with the guard. Sydney didn't need to understand French to recognize the swearwords thrown in, as Griffin whispered, "The guard wants to know what is wrong with the whipped cream already on the dessert."

"Salmonella," Sydney said aloud.

Both men stopped talking at once. Turned toward her. She held up her hand, looking at Griffin, and nodding at the guard, indicating he needed to take that conversation and run with it. "Salmonella," he repeated. And whatever he said next was far too fast for her to understand.

The guard looked at each of them in turn. "*Très bon*," he said, then took a handheld metal detector, indicating that they would all submit to a search.

Giustino held up his hands, the guard ran the wand over

him. When he finished, Giustino picked up the box of whipped cream, started for the door. The guard stopped him, demanded something, and Giustino held the box for him to inspect. The man pulled out a can, popped off the top, sprayed some cream from it onto the lid, smelled it, then dropped it back into the box, motioning for Giustino to step through. He then did the same to Griffin, checked his box, waved him through. He stopped Sydney, however—not because of her dress shoes, which didn't seem to faze him, but because of the black purse, an evening bag with a metal chain, hanging from her shoulder. Unfortunately, he didn't like that she brought a purse, as he pointed to it, demanding something, what, she didn't know.

Everyone paused, looking at her, as though waiting for some response. She had no idea what to say or what was expected of her, and her heart started beating faster. She'd chosen the purse specifically because the chain strap was sturdy enough to carry the weight of her gun and the fake alligator was shiny, giving it a dressy appearance. At the moment, it was actually empty, except for the piece of cardboard rolled inside, inserted to conceal the gun once she put it in there, and to reinforce the thin leather. If he looked inside, found it empty, saw the cardboard, he might think it suspicious. Who knew? Unfortunately, every French word she could think of had to do with food.

Until she recalled something she'd heard years ago. One word that was the same in French as it was in English.

"Tampons." She smiled.

The guard's hand stilled as he was about to open it. He gave a curt nod, ran the wand over her, then waved her in. She looked at Griffin, smiled, then mouthed, *Winging it*, as she followed him in.

A minute later the four walked down a hallway up the circular stone stairs, then entered the huge stone kitchen of the château, where several white-coated men stood working feverishly at the stainless steel counter. One, wearing a chef's hat, looked over, saw them, and started yelling.

Giustino responded, holding up his box, and the two argued. It was only then that Sydney realized that dinner had not only been already served, but the waiters were clearing the dishes, dumping them into large plastic bins. The napoleons were already plated, and were being placed onto serving trays. Sydney couldn't imagine spraying store-bought whipped cream over them, even if such a dessert called for that topping, which this one did not. Apparently the chef thought the same, as he continued arguing with Giustino, then pointed to somewhere beyond the brick oven where a fire burned, presumably telling him where the refrigerator was and to remove the offending ingredients from his sight.

They followed Giustino past the fire, the intense heat warming Sydney's skin. Beyond that stood several stainless steel racks filled with various utensils and cookware. The walk-in refrigerator was just around the corner in one direction, the other way led down another hall, presumably to the main rooms. The four entered the refrigerator, where Donovan and Giustino removed the weapons and phones from the whipped cream boxes.

"What was that all about?" Sydney asked, dropping her gun and phone in her purse, then stepping out of the white uniform, before smoothing out her black velvet Yves Saint Laurent gown, which had taken on the appearance of crushed velvet in some spots.

"He said he would flay us all if we dared touch the dessert with that topping. And who could blame him?" he said, stashing his uniform behind a box of lettuce heads. "I told him it was merely being brought in for an emergency, should the cream filling fail."

Griffin kept an eye on the kitchen, then motioned for Giustino to precede them. "Dumas will inform us once Luc arrives at the train station to meet his buyer. You have thirty minutes to find his office, get into that safe and out of here," Griffin said. "I'll text updates. If there is an emergency, I'll call."

Giustino patted the phone in his pocket, then left.

She and Griffin followed shortly.

"Ready?" he asked her.

"Ready," she said.

They stepped through the doors where they were confronted by the back of a large wide Chinese screen, designed to better conceal the comings and goings of the servants from Montel's guests in the grand salon. On the other side of the screen was a raised platform where a string quintet was playing Schubert. The interior of the château belied its simple eighteenth-century exterior. The parquetry floor of the long salon had been buffed to a glossy sheen that almost mirrored the guests in their chic formal attire. On the spaces between the tall, velvet-draped windows, portraits of purported Montel ancestors alternated with genuine Aubusson tapestries in which muted shades of rose, blue, and green predominated. Their exquisite workmanship, undoubtedly taken for granted by Montel's guests, displayed the recurrent theme of the god Dionysus and his drunken coterie of maenads and satyrs—the only subtle reference to the Montel *vins d'époque*. From the ceiling, which had maintained its pristine simplicity, hung great crystal and ormolu chandeliers. Their myriad glittering faceted pendants reflected the diamond tiaras and jewels that adorned the haute couture satins and velvets of Montel's female guests.

Griffin took Sydney by the arm, escorting her into the grand salon, and when she looked at him, he was the epitome of calm. "What if Luc returns before we get out?"

"He's not expecting us," Griffin said. "People see what they want to see."

"And if he does notice us?"

"We cross that bridge when we come to it," Griffin replied, grabbing two flutes of champagne from a passing waiter, then handing one to Sydney. "Give me a minute to find a party to blend into."

He left her to wander through the guests, pausing beside a group of people, listening to their conversation before moving on, finally stepping into a circle, shaking hands with a middle-aged man and then the woman standing next to him. He finally looked over at her, waving to have her join him, and she realized just how smooth he was in this environment. Much better than she'd been back in Italy, when she'd had to attempt the same with Tex. The moment she arrived, Griffin took her by the hand, saying, "You remember Mr. and Mrs. Johnson, darling?"

"Milan, wasn't it?" Sydney replied, smiling warmly.

"No," Mrs. Johnson said. "We haven't been there in years. Maybe Copenhagen? The pharmaceutical convention?"

"Of course," Sydney replied. "I remember, because the dress you wore was stunning."

"Vintage. I'm not sure I will *ever* again pay retail for a gown I can wear only once," she said, as Griffin and Mr. Johnson wandered off, apparently to join a new group. But when Sydney would have followed, Mrs. Johnson placed her hand on Sydney's arm, stopping her, as she whispered, "I really need a mint before I go in there. A strong one," she said, opening up her rhinestone-edged evening bag. "Dinner was fantastic, but far too much garlic. Damn. Please tell me I didn't leave them in the car."

While the woman searched through her purse, Sydney glanced up, surprised by how far Griffin and the group he'd latched on to had traveled. *Look up*, she wanted to shout. He didn't seem to notice he'd left her behind, and she hid her momentary panic at being separated. Be calm, she told herself. She could do this, act the part of the high-society girl. After all, she'd succeeded this far.

"You don't have any mints, do you?" the woman asked, as the quintet started a new piece and several couples gravitated to the dance floor.

"Perhaps my husband does." She managed to guide the woman over to where the men stood talking, and then she linked her arm through Griffin's, vowing not to lose him again. All she needed to do was play the socialite for the next hour while Giustino found Luc's office and the safe. An easy job, she thought, with little that could go wrong. And as she scanned the room, her gaze landed on a woman at the far side, her short dark hair bouncing in the light as she laughed at something someone said. In that moment, Sydney realized there was a lot more that could go wrong. The woman in the sketch. Griffin's wife, Becca. The woman they were told to bring in at all costs.

Griffin tensed beside Sydney. "Wait here," he said, then started in that direction.

66

December 12
ATLAS Headquarters
Washington, D.C.

Tex walked into the conference room where Carillo was still working. "You sure you don't want to go out on this?"

"Trust me," Carillo replied. "I wouldn't be an asset. First hoity-toity schmuck that made a complaint would find a tray of hors d'oeuvres dumped in his lap. My time's better spent here, doing what I do best."

"Eating stale donuts?" Tex said, nodding at the box from this morning which was nearly empty.

"Sorting through old paperwork, connecting the dots. I'll probably go get a couple sandwiches, bring one to the computer room where Izzy's working." Carillo looked up from his paperwork. "Your guys grumbling about being assigned to dignitary protection?"

"They'll get over it. It's good to have a few quiet jobs every now and then." Carillo's attention shifted back to the paper he held. "What is it?" Tex asked.

"The list of numbers the CIA thinks are tied to Locke-

Starr but can't pin down. I'm pretty sure I've seen this phone number before. I swear I had it in my hand not five minutes ago." Carillo started digging through other folders, sorting through the papers at a lightning pace. "Here," he said, holding up a sheet. "Cavanaugh's phone. Damned number was on *Cavanaugh's* phone."

"Guess that links Cavanaugh to LockeStarr," Tex said. "As if there was any doubt."

"I swear I saw it somewhere else . . ."

Tex turned a dubious eye to the mountain of papers, then walked to the door. "I'll be upstairs monitoring the operation if you need anything."

"Yeah. Have fun," Carillo said, flipping through the files. "Where the hell did I see that number . . . ?"

Carillo finally found the document he was searching for. The list of calls from Senator Grogan's Washington, D.C., office. He scanned the numbers, finding it second from the bottom. Second to the last call Grogan received at his office . . . "Right before he was killed," Carillo said, then dug out his notes. He'd checked the number before, but hadn't been able to cross-reference it to anyone, and so he'd marked it for follow-up.

And now he knew it was linked to LockeStarr.

Carillo leaned back in his chair, staring at the list. What didn't make sense was why someone from LockeStarr would be calling on the public line . . . Not if Grogan was part of LockeStarr. They'd be calling his cell, cut out the middleman, which in this case would be Grogan's secretary . . .

He checked the record of received calls from Grogan's cell phone. The number was nowhere to be found . . .

"Hell," Carillo said, sitting up and reaching for the file box with Grogan's murder case. He dug through the box, pulling out a thick black binder that contained the Grogan murder investigation. He scanned the pages, found the passage he knew would be present, but wanted to verify, because his memory wasn't adding up to what the evidence showed. But no, it was there, just as he recalled. The statement from the secretary, reporting that nothing unusual occurred before

Grogan left for his speech the day of his murder. He had only two calls. His wife to wish him luck and his aide to tell him his car was waiting.

He looked at the numbers, realized the one that *should* be there wasn't.

But memories were faulty, so he looked up the secretary's number from the report and called her. "Hate to bother you again," he said after identifying himself. "I've got a couple more questions about those phone calls the investigators talked to you about."

"Phone calls?" she repeated.

"Yeah. The last few before the senator left for his speech. Just trying to cross-reference them to our list. You told the detective that the senator's wife called right before he left . . . ?"

"That's right. They spoke together for several minutes."

"Several minutes?"

"Something like that. And then his aide called to say his car was ready."

"How sure are you about the order of these calls? That it was his wife who called right then?"

"Very sure. I recognized her voice and she asked how I was doing before I transferred it over. And then when his aide called, I remember the senator telling her, um, that he loved her . . . before he hung up."

The girl's voice shook, and Carillo had a faint recollection of someone mentioning that she and the senator had been having an affair. Had to hurt to know his last words were for his wife. "Thanks for your help," he said. "If you remember anything else, you have my card."

He disconnected, staring at the sheet with the list of CIA numbers, coming back to LockeStarr. And then he looked at the now identified number on Grogan's public line. A dead match.

Carillo walked down the hall, where Izzy sat working the analysis on the computer data. "How sure are you about Olivia Grogan being hit?"

"Hit?"

"Bumped off. Killed."

"Oh, right." Izzy typed something on the keyboard, brought up the screen, then pointed at it. "I mean, it doesn't say killed specifically. It says sacrificed."

Carillo stared at the monitor a full second before it hit him. "I need to tell Tex," he said, rushing out the door. Apparently the CIA had been investigating the wrong Grogan all these years . . .

Which meant Marc and his crew had no idea they were babysitting a woman who was part of LockeStarr.

67

December 12
Château d'Montel Winery
Outside Paris

With every step, Griffin felt his pulse increase, dimin-ishing all sounds but the pounding in his ears.

Becca. Standing there, laughing as though she hadn't a care in the world. As though she hadn't left a grieving husband behind. They'd been separated, their divorce not final when she'd gone with him on that last operation, got caught up in the explosion. But still he'd grieved. He'd blamed himself for her death. And now he had to rethink everything about that day.

Because she wasn't dead.

She was very much alive.

He started in her direction, wanting, needing to see her reaction when she saw him. She was accused of being a double agent. Of stealing and selling this virus research to the highest bidder. The proof was incontrovertible, according to McNiel. The question was why? When had she become so shallow that money became more important than her beliefs? She'd never seemed obsessed by material things, and yet here she was, wearing a strapless burgundy gown that was clearly custom-made, and a diamond necklace shimmering against her pale skin. This was not the Becca he knew, and Griffin stopped in his tracks.

He wasn't ready.

He'd never be ready. All his years in the special forces, the CIA, and finally ATLAS couldn't have prepared him for this moment. There were no instructions on confronting one's wife who was resurrected from the dead, especially when said wife was allegedly guilty of espionage. And there were definitely no instructions on how to do it with a few hundred onlookers.

Suddenly the music started up, and the man to Becca's right placed his hand possessively on her arm, leaned over, whispered something in her ear. She smiled as he led her to the ballroom, where a waltz was playing.

Griffin felt as if a lead weight had filled his gut. Finally he turned, saw Sydney standing there, watching him, and he retraced his steps. "Dance?"

"News flash. I don't know how to waltz. Not part of basic training."

"It's one of the first things they teach you in spy school," he whispered.

"You're kidding."

"Of course I'm kidding." He looked at her. "Your hand."

"Are you serious?"

"Can you think of a better way to get on that dance floor?"

"It's a waltz!"

"I think it has something to do with the price of admission. Charge enough, throw in a waltz, people think it's high-class."

"It is high-class. They're wearing enough diamonds in this room to fund *several* third world countries."

"Which is why they're playing a waltz," he said, taking her by the arm and leading her to the dance floor as several couples swept by.

She cocked her head at him, allowed him to lead her out. The floor grew crowded and he did his best to maneuver

Sydney toward Becca. He had to know whom she was dancing with.

"Maybe," Sydney said, "you should do like they do in the movies. Ask to cut in. Then, as the two of you are dancing, casually mention something like, Gee, you're the last person on earth I would've ever expected to see."

"Sydney?"

"Yeah?"

"Shut up." She looked away, her arm going slack, causing her to misstep, and he immediately regretted his short temper, because he knew what she was doing, trying to lighten things up, put him at ease. "I'm sorry," he said, holding her tighter, feeling the warmth of her through the velvet fabric of her dress. "I didn't expect this. Seeing her in person is different than a composite sketch on paper."

"I can only imagine." She was quiet as he turned her about the dance floor. Then, "What are you going to do?"

"Work our way toward her."

"And?"

"Like you, I'll be winging it."

"Lead away."

Griffin spun Sydney around in time to the music, glad she was able to follow, because the only thing he could concentrate on was leading her across the floor until they passed within a few feet of Becca and her partner.

Becca never looked his direction.

He took Sydney for another turn, trying again with the same result, and then the music ended. When Becca and her escort filed off the floor, he guided Sydney in that direction, feeling as though he should know the man she was with. He'd seen him before, but couldn't remember where.

Arm in arm, Griffin and Sydney meandered about the room. She did an admirable job pretending to mingle, admire, and smile as though she were born to the high-society life, and all the while his attention was on Becca. Finally the man who seemed permanently attached to Becca's side was interrupted by someone who strode up to him and whispered in his ear. He leaned over to Becca, said something to her, then followed the other man from the room, leaving Becca alone for the moment.

"Looks like your chance," Sydney said.

"Keep watch. If he returns, stall him until I get done. I'd like to convince her to walk out with us."

"I'd feel a lot better if Giustino were down here."

"I have confidence in you."

He saw a waiter bearing champagne and he took a flute from the tray, then wove his way across the room to where Becca stood. Unfortunately he was waylaid by the very couple he'd used to crash the party. "Ah," Mr. Johnson said. "Just the man I was looking for."

"And here I am," Griffin replied, quickly glancing over, seeing that Becca was still alone.

"Tell them about the party at the pharmaceutical convention in Prague last year. The one where that idiot spilled the bottle of champagne down the front of the countess's dress."

Never mind that Griffin hadn't been to Prague in years, he had a bigger purpose in mind. "My wife tells it much better than I," Griffin said. "Let me get her."

"Oh, yes, yes," Johnson said. "Wait till you hear this. Hilarious!"

Griffin made a beeline toward Becca. Still alone. "You look like you could use a drink," he told her.

She turned toward him. "No, th—" Her voice caught, and she cleared her throat, taking the glass from him. "Apparently I do."

Although she was a highly trained CIA spy who'd been taught to curb any outward signs of emotion, deep down, Griffin had hoped to see a spark of something more.

And that bothered him. That he still cared.

She gave a bland smile, glancing over his shoulder, saying, "My fiancé probably would not appreciate me taking drinks from strangers, however. I hope he is not too angry."

Fiancé? Griffin turned, saw the man who'd been by her side, approaching from the elevator bank, and he glanced in Sydney's direction. Sydney shrugged, mouthing, *Sorry.* Griffin turned back to Becca, suppressing the urge to say, *I*

wasn't aware you were divorced, instead saying, "Congratu-
lations," just as the man in question walked up. He stood as
tall as Griffin, his dark, wavy hair slicked back and worn
slightly long, brushing the collar of his impeccable tux.

"Darling," Becca said, placing her hand on his arm.

"You look a little pale."

"I feel a migraine coming on. I was just going to take a pill."

The man looked at Griffin, his gaze narrowing slightly.
"And who is your friend?"

"I'm not sure," Becca said, turning a questioning look to
Griffin. "We've only just met."

Griffin held out his hand. "Raymond Zachary."

"Bertrand Leighton," he said, shaking hands, and Griffin
recognized the name immediately. He was one of the CEOs
of Hilliard and Sons Laboratories. In other words he worked
with Luc Montel. "Forgive me, Mr. Zachary, but you seem
vaguely familiar."

Griffin thought the same, but had hoped he was wrong.
"Pharmaceutical convention last year in Prague?"

"One of the better conventions," he said, smiling, then
looked at his watch, a Girard-Perregaux Tourbillon, something that cost more than Griffin made in a year on his government salary. "You'll excuse us, Mr. Zachary," Bertrand
said.

"Of course," Griffin replied.

Becca placed her hand on Bertrand's arm. "I'll join you in
a minute, darling. I need to freshen my makeup and go take
that pill." She smiled at Griffin. "A pleasure to meet you.
Enjoy the party." She started in the direction of the ladies'
room.

Griffin nodded, then walked to a corner of the room where
he wouldn't be observed as he took out his cell phone. There
was a text message from Giustino: "Found it. Might take a
while."

Giustino was probably one of the best safecrackers in
the business, but he was working under a handicap, without the proper tools. Griffin checked the time on the phone.
The message was only about two minutes old, and Luc

wasn't due back for another half hour. Still time, and Griffin relaxed—until he realized that Sydney wasn't where he left her. He immediately scanned the room, looking for threats he might have missed, then saw her standing just a few feet away, speaking to the Johnsons. He was about to start in that direction when a waiter approached. "For you," he said, handing Griffin a note.

He opened it, reading: "Gallery in 10. B."

Assuming he was reading this correctly, Becca was ready to meet.

68

December 12
Washington, D.C.

Each of the guests had been ushered through the metal detectors, then through the various security check-points before being allowed into the ballroom, and Marc stood just inside the perimeter, adjusting his earpiece, wait-ing for word that Lisette and Olivia Grogan had arrived. He saw them enter at the same time he heard Ennis radioing that they were in.

Lisette smiled as Olivia introduced her to a congressman. She shook hands with the man, then followed Olivia past a long table draped in white damask, bearing an elegant ice carving of a swan about to take flight.

A waiter seemed to appear out of nowhere, offering them champagne. It was Ennis. He and the other ATLAS agents also posing as waiters worked the room and would take turns offering Lisette champagne or hovering near her. The real waiters, who had originally been hired to serve the cham-pagne, were suddenly left without a job, and so a quick decision was made to have them walk around serving hors d'oeuvres from their trays—which left the hors d'oeuvres table with its massive swan ice sculpture in the center woefully empty. Marc doubted anyone noticed, or even cared, and he returned his attention back to Lisette. Even though she was wired, the devices failed far too often, hence the backup signal. If anyone saw her with a glass, it was their notice.

Ennis held out the tray. Olivia took a glass, Lisette did not, and when Ennis turned, walked away, Marc relaxed, even though he wasn't expecting anything to happen.

About twenty minutes later, Ennis joined Marc on the other side of the empty hors d'oeuvres table, just behind the sculpture. They stood there, looking around at the nearly two hundred guests who had arrived, and Ennis said, "Apparently Olivia Grogan isn't too happy about our interference. She was bitching that the hors d'oeuvres should be on the table, since that's what she paid for."

"She'll get over it," Marc replied.

They stood there a few moments more, when Ennis said, "I thought this was a simple sit-down tea for seventy-five. Never mind there's no tea. Who are all these people?"

"Damned good question." Marc eyed the guests, everyone from congressmen and senators to heads of major corporations and the handful of socialites and movie stars. "Maybe Olivia got greedy and wanted to make a bigger splash for her announcement to run for office. Looks like the who's who on the political donor list," he said, then paused at the babel of various languages he heard, even catching a few unusual dialects he hadn't expected . . . And that was when he started listening to the conversations. "I don't like this," Marc said, identifying some of the languages. "Some of these guests are from the wobbler countries."

"Wobbler countries?"

"Tex's term. The countries that'll switch sides or start a war with the least provocation. If anything happens to the people in this room, it'd be an international political disaster."

"As in, if this crackpot takes a shot at Olivia, make sure the bullet doesn't pass through her and hit one of them?"

"That'd be a good start."

They stood there a few minutes more, and, not seeing anything suspicious, separated.

Marc wasn't sure how much time passed. Ten, maybe fifteen minutes. It wasn't the time that concerned him, it was the quiet. He looked for Lisette, finding her and Olivia talking with a group of politicians who seemed to be consoling Olivia on the loss of her husband.

Seemed, because he couldn't hear a word.

"Damn it." He keyed the radio. "Is it just me or are we not picking up Lisette's mic?"

He heard nothing but static. No one answered.

Was it his radio or were all the radios out?

He searched the floor for Ennis, saw him near the doors leading to the service entrance, talking with another agent. As Marc crossed the room toward him, his cell phone rang. It was Tex. At the same moment, Olivia Grogan and Lisette disappeared down a short hallway to the ladies' room. "Not a good time," he told Tex. "The radios are out and I've lost visual on Lisette."

"Well, you might want to find her and fast," Tex said. "Because I've got some bad news."

Marc held the phone closer to his ear as he listened to what Tex was saying. "You're sure about this information?" he asked Tex.

"As sure as the evidence in front of me. No one else could've made that call. Olivia Grogan is part of Locke-Starr."

"I'll get back to you," Marc said, worried that Lisette and Olivia Grogan still hadn't emerged from the hallway.

Ennis walked up, holding his tray aloft as though offering Marc a drink. "You weren't transmitting."

"Is anyone?" Marc asked.

"It depends on where you're standing. The channel we're using for Lisette's audio seems to be affected by some sort of interference."

"Hell."

"It's an easy fix. We all switch to channel three."

"Except that we need to get word to Lisette, now. Where the hell is she?"

"Why? What's wrong?"

Marc pulled out his radio, changed the channel, saying,

"Olivia's part of LockeStarr. Tex just called and said Carillo connected her to a number definitely associated with the Network." As Ennis changed his radio over, then gave a hand signal to Stevens to switch channels, Marc looked up to see if Lisette and Olivia Grogan had returned. "Where does that hallway lead to?" he asked Ennis.

"It circles back around. Only thing down there are the restrooms, a couple pay phones, and a courtyard surrounded by an eight-foot wall for the smokers in the group."

They watched. Finally the two women emerged. Lisette's face was calm, implacable. And just as Marc started to relax, thinking all was well, she walked up to a waiter, grabbed a champagne glass, then took a sip.

"Find out what's wrong," Marc said.

Ennis took his tray, crossed the room toward Lisette. Marc radioed the other agents that Lisette had no audio, and had just picked up a champagne glass. When Stevens looked over, Marc angled his head toward Lisette, as he radioed, "Do *not* lose visual. Ennis's making contact with her now."

Marc watched while Ennis backed into Lisette, knocking her glass of champagne, then turned to apologize as he offered her a napkin and a new glass. The two spoke briefly, but Marc's relief was short-lived when he lost sight of Olivia Grogan. He surveyed the room, seeing the top of Olivia's head on the other side of the ice sculpture. She was simply standing there next to the table.

Ennis met Marc halfway, saying, "Olivia told Lisette she needed to sit for a few minutes. It's when she got up that Lisette noticed she was sweating profusely and her hands were shaking. Extremely edgy."

"Maybe the woman's nervous about announcing her campaign," Marc replied, just as a small contingent of Secret Service agents arrived, surrounding Vice President Harrison. "What the hell is he doing here?"

"Damned if I know. He wasn't even on the guest list. It must have been a last-minute addition."

Marc's gaze flew to Olivia Grogan, who was staring toward the door where the vice president stood, greeting those nearest the entrance. *Okay, think.* She was about to announce that she was going to run for her late husband's seat. That was enough to make anyone nervous, surely, so maybe it was nothing.

But then, most people running for the Senate weren't part of a worldwide criminal organization.

And then Ennis said, "What's that in Olivia's hand?"

He looked over, saw she was holding what appeared to be a small vial, and he prayed like hell it was only perfume.

69

December 12
Château d'Montel Winery
Outside Paris

The party at the château had thinned considerably, with only a handful of guests loitering about, by the time Griffin ascended the stairs to the gallery. And with each step he took, he wondered if he'd made a big mistake. Too many emotions roiling through him. A dangerous mix on a mission like this.

The gallery itself overlooked the spacious foyer, where a few guests stood, talking among themselves as they waited for their coats from the footmen. The wall behind Griffin was filled with oil paintings of pastoral landscapes and men and women with powdered hair and satin finery from a bygone era. Three benches were placed evenly around the half-circle space, all empty, and Griffin walked around the balcony, wondering if Becca was going to show.

She was already there, standing in a shadowed corner near a suit of armor that stood sentinel over a darkened hallway. At first, she said nothing, her expression one of diligence, caution. But then it softened momentarily as she asked, "How are you?"

And once again he wasn't prepared for the flood of emotions on seeing her, especially the anger over her subterfuge. "Well, let's see. I painted the kitchen after the funeral. Yellow just wasn't cutting it for me."

"I'm being serious, Zachary."

"Yeah? Well, so am I. It's been two goddamned years. *And* I thought you were dead," he whispered. "How do you *think* I am?"

She ignored his outburst, "You look tired."

Griffin studied her face, trying to assess what she was about. "Let's just say the last few days have taken their toll. So what game are you playing?"

"Game?" she asked.

"The hit man who killed Faas came after us last night. Anything to do with you?"

"Oh my God. If I hadn't sent that package to Faas . . ."

There were a million questions he wanted to ask her about the last two years, but this wasn't the time or place. He needed to get to the bottom of this. "Why Faas?"

"I couldn't think of anyone else, and sending it to the museum seemed so simple. I thought if I mailed it from the lab, it would be lost in the volume of packages." Becca crossed her arms, as though suddenly cold. "The plan might have succeeded, except someone hacked into their system a couple months before, so they were on the alert, and caught the unauthorized shipment—thankfully only after it had been mailed."

"Luc didn't suspect you?"

"No. I heard he suspected one of his special guards, who it turned out was skimming drugs and selling them on the side. Apparently there had been other unauthorized shipments that same day. The guard denied it. His body was found the next morning."

Everything Becca said had the ring of authenticity. But Griffin knew from experience that it was far easier to maintain a lie if the majority of it was framed with the truth. "Is that why you were in Amsterdam?"

"How did you know?"

"We had a witness."

"I had hoped to warn you. Once Luc tracked the package to the museum, he sent Bertrand to retrieve it, and someone to kill Faas."

"Bertrand? Your fiancé?"

She clamped her mouth shut, as though biting back a retort, her eyes sparking. "*Yes*. And I asked to accompany him to do some shopping. I thought if I could catch you before you met up with Faas, warn you somehow . . ."

He'd only seen the man from across the street and in the dark, thank God, or Bertrand might have recognized him. "Wouldn't it have been easier to notify your handler? What was his name?"

"Reggie."

"Or pick up a phone and call Langley? You surely know the number to CIA headquarters?"

"I did the best I could!" she whispered harshly, then stopped, took a deep breath to calm herself. "Look. After the lab's computer was hacked, everyone who worked there was under the microscope. I risked my life to get that package out. And the moment I found out that Luc sent Bertrand to retrieve the package himself from Amsterdam, I immediately arranged for a face-to-face with my handler, so that you could be stopped."

"You're sure this information made it to Thorndike?"

"Positive. I heard Reggie call him. That's how I found out that you'd already left. Thorndike promised they'd do everything in their power to stop you, because they knew you'd be walking into a trap. If you were caught, it would compromise the entire operation."

So now he knew why Thorndike burned him.

Someone pushed open the front door in the foyer below. Cold air and the scent of fresh fallen snow drifted up toward them. Griffin glanced down, saw several people standing in the foyer, before turning his attention back to Becca, trying to decide what direction to take. "Are you aware Reggie is dead? Murdered in his apartment."

Becca closed her eyes and it was several moments before she opened them again, her face turning pale. "He was supposed to meet me here tonight. This was to be our last mission."

"You saw the American newspapers, no doubt. Are you a double agent?"

She turned her gaze toward Griffin, her eyes glistening. "There was a time when you never would have asked . . ."

"That was a *long* time ago. Two years in fact."

"Well, forgive me, but it took longer than I thought to gain Luc's trust."

"And what's so important that you sold your soul for two years?"

"This." She opened her hand, revealing a flash drive. "What I was supposed to be passing off to my handler tonight. Not only is Dr. Fedorov's research on here, but so is the list of every seaport in the Western Hemisphere that LockeStarr has compromised, as well as the security flaws they intend to exploit. And where they're going to release the virus if they recover that missing vial. Luc has never allowed this information on any computer that connects to the Internet. And he intends on selling it. Tonight."

If what she said was true—and he wanted to believe her—then what she held in her hand was the key they needed to bring down LockeStarr, what they'd come looking for. But then her words about the missing vial sank in, and he recalled what McNiel had said about her stealing the virus from the lab. "Who are you planning on selling it to, Becca?"

She stared at him, as though he were insane. "What the hell are you talking about, Zachary?"

"The virus. We know you took it," he said. "There's still a vial missing. Is it being sold to this buyer that Luc is picking up?"

"Luc sent that vial to America. The one I took, I sent to Faas. It was in the cooler. That's what he was supposed to turn over to you. But this is what you're looking for. What I was to turn over to Reggie tonight. When Luc opens his safe and finds it missing, he'll know it was me. I'm as good as dead."

The moment the words left her mouth, he saw Luc and

another man walk in the front door—fifteen minutes earlier than they'd expected—the other man carrying a briefcase at his side. Griffin pulled out his phone, hit the speed dial that would warn Giustino, figuring the man was the buyer, the same one Becca was being accused of selling the information to.

"What's wrong?" Becca asked.

And suddenly he was faced with the decision. Trust Becca or not? "Giustino is in there, looking for that flash drive you're holding," he said.

"Why?" she asked. And then he saw when the realization hit her. What it meant. Not just that Griffin didn't trust her—certainly expected under the circumstances—but for her to know that Thorndike had lost faith. Why else send in a team to do what Becca was supposed to do? And then that look was gone, replaced by determination, and she pressed the flash drive into his hand. "I'll stall Luc. Get Giustino out. Now."

He grabbed her by the wrist. "You're in danger. They know about you. They have to, or why kill Reggie?"

"Trust me," she whispered. "Please."

In a single heartbeat, he let go. And before he could tell her he trusted her, someone stepped around the corner and pressed a gun into his back.

"Don't move."

Bertrand. Becca's so-called fiancé.

70

December 12
Washington, D.C.

There were certain moments in life, Marc thought, when the only thing you could say in the time given is "Oh shit." *This* was one of those moments.

His only advantage was that Olivia Grogan didn't seem to know that they were aware anything was off—an advantage they were bound to lose any second. He carefully backed away, drew his gun, pointed it at Olivia, and told Ennis, "Get the VP out of here. Now."

Ennis radioed Stevens, who then informed the closest Secret Service agent. They immediately ushered the vice president toward the exit. At the same time, Marc stepped around the table, leveled his pistol on Olivia, saying, "Don't move."

But she wasn't looking at him. She was staring at the Secret Service as they yanked the vice president out the door. She took one step in that direction, but the door slammed shut, the sound echoing throughout the room. Her jaw dropped, and she looked around her frantically, as the crowd became aware that something was going down. A few guests noticed

Marc, his gun pointed at Olivia, and a woman screamed, no doubt misidentifying the situation. That was when Olivia finally noticed Marc, or rather his gun. Suddenly she held up the vial, her thumb covering the top, and she shouted, "Everyone. Stop! Stop or you'll all die!"

If there was any doubt in Marc's mind as to the vial's contents, it fled in that moment. Several more guests screamed, and suddenly there was a very wide circle around him and Olivia, and it widened even farther as his agents started moving people back. Apparently Olivia noticed as she held the vial higher, turning about the room, eyeing everyone like a cornered animal. "Don't move," she ordered.

The crowd froze. Marc's team of agents looked to him for direction. He gave them a signal to stand down. He wasn't about to shoot until he knew what would happen if she dropped the thing. Then again, he couldn't think of any way to get that vial from Olivia Grogan and still avoid an unmitigated disaster.

Lisette. He searched the room, saw she'd backed away from Olivia into the crowd and was making her way toward him, slowly, surreptitiously, moving only when Olivia's gaze was somewhere else. Finally she came up behind Marc, half hidden by the melting swan sculpture.

"You think that's the virus?" he asked.

"I'm hoping otherwise."

"If it is, what are our options?"

"Best scenario? It goes straight down and only affects those closest. Still too many people near her, including us. That's if it falls. If she throws it, all bets are off."

"Great." Marc looked around, not seeing any other choice that didn't risk lives. "Sacrifice a few for the greater good."

"And if we're in that few?"

"On the bright side?" Marc replied. "If that happens and there is any fallout, we'll be too dead to notice." He kept the nose of his weapon pointed down. There was no shot. Too many people stood around Olivia Grogan for Marc to take her out, even if he dared. He keyed his radio. "Clear the space behind her."

Ennis radioed back. "To where?"

What was it Ennis had said about that hallway? "En route to the restrooms. Exit the courtyard," Marc replied. "Move as many as you can outside, shut the doors, and do *not* let them back in until it's been cleared. Contact HQ, advise of possible bio threat and your location."

"Ten-four."

Marc felt Lisette standing behind him, though he couldn't see her directly. They'd worked together enough that oftentimes it was as though they could read each other's minds. It's what made them a good team. "Any chance—"

"That I can keep her talking?"

"Yes," he said, even though what he really wanted was for Lisette to evacuate with the others. She would never leave, not while the threat remained. None of the agents would. They were all dedicated. At least Ennis and the rest of the team were far enough away that if Olivia did drop the vial, they might be spared.

Lisette took a step to the side, calling out, "Olivia! Talk to me. What's going on?"

"What's going on?" Olivia glanced at the vial in her hand, then back at Lisette, never noticing that Ennis had started funneling guests down the hallway. "Everything went wrong."

"I don't understand."

"Of course not. How could you?" She looked up to the ceiling a moment, as though blinking back tears, then took a deep breath. "It was supposed to be so simple, but now I don't know what to do."

"I can help you, Olivia. That's why I'm here. You know that."

"How can you help? You don't even know, do you? You were supposed to be gone. All of you."

She started to turn, would have seen Ennis directing the guests down the hallway, but Lisette took a step forward, saying, "What are you talking about?"

Olivia focused on Lisette, giving a manic laugh. "This!" she said, holding up the vial. "You realize what it is, don't you?"

"No. What is it?"

"A virus. A deadly virus. And all I was supposed to do was sprinkle it in the hors d'oeuvres and let everyone have their fill. And then I would just walk away, not eating any of it. But they're not here . . ." She looked at the table, then back at Lisette. "The food was supposed to be on the table, and I would just place a few drops in each tray . . ."

"But you're not going to do that," Lisette said, slowly sidestepping, keeping Olivia's attention on her instead of her surroundings.

"I can't. Even if I wanted to," Olivia said, tears in her eyes. "I would have survived this horrible tragedy. People would have looked up to me. I would have been able to govern where others failed, where my husband failed, and *every-one* would understand that I was *braving* this tragedy for the greater good."

"You wouldn't survive, Olivia. You'll die right along with the rest of us once it leaves the vial and hits the air."

"And how would you know that?"

"It's my job. I'm a microbiologist. Whoever told you this information was just using you."

"You're wrong. My father wouldn't have lied to me."

"Yes, Olivia. That same virus killed the entire crew on a stolen freighter off the coast of Brazil. That vial you have was taken from a lab in France."

Olivia stared openmouthed. "How did you know?" She looked around the room, as though noticing for the first time that everyone was filing out. "He wouldn't lie to me," she said, almost a whisper, never taking her eye off the crowd, or rather what was left of it, thirty guests Marc estimated, including his agents. She looked down at the vial, then back at the people, and Marc's finger instinctively squeezed the trigger to that first click. A hairbreadth more . . .

"He's using you," Lisette said, and Olivia shifted her attention. Marc held his position, kept his aim, willing her to drop the thing.

"The greater good . . . That's what my father always said."

"It's not the greater good, Olivia."

"It is," she said, suddenly facing the crowd and drawing her hand back to throw the vial.

Marc fired. The swan sculpture burst. Olivia jerked back, a look of shock on her face.

Her hand flew open. Time seemed to fragment. The rest of the room seemed to disappear. And all he saw was the vial falling to the ground.

71

December 12
Château d'Montel Winery
Outside Paris

Sydney stood in the shadows at the arched entry-
way that led from the ballroom to the foyer. Her phone vibrated at the very same time she was pulling it out to warn
Giustino that Luc had walked in the door. The call was from
Giustino.

"The safe is empty. The drive's not here."

"Well, Luc is," she said. "Get out. Now."

She looked toward the gallery, but couldn't see Griffin or
Becca from where she stood, and so she moved to the other
side of the arch, giving her a better view. Luc and the stranger
beside him still stood in the entryway, Luc shrugging out of
his coat. Several guests mingled about in the foyer, perhaps
waiting for coats. Suddenly Luc glanced up.

Sydney followed his gaze and saw Becca first, walking toward the stairs, and behind her, Griffin, followed by
the man Becca had been dancing with. He walked closely
behind Griffin, a coat draped over his right arm, undoubtedly
covering a gun.

"Griffin's in trouble," Sydney whispered into the phone, then disconnected.

The longest two minutes of her life stretched into eternity, as she watched the byplay on the stairs. The expression on Griffin's face confirmed Sydney's suspicions when he looked down, saw her just inside the arch, and gave a slight tilt of his head, warning her off. As if she was going anywhere without him. She unsnapped her purse, dropped her phone inside, drew her gun, and held it to her thigh out of sight. At that same moment someone grabbed Sydney by the shoulder, and her heart skipped several beats.

"It's I, *amica*," Giustino whispered, watching over her shoulder as the three continued down the stairs. "This will be *difficile* . . . Too many people milling about. We need a distraction."

She glanced at the fire extinguisher on the wall, partially hidden by the potted palm. "How about that?"

"Brilliant," he said, then casually stepped around her, lifting the extinguisher from the wall mount. He held the canister behind his back, then took Syd by the arm, and the two strolled through the arch into the foyer, as though they were merely a couple of guests on their way out.

Becca was about halfway down the stairs, Griffin and the other man several steps behind her. "I don't understand, Bertrand," Sydney heard Becca saying as she looked back toward the man. "What on earth is wrong?"

"Wrong?" Bertrand said. "I recognized him from Amsterdam. I think you were right, Luc. She sent the package. Not that guard you suspected."

"She had nothing to do with this," Griffin said.

"Indeed?" Luc said. "And who are you to say?"

"The man who stole the data from your safe." He held up the flash drive, looked right at Sydney and Giustino.

Giustino hurled the fire extinguisher into the foyer. As it clattered across the marble tiles, drawing Bertrand's attention, Griffin pivoted. He rammed Bertrand's gun arm, the weapon flying from his grasp. Griffin jumped down several stairs, grabbing Becca's hand, taking her with him.

A gunshot shattered the air, echoed across the foyer. And Sydney couldn't tell where it came from or who fired. Or whether it was Becca or Griffin who stumbled. Or who pulled who to the ground. But Griffin was on top of Becca, clearly protecting her.

Sydney saw Luc with a gun. Guests screamed, ran out the door, blocking Sydney's aim. Giustino swore, unable to get a clear shot. And suddenly Bertrand was back on his feet, his gun in hand. Two guards burst through the front doors, both with weapons drawn. "The man on the ground," Luc cried. "Get the flash drive from him."

They were outgunned. And then she saw the fire extinguisher on the ground. She aimed. Fired. It went spinning, spewing forth a white cloud that instantly filled the room.

Giustino darted in, dove through the vapor toward Becca and Griffin, dragging them back to the ballroom.

And as Giustino helped Griffin and Becca to their feet, and to the hallway that led to the kitchen, Sydney kept her gun trained on the haze-filled room, hearing the screams, hearing Luc shouting, "Find them!"

She turned, hiking up her dress as they raced through the kitchen. Donovan had parked the van right next to the kitchen door, the engine running. Giustino threw open the cargo door, helping Griffin and Becca in. Sydney covered them, her gun out, aiming it toward the front of the house, then to the kitchen as she backed to the van.

And as she climbed into the passenger seat, she looked down, and saw a dark trail of blood.

72

December 12
Washington, D.C.

Olivia Grogan lay sprawled on the floor, moaning as she pressed her hand against her right shoulder, blood seeping through her fingers. Marc kept his gun trained on her, ready to shoot her again if she reached for that vial that had fallen just a few inches away from her. His sole purpose had been to keep that vial from the crowd, and as much as she probably deserved to die, he wondered how they'd even render aid to her if she was contagious. From his peripheral vision, he saw Ennis and the other agents still moving the guests down the hallway. Marc switched his radio to the main channel, called for an ambulance and a hazmat team, then ordered Ennis to continue evacuating the guests.

He would have given anything to avoid exposing Lisette. For all the years they'd worked together, he could never have asked for a better partner, and that included the heartache of their brief relationship and the breakup that followed. "You okay?" he asked her.

"Yes. I just didn't expect this. Not in a million years." Her sigh was one of resignation, a bittersweet sound that nearly broke his heart, especially when she reached out, touched his arm, whispering, "No regrets, though."

"No regrets," he said, wondering how long it would take for the first symptoms to appear if they were infected. Fedorov died within a week. A very long week, undoubtedly. Time seemed to be at a standstill and he looked around, saw that everyone had been cleared from the room. "Where the *hell* is that hazmat team?"

Lisette didn't answer, and he wished he hadn't sounded so harsh. He glanced over, saw her studying the scene, probably determining how best to keep contamination down to a minimum. "Oh my God," she said, dropping her hand, and taking a step forward.

"Lisette?"

"It's still intact."

"What is?"

"The vial." She took another step forward. "The top's still on." Her gaze swung to Olivia, still lying in the same spot. "You didn't remove the stopper."

"I couldn't," Olivia said. A sob escaped her throat. "I told you . . . Everything . . . w-went wrong . . ."

73

Griffin, his arm around Becca, felt as if his limbs were made of lead, trying to balance upright in the back of the van as Donovan sped up the hill and away from the château.

"Giustino?"

"Amico?"

"Take it," he said, holding out the flash drive.

Giustino was at the back of the van, giving them space. He leaned forward, took the flash drive. "How bad is it?"

"I'm fine . . ." Becca said.

But Griffin saw the blood pooling beneath her, and he pressed his palm against the wound, trying to stop the bleeding. He didn't want to say how bad, didn't want Becca to know. He'd seen men go into shock with less serious injuries because they thought it was worse than it was. "We need to get her to the hospital."

"I'll call Dumas. He can arrange for an ambulance."

Griffin pulled Becca closer, trying to get more pressure on her wound.

Her mouth parted as she took a shuddering breath.

"Am I hurting you?" he asked.

"No." But he knew she was lying. He knew that every bump they drove over as Donovan raced to the hospital had to be agony. "Zachary . . . ?" He waited, and she said, "I'm sorry."

"For what?" he asked.

"Not . . . telling . . . you."

Griffin leaned his head against the side of the van, and for some reason glanced over, saw Sydney watching him, her face filled with worry. He turned back to Becca, willing for her to hold on. He didn't want her apologizing. He wanted her to be fighting, and he took a deep breath, wondering if a prayer at this late date in his life would have any hope of hitting home. "None of that matters now."

"What color?"

He looked at her, trying to see her in the dark. "Color?"

"The kitchen . . ."

He closed his eyes, wishing he could take back so many words. "It's still yellow. Just like you left it."

She was quiet for so long, then, "Thank you . . ."

"For what?" he said, looking down at her, telling himself that the pool of blood beneath her was *not* getting larger.

"For getting me out of there . . . I didn't want to die alone . . ."

"You're not going to die."

She made a sound, a laugh, he thought. "Always were a good liar."

"Don't . . ."

"Promise me . . ."

"What?"

"You'll finish this. LockeStarr . . . the Network . . ."

He tried to answer, couldn't, and swallowed past the lump in his throat. "I will."

He held her closer, bent down, breathed in the scent of her hair, trying to remember the good times of their marriage before it had disintegrated. All he could think of, recall, was that photo on his desk, of them skiing. She loved the thrill, reveled in the competition, the very things that made her a great agent. But when it came to relationships, she was clueless—not that he was much better—and as he looked back, he realized there weren't very many good moments during their time together. Even though he'd tried to deny the fact, they both knew early on that the marriage was doomed.

That didn't make this any easier, he thought, stroking her cheek, telling her to hang on, help was coming soon.

Her breathing seemed labored, shallow. It was too dark to see her face. But he knew he was losing her. He'd seen death, heard it, and right now, he could feel her life slipping away. And all he could do was sit there, hold her, be there for her. Eventually the pool of blood below her stopped spreading. She took her last breath and he didn't move.

And Donovan kept driving.

74

December 19
ATLAS Headquarters
Washington, D.C.

There was no funeral for Becca. Griffin wanted to say
good-bye alone, and so he'd taken her ashes, flown to
Gstaad, and scattered them from the slope where they'd last
gone skiing the year before she'd left him. It was, Sydney
had learned from Tex, Becca's favorite spot. The place she'd
loved best, and one of the last happy memories Griffin had
of their marriage.

And so it was that, a week later, when Syd arrived in
Washington, D.C., for the debriefing on the mission, she
didn't expect to see him there. Even so, when she and Carillo
walked into the meeting room, saw Tex seated at the table,
and no sign of Griffin, she was disappointed. It didn't matter
that she wasn't sure what she'd say to him, she thought as
Tex pulled out the chair beside his so that she could sit. He
smiled at her, then eyed Carillo. "What? No donuts?"

"Ate 'em before we got here."

Tex looked at Sydney. "You eat donuts?"

"Any chance I get," she said as Marc and Lisette walked in, followed shortly by McNiel and Pearson.

McNiel looked at the clock. "Thorndike called, said he'd be late, so we might as well get started, since he already has this report from Pearson. The Bureau served the search warrants on the San Francisco office of Hilliard and Sons Laboratories, and the DST did the same on the Paris office as well as Luc's château," he said, referring to the French equivalent of the FBI, the Department of Territorial Safety/ Security. "And," he continued, "I thought you might like to see this." He opened up a French newspaper, the headline reading simply, "*Espionnage*." Below it, a photo of Luc being led from the château in handcuffs.

"Bertrand as well?" Tex asked.

"Without incident," McNiel said, and it seemed the room breathed a collective sigh of relief. There wasn't a person seated there, Sydney included, who didn't wonder if Griffin wouldn't attempt to exact revenge on both men for the death of his wife. Especially considering the fact neither had been arrested right away and were merely kept under surveillance until after the search warrants were served.

"Moving on," he said, pushing the newspaper aside to read his agenda, "Olivia Grogan will apparently survive to stand trial with her father, so expect subpoenas to be forthcoming, unless they decide to plead out."

"Not likely," Marc said. "Olivia, unfortunately, is saying her father is innocent, she worked alone, and that Cavanaugh was on her payroll. She also admitted to hiring the two hit men who came after Izzy, and who killed Cavanaugh. Of course she and her father both refuse to give up the names of other Black Network members."

"Job security," Carillo said, just as the door opened. Sydney glanced up, expecting Thorndike.

It was Griffin. He appeared tired, worn, the circles beneath his eyes darker. He looked over at her, and though he didn't smile, she had the feeling that her presence was welcome, that maybe he was glad to see her.

And then he walked into the room, handing a folder to

McNiel, saying, "My finished report on Amsterdam and France."

"Thanks," McNiel said, taking the paperwork. "We're just starting the debriefing if you want to stay."

"Actually, I came to apologize. To Marc," he said. "For compromising your safety. I should have been there as ordered."

"Had it been Lisette," Marc said, clasping him on the shoulder. "I would have done the same."

The two shook hands, and then Griffin left. And how could she blame him? To sit there during the remainder of the session, hearing after the fact that Becca *was* a hero? That everyone had been wrong about her? The recovered flash drive contained everything she'd claimed and more, crippling LockeStarr completely. As disappointed as Sydney was that Griffin did leave—primarily because she had no idea when, *if*, she'd see him again—she couldn't blame him. That, she thought, as she left the meeting, was too much to ask of any man.

She rode the elevator down with Tex and Carillo to the lobby, and when the door opened, Griffin was there waiting.

For her, she realized.

She walked up, and he said, "I was wondering if we could talk a few minutes?"

"Yeah, sure," she said, just as Thorndike walked in the lobby door.

He seemed taken aback at the sight of Griffin. "I'm, uh, sorry about Becca. About everything . . ."

Griffin tensed beside her. It was several seconds before he responded, and she had the feeling he was mentally counting to ten, before he finally asked, "Who did you bury in her grave two years ago?"

"No one," Thorndike said. "The casket was empty."

Griffin stood there, his jaw clenched. And then he took a breath, as though trying to calm himself. "I wanted to kill Luc. Go back there and put a bullet through his head, your investigation be damned."

Thorndike nodded. "I'm glad you didn't. Becca was a hero. She would've—"

Griffin slammed his fist into Thorndike's face.

Thorndike staggered back, falling into the row of chairs against the lobby wall. Everyone froze, staring as Thorndike sat there, stunned, reaching up to run his hand across his jaw. And then Carillo made a show of examining his watch. "Geez. Look at the time . . ." he said, heading toward the door. "Late for a meeting . . ."

"Yeah," Tex said, hurrying out after him. "Forgot all about that."

And Thorndike picked himself up, crossed the lobby, keeping a wide berth around Griffin as he walked to the elevator and got on.

Sydney looked at Griffin, who took a breath, as though some weight had been lifted from his shoulder. Finally, she asked, "So what did you want to talk about?"

"Nothing in particular." They stepped outside, the sun shining on the dirty, melting snow. "Just wanted to talk."

"Nice hook, by the way."

"Thanks."

Talking, she thought as they walked down the sidewalk, was a good thing.

Fact or Fiction?

The Cold War may have ended decades ago, but the lethal remnants from that era remain a very real and present danger to all mankind should they fall into the wrong hands. Perhaps one of the most frightening aspects is that one of these threats, a potential bioweapon, can't be seen with the naked eye, and by the time anyone recognizes it, it's too late.

What is it? Smallpox.

Back in the day, children were vaccinated against smallpox, not because of any bioweapons concerns, but because, like many other diseases, it sometimes happened in the natural course of life. But this is one case of man versus nature where the scientists fought it and won.

Like many readers, I bear a small, unusual scar from the smallpox vaccination on my upper arm that looks like someone branded me with the round tip and pins from a computer accessory plug. My children, however, do not have such a scar. Smallpox was eradicated because of the successful vaccination program, and the last known naturally occurring case of the disease was in Somalia in 1977.

Fast forward to the present day and the fact that no one—not even those who were once vaccinated—is immune to smallpox, a disease which carries the distinction of being the single biggest killer in human history. Should it somehow rear its ugly head, perhaps find its way out of the freezers in Russia or the U.S.—where the only *known* laboratory stocks are held—and into the hands of terrorists, the devastation to human life is unimaginable.

There isn't enough vaccine to go around.

My mind started spinning with the basis of a plot, and I worried about the smallpox stockpiles that somehow ended up being unaccounted for. The world's scientists decided *not* to destroy the remaining viruses, because there was still that nasty but less lethal monkey pox floating around that could mutate into a deadlier form. They needed to keep those stockpiles handy for studying, just in case. But in this world we now live in with the very real threat of terrorism, what would happen if one of those missing and unaccounted for smallpox strains ended up in the wrong hands? What if someone combined it with another virus, perhaps an even deadlier virus, thereby rendering any existing vaccination ineffective? Would anyone be foolish enough to release such a virus on the world? More important, would anyone be foolish enough to *create* such a virus?

The answer to that last question is yes. In fact, it has already been done, at least according to Ken Alibek, a former Vector scientist from Russia. Around 1990, Russian scientists from a bioweapons program known as Biopreparat worked to turn the already extremely deadly smallpox virus into a more lethal and virulent form by altering the DNA or the RNA from that virus and another deadly virus, then splicing them together to create a recombinant chimera virus. ("Chimera" derives from Greek mythology, a monster with a lion's head, a goat's body, and a serpent's tail.) Since smallpox happens to be a virus that is amenable to genetic engineering, it was a natural choice. The other virus, it seems, was chosen simply for its fear factor: Ebola. Although this has been denied by other Vector scientists, Alibek reports that this Ebola-smallpox chimera, known as blackpox, or hemorrhagic smallpox, was created for use as a bioweapon.

Of course the biggest problem with bioweapons happens

to be the dispersal method, since heat (especially if disbursed by missile) and exposure to the sun (unless one ensures it is disbursed at night) actually degrades the bioweapon, often rendering the biological agents ineffective. Add to that the deadliness of throwing this new blackpox out there in the wild—how does one stop the unstoppable?—thereby endangering the entire human race, well, it probably isn't the first choice of those countries capable of creating such a weapon. (Heaven forbid any current or genetically-altered diseases make it into the hands of radical terrorists.)

Clearly there needed to be a genetic alteration to the genetic alterations to make sure this new deadlier virus can be controlled. Or, in the case of those who hope to make a heartier weapons-grade virus, an alteration to allow it to withstand the high temperature should it be dispersed via missile. But where does one find such a virus that can be manipulated so readily?

Enter the (fairly) new theory that life may not have begun with a big bang in space, but at the opening of the world's deepest hydrothermal sea vents, which are teeming with newly discovered viruses and bacteria that thrive in temperatures exceeding 600 degrees Fahrenheit. One need only to splice them into the chimera viruses, altering them even further, whether to allow the weaponized viruses to live at such extreme temperatures or to eradicate themselves after a certain time period to render them ineffective. Maybe it hasn't *yet* been done, but the science is there, and the point is, it *can* be done. There are numerous scientific articles on hydrothermal vents and the new life found there, each one fascinating. For further reading on genetically altering viruses for bioweapons, I recommend *Biohazard: The Chilling True Story of the Largest Covert Biological Weapons Program in the World—Told from Inside by the Man Who Ran It* by Ken Alibek and Stephen Handelman. And for more information on smallpox, delve into *The Demon in the Freezer: A True Story* by Richard Preston.

Happy reading.

Keep reading for a sneak peek at

ROBIN
BURCELL's

THE BLACK LIST,

the next suspenseful thriller featuring

FBI Special Agent Sydney Fitzpatrick,

coming January 2013

FBI Special Agent Tony Carillo tossed his keys on the table in the entryway of his condo, dropped his coat over the back of the sofa, then walked into the kitchen. It had been one of those days, the sort where what could go wrong, did go wrong, starting with the arrest of the bank robbery suspect, who decided to run at the last minute—right into an oncoming SUV.

Carillo opened the fridge, anticipating the leftover Christmas turkey dinner that his neighbor Mrs. Williams sent over, when he heard a rustling noise coming from the spare bedroom he used as his office. He quietly closed the refrigerator door, drew his gun, then stepped into the hallway, careful to avoid the one spot in the hardwood floor that creaked as he made his way to the back of the house. He paused just outside the office door to listen.

There it was again. The sound of rustling papers.

Finger against the trigger guard, he swung into the room.

His wife looked up, saw the gun, her eyes going wide as she dropped a book. "Tony . . ."

"What the hell are you doing here, Sheila?" he asked, holstering his weapon.

"I—I was just looking for something to read."

He saw the envelope addressed to his former partner, Sydney Fitzpatrick, still sealed, thank God. Sheila wasn't exactly known for keeping out of things that didn't belong to her. "I mean what are you doing here. In my house."

"It's *our* house."

"Until your lawyer finishes sucking me dry," he replied, casually straightening the papers, making sure the envelope was covered. "You need anything else to help him accomplish that? Blood type? DNA sample?"

"This isn't easy for me, Tony." She tucked a long strand of blond hair behind her ear, her hand still shaking, probably from seeing him pull a gun on her. "I'd like to speed things along, especially now that I'm getting married."

"Word to the wise, Sheila," Carillo said, walking out of the room, trying to keep his temper in check, as she followed him out. "Wait for the divorce to be final before you tie the knot. Less problems that way."

"You're such an ass."

"What are you really doing here?" He entered the kitchen, stopped in front of the refrigerator, then looked back at her.

She turned away, unable to meet his gaze.

"I need a place to stay until Trip gets out of jail." Jefferson Colby III, or Trip, as Sheila called him, was her current boyfriend. A real piece of work, this one, having been arrested for allegedly embezzling money from his employer, a charity no less.

Carillo eyed the six-pack of Sierra Nevada on the shelf, figuring it wasn't nearly enough. He grabbed a bottle, closed the door, then faced her. "No."

"Aren't you going to offer me a beer?"

"No, because you're leaving."

"I can't. There are people after Trip. They might come after me."

"So Trip *is* guilty of stealing money from his employer?"

"No. Of course not. But you don't understand."

"You're right. So fill me in."

"The charity he works for. He thinks it might be a front for some criminal thing."

"A criminal thing? Really, Sheila? Something beyond the fact Trip was skimming money from it?"

"It's like I'm talking to a brick wall! Why do I even bother? They set him up."

"Of course they did."

"At least talk to his friend in Washington, D.C., Dorian Rose."

"What is that? The name of a ship?"

"His friend who got him the job."

He took a long drink, wondering where she was going with this.

"I'm serious."

"Dorian Rose. Washington, D.C. Anything else?"

Sheila narrowed her gaze, took a frustrated breath, and said, "Dorian Rose works for a sister charity in Washington. One of his and Trip's friends was killed in a car accident after he found some discrepancy in the books and reported it. I mean, it was a real accident, so they don't know, but before he died, he told Dorian to have Trip call his brother-in-law in England and have him see if the same thing was going on there."

"What thing?"

"I have no idea. Whatever it was, Trip thinks it's going on here. And now Trip's brother-in-law won't call him back, and then Trip was arrested, and I think I'm being followed."

Carillo stared at her a full second as what she was saying sunk in. "And you, of course, decided to keep all this from me because . . . ?"

"Trip told me I couldn't tell anyone. He said it was too dangerous."

"What the hell do I look like? A Boy Scout? That's my job, Sheila. And it helps when people tell us *exactly* what is going on so we don't *goddamned get ourselves killed.*"

"You're yelling at me."

"Yes, I'm yelling at you! What the hell were you thinking?"

"That maybe Trip would tell you?"

"Jesus," he said. "He's in friggin' jail, so I think the likelihood of him mentioning it to me is about nil. Which is not to say I believe you."

"Does that mean I can stay?"

He took a deep breath, then looked at his wife, wondering

how it was he'd stayed married to her as long as he had. He'd loved her once. Hell, he still loved her, even though she'd slept her way through half of his friends over the years and, after the most recent round of counseling failed, he knew when it was time to let go. Past time. "You can sleep on the couch."

She rushed forward and hugged him. "Thank you, Tony."

"Yeah," he said, holding his beer away to keep it from spilling, and wishing he'd had the foresight to bring home a case of the stuff. "Write down everything you know about this charity, this Dorian Rose guy, how we can get ahold of him, and anything else you can think of."

Sheila took a pad of paper from the drawer, then started writing, and he tried to ignore the occasional tear running down her cheek, since each one made him want to drive out to the jail and strangle Trip until he confessed to exactly whatever the hell was going on. One thing was certain. He knew when Sheila was keeping secrets, and he was sure she hadn't yet told him everything—a fact confirmed the following morning when he discovered that not only was Sheila gone, but so was his ATM card.

Sydney Fitzpatrick tossed the newspaper on the coffee table, disgusted at the California State Legislature's latest efforts to balance the budget—the early release of prisoners into the parole system, because the jails were too full. Apparently someone forgot to mention to the lawmakers that they'd already laid off hundreds of parole agents earlier in the year due to lack of money. Never-ending circle, she thought, as her eleven-year-old half sister, Angie, rolled a tennis ball across the floor near the Christmas tree, hoping to teach her shepherd-mix puppy to fetch. But try as she might, Sydney couldn't stop thinking about the news article. The same thing was happening on the federal level, too, even at the FBI where she worked. They'd frozen all hiring, and she'd heard rumors that they were canceling the next recruit class for new agents.

"Watch, Syd," Angie said.

"I'm watching."

Sarge scrambled after the ball, stopped when his tail hit an ornament, turned, eyed the shiny orb swinging from the lowest branch, then jumped up, trying to nip it. Angie dove forward, catching the pup, shaking her finger at him. "No, Sarge. No!"

"Angela!" her mother said, walking into the room just in time to see her precious collection of decorations threatened by the dog's antics. "Be careful. Those are older than you are."

"Everything's older than I am, Mom. Maybe you should be more specific."

"Is playing with your dog outside specific enough?" she asked, constantly challenged by her youngest daughter, a change-of-life baby who was far too intelligent for her age. "Do *not* play near that tree again, or the dog goes out," she said on her way up the stairs.

Any retort her sister had planned died at the sound of a sharp rap at the front door, and Angie jumped to answer it, Sarge bounding after her. She threw open the door before Sydney could remind her to check out the peephole. All Sydney could see was a dark suit as her sister hugged the man, saying, "I was hoping you'd come."

"Hey, squirt."

The voice belonged to Tony Carillo. She and Carillo had been partners before she'd transferred from the San Francisco FBI field office to the FBI Academy at Quantico to teach forensic art. Angie opened the door wider and dragged him in by his hand. "Look who came by to see *me*."

"I was in the neighborhood. Bank robbery in Marin yesterday. A couple houses I want to check on a tip we received."

Sydney glanced out the window. His blue Crown Victoria was parked in the drive, the front seat empty. "You're by yourself?"

"I was thinking maybe you'd like to go with me."

"Hard as it is to believe, I did not fly all the way out from the East Coast so I could work a bank robbery with you."

"I'll go if she won't!" Angie said.

Carillo grinned at Angie's enthusiasm. Her dream was to be a cop and he loved to encourage it. "Let's talk your sister into coming, first, eh, Angie. We wouldn't want those skills of hers diminishing now that she's sitting behind a desk in a classroom all day."

"If anything," Sydney replied, "my skills have been sharpened these last few months. Besides. It's Christmas."

"Last I checked, it was the twenty-seventh."

"And I'm off until New Year's."

Angie's mouth dropped open as she looked at Sydney. "You *can't* let him go alone! What if something happens?"

"Yeah," Carillo said. "You don't want something to happen to me."

"I am doing nothing today and enjoying every second—"

Her mother came down the stairs carrying a basket of dirty clothes. "Hi, Tony. Are you staying for lunch?"

"Sorry, Mrs. Hughes. Working a case. But thanks."

She hefted the basket on her hip, then pinned her gaze on Sydney. "How about running Angela down to her ballet lesson, then basketball practice? It'll give you two some good quality time together and I can get some laundry done."

Vegetating between ballet *and* basketball? *Definitely* not on her list of how to spend the rare day off. "Geez, Mom," Sydney said, standing. "I'd love to, but they're running shorthanded at work, and Tony needs my help."

"Bank robbery," Angie said solemnly. "FBI stuff."

Her mother gave a sigh, then continued on through the hall into the laundry room just off the kitchen. If she'd had her way, Sydney would be teaching kindergarten at some secluded private school where nothing bad ever happened.

Carillo turned a triumphant smile Sydney's way. "Get your gun, Fitzpatrick. We've got a bad guy to catch."

"This is for you," Carillo said, once they were in his car. He handed Sydney a thick envelope.

"Gee, and here I was hoping for coffee and a donut. What is it?"

"The BICTT numbers. Figured it was safer to give it to you in person, what with Sheila snooping around."

Sydney fingered the envelope. The acronym stood for Bank of International Commerce Trade and Trust but was better known in their world as the Bank of International

Crooks, Terrorists, and Thieves. Even the CIA had used the bank, which had caused a major government scandal a couple decades ago, before it was shut down. Sydney had stumbled across several players in the BICTT coverup while investigating her father's murder, and found the original set of numbers, which the government confiscated. Carillo, being a firm believer in governmental conspiracies, made a photocopy of the numbers, feeling that somewhere, sometime, they might come in handy. Now all they had to do was figure out what they meant. "Any idea what I'm supposed to do with these?" she asked.

"Well I sure as hell wouldn't flash them around. And for God's sake, don't start running them on any computers. Doc figures if you do, you might as well hold up a sign asking the CIA to come knocking on your door," he said, referring to his current partner, Michael "Doc" Schermer.

"Lovely." She tucked the envelope beneath the seat. "So why'd you really want me to come with you?" Syd asked as they drove south on the freeway toward San Francisco. "You caught that bank robber yesterday. I read about it in the paper."

"Doc's out of town," he said. "Wasn't anyone else I could ask. It's about Sheila."

Carillo and Sheila were in the midst of a contentious divorce battle over the "custody" of Carillo's modest condo. It was, as far as she knew, the big holdup in why they hadn't finalized the divorce.

"What'd she do this time?"

He glanced in his rearview mirror, then changed lanes. "You remember that boyfriend she had back when we were working your father's murder?"

"The guy with the mansion?"

"Not him. The other one. The guy from England."

"Must have missed that update."

"Yeah, you might've been in Mexico dodging a few bullets at the time." He signaled for a right turn, glanced over his shoulder to check for traffic, then gave her a pointed look before turning his attention to the road. "She's talking marriage with this one."

"Bigger checkbook?"

"Bigger something," he said. "And as much as I'd like to move on, get Sheila out of my hair, the guy bugs me."

"He's not you?"

"Aren't you the funny one. He's being investigated by the locals for skimming money from the charity he works for, and Sheila's insisting I look into it and clear his name."

"Only a minor conflict of interest, eh?"

"I called the detective investigating it. Clear-cut case. Not a lot I can do, even if I was so inclined—which I'm not."

"So she's involved with a dirtbag. That can't be the only reason."

"She took off last night. Said she was scared, wanted to spend the night at my place because she thinks someone's trying to kill Trip."

"The boyfriend who's in jail?"

"Right. So, I let her. Only she took off with my ATM card. Guess I probably should have changed the PIN when she moved out."

"I'm assuming you called the bank?"

"She last used it at the market about a block from her house for cash."

They drove across the Golden Gate Bridge, through San Francisco, then on to San Mateo, and he pulled in to a subdivision of houses that had to be worth a small fortune, parking at the end of the street. He pointed to the last house on the block.

"That's Sheila's house?" Sydney asked.

"It is."

"What is this guy? The CEO for the charity?"

"No. Apparently the charity owns the property. Isn't it nice to know when you donate money, it's being spent wisely? They lent it out to him."

"Nice. And here we thought working for the Feds was cush because we get paid holidays. So what are you planning to do?"

"Find Sheila and talk some sense into her head. She doesn't have to save every stray that wanders into her fold."

"That what you were? One of her strays?"

"Except I couldn't be saved." Carillo walked up the hill, stopped in front of her house. A white BMW convertible was parked in the driveway. "Well, her car's there," he said. "Can't wait to hear what she has to say."

The two walked up to the door and Carillo rang the bell. No answer. He looked in the leaded decorative glass of the door, then pulled out his cell phone and called her. "Still not answering. Something's up. This is too weird, even for Sheila." He headed to the side gate, opening it to allow Sydney to enter first. "I think we could jimmy one of the dining room windows back here. These are nice and low. Easy to climb in."

"How sure are you about this?"

"I'm not sure about anything. Sheila's a ditz, no doubt about it, but she seemed genuinely upset last night." He took a pocket knife and slid it into the window, popping it open. "I told her these windows were crap and that she should secure them better. But no. She didn't want to waste the money when they were only going to be here until the divorce was final and she got her claws on my condo."

"So what are you trying to say? She's a gold-digging stray saver? Which is going to sound so good when we get picked up for felony breaking and entering."

"Nothing's going to happen." Carillo drew his gun, sat, then straddled the window ledge, one foot inside, one outside. "Besides. I hear the water running upstairs. She's probably in the shower."

"That'll go over good in divorce court," she said, drawing her own weapon, then following him in. "We're the FBI, Your Honor. Breaking into estranged wives' houses while they shower is what we do."

Everything looked neat and tidy, she thought as they walked through the kitchen toward the living room. No sign of a struggle or any trouble.

Carillo stopped. Listened. "Definitely coming from the second floor. Which maybe explains why she didn't answer her phone." He holstered his weapon, appearing much more relaxed now that they knew she wasn't lying dead somewhere with a knife-wielding suspect standing over her.

They started toward the stairs. Carillo stopped when he saw Sheila's purse on a table in the hall. He reached in, pulled out her wallet, found his ATM card, and shoved it in his pocket. She was surprised he didn't take the two hundred bucks Sheila had withdrawn from his account along with it.

The upper story consisted of four rooms—two unfurnished bedrooms, an empty bathroom, and the master bedroom, where the sound of running water seemed to originate. He and Sydney stood on either side of the closed double doors that led inside. Carillo, his free hand on the doorknob, looked at Sydney. She nodded and he unlatched it, then used his foot to push it open. They peeked in. The room appeared unoccupied, the bed neatly made. Two doors on the far wall, both closed, faced them as they entered. A thin strip of light reflected beneath the door on the left, undoubtedly the bathroom. The other, she assumed, was the closet.

"Time to find out what's going on," he said.

"Sure you don't want to wait until she's done?"

"If I thought she wouldn't run off, yeah." He crossed the room, his footfall silent on the off-white carpet.

Sydney hung back, fairly certain that Sheila was not going to like that her soon-to-be-ex was about to burst in while she was showering, especially with a spectator in the room.

He opened the door, then pointed for Sydney to enter.

"Me?" she whispered.

"You think *I'm* going in there?"

"You're married."

"By a technicality."

"You are *so* going to owe me." She gave him a look, then pushed the door open the rest of the way, the hot, moist air hitting her face as she stepped in. She stared at the steamed-up glass enclosure. Empty.

"What's wrong?" he asked.

"There's no one here."

"What?"

He pushed past her, moved inside, opened the glass door. "Where is she?"

Sydney glanced out into the bedroom. "A better question is why is she hiding from you?"

"Because she stole my ATM card?"

At which time they both looked over at the closet, still closed.

He and Sydney flanked it. "Sheila?" he called out.

Sheila, however, was not in the closet. She was under the bed, poking her head out from beneath the bed skirt, and looking imminently relieved when she saw Sydney and Carillo standing there.

"What the hell?" he said.

"I'm sorry!" she said, crawling out. "I thought you were them."

"Them who?"

"I told you last night. The ones after Trip."

"Isn't he in jail?" Sydney asked.

Sheila sat on the bed, her hand to her chest as she took a deep breath. "He got out this morning."

"And what?" Carillo asked. "You needed my ATM card to welcome him home?"

"No," she said, turning an angry glance his way. "I needed it so they couldn't trace my movements and find me, thereby finding him. Don't you think it's odd that they dropped the charges right *after* they learned I asked you to look into it? Like they *knew* you'd find out they were setting him up?"

"Great. He's out. So where is he, then?"

"In hiding."

"Hiding? Under the bed with you?"

"My God, Tony. What part of this don't you get?"

"The part where you go sneaking off and don't answer your goddamned phone so I think you're lying dead somewhere."

"You mean you actually care what happens to me?"

"Finish your goddamned story so I can figure out what's going on."

"Fine. I heard a car pull up and looked out my bedroom window, expecting to see the maid's car, but saw yours instead. I freaked."

"Because you saw *my* Crown Vic, the same one I've been driving every day for the past year?"

"No. Because, A, my maid has been coming here for six

months at seven-thirty in the morning and has *never* been late until today, and, B, I wasn't expecting you. Naturally I thought you were the guys after Trip, so I hid. Happy?"

"Ecstatic. So what now?"

"Now I pack a few days of clothes and go to meet him. And then we need to get a hotel or something so they don't find us. I don't suppose you'd let me use your credit card?"

Sydney, trying to ease Carillo's frustration, asked, "What makes you think someone's after you?"

"Trip. He told me."

"Why does he think this?" she asked.

"I have no idea. I only know that he's too scared to come to the house."

"And yet," Carillo said, "he had no problem sending you here?"

"He'd be furious if he thought I was here. He thinks I'm at your house."

"He just went up a few notches in my book."

"So I *can* use your credit card?"

"Tell you what, Sheila. Assuming any of this is true, I'll follow you to your hotel, pay the bill, then sit down with Trip and get to the bottom of it."

"You'd do that for me?"

"If it will bring me peace for an afternoon, yes."

She got up off the bed, put her arms around him. "Thank you, Tony."

"Yeah, yeah," he said. "Get your things together. Sydney and I will wait for you downstairs."

He and Sydney walked out, and he closed the door behind him.

"You buying that?" Sydney asked.

"I think she watches too much TV."

"At least Trip's off the hook for embezzlement."

"What more could a prospective wife ask for?" Carillo said, as he and Sydney started down the stairs.

The doorbell rang, and they heard Sheila call out, "It's probably the maid. She's got a key."

"She gets a maid, I get the bill," Carillo muttered as someone turned a key in the lock, then opened the door.

A small woman in dark clothing stood there, shoving something in her pocket before turning around to pick up a caddy filled with cleaning supplies. She straightened and looked right at them, her eyebrows shooting up, not in fear, but in inquiry. "Are you Trip?" she asked, focusing on Carillo.

Carillo froze. "How long did Sheila say she was the maid here?"

"Six months," Sydney answered.

No sooner had the words left her mouth, Sydney saw the woman reach into the caddy, pulling out a black semiauto.

Before the woman's gun cleared the bucket, Sydney drew and fired. She heard Carillo's almost simultaneous shots. The woman fell back, looking surprised as the bucket and gun clattered to the floor. The two agents approached, keeping their weapons trained on the woman. Carillo opened the door, looked outside, checking for more suspects. Sydney kicked the woman's gun away, and it went sliding. She reached down, checked the carotid for a pulse. There was none.

Sheila, hearing the gunshots, ran out of her bedroom, stood at the top of the stairs, then screamed.

She sank to her knees. "Oh my God . . ."

"I take it that's not your maid?" Carillo asked.

She shook her head. And when she recovered, said, "Now do you believe me?"

Sydney took out her phone to call 911. As she punched in the numbers, then put the phone to her ear, she looked at Carillo. "This is *not* how I wanted to spend my Christmas vacation."